THE PLANTATION

A SULFUR MOUNTAIN SERIES

Book 2

By

VICKI ADRIAN

<u>Content Warning:</u> this book contains adult language, Sexual situations and situations of emotional abuse. Please use caution when reading. This book is meant for 18+ ONLY

INTRODUCTION

The Plantation is the second book in the Sulfur Mountain Series. The first book to the story is *"Devils Attic."* The story continues from Devils Attic through this book and will continue into the third book.

You can pick up a copy of Devils Attic and The Plantation in Paper copy or Digital download from Amazon.com.

TABLE OF CONTENTS

Dedication

This book is dedicated to my family, for there support. To the great friends that have supported me through the second book and loved the first one.

Marti Jones, Louise Eaton, Phyllis Adrian, John Eaton Sr., Steve and Marie Nichols, Debra Kirk, Carlos Franco Beja,Dr. Sastry, Ron Lawley, Don North, Elsa Chandler, Cindy Blanton, Lucas Walker, Tammy Pitts Dukes, Angel Pratz Hobbs, Bobbie Medders Malory, Barbara Hancock, Diana McIntosh, Sue Soares for her awesome editing,.

Kyle Eaton for helping me write this book and putting up with the craziness for the past year to achieve this goal with this book couldn't have done it with out you. Thank you John and Louise Eaton for letting me use their property and their dog Hurley to write the series. Couldn't have done it with out you. And everybody that I didn't mention that has supported this journey so far. Thank you!!

To my dad Virgil W. Adrian 1932-2001 love you and miss you still.

To my baby boy Jessee James my first boxer baby miss you everyday Jessee mom still loves you so much. 4/3/2003-11/21/2014.

E-book ISBN: 10:0-9905253-5-6

Paperback ISBN: 13:978-0-9905253-6-3

In the very earliest time,

When both people and animals lived on earth,

A person could become an animal if he

Wanted to,

And an animal could become a human

Being….

All spoke the same language

Knud Rasmussen, poems of the Inuit Indians

CHAPTER 1

"The Ceremony"

"Let's get you into a room, Kia, so you can put on something more comfortable," Dr. Redbone says as he leads them back to a room. "Put on the medicine robe and come out when you're done."

Kia closes the door and slips off her clothes except for her bra and underwear. She wraps the medicine robe around her. Walking out, she sees Victor and the two doctors laughing and carrying on.

"Follow me, Kia, so we can check you and your babies." Dr. Redbone says.

They walk down a corridor to another room. This room is set up like the inside of a teepee with animal skins on the floor, a fire pit in the middle and several other people sitting around it. Herbs and stones hang all over the walls and from the ceiling. One of the guys smokes a pipe.

They walk in and move around the fire pit. Dr. Redbone places Kia between him and Dr. Whiteriver with Victor on the other side of them across the fire pit. He instructs her that the other people are shifters. "My staff is here to help you. Please pull off the robe and lay back."

He takes a smudge and places a black symbol on her belly where the babies are. He places an arrow symbol on Kia's forehead and a hand symbol on her chest, standing for success in battle. On her stomach area, several symbols are placed as the clan chants softly.

The first symbol on her stomach is the wolf for strength, endurance, instinct, intelligence, family values; this is placed under her breastbone. The next symbol is the moon, protector, and guardian of the earth. Following that is the eagle for courage, wisdom, and strength. The butterfly, for transformation, the symbol of mother and twins is placed between her hips. Hand and eye symbol is placed the furthest down.

Dr. Whiteriver motions for Victor to come and sit at Kia's head. "Place her head in your lap; the spirit animals are joining us to choose the babies."

Victor gently places Kia's head in his lap, gently stroking her hair on the sides of her face. The others continue to chant a little louder now.

Dr. Redbone places a small stone on Kia's head while Dr. Whiteriver moves a smudge of sage back and forth above Kia's body; the others in the circle chant in the background.

Victor looks up and sees the guard from the gate when they pulled in, now standing next to the doorway, straight as an arrow with his big muscular arms crossed. He is tall and has a tattoo on his arm, high up by his shoulder. It is the wolf clan and a half moon symbol. He must be an alpha male in the clan.

White streaks blast through the doorway; several circle just above the fire and then settle above each individual. They are the spirit animals of each member. They all stare at Victor and Kia. One spirit animal, not part of the ones that came in, moves around the circle. This one moves slowly and looks at each person as it passes by.

It stops above Kia and looks at her. It smiles and moves down until it's hovering above her a few inches. It looks at Victor; he notices it is a fox spirit animal with two different colored eyes — a green and a blue. She must be Kia's spirit animal guide. *They look alike.*

Kia still has her eyes closed. The spirit animal places her hand just above Kia's belly. A white light comes from her belly to the spirit animal's hand.

The fox spirit animal motions her hand and another spirit animal flies through the circle, spins around, and hovers to the left of Kia's spirit animal. The fox spirit animal looks at Victor and holds her hand out for him to touch hers. He holds his hand up and a burst of blue light shoots out across the room horizontally. Then a green light bursts out vertically straight up to the ceiling and vanishes into it. As soon as the light vanishes into the ceiling, a spirit animal drops down and hovers to the right of Kia's spirit animal.

With both of their faces distorted and eyes closed, Victor and the others cannot see what spirit animals choose them.

"When two lights flash, it usually means two children." Dr. Redbone says, leaning over towards Victor.

"Twins of the opposite sex when there are two different colors; one is male and one is female, or the lights would have been of the same color." He whispers to Victor.

One of the faces changes as if vibrating in high speed, distorted. Then it stops, blank, with no features on it at all. They watch and it slowly takes form. First, they see a black spot and it grows outward, brown-colored fur forms behind it. It moves rapidly up, down, and to the sides of the fur. A partially human jaw forms under a strange-looking mouth, the eyes open and the forehead and head rapidly take shape like water running backwards, but moving up.

They watch intently, waiting for a clear vision. They notice two circle areas on the sides of its head, and something spins in a spiral motion out and upward in a hook-type movement.

Victor, Dr. Redbone, and Dr. Whiteriver sit in amazement as they watch the transformation happening in front of them.

The face becomes clearer; the black circles are now obviously horns. The fur on the head and down the back is thick like fur of the buffalo. It opens its eyes and looks directly into Victor's, as if it is a part of him.

"It is a buffalo spirit animal." Dr. Whiteriver says to everyone.

The buffalo stands for endurance and survival, has great healing powers, knowledge, serves for the greater good, lives in harmony and love, and brings good to all living things.

The eyes change from deep brown to an emerald green. They look to the second spirit animal and the face does the same. Shaking rapidly, distorted and then it stops with a blank face.

A swirling fog surfaces its blank face and spins around in it. They can't seem to see how this one is forming. It's a thick fog. Suddenly, Victor jumps from a flash of blue light and the fog recedes to show a head of a horse on a human torso with fur on the body. Its arms, chest, and neck look like a ghostly image of a human horse.

The eyes are closed. Victor's mouth opens in surprise at what he is seeing. The eyes open slowly; they are also a deep brown color. The spirit animal shakes itself as a horse would do, and stretches out its head in Victor's direction as if to sniff him.

Victor reaches out his hand to touch the nose of it as it has its head outstretched. As soon as his hand touches the ghostlike fog, a flash of white light echoes through the room suddenly. Victor flinches and the eyes open wide on the horse spirit animal, now changed to a blue eye and an emerald green eye. A flame of ember fire flickers within the eyes. The sight of it captivates Victor. *How magnificent the creature is.*

Victor turns and looks at Dr. Redbone and Dr. Whiteriver and smiles. Dr. Whiteriver tells Victor that the horse represents many great things for the child.

"The horse spirit animal is the guardian of travelers, courage, freedom, power, clairvoyance, earth and moon, magic, governs the cycle of life." He tells Victor.

The chanting stops and the two spirit animals look at each other and then down at Kia. They move closer to her and reach out towards her, touching her stomach area. Kia's body arcs upward. Victor holds her shoulders down gently. A reddish pink light forms around the hands of the spirit animals and Kia's stomach.

Swirling in a circle, a white light forms and connects the hands to her belly while the reddish pink light grows wider. The light shines so bright everyone has to turn away. Then suddenly it stops. The two spirit animals move over and one hovers on each side of Victor's shoulders.

Everyone in the room bows their head. The spirit animals move together in a circle, following the fox spirit animal of Kia's. They pass behind each person in the circle and move out the doorway, nodding their heads to the big guard at the door.

Dr. Redbone tells Victor to wake Kia. Victor bends down and kisses her on her forehead. Rubbing his thumb around her lips gently, he whispers in her ear.

"Wake up, my love."

Kia opens her eyes slowly. Looking up at Victor, she dons a big smile on her face. She reaches up her hands and grabs his.

"It's over, Kia." Victor tells her.

"Is it already? It seems like we just came in here." She tells him.

Dr. Redbone puts his hand on her shoulder and says, "You and the twins are perfectly healthy. I have to tell you, Kia, your twins are not just any babies. They are what we prophesied, what we have been waiting for. The ones that can help us in time of need, they will train to be great warriors and lead us to many great battles against the evil that threatens our tribes and all the shape shifter clans."

"What are they, two boys?" Kia asks.

"A boy and a girl, honey." Victor interrupts.

"They each have their own spirit animal guide. They will show them, protect them, and they will learn from them. They are growing fast so you will need to come back at least once a month until they are ready to see this world." Dr. Redbone tells her.

"I will do as you ask, Dr. Redbone. How long will it take? I mean, when do you think I am due to deliver?"

"About six more months, shapeshifters have shorter pregnancies. Unlike the normal humans, our bodies have DNA of different animals that speeds the process."

"There is no problem with bringing her back, Dr. Redbone. I will bring her back as often as you need to see her. She will be moving in and living with me." Victor tells him.

"That will be the best thing for her. She is going to need a lot of help and support through this. She is going to have a lot of difficult days with her body changing to compensate for two shape shifting offspring." Dr. Redbone states.

Everyone around the circle gets up and Victor helps Kia stand. They place the robe back on her. Dr. Whiteriver gently rubs Kia's belly, feeling the movement within her.

Each person in the ceremony walks up to Kia and Victor, placing a hand on her belly so they can offer protection and bond as family with the twins. As each one touches her belly, they feel a tingling feeling of warmth and two tiny hands.

"Welcome, my sister and my brother," People say as they greet them.

Victor and Kia follow Dr. Redbone and Dr. Whiteriver to the doorway. When the two doctors pass the guard, he steps in front of Kia and Victor still standing very tall and straight with his arms crossed at his massive chest. Kia looks up to him and takes a deep breath as she looks into his beautiful blue eyes.

19

He unfolds his arms and places his hand out. Victor stands behind Kia holding her by the shoulders for security. She takes the guard's hand and places it on her belly. His expression changes from serious to a very soft look, in awe over the feeling he receives from the twins. He takes Kia's hand and kisses it. She looks away bashful then back up into his blue eyes.

"My name is Kane. I will be your guard."

He steps back out of the doorway and they walk past him. He turns and follows behind Victor.

"Oh, I see you've met Kane. Yes, he will be your protector." Dr. Whiteriver tells them.

"But I'll protect Kia." Victor says.

"I'm sure you will, my son, but you will have your hands full with her and the twins on the way, especially when they arrive. You will not have a clear mind. Kane is a great warrior and protector in the wolf clan. He will strictly protect Kia and the twins." Dr. Whiteriver tells them both.

"Do you know what type of shapeshifters they will to be?" Kia asks.

"No, my dear. That will be up to them as they grow. Each child born with silver-blood has the ability to have multiple DNA. As they grow older, they can take many different forms. It is going to take a lot of guidance and training to teach them how to use it and how to change into all the ones they have in their blood."

"How will they learn?" She asks Dr. Whiteriver.

"They will come here to train at the age of change."

"What does that mean, Doctor?"

"When their bodies go through puberty, they will be ready to be schooled. I am going to send a care package with you of herbs and natural remedies for the twins. You are to drink the teas as I've instructed on the note inside. Dr. Redbone has instructions on the other items for you. Remember, Kia, every month."

"Yes, sir, Dr. Whiteriver, and thank you, Dr. Redbone."

Kia hugs them both and Victor shakes Dr. Redbone's hand and hugs Dr. Whiteriver.

"Nice to see you again, my son. I will expect to see you often."

They walk out of the clinic. Victor's car is parked outside with Kane driving.

Victor helps Kia into the backseat and she lies down. Victor gets into the passenger seat and they head out the driveway towards Virginia.

The dawn is rising in the eastern sky…

CHAPTER 2

"Alexis Ravenworth"

Massive iron gates and a brick wall stand tall around the huge Plantation, reaching heights of sixteen feet.

The iron gates are each twenty feet tall, with a raven made of iron mounted in the middle of each one. The iron ravens are six feet tall alone. A black iron mesh curtain hangs behind the iron gates blocking the view from the outside.

People gather on the outside of the gate waiting to get in. There are guards on the inside of the gate that allow the select few into the Plantation every day.

Alexis Ravenworth watches over her garden from her office window, three stories up in her seven-story castle with over seventy-five rooms inside.

Inheriting her family's castle and business, Alexis is the heir to a multimillion-dollar fortune. It has been in her family for over four-hundred years.

She asks her head servant Gabriel to tell the guards to prepare to open the gates, "You choose the twenty-five people to come in for the day. Have the other servants send out the animals to tend the grounds and the gardens."

"Yes, My Lady, as you wish." Gabriel replies to Alexis. Standing with his head down and his arms behind his back with his feet together, Gabriel bows to her and walks quickly out of the office.

Alexis walks over to the giant mirror that is hanging behind her desk and makes sure she is perfectly presentable.

Alexis' office is made completely out of oak. The walls are littered with bookshelves and filled with books, the shelves are two stories tall in her library within the office. A stairway leads up to the second story and has a big sitting area completely equipped with a kitchen and full-sized bathroom. A large reading area is also upstairs with the finest leather and marble furniture from around the world.

Her desk comes from Scandinavia in the late 1500s handmade from oak with dovetail tongue and groove joints — no steel screws or nails. The handles are made of ivory carved specially for her family in the late 1500s.

Chandeliers hang by chains from the ceiling; lamps made from exotic animal hides are perfectly placed on tables with marble tops throughout the massive office.

Couches and chairs made from the finest exotic leathers from around the world fill the room. Priceless collectable artwork hangs from the walls, statues occupy the corners, and sculptures scatter throughout the two-story office.

Portraits of her family over the past seven hundred years are mounted on one large wall behind her desk.

Opening the double doors to walk out of her office, one of the other servants, Ada, greets her.

"Good morning, My Lady. I have a message from your sons."

"Well, what do they have to say?" Alexis responds.

"My Lady, Malik says they have found what you're looking for and they will need time to gather the stuff you asked them to get. He will need money wired to Beaver Creek so he and his brothers can complete the job."

"Very well, do as they ask. Tell Malik not to disappoint me this time." Alexis says.

"Yes, My Lady, as you wish."

Alexis walks down the long hallway to her personal elevator with two large bodyguards. Ada turns and heads to the servants' stairs.

The guards tending the gate stand ready for Gabriel's command. The grounds and gardens have the animal servants tending to each area.

Gabriel monitors his watch on his arm so he can precisely open the gates at 10:00 a.m. He motions to the two guards tending the gate to open them. He walks through and stands on a small podium. He announces he will only take twenty-five people today. The people yell and shout as he talks.

"Anyone with green clothing, move forward towards the gate, please." Gabriel announces.

Behind Gabriel, a line of armed guards controls any misbehaving crowd member. The guards in full suits of armor hold razor sharp swords in their hands. Pointing straight towards the sky and close to their body, the blades sparkle and shine in the morning light.

Each guard stands over six feet six inches tall. They are hand-selected for this job and train very hard. They serve and protect the grounds, gardens, and the animal servants within the castle, along with their master Alexis.

Gabriel picks the chosen and tells the guards to close the gates. The guards push the massive gates closed and turn to face the walkway to the garden where Gabriel leads the chosen.

They stop in the circle of the first stone pathway. Everyone takes in the beautiful gardens of flowers in every color one can imagine, perfectly bunched, and manicured hedges and lawns.

Hedges and shrubs of every kind line the small stone walls that wrap the walkways throughout the entire place. Some hedges are cut in shapes of animals, people, and cartoon characters.

Suddenly, everybody turns and looks at an elegant woman walking towards them. They can't help from looking at her. One girl whispers to her friend, "She looks like a queen."

She is a tall thin woman with black shiny hair laced with white highlights that perfectly accent her emerald green eyes. She dons a silver necklace and earrings, with a bracelet and ring to match. The necklace has a black stone cut in the shape of a raven. Her dress is made of a soft leather fabric, with a corset top and lace sleeves. A leather belt wraps around her small waist and one side attaches to the leg like a holster for a gun. She looks like she just stepped out of the Renaissance era. Her makeup is perfectly done and her fingernails long like claws match her eye shadow.

Alexis steps up in the middle of the crowd that circles a stone platform. "Welcome my friends. Welcome to the Plantation. I am your host and the owner of the Plantation Alexis Ravenworth. We will be walking through all the gardens today and you will learn about the different creatures raised here at the Plantation. You will be served a five-course lunch in the castle, arranged on an extraordinary buffet. You can eat as much as you'd like. Feast like a king, as we say here at the Plantation. Please follow me and we will get started."

Alexis steps down from the stone and the people follow her. She has two guards that walk directly behind her, separating her from the people. Two more guards follow behind the crowd of people, keeping everybody in check.

They walk out of the circle and down the long white stone path. It is as wide as a single roadway. The pathway circles and winds through the entire Plantation.

Alexis mounts her headset with a Bluetooth microphone on her left ear. When she stops at each garden, her guests can hear her talk about the area from the speakers placed throughout the Plantation.

She can also communicate with her servants on the grounds.

She walks them through each plant in the garden, what it is and what uses it has in every form: teas and medicinal properties. She tells them the botanical names of the plants as well.

In some of the gardens, she explains different mammals in existence. She tells them how they coexist together for the best in both plant and animal. The perfect chemistry between them makes strong, health plants and animals.

"Some of the plants along with the mammals were given to her family hundreds of years ago by the empire of China, the King and Queen of Wales, and others from around the world. Statues from famous artists were made specifically for the family, exotic plants and animals in the finest detail of artwork." Alexis tells the crowd.

Each garden has one of these statues of a human with animal characteristics, along with a plaque explaining what they are and how they are so rare.

The Garden of the Crows is midway through the tour; about an hour has past now. A Crow warrior tends the garden dressed in a pair of deerskin pants. He wears a chest plate made of bone and beads. Black feathers stick straight out of his scalp and around his head as if they are his hair. Shining bluish black in the sunlight, the feathers are longer down his back. They seem to follow his spine all the way down almost like a headdress, but Black Crow feathers instead.

People whisper amongst themselves regarding how real his feathers look as if he and the crow are one being.

The Crow warrior greets Alexis with a nod and a bow. He demonstrates without any words how he and the Crows picking the grounds are as one with each other.

He makes a perfect Crow call and holds his arm out to his side. Several Crows fly up and land on his arm. Standing in the shade up by the giant shrubs that are almost fifteen feet in height, they separate the gardens.

Alexis explains that the warrior and the Crows were a gift from a Crow Chief over a decade ago. They came from the Crow reservation.

The Crow warrior has a tattoo of the Crow clan on his right arm up by his shoulder. His eyes look exactly like a Crow's eyes, completely inhuman, distinct, and round. Dark brown almost black, making his appearance even more exotic.

Just before they are finished with the presentation, a solid black figure steps from the shrubs and grabs the Crow warrior from the back by his feathers on his head. He doesn't even try to struggle. Everybody gasps and jumps.

The black figure pulls out a long dagger type of knife and cuts the feathered scalp of the Crow warrior in one swipe.

The face of the black figure is unseen; it has no features to see. The Crow warrior falls to his knees with his head hanging down as if he knows what has come and accepts it.

Blood runs down his face and drips on the ground. The black figure puts the dagger into its black robe, grabs the Crow warrior by the back of his neck feathers, and drags him into a doorway in the shrubs.

Everybody is talking amongst themselves horrified at what has taken place in front of the.

One guy yells out. "It is just a show, people."

Alexis tries to calm everybody down by announcing it is just a show and they are acting.

"Oh...," everybody sighs with relief. They watch the black shadow disappear in the doorway.

One girl whispers to her friend, "Where did that doorway come from? I didn't see it there when we walked up. Look, it is gone again. How did they do that?"

"It has been there the whole time, dear. You just never looked in the correct spot."

Shocked, the girl is amazed Alexis could hear what she said that far away.

"I hear everyone and I read everything, my dear. Nobody hides their thoughts around here." Alexis says to them all.

They continue, garden after garden, noticing each one has a human dressed up as if it is half human and half animal. One person asks her why the panther has a person that looks like a human panther that cares for the area. She explains they accept them this way. They sense him as one of their own.

They are all amazed at how connected they all are with the animals and plants in the Plantation and how real they look. People comment on how the makeup is so real.

Alexis gets a call through the Bluetooth headset from her head chef telling her that lunch is ready.

She walks the group towards the castle. Everyone takes pictures, astounded at the massive size of it. The closer they get the bigger it is.

Alexis motions the guard to lower the gate across the water moat that surrounds the castle. A large wooden gate with huge iron chains moves towards the ground in front of the crowd. Once it is down, two more guards walk across and relieve Alexis from the crowd to tend to the lunch staff.

The two guards escort the group of people inside the castle; two more guards hold the fourteen-foot tall doors as the group enters into a huge lobby area.

Ada, the head servant for the house greets everyone explaining that lunch is almost ready to be served. "There are washrooms on each side of the lobby, with plenty of room for everyone to clean up for lunch."

Everyone heads to the washrooms, reminiscing about the garden and the events in each one, especially the Crow garden.

"This place is so cool; I wonder how you get a job here?" A young girl asks one of her friends as they walk past Ada to the washroom.

"We are accepting applications for a few college interns," Ada reveals.

"Really?" One girl says as she turns to Ada. "Where do we fill them out?"

"In the office to the right of the lobby. I will be there after you eat lunch. Stop in and you can fill one out." Ada tells them. Excited, the girls turn back to go to the washroom.

Chapter 3

"Lily's Message"

Riding through the logging trails in the mule with Hurley running through the woods chasing whatever he can stir up, John checks the cameras throughout the property and the cave.

The sun is just falling behind the mountains as he walks in to the cave down by the creek. Hurley is swimming down the creek smelling all the scents left behind from other animals that have passed through.

Putting on his head light and his flashlight in hand, John walks into the cave and decides to start with the furthest camera in the cave and work his way towards the front. The sun is dropping and he feels uneasy walking into the cave as it gets later and darker out.

Walking through the cave, he notices the air smells stale. There is heaviness to it, moist and with an odor. *Hmm more of a stench than an odor*, he says to himself. *What is that smell?* The further he walks in, the stronger it becomes. It smells earthy, and something rotting, mixed up with a smelly dirt dog smell. *I have never smelled that before down here. I wonder if it could be Benny Saxon.*

The further he walks, the more he takes notice of the different things in the cave. The rocks that line the walls as he walks past are three different colors of red and brown. The walls are wet with moisture and water trickles down in some areas. There are stalactites, and stalagmites all around that are growing rapidly with all the rain that has been coming into the area.

He looks down at the ground with his flashlight noticing the mud is damp, but just enough to leave an impression as someone or something walks on it. He sees tracks in the mud, from some type of animal. He stops and bends down to view them better.

It looks like a dog has been in and out of the cave several times. On the other hand, maybe a few of the same animal came in and went back out. The prints are larger than a dog's even for a large one.

John places his left hand over the top of the track. It is as big as his hand. *Wow, that is a large track to be as big as my hand. I have big hands.*

It isn't a bear track and it isn't a cougar or big cat track. It looks like an extremely large dog track. What could be that big and be in these woods without being noticed? I still want to discover so

36

many things in these woods. So many creatures and shapeshifters hide in plain sight. Whatever this thing is I am going to have to ask Victor and Kia about it. Maybe they will know what the track is.

John takes out his cell phone and snaps a picture of the tracks and then one with his hand to measure the size of them. Hoping that the cameras have picked up something, he hurries to the big cave.

Checking the camera in the big room and changing the SD cards, John is amazed how many pictures are facing the pond area. *One-hundred and seventy-eight images on just this one. Wow, that should have caught something*, he mumbles to himself.

Finishing up with the camera in the ceremonial room, he feels as if he is being watched. The hair slowly stands up on the back of his neck. Unsure of what it is, he turns around. Then John hears a woman's voice humming that tune again. *It must be her. Kia told me about Lily, but is she really a mermaid? Mermaid is very farfetched. How could a mermaid get in here in the first place? I still can't get past the fact they are a myth, something not real. But then again, there are many things proving me wrong lately about what is real and what is myth.*

The voice continues to hum. John listens to her wondering if he should address her or just let her be. She has to know he is there. Maybe that is why she is singing. What would it hurt to see if she would show herself?

"Lily? Is that you, Lily? It's okay, Lily. Kia told me about you. I would really like to meet you, Lily. My name is John and I own this cave and the property around it. I would love to understand why you are in here." John calls out.

The singing stops. John waits to see if she shows herself or answers him. He walks closer to the pond and looks across the water with the flashlight. He sees nothing.

Suddenly, a small ripple of water moves like an arrow towards him. It looks as though something is moving his way. He steps back a few inches unsure what it is, or if it is Lily, will she accept him around her domain.

John waits to see if the ripple will bring anything. He waits a little longer and still nothing. No singing, humming, no Lily. He decides to head back out and finish checking the cameras.

"Hi, John,"

He hears a voice of a woman.

"Lily, is that you?" John asks.

"Yes, it is I." She replies.

"Where are you, Lily?" He asks her.

"I'm right here." She says.

John moves the flashlight around the water, but doesn't see anything. Her voice sounds like she is right in front of him.

"No, over here." She tells him.

John shines the light to the sound of her voice. When the light hits her, he is amazed at what he sees. A beautiful woman with long red hair past her buttocks, pearl white skin that glistens in the light. Her eyes are a beautiful blue with pink reflecting from the light. The bottom half of her body is that of a fish. Scales of multiple blues, aqua, green, white, and black running on the outer side of the tail fin.

"Oh my God, you are!" John tries to spit the words out.

"A mermaid. Yes, that is what I am, John." Lily says.

"I can't believe it! I mean no disrespect in anyway, Lily. I never knew you existed in real life.

39

You are the most beautiful creature I have ever seen." John sputters.

"This is our little secret, John. Nobody, I mean nobody can know that I live here or my life will be in danger." She tells John.

"Of course, Lily. I am here to help protect the creatures and animals that are down here." He tells her.

"I need to explain something to you." She asks.

"Of course. I am listening." He replies.

"The tracks you saw when you came in… they are of a very bad animal. They mean harm to all the creatures that are here and still on their way. I need your help to protect them and myself, along with my offspring." She says.

"I understand. I will help in every way I can." John replies.

"I need you to take this information to Kia. I need her to come here. She is the only one that will help us from the evil that has found this cave. They have the scent of her and the others here; they will be back." Lily tells John.

"What are they, Lily?" John asks.

"They are bad news, deadly news for all us shifters. Please, John, I need Kia to come as soon as possible. I need to speak with her." Lily tells him.

"Okay, I will go call Kia and tell her as soon I get to the camper." John tells her.

"Thank you, John. I will talk to you again." Lily says as she slides back down into the pond and disappears.

John, still amazed that he just talked with a real live mermaid, makes his way back through the cave, checking the cameras as fast as he can.

"Hurley, load up," John yells, waiting for Hurley to jump in the back of the mule. Hurley jumps in and they head for the camper. John is excited yet worried that whatever it is that has found the cave will be lurking in the woods waiting for the creatures and shifters to come out to attack or kill whatever it is here to do. *How is Kia going to solve all this?* John wonders. *This girl really must be something special to them.*

John looks at his cellphone for a signal while standing outside the garage, John can smell that weird odor again in the breeze blowing gently through the field.

"Hello, Victor, how are you doing? This is John Smith.

"Good to hear from you."

"Victor, I need to speak with Kia. Is she available?" John asks.

When Kia gets on the phone, John asks how she is doing. "I have a strange request of you." John announces.

"Strange request, John? What do you mean?" Kia asks.

"Remember Lily? Well, I just saw her down in the cave. She really needs to speak to you. She said it is very important to her and your lives. That is all she really told me." John tells Kia.

"Okay, John. I just got settled in Victor's house in town. I guess I could come out tonight, that is if Victor and Kane will allow it. I will have to call you back. Is that all right, John?" Kia asks.

"Sure, no problem." John replies.

He hangs up and walks inside so he can start dinner, shower, and see what pictures are on the cards.

CHAPTER 4

"The Brothers"

Malik, one of Alexis Ravenworth's sons, checks into the Beaver Creek Motel. He gets two rooms adjoined for seven days.

Damien, Luther, and Lucius are waiting in the car for their brother to come out. They are waiting to hear from their mother's servants, Ada or Gabriel. She never calls herself; she always sends someone that works for her to take care of them.

They get their suitcases out of the trunk and walk towards the motel door.

"Luther and Lucius, you two are in Room 8. Damien and I are in Room 7. A door connects the rooms so unlock it when you get in." Malik tells them.

"So how long are we in this joint?" Damien asks.

"Until Mother has her slaves call and tell us where they have rented us a place to hang for a while. It surely isn't going to be in this place. Especially for what Mother is asking us to do. We could never get away with that here." Malik tells them.

"What is on the agenda, bro?" Luther and Lucius say simultaneously, then laugh and punch each other.

"Stop copying me, Lucius. Damn it!" Luther says to Lucius.

"No, you stop copying me. I said it first." Lucius says to Luther.

"Bullshit, dude." Luther replies.

"Hey, you two idiots, knock it off already. Grow the hell up. You two are twenty years old. It's time to act like it." Malik scolds them.

"Back to business. I will scope out the place, take a midnight run to survey the scent of any other animals out there. We need to know what we are looking for is here. We can then tell Mother what we have picked up on." Malik tells all of them.

"Sounds cool to us, right bro?" Lucius says and high fives his twin brother. Malik just shakes his head.

"Okay, in about six hours, we will be going on our run. I suggest you get a little shuteye, especially you two. Make sure Luther and Lucius are ready when I come wake you." Damien tells them. Malik just looks at Damien. Damien just rolls his eyes at Malik and walks past him, bumping his shoulder into his. Malik doesn't budge, as if Damien never even touched him.

Malik is the dominant one in the bunch. At twenty-five, he is the oldest brother. Standing at six feet five inches with straight hair almost to his shoulder, his body is muscular. He wears his beard tracing his jawbone in a thin line and a neatly groomed goatee. He has blackish brown hair and light brown eyes almost a reddish tan color.

Damien is the second oldest and has a bad attitude he cannot control. A lot of his aggression is jealousy towards Malik. He is twenty-three, and not quite as tall as his older brother. He is only six feet tall and that pisses him off to no end. He always has to look up to his brother, even when he doesn't want. Damien is the perfect Damien. Dark brown eyes with a light amber color ring around the pupil. When one looks him in the eyes, one is taken aback at how strange they look. He has shoulder-length, jet-black hair and not as muscular as Malik.

Luther and Lucius, they are identical twins. They have always finished each other's sentences. They are different from the other two. They are tan-skinned, long blond hair down past the middle of their back, straight and thick, and bright blue eyes with a light brownish tan ring around the pupil. They have no facial hair. Nicely built with not too much muscle, but lean and fit, they are shorter than the other two at only five feet eleven inches. These two go with the flow of things, no arguments unless it is with the other twin. They are a lot like two surfer dudes. They are only twenty.

Damien and Malik have always butted heads. In a fight for dominance, Damien hates Malik for ever being born. Malik doesn't feel that way about Damien. They even had to be separated for a few years growing up because Damien tried to stab Malik several times. Despite his hatred Malik, Damien loves his younger brothers; they just drive him crazy.

Damien sneaks into Luther and Lucius' room. It is almost midnight; he knows that they are asleep. He softly walks in and stands in between the two beds. Hitting the wall and yelling, "Look out!" at the same time, Luther and Lucius jump up and yell for Malik. Looking around the room, they see Damien standing in between the beds, laughing so hard he is crying.

"That shit isn't funny, man." Lucius yells at him.

"You should have seen the looks on your faces… priceless." Damien says laughing hard.

"What the hell are you guys doing over here? Are you trying to wake up the whole motel?" Malik says as he walks into the room.

"It is Damien's fault!" Lucius replies.

"I don't care. You need to calm down and get your asses in the truck. We have work to do and only a short time to do it tonight. We already have the scent; we need to find where they are hiding." Malik tells the others.

They all get in the truck and head out. Luther asks if they can drive through McDonalds to get some food. He is hungry. Malik agrees.

Turning down the dirt path that leads to the ledge above the camping areas by the creek, Malik pulls the truck a ways into the woods and turns it to face outward just in case they have to leave in a hurry.

They get out of the truck and stand at the back tailgate.

"Are you all ready for this?" Damien asks his brothers.

Malik lets them smell the scent he has. "Remember this is the scent we need to find. Mother says this one is the most important one for Monroe. Anything else we find, make a note of it, and we will let Mother know what we have gathered. Understand?" Malik says to his brothers.

They all run and soon they are transformed into huge massive animals. Damien runs in second place, allowing Malik, the pack leader and alpha male to move ahead of the pack. Lucius and Luther run side by side as always. Twins stick together even when they are in shifted form.

They stop at the creek edge. Malik smells the air. It is blowing in from the west. He looks at the rest with his amber yellow eyes and snarls. The others know what he is saying, that he has picked up the scent of another shifter.

They take off running between the creek and the tree line along the creek edge. Damien, the wild card, runs slightly ahead of Malik. Malik looks over at Damien; he notices that Damien's eyes are slightly different. Malik slams into Damien, reassuring him that he never challenges the leader of the pack especially the elder and alpha male.

Damien bounces back and again challenges Malik for lead position. Now angry, Malik slams Damien harder, hoping it will send him in a roll to slow him down and make him focus. Instead, Damien senses Malik's move and compensates for it, tripping Malik and then grabbing him by the neck. They both roll and tear into each other.

Luther and Lucius stop and watch their two brothers viscously fighting. Neither one backing down, Luther finally shifts into his human form and yells at them.

"Stop it, you freaking idiots! What the hell is wrong with you two? Is this how it is going to be every time we go to work? I am so over you two. If Mother were here or even knew about you two fighting constantly, she would remove one of you. Damien, I bet it would be your stupid ass!"

Damien looks at Lucius for a split second. His eyes turn orange and he lunges for Luther! Malik grabs ahold of Damien by the back between his shoulders with his furious teeth. Damien still tries to pull out of Malik's grip to attack Luther. Lucius leaps in front of Luther protecting him from Damien. Malik tightens his hold on Damien and finally he backs down. Malik still holds on to Damien until he shifts into human form.

"What the hell is your fucking problem, you piece of shit?" Malik yells at Damien.

"I don't know something came over me when I caught the scent down the creek. I don't remember anything after that until now." Damien replies.

Luther and Lucius stand back watching the two argue. Now they are all in human form. Malik walks over and slaps Damien in the back of the head.

"You better get your head cleared out, brother, or else I am going to have to hurt you next time. This was worse than it has ever been before. We are not kids anymore, Damien. You need to learn how to control the hell burning inside you. Respect the leader; respect the alpha male. That is how we stay a pack. Now are we done here? I got that scent and it seems to be coming down stream a few miles?" Malik asks the boys.

They all turn and run, leaping into the air and shifting into their hellhound forms again.

CHAPTER 5
"THE SHIFT"

Kia sits up in bed watching TV while Victor sleeps soundly next to her. The twins grow rapidly and her appetite seems to be matching their speed.

These sleepless nights. Why don't you two let Mom sleep a good night for once?

Looking over at Victor, Kia gets up and decides to walk outside hoping the fresh air will help her and the twins relax.

She opens the slider door and walks out on the porch that adjoins the master bedroom.

Looking up at the moon and stars in the sky, Kia thinks about how clear it is and how beautiful the night sky is here. The colors from the horizon are black and fade upwards into a deep dark blue, filled with tiny bright white lights. The moon is almost at the fullest, glowing like a light over the yard. The wind is blowing slightly to the east and the temperature is perfect out.

Kia remembers when she was little her Grandma and Grandpa used to take the kids out on the full moons to bathe in the moonlight. 'It is very

healing for the mind and body of all living creatures,'
Grandpa Moon used to tell the kids. Back then, she
never understood it, but tonight she can feel exactly
what Grandpa Moon talked about. *It is like the
sunshine on your face. You can feel the mood lifting
and changing your skin and your mind. It feels like it
is cleansing you, pulling all the bad out through your
skin, and rejuvenating your entire body. Oh, what a
feeling. How wonderful. Why don't we appreciate
things like this when we are younger?*

Relaxing with her eyes closed and leaning on
to the railing of the porch, Kia's mind clears and then
she gets a vision. She grips the railing tighter. She
opens her eyes and looks out across the yard. She
can see water, trees, and rocks moving quickly past
her, as if she is looking through someone else's
eyes.

Her heart rate increases and she can feel the
twins restless inside her. She tries to breathe deeply
and exhale slowly to bring her heart rate down. In a
flash, she is standing in the middle of the creek in
her nightgown. She looks around and it is pitch black
outside. Terrified, she feels danger is near. She
never knows what is going to happen in these
visions; they seem so real sometimes.

Kia crouches down and runs up to a big tree
on the creek shore, hopefully hiding from whatever it

is that is out there. Looking all around her she feels her shift coming on.

Oh no…please not now. Not while I am pregnant! This is not good. Why can't Victor feel my cries? Kia whispers as she cries.

She looks down at her arms and a glowing light ripples down her arm. In a shake, she has shifted. Still half-human she has all the reactions and senses of both. She looks like she is a human with a whitish-brown fur covering her body and black fur around her two differently colored eyes.

She smells something in the air. She knows this scent. Her fur rises on her neck all the way down to her back. She suddenly realizes it is the hellhounds. They have made it to Beaver Creek. She takes off running at a fast speed, bouncing high off the rocks under her and finally reaching a field.

Kia stands there looking through the open field in the moonlight. *I know this field,* she says to herself. *This is…* Suddenly she hears water splashing and growls coming from down the creek. She smells them coming. They are getting close. She takes off running low to the ground, darting around the field to fool the hellhounds.

Kia reaches a bridge she doesn't recognize and stops. She gets a whiff of another scent. This scent is familiar also, but it is a good one.

"John, it is John's scent. I must be on John's property." Kia whispers.

She dashes across the bridge that runs over Beaver Creek and keeps going until she reaches a road. Not sure what road it is, she runs away from the scent of the hellhounds.

She stops at a crossroad. With her keen hearing, she listens to see if she can hear them anywhere. Listening, she doesn't hear them. However, she hears what sounds like two dogs fighting. *What is going on*, Kia wonders.

Not sticking around to wait, she tells herself and off she goes heading west.

Finally, she notices where she is. It is the town of Beaver Creek. From there, she knows how to find home.

Wishing Victor would wake her from this vision before something bad happens to the twins and her, a sharp pain wraps around her side bringing her down to the ground. She tucks and rolls so she doesn't land on her stomach. Kia yells in pain and calls for Victor just before passing out.

Victor jumps up in the bed. *Kia*, he looks to the other side of the bed and she is gone. He leaps out of bed and runs out the open slider. Standing on the porch in the moonlight, he feels something is wrong.

Racing across the field towards the town, Victor runs as fast as he can. He stops suddenly in a crossroad. Focusing all of his energy, he places his hands in the center of his stomach. With his head down, a bright light emerges from the center of his chest and shoots out across the area. His arms now out to his side and head straight up, he summons the earth elements and spirit animals to help him. Within seconds, he opens his eyes, surrounded by spirit animals. He nods his head to them all and they all scatter in different directions in search of Kia.

He hears something coming up behind him. Victor turns around and sees a big black figure running at high speeds right towards him. Victor puts his hand out ready to blast whatever it is. Then he sees the crystal blue eyes. Kane.

"Kane, is that you? Where the hell have you been? Where is Kia?" Victor says.

"I don't know, Victor. I was sitting in the chair in the living room, when I awoke to a scream. Kia's scream. I looked in the bedroom and noticed you guys were gone. I ran out the door and tracked your scent to here." Kane replies.

"Can you smell Kia, Kane?" Victor asks.

"No, that is what is weird. All I smell is a rotten, foul smell like a dirty dog that rolled in something dead. I can tell it is not a good smell. Whatever it is, it's bad." Kane tells Victor.

"Okay, let me see if I can connect to the spirit animals that are searching for her." Victor tells him.

Victor places his hands together in the center of his chest and closes his eyes, waiting for one of the spirit animals to give him a sign.

Victor takes off running in a high speed. Kane follows right behind him. They come up on Kia's spirit animal hovering over Kia with her hand on her head. Victor looks at the spirit animal and she has a panicked look on her face. She flies up above them both and circles as if something is wrong. She points towards the east and flies back in front of Victor.

She places her hands on each side of his head. Suddenly, Victor sees something.

Yellow glowing eyes looks like they are running towards them. Victor jerks out of the spirit animal's touch. Shaken by what he saw, he bends down to Kia gently rolling her onto her back.

"Kia, honey, you must wake up now." Victor says to her.

"Kia, come on, baby. Get up. We are in danger; you must wake up. Kia. KIA!!" Victor shouts her name.

Kia wakes up startled, scrambling to get away from Victor. She doesn't realize it is he. She crouches on her knees in fear until she finally realizes it's Victor touching her.

"Victor, something... something is after me! I could smell them again, I could hear them, and I could feel them. They are after me. They aren't after the other shifters they want me." She says as she cries. "Kia, I know something isn't right. We need to go and get you back to safety."

Both Kane and Victor move to pick up Kia. Kane steps up and tells Victor, "Victor, let me take her. I can carry her home. I have the strength and speed to do this in my shifted form."

"Okay, please be careful with her." Victor says.

Kane picks up Kia and her aura shifts before he takes off running at speeds Victor can't keep up.

Finally, they get back to the house. Kane puts Kia in her bed.

"Kia, are you all right?" Kane asks her.

"Yes, Kane. I am now, thank you." She says.

"Kia, if you don't mind me asking, what the hell were you doing out that far alone? How did you sneak past my guard? I never even sensed you were up and gone until Victor came in."

"I walked out in the moonlight and the next thing I knew, I was standing in the middle of Beaver Creek! I sensed danger and shifted. Not willingly, it just happened. I had no control over it at all. I couldn't get back fast enough to take the herbs Dr. Whiteriver gave me in case I felt I was going to shift. I don't understand how I ended up there!" Kia tells him.

"The next thing I knew I was running as fast as I could and ended up by town. I could see these glowing eyes chasing me, and then I heard Victor yelling at me. That is when I saw you two." She tells Kane.

"We need to lock up the doors and get the sensors so when one opens, I know about it!" Kane says in a deepened tone.

Victor finally comes in the bedroom slider, closing and locking it behind him. He turns and shakes his head at Kia.

"I know I screwed up, but before you yell at me at least, let me explain." Kia says.

Victor stands next to her on the bed and waits for her to tell him. She explains she had another vision, but somehow ended up in the middle of Beaver Creek. Victor doesn't bat an eye; he just stares down at her angered.

"Let me tell you how close you came to being taken by whatever the hell is out there. Kia, what the hell? Do you not care about the twins? You are grounded and I mean it! You will not leave this room at night if I have to sleep on the couch and leave Kane in here with you every night. You are not to leave this house unless one of us goes with you. Do you understand, Kia?" Victor says in a loud voice.

Kia agrees and cries.

"I am sorry, Victor. I didn't have any control over it. I swear I wasn't trying to hurt the babies." Kia says sobering.

Victor sits down on the edge of the bed and hugs Kia while she cries. Kane exits the room for a few moments just to come back with a chair and a table and sets in front of the slider door in the master bedroom.

Victor looks at him and rolls his eyes,

"Seriously you're going to sleep in here with us?" Victor says.

"Yes, sir. I am! I was sent here to protect her and she will not leave my sight like that ever again." Kane says to both of them.

Victor agrees.

CHAPTER 6
"GABRIEL"

"Gabriel... Gabriel... come here!!" Alexis Ravenworth yells through the Bluetooth intercom system in her mansion.

Gabriel runs up the flights of stairs to Alexis' office on the third floor. Sliding to a stop in front of her office door, Gabriel takes a deep breath and opens the door with a smile on his face.

"Yes, My Lady. What can I do for you?" He says.

"Have my sons called today?" She asks.

"No, My Lady. I don't believe they have called today. Would you like me to go check with Ada, My Lady?"

"Those four bastards... they better not mess around. They better do their goddamn job!" She says in an angered voice.

"Yes, My Lady. I do hope they are." Gabriel replies.

"Take this letter to Monroe and tell him I need another Crow Warrior and soon. We used the one the other day and we need another one to take its place. He should have had him already prepared, but I see the Crow area is unattended. We have to entertain the guests in less than twenty-four hours. I want the Crow Warrior in his place." Alexis tells Gabriel.

"Yes, My Lady. I will do it right now. Is there anything thing else I can do for you, My Lady?" Gabriel asks.

"No, that will be all for now." Alexis says.

Gabriel turns to leave the massive office and he hears Alexis say something.

"Gabriel, make sure Ada informs me when Malik calls today. I want to speak with him." Alexis tells him.

"Yes, My Lady. I will." Gabriel replies as he bows before turning to the massive wooden doors.

Gabriel walks down to the basement of the mansion where Monroe performs his experiments. Hitting the buzzer outside the laboratory, Gabriel smiles at the camera waiting for Monroe or Dr. Brack to unlock the door.

The door pops open and Gabriel walks into the lab. He hates to come down here; there are so many strange things inside the crates, containers, and cages inside the lab area. *It is always cold down in the lab and smells bad.*

"What can I help you with, Gabriel?" Dr. Brack says.

"Hello, Dr. Brack. I have a letter for Monroe from Lady Alexis, sir." Gabriel lays the letter on the edge of the stainless steel table. Gabriel can't help himself from looking at what they are working on as he peeks over the side of Monroe. Monroe feels Gabriel behind him and slowly turns his head to the left looking at Gabriel out of the corner of his eye. Gabriel has no clue that Monroe is looking at him; he is too shocked at what they are working on.

"Can I help you?" Monroe says with his deep voice. Monroe is a big man. Blond hair and brown eyes, he has a very deep voice and intimidating. Gabriel jumps, startled.

"No… no, sir. I was just delivering the letter; that is all." Gabriel says as he takes a few steps backwards.

"What's wrong, Gabriel? Do you remember this? You were on this slab of steel before." Monroe says sarcastically to him and grins.

Dr. Brack tells Monroe to concentrate on the patient not him. Gabriel turns slowly, looking around at all the specimens they have on the various tables in the laboratory. Eyes widen in fear; he remembers being strapped down to the table and Monroe doing experiments with different DNA on him until they made the combination that was needed to make a good servant to Alexis.

The fear inside never leaves you.

Monroe and Dr. Brack look at each other and smirk.

"I would say he remembers something from his past. Wouldn't you agree, Monroe?" Dr. Brack says.

"I would have to agree with you on that one, Doctor." Monroe answers.

"Gabriel, what is wrong?" Ada asks as she passes him in the corridor to the first story gallery.

"Nothing!" Gabriel says as he passes with his head down.

"Wait a minute! Something is wrong; what is it? You can tell me." Ada says turning around and watching him walk past her.

Gabriel stands for a moment before turning around and slowly raising his head up to look at Ada.

Staring at each other, Ada senses something is horribly wrong with Gabriel. She doesn't say a word and walks towards him. Gabriel has tears in his eyes and his color is pale.

"You look like seen a ghost, Gabriel. Please, what is wrong? What happened to you?" Ada pleads for him to answer her questions.

"I had to deliver a message to Dr. Brack and Monroe in the lab. I…ah." Ada cuts him short.

"Don't tell me they made you come into the lab to give them the message? What is wrong with them?" Ada says loudly.

Ada grabs Gabriel and hugs him caringly.

"It is in the past. Try not to think of it. Think of the good times now, okay? The past isn't where we need to be or even remember. It was a very bad time for us and even though they try to erase the memories from us, they never will delete them all. However, Gabriel, you mustn't let anyone know you have any memories, especially Monroe and Dr. Brack. You know what will happen if they even suspect you remember anything."

"I know, Ada, but I couldn't help it they…I mean I saw."

"Ssshhhh!!! You must not say anything, Gabriel. I know what you saw, I know how awful it is, and how awful it was for all of us to go through the stuff we all went through. But you must remember if we don't watch out and take care of each other, we will be the next one on the list... if you know what I mean?" Ada says whispering into Gabriel's ear.

Ada steps back and grabs Gabriel's hands. Holding them in hers, she bows her head to him and he returns the gesture.

"Take care, my friend." Ada says letting go of Gabriel's hands and turning away.

Gabriel stands watching Ada walk down the corridor back towards her office, thinking about what she said. *She is right about not letting anyone know he remembers what happened to him. Alexis would have him taken and...* Suddenly he hears a voice come through his radio.

"Gabriel, I need you to meet me in the fourth floor parlor." Alexis instructs him through the mic he wears in his ear. Gabriel panics, turns to the left, and goes to walk. Then he realizes he is going the wrong way. He turns back around and heads to the stairwell in the middle of the first floor corridor between the lobby and the guest area.

Flustered that she has overheard him talking, Gabriel prepares for the worst as he takes a deep breath and walks up the stairwell. Just then, he realizes he forgot to tell Ada that Alexis wants to talk with Malik when he calls. Frustrated, he knows he doesn't have time to go to Ada and tell her. Hopefully, she won't talk to Alexis until he gets back.

CHAPTER 7

"Pieces of the Puzzle"

Hurley whines at the door wanting back in from his early morning walk around the property. John opens the door of the camper and lets him in. Hurley shakes before John realizes he is all wet from the dew on the grass and weeds throughout the field.

"Damn it, Hurley!" John says aloud. "You shook water all over my laptop and in my coffee. Thank you, you're too kind sometimes, my friend." John says as he grabs a rag and wipes his laptop off.

It is still dark across the pasture at 4:45 a.m. in the morning. John sits down in his chair and starts his laptop, sipping on a fresh hot cup of coffee.

Eager to view the SD cards from the cave, he got up early before heading out for the morning rounds. Kia and Victor are supposed to be here today to see Lily. Hopefully they will.

Going through the first card from the first camera, John doesn't see much that he can notice. Many of the images are smeared or not in focus. He moves to the second camera's SD card, thumbing through the images quickly to see anything unusual.

He stops and clicks on an image that looks strange. Red lights moving like a streak, he tries to see what it is, but it is very hard to make out. He clicks to the next image and then the next. There it goes again — red lights like streaks. *They must be eyes.* Image after image, he finally sees a person in the cave looking right at the camera. John clicks on the image and enlarges it.

"I can't believe this." Johns says aloud. He sees a woman dressed in black with a black lace veil staring right into the camera. She looks like she came straight out of the 1800's. Could this be Anne Stellar, John wonders. Or someone is snooping around the caves again? Funny thing, I didn't see anything strange in or outside the cave as far as a woman's footprint. Well, maybe when we looked for Hurley, we saw some, but those were Lily's, I thought…

He clicks and downloads the image to save it on his computer. Next SD card from the third camera reads Empty.

"Well, how can that be?" John says.

Pulling it out and putting the next one in for camera four, "Card error" comes across the screen. John is getting frustrated.

"How can this be happening? Ten damn cameras and only one image I can use so far. I hope the other six have something on them."

SD card five starts to load images. Finally... Finishing his cup, he gets up to refill it while the images load.

Turning around and stepping from the kitchen area over to the laptop, he sees something on his screen. It freezes him in his tracks. John stares at an image on the screen he has never ever seen before. A huge creature stands in the entrance of the big room. Glowing yellow eyes stare right through the camera and watch John. He can feel it. He drops his coffee cup and it shatters on the floor. Hurley jumps up from a sound sleep startled.

"Shit! Damn it! I'm sorry, Hurley boy. Did I get hot coffee on you?" John says bending down to pick up the pieces of the broken cup. Reaching for the paper towels, he gets a strange feeling. He stops and slowly turns to the window behind him. Knowing he shut the door to the garage, there can't possibly be anything in here. However, he feels something watching him. He walks slowly over to the window and looks out. Pitch black in the garage he can't see anything. He laughs a bit and shakes his head looking one more time out the window to see he was just letting things get to him. Right then, a pair of yellow eyes appears in the window. John jumps back. This time he got a good look at the dark face behind the eyes.

He runs over and turns the outside light on for the camper. Looking out the window, he doesn't see anything. He runs back to the window and doesn't see anything. Looking through all the windows checking all around the camper, he doesn't see anything.

Hurley looks at him as if he has gone mad.

"Don't just lay there like you didn't notice anything. Don't you smell anything? No, it is all me again, huh?" John says to Hurley.

"I guess it is just me. That is what I get I guess from all the strange things that have happened lately."

Looking at the image on the computer, he saves it so he can show Kia, Victor, and the sheriff. The next image comes up and four big creatures now stand in the entrance of the big cave. The other three look towards the pond and the one still stares right through the camera. Except now, he is closer. The other three seem to be looking at or for something. He downloads it and moves to the next image. The image comes up and John jumps back in his chair.

'Wow, that is.. The exact image I just saw outside the window", He mumbles.

'How did I see it in the window before I saw it on the computer?' He wonders. Sitting back up, he clicks through the images. It is night vision so it is a little hard to make out exactly every detail of these creatures. They are huge with yellow eyes. They resemble an extremely large dog or wolf except the hair looks longer and they have something around their neck down by their chest. It seems to wrap all the way around them and glowing orange, almost like the color of flames in a fire. They also have an orange yellow hue tone to their eyes now. Clicking through image-by-image, he realizes that they are searching for something.

"I bet this is what Lily needs to talk to Kia about." John mumbles looking down at his clock. It is almost 8:00 a.m. already. John quickly downloads the images he has found and turns off his laptop.

Getting up from the chair, he turns and calls Hurley. "Come on, boy. Let's go make some phone calls and take a ride around the property." John says walking out the door of the camper.

Kane and Victor wait in the kitchen for Kia to come out. They are heading to see John this morning. After all the events that happened last night and Kia shifting herself to another place, Victor is very worried that she doesn't have control over what is happening to her. He wonders what is causing this bizarre shifting. Possibly the twins, but they are still so young they wouldn't have any control on her powers of shifting, he wonders as he leans up against the kitchen counter.

Kane seems worried also. For the first time, he feels as though he might not be able to keep Kia and the twins safe. For a werewolf, this is very degrading to his inner being. He sits with his head hung down, staring into a cup of coffee. He can hear Victor talking in the background on the phone. He contemplates whether he should contact Dr. Redbone and Dr. Whiteriver about what happened last night.

"Well, don't we look like we lost our best friend?" Kia says to Kane. Kane snaps his head up and looks at Kia. The light from the morning sun is just gleaming through the large kitchen window shining on Kia's face and down the front of her. Kane's eyes slowly travel down her body studying every inch of it. He can feel the wolf inside him lusting for her desire. He makes a deep sound in his throat like a low growling sound. His eyes move

73

back up her body. He can't help from staring at her. She's so beautiful; she has a glow that glitters like a light beaming off her skin like an angel. He can feel the warmth of her body from across the table.

His eyes lock together with Kia's they sit staring at each other without saying a word.

"Good morning, Kane." Kia says. However, Kane just stares at her.

"Are you all right?" She asks.

"Oh….yeah. Good morning, Kia." Kane replies. Flustered, he jumps up out of the chair.

"How are you feeling this morning?" Kane asks.

"I'm fine, but I'm a little concerned about you, hon. You sure everything is all right?" Kia asks him.

"Oh yes, ma'am. I was just in a state of thought, sorry." Kane replies.

Victor walks up behind Kia, kissing her on the neck and wrapping his arms around her growing belly.

"How are all my babies doing this morning?" Victor asks her.

Kane walks to the kitchen sink, pouring out his coffee.

"We are fine, dear." Kia replies to Victor.

"Are we ready to go then?" Kane asks walking towards the door. Kane opens the door and waits for Kia to walk out to the car.

Chapter 8

"Family never gets along"

Back at Beaver Creek Motel, Lucius and Luther sit outside watching the sun come up, waiting for Damien and Malik to come out.

"What the hell happened last night, bro?" Lucius asks.

"Dude, I don't know. I guess Damien caught a scent and he snapped. I know Malik has had it with Damien and his evil tendencies towards him." Luther says.

"He almost had your ass, man. If Malik didn't grab him by the neck from behind and sling him, he would have attacked you. Why did you shift anyways?" Lucius asks.

"I was going to talk them down, but when Damien turned around. I saw his eyes were like two glowing flames. They changed and I knew he was in a rage to kill. I knew if I shifted back, he would see me as more of a threat and become more furious." Luther explains.

"I'm sure Mother will hear about this today when Malik makes the call. Malik has to report what we found. I'm sure that is what the meeting is all about this morning." Lucius says.

They both turn when they hear a door open. Two young pretty girls walk out talking and laughing from the room next to theirs. They both watch the girls walk past them and open the doors to their car parked next to boys' truck.

"Good morning, ladies." Luther and Lucius say at the same time.

The girls giggle.

"Oh, good morning, boys," the one girl says as she smiles and winks at them.

The other girl across on the passenger side waves. "Good morning. Are you guys staying for a while?"

"Why yes, ma'am, we are. How about you ladies?" Luther replies.

"Yes, we are here for a few weeks. Maybe we can hook up later?" the one girl says.

"Yeah, for sure. We will be here." Lucius says.

They watch the girls pull out, waving as they leave. About that time, they hear the door to Malik and Damien's room open. Malik walks out and stands in front of the truck. Damien slowly comes out leaving the door open. He stands in the doorway and leans against the frame.

Neither one say a word to Luther or Lucius. Damien crosses his arms to his chest and hangs his head down looking at the ground. Something is different about him. Luther and Lucius sense something strange and stand up, moving away from Damien. Something uneasy in his vibes is scaring the two younger brothers. It doesn't bother Malik at all. Damien watches Luther and Lucius move away from the top of his eyes. His eyes have a hint of red glowing in them. Rage and anger unsettled within.

Malik looks in perfect control as always. Never shows fear, never shows doubt. "So do we all want to discuss what happened last night?" Malik says.

Lucius and Luther agree, but Damien still doesn't say a word. He just stares at the ground.

"Okay, what did you guy's pick up on last night? Malik asks

Luther is the first to speak. "I sensed a creature of the water shifters and several others I think Mother will be interested in."

79

"What other ones did you sense, Luther?" Malik asks.

"I sensed a female scent, like she is attracting a male species. It was a sweet rotten smell. Made me think what kind of shifter it could be. I never picked up on that before. The other was human like, but not human. It also had a rotten smell to it." Luther says.

"Yeah, that is exactly what I smelled." Lucius comments.

Damien snickers under his breath shaking his head as if he knows something and they don't.

"What about you, Damien? Would you like to share your personal joke with the rest of your family?" Malik says.

"You want to know what I smelled. I sensed a bitch with child that was so fucking irresistible. It was strong, intoxicating; all I wanted to do was find it and nothing was going to stop me. That is the scent Mother is looking for — a special shifter carrying offspring. Isn't it, Malik?" Damien replies to them.

"I smelled the same scent and no doubt it was intoxicating. However, it didn't make me lose control and turn into a wild beast trying to take out my younger brother and challenging the leader of this pack! So you want to tell us all what the hell is wrong with you, Damien!" Malik says in an angered voice, walking up to the front of Damien.

Damien just snickers and looks up to Malik knowing it is going to piss Malik off if he acts as if he doesn't give a shit

"We are here to do a job and I will see that it is done and correctly, without harm to us or the shifters we seek. Now if you have a problem with me, Damien, we need to settle it ourselves. Don't take it out on someone else or your own brother. Now you have authority issues since you were younger, you're an adult now. Grow the fuck up and get over it. I am the alpha and I am the leader of this pack, like it or not!" Malik says.

Damien looks up at Malik with a glowing red in his eyes. Malik knows that he is going to have to tell mother about the events that have taken place. Something needs to be done with Damien or they need to put him on some kind of drug to help control his anger issues.

"Hey, do you guys want to hear some good news?" Luther asks.

"Yeah, sure. What is it?" They all respond. Everyone except Damien. He just keeps his head down and looks at them from the top of his eyes.

"Two young girls are staying for a few weeks next to our room. Maybe they can bring some other girls and we all can hook up." Luther suggests.

Damien uncrosses his arms and asks, "How'd they look? Sweet, sexy, and nice bodies?"

"Oh man, yeah. Sweet as sugar and hot bodies willing to take us on. I could smell them; they wanted sex." Luther replies.

Malik changes the subject asking if they are ready to get some breakfast. They all reply yes. They get in the truck and head to the nearest restaurant in town.

"Hey, look at that place. It looks good." Lucius points over to Nell's Diner. Malik pulls in to the parking lot. Luther notices that the two girls from the motel car are parked over on the other side of the lot.

Walking in, Luther elbows Lucius and nods towards their car in the parking lot. Lucius realizes what Luther is doing and sees the girls' car, giving a high five to his brother.

Chapter 9

"HEED THE WARNING"

Kane opens the door for Kia and helps her get out while Victor greets John and Hurley.

"Hi, Hurley. How are you, boy?" Victor pets Hurley on the head. "Hi, John, how are you doing?" Victor shakes his hand.

"I'm good, can't complain. I am glad you guys could make it. How is Kia been doing?" John asks.

"She is doing okay. She pulled a strange stunt last night that had Kane and me scared. Oh, I didn't introduce Kane to you yet, John. This is Kane. He was sent to help protect Kia and the twins." Victor introduces them.

Kane shakes John's hand and John hugs Kia, introducing Sheriff Taylor to Kane. John explains to them that he was down in the cave checking cameras when he finally met Lily. "She was desperate to talk to Kia. Almost demanding," he explains.

They all get in the mule and head to the creek. Kane sits in back with Kia and Sheriff Taylor while Victor rides in front with John. Hurley, well, he is bouncing through the field leading the way as usual.

They make their way across to the cave. John, Sheriff Taylor, Victor, Kia, and Kane walk in the entrance. Suddenly Kia feels someone grab her by the arm and pull her back out the cave.

"What the hell? What are you doing, Kane?" Kia asks in a demanding voice.

"You need to leave this minute! Kia, you are not safe here. There is something very bad in that cave. Evil, Kia. I am not joking around here. Victor??" Kane yells.

Victor comes running out. "What's going on?"

"I smell something very evil inside the cave. Kia needs to get out of here right away. She can't stay here." Kane explains.

"Kane, it is all right. Kia has been in the cave many times before this." Victor tries to calm Kane's fears. However, he refuses to accept that for an answer. He wants to take her out of there immediately.

John can't help to hear them arguing about what is inside the cave as Sheriff Taylor keeps walking. He decides to tell them what he saw on the SD cards hoping that it make it easier.

"If I could interject. Perhaps it will help if I explain to you all what I have seen. Four very large animals that looked like jumbo-sized wolves on steroids, with glowing yellowish orange eyes and the same flow around the chest and under the front legs. One keeps staring at the camera as if he knew it was there. The others went to the pond.

"If you come further in the cave, you can see the tracks. I saw them when I went down to check the SD cards yesterday morning."

They decide to walk in and look. Kane believes he might make out the tracks and the smell may be stronger inside.

"The only thing is I have to shift. I don't know John." Kane says nervously.

Kia reassures Kane, "John is the best friend we have. He is completely fine."

Kane turns and walks into the entrance of the cave. As he walks, he shifts into a black wolf with bright blue eyes. John is amazed. He has never seen one before.

"Those other four creatures in the cave looked similar to Kane except they were even larger than Kane is." He tells Victor and Kia.

They all follow Kane into the cave. Going all the way back to the big room, Kane stands in the entrance and his hair rises on his back. His stance becomes threatening, humped up with his head down. Then they hear a rumbling deep growl that shakes the air. It vibrates through the whole cave. Anything and everything in the cave could feel it.

Kia holds on to Victor tightly as they wait for Kane to allow them to walk through. Finally, Kane shifts so fast the air moves like wind blowing forcefully past them.

"It isn't just the four of them. Something else is in the cave somewhere. I know they are evil and the one doesn't seem to be the eminent danger." Kane tells them. He is extremely worried about the other four. He can't take on all four of them.

"So it is safe now? I can go find Lily?" Kia asks Kane.

"Yes, ma'am, but I have to be with you. I can't let you go anywhere in here alone, understand?" Kane says in a deepened tone.

"Okay, that is fine just don't freak out when you see Lily, okay?" Kia quickly responses to Kane. Kane looks at Kia shocked by her comeback.

Kia walks over to the edge of the pond and reaches down to the water. Placing her hand in the water and swirling it around, Kane stands next to her watching across the water for anything to come out. Victor and John stand on the other side of Kia.

Kane slowly reaches down and puts his large hand on Kia's shoulder in a protective stance. He stares out across the pond. Kia slowly gets up and they all watch the water. Then they hear a woman's voice humming John's favorite tune. Kane tightens his grip a little on Kia's shoulder, slowly pulling her back away from the water.

"Kane!! It's all right. It's Lily!" Kia says with a harsh whisper.

Kane loosens his grip, but keeps his hand on Kia. Victor watches Kane with concern. Knowing he means well, he still fears he is becoming more than a protector to Kia. The way he looks at her and different ways he tries to protect her seem a little more than his job.

John and Sheriff Taylor shine the lights across the water waiting to see Lily. Kia calls for her and a small wave moves towards the shore of the pond by where they are all standing. Kia walks over to the water, with Kane right beside her watching every movement and sensing every smell in the cave.

"Kia, is that you?" They hear a voice call from the water.

"Yes, Lily. It is I, Kia. Please come out, Lily. I came to see you." Kia replies.

"I smell an unpleasant odor with you, a threatening one, Kia. Who is with you?" Lily asks.

"John, Victor, and Kane are here to protect me and the twins. It is all right, Lily. Nobody here will hurt you, I promise." Kia tells Lily as she looks at Kane with a glare in her eyes.

John shines the light towards the big rock on the side of the pond. They see the face of a woman; it is Lily. She slowly moves up towards the shore in the water. Walking towards them, Kia feels Kane loosen his grip on her shoulder. She quickly grabs Kane's hand, holding it tightly. Kane spins his head around with a surprised angered look on his face. Kia motions her head in a "No" response. Kane turns back and looks at Lily he is amazed at how she looks. John, Victor, and Sheriff Taylor just stare at her as she moves from the water towards them. She has shifted into human form to greet Kia.

Her skin is pale white with a soft fish scale texture to it. It has a glow of radiance from it like the Mother of Pearl. Silvery white with pink, blue, orange, and yellow glow to it. Her hair is very long and orange-red color. Her eyes are as blue as the ocean, bright and bigger than normal human eyes. She shies from the light that John holds towards her. The light hurts her eyes.

Kia releases Kane's hand, walks over to Lily, and hugs her.

"Lily, you are so beautiful. How are you doing?" Kia asks.

"Kia, I am fine. I can feel the life growing inside you." Lily touches Kia's stomach to feel the babies inside of her.

"They are growing fast and they know more than you think they do." Lily tells her.

"Lily this is Kane, my guard, John you know, Victor the twin's father, and Sheriff Taylor." Kia introduces everyone.

"It is nice to meet you all." Lily says.

"Lily, what is going on? Why did you need to see me?" Kia asks.

"I need to warn you, Kia. They are here. They are looking for you. They have been coming into the cave smelling everywhere, searching for different shifter creatures. I overheard two talking that they need to find the one with the great child to bring back. Right away I knew they were looking for you." Lily tells them.

"But I have all these men that are protecting me, Lily. There is no worry. I am safe here with them." Kia replies.

"No, Kia, no... Heed my warning, Kia. If you stay, they will find you. If they get you, they will take you and imprison you in a cage, take the babies from you, and harm them. You must leave as soon as possible. Immediately! All these men have no power over them. They are very evil creatures, Kia. They are hellhounds." Lily says.

Kia's eyes widen. She remembers a vision she had a while back about the four images on the ridge of the mountain while Victor and she were in the field. She remembers that smell in the air. Suddenly she looks around and takes a deep breath.

"OMG!" Kia says loudly.

Kane grabs Kia's arm and places half of himself in front of Kia. Putting himself between her and Lily. Victor steps to the other side of Kia and grabs her arm.

"What is it, Kia?" Victor and Lily say at the same time.

"I remembered a vision and what was after me the other night? I can remember the smell of them. They were hellhounds, and I just smelled the same scent in here!" Kia says.

"You must take her far away from this place until the twins are born. Don't bring her or the twins back together. Kia can come back, but it is too dangerous for the twins until they are older or the threats are gone." Lily says to them.

"I will take her away from here. She is under my protection and my watch. I am not taking any risks. We will leave immediately." Kane says in a determined voice.

"Wait, wait, a minute." Victor says.

"I can handle them. I am a warlock, Lily. I have powers they cannot deal with. Kane... he is ferrous also. There might be four of them, but between my powers, Kane, and Kia's help, they are not going to get to her." Victor replies.

"I am taking Kia out of Beaver Creek. End of story!" Kane decides. Victor steps aside, knowing Kane is right. The slightest chance of them getting Kia is a threat to the twin's lives and he will not allow that to happen. Victor agrees with Kane.

Lily hugs Kia and tells her to hide until it is safe for her to come back. "I will be in the cave hiding. They will not get to me," Lily says. "A number of different shifter creatures have been hiding in the cave until the hellhounds showed up. Now they come in and leave." Lily tells them.

"If you don't find some other cave system to hide in, you could be in grave danger," Lily says.

Lily turns away and walks back into the water. Kane grabs Kia gently by the right arm and walks her out of the cave. Victor follows behind them while Sheriff Taylor and John follow behind.

Victor looks at Kane, "So what do you think, Kane? How bad is it really?" Victor asks.

"There is no way Kia is staying here another minute. If you want, you can go pack up her stuff and meet us in North Carolina. I am leaving as soon as we get back to the vehicle." Kane says in a demanding voice to Victor.

Kane is taller than Victor, and he knows that intimidates him. Even with Victor being a warlock with great powers, he can't underestimate the size of

Kane and the powers he has as a werewolf. Victor knows that wherever Kane takes Kia is the safest place she could be.

Chapter 10

"Mother"

"My Lady, your son Malik is on the phone." Ada tells Alexis.

"It's about time, Malik! What have you four been doing?" Alexis says picking up the phone in her office.

"Good morning to you, Mother, Nice to hear your voice." Malik says.

"How is Damien holding up? Is he getting out of control again? Alexis asks.

"No.....Mother, I have everything under control. Damien and the boys are doing well they're eating breakfast right now. I stepped out to call you and tell you what we have found." Malik tells Alexis.

"Well, I hope you found something, Malik. We need a silver-blood to synthesize the DNA and build…" Malik interrupts Alexis while she is speaking.

"I know, Mother. If you'd just listen to me once, you would know that I have found what you're looking for." Malik says.

"What? Where? You captured a silver-blood?"

Alexis asks excitedly for the first time in a long time.

"Last night, we went for a run and we picked up several creatures' scents in the woods. One is the creature you're looking for, but the other is very, very rare. You will really appreciate the item I am mailing you today. It should be there tomorrow. You need to take it right down to the lab to see how fresh it is." Malik says.

"Malik, what did you find? You're making me wonder and I don't like to wonder, you know." Alexis tells Malik.

"We all smelled different scents, but the silver-blood was so close and then…" Alexis cuts Malik short.

"What do you mean it was close and then! Malik if you lost this silver-blood shifter again like last time, I will put you all out to pasture! Do you hear me, son?" Alexis says yelling into the phone.

"Yes, we found the silver-blood and we followed the scent for a while. Then it disappeared on us. I know… like last time. But listen to me first, Mother. This one is pregnant! And the other scent we found was very rare; actually a few were very rare."

"If you lost this one, Malik! You better capture this silver-blood or I will send out Phooka to clean up your mess once again, Malik." Alexis yells through the phone to him.

Malik falls silent for a moment. Alexis knows he doubts that his brothers and he can bring back the creature she wants. Silver-blood shifters are very smart, very protected, and once they feel or sense a threat, they disappear without a trace.

"I see. Well, at least you have found it now. Hopefully, it hasn't fled the area and gone into hiding again like the last one. Not this time, Malik. This time you will listen to me or I will be done with all of you! You hear me????" Alexis says to Malik, angrily.

Malik answers Alexis and agrees. They will wait for Phooka and once he comes, Malik will bring other creatures she is looking for back to the Plantation as Alexis has instructed.

Malik hangs up the phone with his mother Alexis just as the door to Nell's opens and Lucius walks out holding the door for his brother Luther.

"Hey, Malik. Luther got those girls' number and names. They said they are having friends come to their hotel room for a party. Can we go? We can score, man." Lucius tells Malik as he walks past him.

Malik puts his head down for a moment then looks up at Lucius and tells Lucius he doesn't care as long as they are careful and nobody finds out what they really are.

"Other words, Lucius, make sure when you're fucking that chick, you don't let your hellhound come out. Control yourself if you find a girl that will fuck you." Malik grins at Lucius, who doesn't find that funny at all. Lucius turns around and walks away pissed.

"If a girl would fuck me!" Lucius says under his breath as he walks towards the truck.

Luther comes out behind Lucius, strutting like a rooster that just banged the hen, proud of himself for talking with the two girls and getting the phone number of the one girl Elsa.

He smiles at Malik as he walks past him. Malik smiles and nods his head at Luther. Luther walks towards the truck saying, "I got her number, brother. You were a chicken, dude."

Last but not least, Damien strolls out the doors. He looks to the left purposely to show Malik he doesn't obey Malik and doesn't respect him as the alpha of the group.

Malik looks at Damien and squints his eyes enough to let Damien know he's pushing Malik's limits. *I am so over Damien and his bullshit attitude towards him and the two brothers. When we are done with this job and back home, I am kicking Damien out. This will be the last time he hunts with this pack.*

Malik and the others get in the truck and head out of Nell's Restaurant. Lucius asks Luther what the names of the two girls are. He likes the one with the long blond hair and the brown eyes.

"Dania and Elsa. I got my eye on Elsa; she is the one with the long black hair and the green eyes. Dania is the blonde." Luther tells Lucius.

"Too cool, bro." Luther says to Lucius and they do a high five.

CHAPTER 11

"LIZZIE AND THE BOYS"

Lizzie pulls onto Beaver Creek Road with Jake and Kyle. Finally, she has a chance to see the property and hopefully Jake will get his act together. He has been getting in trouble almost every day at school and then the cops picked him and some of his friends up for suspicious activity, breaking and entering into a home while the owners were on vacation. He escaped jail time, but had to do community service and pay fines for almost twelve months.

Lizzie is hoping that Jake will find himself while out adventuring on their 100+ acres in the middle of southern Kentucky. Kyle has always been the good son — never gets in trouble, does excellent in school, and is a lot like his father. He loves the outdoors and building things.

"Hi, honey. Where are you guys?" John says when he answers the phone.

"Hello, stranger. We are just pulling on to Beaver Creek Road. Heading your way. I am not sure where to go. Is there any way you can meet us out at the road?" Lizzie says to John on her cell phone.

"Hurley and I will meet you guys at the road in the mule. You are about five minutes away." John tells Lizzie.

"Okay, see you then." Lizzie says and then hangs up her cell phone.

Hardly speaking to Lizzie or Kyle for the whole trip, Jake sits in the front seat. Lizzie feels uncomfortable about it, but realizes he is going through a lot and he's only fifteen years old. The teenage hormones have well kicked in on him. Maybe he will find a girlfriend while he is out here. Lizzie is thinking of leaving him here with his dad for the first part of the school year coming up soon. Maybe it would be good to work on the farm and help his dad, instead of coming home after school and going hiking or skateboarding with his friends in Colorado. The kids are a lot different here in Beaver Creek. Most of them have chores and farming work to do.

Lizzie sees John and Hurley sitting in the mule by the red Iron Gate. Lizzie pulls in and follows John down the driveway and up to the garage.

John has had two cabins finished and one almost completed, yet still has a few more to go. It has one set up for the boys. This way they can stay out there in their own space. Built by the southeast side of the pasture, the cabins are down near the blue hole and the cave. The blue hole is a nice swimming area in the creek where it looks bluish green. The cabins are alike: they have a small living room with a dining area, with a small bathroom and shower. There's a bedroom downstairs and a loft bedroom upstairs that is open from the balcony. There is a porch that wraps the whole area downstairs and a porch that opens from the loft bedroom to see the creek down below.

Lizzie is not crazy about the idea of them staying alone out there, but she would really like to be alone with her husband John. They haven't seen each other for almost a year.

John helps Lizzie out of the truck and hugs her tight. Kyle is the first one out of the truck and he scratches Hurley's head and then hugs his dad. Jake just grabs his bag out of the car and walks towards the garage.

John yells at Jake and says, "Jake, son, you have grown a lot." Jake just glances at his dad and then looks back to the ground. John looks at Lizzie and Lizzie rolls her eyes.

"Yeah, this is what I have to deal with every day, John. You need to keep him here and straighten him out. I am at my wits end. He acts as if I am the enemy when he is the one getting in trouble with them boys he hangs out with all the time. I am not bringing him back when Kyle and I leave. He needs to stay here and learn what it's like to get up and work before going to school. He has had it too nice and he expects us to give him everything. His attitude is like we owe him." Lizzie says to John in a low angered tone.

John just shakes his head in disgust. He knows he has to work on Jake hard or he will just become a problem. If he doesn't realize it, he will get into trouble one day that could put him in jail or cost him his life.

"Jake, let's take a ride. I want to show you and Kyle something." John says to them.

They all get in the mule, drive down the logging trail around the pasture, and pull up at Cabin 1. Kyle is amazed how cool they are. Jake doesn't say a word.

"Come on, I want to show you something." John says to them.

John takes them into the cabin. It is fully furnished with satellite TV, Wi-Fi, food. You name it; John put it all in here, including a brand new Xbox station for them to play at night. Jake walks behind and looks around. He has the slightest grin on one side of his mouth. John sees it and smiles under his breath. He knew this would cheer him up a bit.

"This is so awesome, Dad!" Kyle exclaims.

Jake throws his bags on the couch and grabs his cell phone from his pocket. Checking to see if he has a signal, he doesn't have a cell signal but he has Wi-Fi.

"What is up with the phone service out here?" Jake says.

"Well, it's simple, Jake. There is barely a signal here. If you walk around the property, you might find a better area for reception. Otherwise, you will have to wait to call your friends. You're here to relax, think about where you're heading in your life, and learn how to run the farm with me." John tells him directly.

Jake just walks to the bedroom with his bags and his head down. Kyle walks up and puts his arm on his dad's back and smiles at him.

"Kyle, there is a cave down on the other side of the creek. I will have to show you two, but you can't go in there alone. I found a body of a young girl that was killed and we are not sure what killed her. I will have to show you guys some of the videos and pictures I have from the Native American spirits and shape shifters out here." John tells Kyle.

Kyle is all excited. Jake yells out from the bedroom. "Really, Dad? You think I am going to fall for your fantasy fairy tales? I thought you were an adult, not some teenager living in a movie fantasy like Twilight or something."

Kyle rolls his eyes to his dad over what Jake is saying. Kyle tells his dad that he believes him. He knows there are different things out there and he would love to see them.

"Jake, would you like to go down and see the blue hole where the kids from town come and swim?" John calls out.

With no reply from Jake, John walks in the bedroom and looks at him. He is already on his phone texting his friends. John turns and walks out of the cabin with Kyle and they leave in the mule. John puts it behind him. He will give Jake his space for now, but when Lizzie leaves, he will be busting his balls to work with him every day until school starts. Then he will work every day after school and on every weekend.

John and Kyle get in the mule and head down to the creek. John tells Kyle everything that happened when he was down here exploring in the creek. Kyle was taken back he was actually very interested in everything his dad was telling him.

"How cool, Dad! Do you think I will see some of the animal spirits and shapeshifters?" Kyle asks excitedly.

"We will have to set out by the garage every night and they might just come up. That is what they do. I never called them; they would just appear. There are also some bad things on the property, Kyle. When I say, 'don't go in that cave without me,' I mean it. There is some sort of creature that lives in there. It is called a banshee and she has already killed one young man and believed to have killed the young girl. She is also believed to have turned another young man that fell into another cave Devil's Attic into some type of cave-dwelling creature. So please don't wander alone unless you are going for a swim. Let me know and don't go by yourself. Okay? It can be dangerous. You never know when the creek will pick up and if it does when you're not expecting it, it can pull you down the creek over trees and rocks like rapids." John explains to Kyle while they walk across the creek to the cave.

John and Kyle walk into the cave. John gives Kyle a flashlight and tells Kyle to follow close behind him. They walk through the cave slowly when John stops in front of Kyle.

"What is it, dad?" Kyle asks

"Ssshhh" John says. "Listen. Do you hear that?" John asks.

"Yeah, I hear something. What is that smell? It smells like something dead." Kyle says.

They both start walking again. John looks down at the ground of the cave with his flashlight. He notices human footprints along with a bunch of different animal tracks, more than he has seen before. He doesn't stop; he doesn't want to scare Kyle into thinking something is wrong. John knows that the tracks belong to Tori. He was hoping she left or something got her. Now John is worried because he knows she looks for males to mate. When she does, she usually sucks the life out of them. They continue through the cave until they get to the big room.

John notices when he shines the light around the cave, it has a different feel to it. He realizes Lily isn't around and something else is there. His hair stands on the back of his neck, like when someone or something is watching, but is invisible. John thinks it is probably Benny Saxton. He tries to blow off the feeling and show Kyle what they believe is like a sacrificial area in the cave with the granite table.

Kyle stands at the steps that lead up into the area looking around with the flashlight amazed. John watches as Kyle looks at every symbol on the wall and herbs hanging.

"What do they mean, Dad?" Kyle asks.

"I don't know all of it. I do know there was a house built down the creek in 1839 and the lady was burned, accused as a witch. Then they hung her husband and took the children. Another witch came about later and bought the place with her son. The marshal burned the lady and hung the husband. He also killed this other lady accused of witchcraft. I believe this has been used for the American Indians and others. I don't know how old it is, but it is very old."

Kyle listens and absorbs everything his dad tells him. They turn and walk down to head out of the cave when Kyle hears something above him and screams.

"What is that, Dad?" Kyle says in a frightened voice.

John hears it, but he didn't want to jump and scare Kyle. Hoping Kyle didn't hear that, John holds him behind him, "Stay close; it will be all right. It is probably the pack rat that lives in the cave."

Kyle says, "No, Dad. This was a growling sound, a deep rumbling sound that went right through me."

John tries to calm Kyle down when suddenly they hear a high pitch scream coming from the other cave entrance up above the sacrificial area. John turns and shines the light up to the entrance, but sees nothing.

"Okay, Kyle, I think it's time we leave. I believe something is back in the cave that I thought had left a while ago." John tells him.

"What is it, Dad?" Kyle asks.

"Just some creature that doesn't like people disturbing it or the area it lives in." John explains to Kyle.

They both walk slowly out of the cave and back over to the mule. John takes Kyle over by the old foundation and shows him where the Stellars use to live.

"This is the Old Stellar remains of the cabin. The witch I was telling you about in the cave? This was the cabin they built and lived in. They had two daughters also that disappeared after they came and burn their mother they came back and hung their father Mr. Stellar up on the big old walnut tree on the hill I will take you by and show you on the way back to the garage."

"How did they disappear dad the two girls?" Kyle asks.

"They were being taken back to the church in town to the orphanage when something happened.

They say the oldest girl escaped and fled into the woods and was never seen again, the youngest was going to be assaulted by the deputy marshals, but something came out of the water they stated a grey creature and grabbed her and pulled her under and they finally found her body, but she was dead. That is why I don't want you coming down here alone." John tells him.

Driving past the old Stellar foundation he heads down the creek a little further and parks by the shore.

"One day I was down here at the creek with Hurley after digging in the old foundation I had found a finger bone with a ring on it and had it sent off to a lab. I was bent down washing my shovel and hands in the creek and seen something in the water so I reached down and touched it and it was pretty big I traced it with my hands and couldn't believe what it was."

"What... what was it? A creature or something like that?" Kyle asks.

John laughs.

"No it was a human skeleton."

"No way!" Kyle replies

"Yes not just a human skeleton it was an American Indian warrior."

"Oh cool what did you do with him?" Kyle asks.

"Well, that is the tricky part. See them rocks over there?" John points to an area of small river rocks lined on the ground and stacked as if someone had placed them in a large formation.

"Yeah is that were you put him?" Kyle asked.

"Yes, I took him and every bone I could find around him, and buried him. He still had a bone chest plate on him. When I did this, the trees bent and swayed from the blowing wind. The clouds became very dark and something spoke to me. It said never to say anything of this. You must promise me, Kyle, never to tell this to anyone else. I trust you, because you are my son." John tells him.

"I understand, Dad. I will keep this our secret." Kyle replies.

"I think it's just about dinnertime, don't you?" John says and heads back to the cabin to check on Jake before going to the garage. On the way, they go past the old walnut tree and John shows Kyle where they hung George Stellar.

"Jake, you want a ride up to the garage we are going to grill some steaks and chicken for dinner?" John yells from the front door.

He gets no response so he walks in and finds Jake asleep on the bed. He decides to leave him. *I will leave a note for him. I will wake him when dinner is ready.*

Kyle is anxious to see the photos and videos his dad has captured from the cave and around the property.

John and Kyle pull up to the garage and Lizzie is already cooking everything else for dinner.

"Where is Jake, John?' Lizzie asks.

"He is asleep on the bed. I will get him when dinner is done." John tells her.

"Mom, Dad, and I went in this cave on the other side of the creek and there's something in there. A creature, Dad said. A bad creature." Kyle says to Lizzie.

Lizzie spins her head over to John and gives him a glare with her eyes. John smiles and says, "It is nothing. The boys know not to go in the cave unless I am with them." Lizzie looks at John, turns, and walks away angered. John hasn't had a chance to explain everything that has happened. If he had told her everything, she would never have come out with the boys.

"John, dinner is almost done. Get Jake for dinner." Lizzie yells out at him while he and Kyle are sitting in two chairs looking across the pasture. It is dark now and Kyle wants to see if he can spot some spirit animals darting across the field into the woods. He sits and watches contently while John gets in the mule and heads over to pick up Jake.

"Jake, you up? Dinner is ready." John yells from the front door.

He gets no reply from Jake so John walks into the bedroom and finds the bed empty. He calls for Jake again and looks in the bathroom. No Jake. He goes upstairs to the loft bedroom, thinking he is probably up there on the balcony looking out. No Jake there either. John walks back downstairs and walks around the porch calling his name, but no answer. John thinks he is playing one of his games. He probably went for a walk up to the garage. John gets in the mule and heads back to the garage.

Lizzie comes out to set the table. She looks at John strangely.

"Where's Jake, John?" She asks.

"Isn't he here?" John asks her.

"No... Why would he be here? You went to pick him up." Lizzie says.

"He wasn't there. I figured he walked up here and I missed him on the way to the cabin." John replies.

"No, he's not here. I haven't seen Jake since you took the boys to the cabin. Where did he go, John?" Lizzie asks.

John becomes a little uneasy, but doesn't want Lizzie to know. He knows he saw Tori's footprints in the cave and he heard her scream inside the cave. Thinking Jake is wandering around the property in the dark probably looking for a better cell signal to call his friends, John jumps in the mule and calls Hurley to follow him.

John races back across the field and down to the creek. Yelling for Hurley as soon as he steps out of the mule, John asks Hurley where Jake is.

"Find him, boy. Where did he go? Did Jake come down here, Hurley?" John says.

Hurley looks around and then heads down the side of the creek away from the cave. John shines the light and watches Hurley. Hurley puts his head down and follows a trail of something. Hopefully it's Jake. John watches as Hurley gets further down the creek bank and sees him dart up an old trail. John jumps in the mule and follows Hurley. This trail leads to the other side of Devil's Attic. He gets the strangest feeling Jake could have walked towards it and didn't even know anything about the deep hole in the ground.

John thinks he should have blocked off around it so the boys didn't just stumble upon it and fall in. He doesn't think about it with all the stuff happening out there and now something coming for Kia. Boy, if Lizzie finds out everything, she will leave tonight with the boys.

John gets up to the top end of the pasture. He shines the light around for Hurley. He doesn't see or hear Hurley so he yells for him and then Jake. Knowing Jake will not answer him, Hurley will usually bark or come close enough so John can see where he is.

John takes a flashlight and walks towards Devil's Attic. On the way up the trail, he hears something. It is not Hurley. He stops and listens. It's that high pitch scream again. He listens for a few minutes then hears another scream. This time he hears one and another one with a different tone follows it. Like they are talking to each other. *It has to be Benny and Tori,* John says to himself. I hope to God Jake walked the other way.

John reaches the opening to Devil's Attic. He bends down and shines the light down into the darkness. It is so deep he can't see anything. He listens to see if he can hear movement anywhere in the cave. Sometimes at night, the echo is better and travels a lot further.

John leans closer into the opening, listening for something, anything. He gets a strange feeling as if he is being watched. He jumps up and looks around the woods with the flashlight. Nothing is there that he can see. He has been out there a lot and has never had a feeling like that. Once again, the hairs on the back of his neck stand up and the feeling moves upwards from his feet to the back of his neck. He knows it is not a good sign when it does that. His body senses something, but he doesn't know what yet.

Hurley comes bouncing out of the woods on the butt end of a rabbit. The rabbit is giving Hurley a run for his money. John snickers for a second, and then looks back to the opening of Devil's Attic. Trying to figure out where Jake is, he turns and walks back down the hill. Suddenly he hears what sounds like a human voice yell. John spins back around and looks into the woods. He stays still and listens. Nothing makes a noise except the crickets chirping.

John turns back and heads out in the mule to the garage, just to check if Jake has shown up.

It has been over an hour since John went looking for Jake. He pulls up and sees Lizzie standing there. He knows by the way she is acting Jake isn't there. *Where the hell did he go?* John wonders. *And what am I going to tell Lizzie?*

John gets out of the mule and walks up to Lizzie.

"Well, where is Jake?" Lizzie says with an angered tone.

"I can't find him, Liz. I guess he went for a walk on the property. I told him that the only signal for his cell phone is on the property. He would have to find the spot because there was no signal in the cabin. He probably is out looking for a sweet spot so he can call his friends." John tells Lizzie.

"He better show up, John. I don't think Jake is the type to just go wandering off through the woods. Alone!" Lizzie snaps back and says.

"Kyle can stay with us and maybe when Jake gets back to the cabin, he will walk up here so he doesn't have to stay out there alone." John tells Lizzie.

Chapter 12

"KIDNAPPED"

Kane heads out with Kia, leaving as fast as he can out of Beaver Creek. Kia is still a little frightened from everything happening so fast. She is a few months pregnant, but when you're a shifter, your offspring develop much faster than a normal baby. The also grow up faster than normal humans; that is why they have to be schooled with other elders in the clan.

"What about Victor, Kane? Is he coming to join us? Should we call Dr. Whiteriver and Dr. Redbone and let them know we are coming?" Kia asks.

"I will call them later and Victor said he would go pack up your things and meet us there later tonight." Kane answers swiftly.

They head out Route 167 towards Hwy 90 and over to North Carolina. Kia feels discomfort coming from the twins. She grabs her belly. When Kane looks over and sees she is in pain, his senses go on high alert right away sensing what is wrong. Kia looks over at Kane about the same time Kane looks at Kia when all of a sudden something hits the vehicle and causes Kane to run off the road.

Kia screams and holds on while the car crashes into a ditch knocking Kane out. Kia had a seatbelt on keeping her from hitting her head on the dash. Kia tries to unhook the seatbelt so she can get to Kane, but it's stuck. Kia fights with it and yells at Kane.

"Kane! Kane! Wake up! Kane, are you all right?"

Kane is still out. Finally, she gets the seatbelt unhooked and reaches over to Kane to wake him up when something grabs Kia around the waist and pulls her out of the vehicle. Kia panics and screams. Her eyes change color; she is shifting when she shouldn't be. She is too far along in her pregnancy to be shifting again.

Kia tries to see who has hold of her when she feels a sharp stabbing in her arm. It is a needle and she passes out.

Kane wakes up to the sound of Victor yelling. Disoriented, he doesn't know what has happened. Victor is in a panic yelling at Kane, but Kane doesn't have a clue what he is saying. It is as if his ears are muffled with something. Kane shakes his head and realizes he has a splitting headache.

Kane looks around and then looks over to the passenger seat when he realizes Kia is not there. Then he hears Victor.

"Where is Kia? Kane, what has happened to Kia? Where did she go? Is she hurt?" Victor yells.

"I don't know. I was driving when Kia started feeling pain in her belly. I looked back up when something hit the vehicle and we ran off the road slamming into the ditch. Kia had her seatbelt on. There is no blood in here from her. I don't know where she went. She was...." Kane stops in mid-sentence. Victor stops talking and looks at Kane. Kane's face changes, shifting into his wolf form.

"What is wrong?" Victor asks Kane. He makes a deep sound in his chest like thunder in a distance.

Victor knows something isn't right and he knows Kane senses it too. He watches Kane to see what he does. Kane walks around the vehicle until he gets to the passenger side. He takes a deep breath, spins around, and looks off across the woods. Suddenly Kane shifts into a huge wolf and takes of like a streak of lightning. Victor yells for Kane, but he doesn't stop.

Victor closes his eyes and holds his hands in front of him trying to tune into Kia's thoughts. It has been a while since he has done this from a distance. Usually she is standing near him. He hopes it works.

120

A few minutes pass and Victor swings his arms up above him and his head goes back. His eyes change to an amber color. He talks fast under his breath.

"Oh sister wind, blow to me and lift me up,

Take me across this land.

Oh sister wind, send me the force of your wind

To find this soul I seek

Oh sister wind, please guide me to find the twins.

Oh sister wind, send me your strength, lift me up and

Carry me over the lands and through the trees.

Oh sister wind, please help me find the soul I seek."

A white light forms around Victor as he chants. Then it moves like the wind high above the trees and disappears. Victor drops to his knees next to the car in the ditch. With his head down, he doesn't move a muscle. It is as if he left his body and the shell of it has fallen to the ground like an empty sack of skin.

Kane stops at the edge of the forest's tree line some fifteen miles from their vehicle. He hears a strange noise and turns quickly behind him to see the trees blowing and whipping in the wind as if a tornado is coming. Trees slapping each other with force, limbs are breaking and falling to the ground after they are tossed a distance from the tree.

Kane backs out of the trees and into the field looking at the wind moving up towards him and he sees a bright light behind the wind. He shifts to his human form and backs up fast into the field. Not knowing what is coming, Kane leaps in one swift jump and lands into his wolf form, racing ahead of the force of the wind and light.

He can sense that it is something supernatural, but he has no idea what it is. He darts to the left and runs into a different area. Realizing it is moving straight ahead, Kane watches it. He notices a strange form inside the light traveling behind the wind, but he can't tell what it is.

Kane runs over to the center of the field and sniffs the air. He has lost the trail to Kia. He shifts back to his human form again. Standing in the field, he looks all around him trying to figure out what has happened. *Who could have taken her? And where did they take her. Was it the wind and light racing up behind him?* The scent he picked up was very odd. He then remembers. When he was a young kid, he and Warrick were out with their father running in the woods. When his dad stopped suddenly, he turned and growled at him and his brother, forcing them to run back home. Before they turned back around, Kane remembers a strange scent the wind brought. It sent the hair up on his back and made him feel like it was very evil, whatever it was. He now has the same feeling.

Oh no! Kane says under his breath and falls down on one knee. He remembers more of the event when he was younger.

When he and Warrick turned around and ran back towards their home for safety, they heard their father make a fierce growl and attack something. They could hear their father fighting something and then heard him scream. Kane and Warrick ran faster and faster with every sound that they heard from their father. When they got back to their home, they ran inside to hide. Their mother asked what was wrong and where their father was, but they were so frightened, they couldn't answer her. Their father was never seen again.

A tear runs down Kane's check, knowing now that this is the same evil that had taken his father's life years ago.

What am I going to tell Victor? What am I going to say to Dr. Redbone and Dr. Whiteriver?

Getting up, Kane turns and walks back to where he left Victor, with his pride hurt. Even worse, he let something take Kia, the one he was sent to protect until death. She is the chosen one of the tribes. *How am I going to face the Wolf Clan after this event?*

Returning to the vehicle Kane finds Victor standing next to his truck. "Did you find anything, Kane?" Victor asks.

Oh, the dreaded question, Kane feels it go right through his heart.

"No, sir. I did not find her. I had the scent and then this force of wind came from behind me and I ran the other way. It was a supernatural force of some kind. I have never seen it before." Kane tells him.

"I found what it is and I found where it has taken Kia." Victor tells Kane.

"How did you do that?" Kane asks concerned.

"I was the force of wind not to be reckoned with Kane. I am a warlock or did you forget that and the powers I hold." Victor says swiftly back.

"No, sir. I did not and I do not mean any disrespect, Victor, but may I ask what it is that has taken Kia?" Kane asks.

"It is a very old creature; it is usually used by a very evil force. One with lots and lots of power. Power in every way and form. It is only sent out when one fails to bring back the prize the master is looking for. It is very powerful itself and only comes when summoned to the call of its master to finish a job or collect the being or soul of one that is impossible to catch. This is the work of Phooka." Victor tells Kane.

"PHOOKA!!" Kane says loudly.

Victor looks at Kane and notices the fear in his eyes. He isn't supposed to have fear; he is of the Wolf Clan. The leader, he is to be fearless. Victor is unsure why Kane is so filled with fear from the name. It is an ancient creature that shape shifts between animals, humans to Phooka.

"Tell me, Kane, why do you fear Phooka? Have you come across him before?" Victor asks.

"When I was very young, my father took me and my brother out for a run. While ahead of us, he suddenly turned, stopped, and growled for us to run, run like the wind back to home. That was what my brother and I did, but before I turned, I smelled something in the wind blowing towards us. It hit me right in my face, a smell I will never forget. I have been waiting years to find this smell again. When I finally turned to run, I caught a glimpse of something

125

tall and skinny that looked like a head of a goat with the body of a man. The creature, with its long dangly arms and sharp claws, walked up behind my father while he forced us to run to safety. After that, we ran as fast as we could and we heard my father fighting with something and then scream. He never ever came home and we went looking for him the next day, but never found a trace of him. I have been waiting for this creature to seek revenge for my father for years and now it's here and it has taken Kia. I fear the worse, Victor. We have to find her." Kane tells him and the tears roll over his cheeks.

Victor puts his hand on Kane's shoulder, "We will, my friend. Don't worry; we have a lot of people that can help us and these people are more powerful together against this creature. This is how we will get her back. Trust me, Kane. She will be okay." Victor tries to comfort Kane, knowing as a wolf, he will be dishonored for these actions that have taken place. Even though it wasn't his fault, he was knocked out during the incident.

"Come on, Kane. We need to head to North Carolina. We need to get some help to get Kia back." Victor tells Kane.

They both get in Victor's truck and speed off down the road to Dr. Redbone's clinic.

Chapter 13

"Jake"

Lizzie wakes John in the middle of the night. She can't sleep with the thought of her son out there alone somewhere. John really can't sleep either. He sneaks out past Hurley and Kyle sleeping in the foldout bed that doubles as the couch in the camper.

John decides he will walk through the field with the flashlight and check the cabin to see if Jake has made it back. Strolling across, he looks all around to see if he might spot him walking around or just anything. *Where are you, Jake?* John says under his breath. *Damn it! Why do you have to be so bull headed about everything?*

John reaches to turn the door handle and notices the door isn't closed.

Now I know I shut this door last night. It wasn't locked, but I heard it close.

Stepping slowly into the cabin, John turns on the lights in the kitchen/living room area and looks around. He sees nothing out of the ordinary. The boy's suitcases still sitting in front of the end table, so he walks through the cabin to the bedroom Jake claimed. His computer backpack is still sitting on the bed. John decides to go through the bag to see if there is something that might help him figure out what is going on.

John pulls out Jake's laptop, some notebooks, and two charge cords. Digging through the front pocket, John discovers Jake's cell phone is in the bag.

"What the hell?" John says.

John can't believe what he just found. He pulls out the cell phone and looks at the screen. *There is no signal, but why would he leave his cell phone behind? I don't understand this; this is unlike Jake all together. Then why did he wonder outside the cabin?* John wonders as he holds Jake's cell phone in his hand. John sets it down on the bed and walks out of the bedroom, beside himself, trying to figure out the situation. John decides to walk up to the loft to see if Jake might have gone up there to sleep. Reaching the top of the stairs, he notices the door to the balcony is open.

"Jake... Jake... are you out there, son?" John calls.

No reply as usual, so he walks over to the door and flips on the switch that turns the light on outside on the balcony. John installed a light that is made of black iron and looks like a tree. The leaves on it are little lights. When lit, it is very bright. No

Jake anywhere on the balcony. John walks over to the railing that borders the area partially covered by a roof. He looks over the balcony and shines his flashlight around.

Hoping to see something moving, particularly Jake, but he finds nothing.

"Damn it, Jake. Where are you?" John says.

John turns to walk back into the cabin when he catches a glimpse of something. He turns quickly back around just to see a pair of eyes. Then they disappear. John knows those eyes; they are Benny's eyes. He must be out prowling tonight.

"Benny, Benny... wait!" John yells out.

He knows Benny is curious of John and the sheriff by the way he acts when they call his name. He remembers something and seems to want to communicate with them, but he doesn't know how.

John runs down stairs and around the porch, down through the back of the cabin to the tree line. He shines the light out into the woods. Nevertheless, he is gone. John calls Benny a few more times hoping he will turn around, but he doesn't.

John turns and walks back towards the cabin to turn the lights off except for the porch. Maybe

Jake will see them from wherever he is and follow the light to the cabin.

John walks back up to the garage through the field. Suddenly he hears a high-pitched scream again. He turns around; the sound makes the hair on the back of his neck stand up. It is an eerie haunting scream. Something one doesn't want to hear in the middle of a dark field. It isn't too far away from John, so he turns back around and picks up the pace back to the garage.

The cameras! They must have something on them if Jake walked down into the cave. I will get the mule and head down there at first light this morning.

"Did you find Jake, honey?" Lizzie asks in a sad tone.

"No. I looked all through the cabin and I found nothing." John tells her.

John doesn't want to mention that he found his cell phone. That will just make Lizzie panic even more or about the red eyes he saw in the tree line.

"Where could he have gone, John?" Lizzie says with tears flowing out her eyes.

"Don't worry, Lizzie. We will find Jake. He is a smart young man, stubborn as hell and bull headed. That is probably why he is doing this, to make us worry about him. You know how kids are at that age. We were there at one time in our lives. We get mad at our parents and want to just disappear to make them feel guilty for punishing us or yelling at us." John tells her.

John sits in a chair outside the garage waiting for the sun to rise up and bring some light to the property. *Maybe he is lost in the caves and can't find his way out. Maybe I should call Sheriff Taylor and tell him that Jake wandered off.*

John picks up his phone and looks at the time — five forty-eight a.m. The sheriff doesn't usually get in until about six thirty a.m. *Maybe I will take a drive into town and down a few of the back roads around here to see if Jake is walking.*

John jumps in the truck and heads out the driveway to town. Slowly driving down Beaver Creek Road, he looks out the window to see if he might spot Jake standing off in the woods.

Reaching the end of Beaver Creek Road, John turns right and heads to town. Driving through the old part of Beaver Creek, passing the library, the museum, farmer's market pavilion, and the theater in the stripe on Hwy 90. With all the lights on in town, there is nobody out on the streets. There are hardly any cars this early. John continues up and out of the old part of town. Since he is in town already, he heads to the sheriff's office to hand him a photo of Jake so the deputies can keep an eye out for anyone fitting his description.

"Hey, John, what brings you here, especially this early in the morning? Did you find another body?" Sheriff Taylor says as he pours himself a cup of coffee in the lobby of the sheriff's department.

"No, no, Sheriff. I wanted to drop off this picture of my son, Jake." John says.

"John, for God's sake, what is wrong?" Sheriff Taylor asks.

John and Sheriff Taylor have developed a very close relationship since John bought the property off Beaver Creek. Sheriff Taylor doesn't have many friends or he doesn't consider anyone as such, but John and he seem to just hit it off. They respect each other on a professional and personal level. John has gone to Sheriff Taylor's house and had dinner with his wife and daughter several times in the past few years. John knows he can call on Sheriff Taylor anytime he wants and he would drop everything to help him. John feels the same way about Sheriff Taylor.

"My wife Lizzie and my two sons Jake and Kyle came in yesterday morning. I set them up in one of the cabins down by the creek. Jake has been in trouble back at home in Colorado. Lizzie thought bringing them down and leaving Jake here with me for the school year would get him away from the bad kids he has chummed up with back home. When Kyle and I went down to the creek and through the cave, Jake didn't want to go. He wanted to stay at the cabin and play on his cell phone.

"When Kyle and I got back, Jake was asleep. I let him sleep until dinner was done and I went down to get him, but he wasn't anywhere around. I looked all over the property, the cave, even went to Devil's Attic, and called for him. He hasn't shown up yet. I walked to the cabin this morning at 3:45 a.m. and found the door was not latched. I made sure, when I left a few hours earlier, I latched the door. I walked in and through the whole cabin couldn't find a trace of Jake except one thing is strange. He left his cell phone in his computer bag, something this boy doesn't do. It is glued to his hand.

I decided to drive up the road this morning, hoping he was walking the roads to town or something, but I can't find him anywhere, Sheriff. I am really getting worried. I heard those high pitch screams in the cave yesterday. You know the ones we heard about a year ago when we found the big room and saw Benny down there?" John tells him.

"Yeah, I remember and I know what that means also. Here, let's go back to my office, John, and talk for a bit." Sheriff Taylor says as they both walk towards his office.

"John, have a seat please. Why didn't you call me when you found he was missing? I would have gone through the cave with you. I will get some of the deputies this morning as soon as they clock in and we will meet you at your place. I will send the deputies out through the property and you and I will go through the cave by the creek. I will bring some rope. I want to go up through that opening above that room by the pond." Sheriff Taylor tells John.

"Okay, Sheriff. Sounds like a plan. Thank you for helping. I know you have procedures to follow about missing pers-" Sheriff Taylor cuts John off.

"John, you're like family. No problem." Sheriff Taylor assures John.

John walks out of the sheriff's station and gets into his truck. Heading back to the property, John gets a phone call from Lizzie.

"Where are you, John?" Lizzie frantically yells in the phone.

"I am in town leaving the sheriff's office. Why? What is wrong?" John asks.

"It is Jake! Hurry, John! HURRY!!" Lizzie says.

John hangs up the phone and speeds back to the property as fast as he can. Pulling up to the garage, he finds Lizzie kneeled down next to Jake and Kyle standing next to Lizzie. Jake is lying on the slab just out from the garage. He has blood on him and his clothes are mostly torn off him.

John leaps out of the truck and runs to Jake.

"What happened?" John yells.

"I don't know. I heard Kyle screaming for me when I was cooking breakfast. I ran out here and found Jake like this." Lizzie tells John.

"Has he moved or opened his eyes?" John asks.

"No, no, he has been lying here just like this. Oh my God, John, what has happened to him? Look at him. He has deep wounds all over his body. What could have done this to him?" Lizzie asks.

"I don't know, honey. I don't know." John replies. Actually, John knows exactly what has caused Jake's wounds. He just didn't want Lizzie to know about it and rush back to Colorado, never letting the boys stay here.

About that time, Sheriff Taylor and two deputies pull up to the garage and see Lizzie and John near Jake's body lying on the slab. Sheriff

Taylor rushes out of his vehicle and tells one of the deputies to call the ambulance.

Sheriff Taylor asks John and Lizzie what happened. While they explain, the sheriff tells Lizzie to get some cold water and a rag so they can clean some of the wounds and stop the bleeding. John tells Lizzie the only thing he has is a first aid kit under the sink in the camper. Sheriff Taylor tells Lizzie to find a shirt and rip it into sections to tie up some of the deeper wounds until the ambulance gets here.

They dress Jake's wounds the best they can. Jake still is unconscious when the ambulance pulls up. They load him up and head to the hospital. Lizzie, John, and Kyle follow them. Sheriff Taylor and the two deputies escort the ambulance through to the emergency room. They unload Jake and rush him in. John and Lizzie sit in the waiting room until they can see Jake.

Chapter 14

"What is this place?"

Kia wakes up and tries to sit, but she can't. She tries to move her head so she can see what is tying her arms down. She suddenly realizes she is strapped down to a table. She can see out of the corner of her eyes that she has IVs in her arms and it looks like she's in a lab somewhere.

Kia tries to force herself to shift, knowing she could escape the straps. She tries and nothing. She tries to concentrate harder! Still nothing. *The twins, they are not moving. They must be feeding me some type of drug through the IVs. It is keeping me from shifting.*

She hears somebody talking. It's getting closer. She closes her eyes and acts as if she is sleeping. She feels someone touch her belly and say she is due in a few months. *How do they know this?* Kia wonders.

"Alexis will be happy to know she has finally found her silver-blood, and she's pregnant."

Kia's mind races. *Who's Alexis? Moreover, what does she want with the twins and me?*

She hears them say that the DNA they took earlier from her is outstanding. "It is perfect. Hopefully the new patients we inject will become a new breed of shifters. We have been working all this time trying to perfect it and finally we have someone that will take it all the way to the highest level of DNA splicing. Yes, this one is the key factor we needed. Thanks to Phooka for a fine job."

"The boss will be down here soon, I am sure. She will want to see the silver-blood herself. She has been chasing one for a very long time and finally captured it."

"Yes, Dr. Brack. It will." Kia hears them walking away and a door open and close. She opens her eyes up again. Struggling even harder to pull herself from the straps to get free, she gets her head turned enough to the side she can see it is a lab. There are more people in there with her, in the same situation as she. Lying on a slab strapped down, some of them have tubes running in their arms, mouth, and other places. She turns back and fights to turn her head to the right. She sees cages for something — they must be for animals, but they are huge. *They must work on many big animals in here,* Kia wonders.

"What the hell is this place?" Kia says softly looking around. She can hear the sounds of different creatures and strange sounds like cries or screams.

Sounds she has never heard of before. They sound distressed or injured. They seem to be coming from a different room near the one she is being held.

Kia closes her eyes and tries to send a message to Victor. Maybe he will hear her. Because of the sixth sense they share, he can pick up when she is in trouble. She hears people talking again and the door open. It is a woman's voice this time.

"Where is she? I want to see her." She hears the woman say. Kia doesn't recognize the woman's voice.

"Over there, My Lady." Some man says; it sounds like one of the men who were in talking earlier.

The voices and footsteps get closer and closer until… She feels someone touch her belly again and push on it hard, palpating it to feel the twins. Kia tries to act as if she is out from the drugs, but it hurts badly. She holds back her cries so she doesn't jeopardize her and the twin's lives.

"This is the silver-blood you have been looking for, My Lady." A man says.

"She is beautiful. I should have guessed she would be an American Indian. Now I know why we haven't been able to catch one." The woman says.

"She's pregnant, My Lady. As you felt, she is due in a few months. There are twins, My Lady."

"Really? Well, that is even better. That means this offspring she is carrying is very valuable. Priceless! These babies will give the supreme DNA we need for the perfect shape shifters. You boys haven't a clue what you're in for when you test the DNA of the offspring she has. They will be faster, stronger, with unbelievable powers. Powers you two can't even imagine. Take the DNA directly from the offspring. This will prove to be much more beneficial to us. We will capture more qualities in the un-born's DNA. When you splice the DNA with these, watch the magic happen, boys." The woman tells them.

"Yes, My Lady. We will do that right away." A man with a deeper voice says.

"Good, then carry on!" the woman tells them as she turns and walks away.

"Wait, excuse me, My Lady, but is Malik bringing us new prospects for the DNA transformation? We are in need of new test subjects, My Lady." The one man asks.

"Yes, Malik will be here in a few days. You have plenty to do until then. I will call and have him put a rush on things for you, Dr. Brack." The woman says.

Kia hears them all walk away from her.

"Remember, I want the supreme shifters only! They are not to go out into the Plantation. I have a place ready for them under the lab here. Anything else, feed to the carnivores." The woman tells them.

"Yes, My Lady. Thanks for your advice. Have a great day, My Lady." The men say.

OMG! Kia says under her breath. She thinks this lady is insane! She's a female Hitler building a supreme shifter race. Why? What the hell would anyone want with a supreme shifter race? Kia hears the two men come back and once again, she acts as if she's asleep.

She feels them pull her shirt up and expose her belly. They push and manipulate her, feeling the twins inside her. She feels a cold wet hand rub jelly-type stuff on her, then a cold instrument. They move it back and forth on her belly. *They must be doing an ultrasound of the twins.*

"I see them, Dr. Brack. They are positioned exactly across from one another. They are on either side of her belly. I will mark a spot on either side where you can enter." The man with the deep voice says.

Kia feels the guy make a mark on her belly. Then she feels something stabbing her. She feels more and more pressure with more pain as it goes deeper. She can feel it going in through her stomach muscles. The pain is so great. Kia tries so hard not to make a sound or move a muscle. She is scared with the needle or probe they have in her. If she moves, it will injure the twins.

She can't take it anymore. The pain is so great Kia opens her eyes and looks at the two men. Her eyes widen in fear when she sees the instrument they have sticking in her belly. It isn't one; it is several. Kia panics.

"What are you doing to me?" Kia screams.

"Put her out. Put her out, Monroe! Hurry!" A man yells.

Kia feels something ice cold running into her right arm through the IVs. She can feel it moving up her arm closer and closer to her neck. *It must be a drug in the IV to put me out.*

She feels funny; she can still see the men and they're talking. She feels like she is falling backwards down a hole. They sound like they are in a tunnel. Deeper and deeper, she feels herself falling. The lights above fade further and further as if she is falling in slow motion. She tries to yell, but her mouth barely moves.

"Is she out? Yes, finally." Monroe says to Dr. Brack.

"That scared the hell out of me!" Dr. Brack says.

"Yeah, it scared me also. I can't believe she woke up. I put a heavy duty tranquilizer in her mix before I hung the bag." Monroe says.

"Sometimes they snap out of it like nothing. Amazing what the mind does to the body. It can bypass stuff when it feels it's in danger." Dr. Brack says.

Chapter 15

"Lesson Learned"

Lizzie and John finally see Jake. He is awake, but resting. The doctor had to stitch some of the wounds on him that were deep, especially the ones on his back and the bites on his neck. They sit in the room waiting for him to wake.

Lizzie sits next to Jake's bed holding his hand and still crying. John and Kyle sit on the other side of the bed watching motocross on TV.

Sheriff Taylor opens the door to see if Jake's awake yet and see how everyone is doing. He motions for John to come out in the hallway. John gets up and walks out of the room.

"I just got a call from Victor about an hour ago. Seems that after they left the other day, something hit Kane's car as they headed down the road. Ran them off the road and into a ditch. It knocked Kane out, but Kia was missing. They know who took her, but Victor wouldn't tell me. He said he wanted to speak to you. He gave me his cell number just in case you didn't have it." Sheriff Taylor says.

"What the hell is going on, Sheriff? I guess Lily wasn't kidding about something coming to

Beaver Creek. It is one thing after another. Who the hell could have kidnapped one of the most protected persons we know? It had to be as Lily said; their powers alone won't stop the force that is coming. But how did this force know that Kia was leaving Beaver Creek?" John asks.

"I don't know, John, but something is happening. I just wonder what to expect next. It was calm here for a little while, but now everything is starting all over again. Thank gosh Jake is alive; he could have easily been another Abigail Flynn." Sheriff Taylor says.

"I know, Sheriff, I know. I have to tell you something I saw the other night when I went looking for Jake at the cabin. I was up on the balcony and heard that high-pitched haunting scream as we heard before. Then when I went to turn away, I saw two red eyes in the tree line watching me. I know it was Benny Saxton. I yelled out for him, but he disappeared in the darkness. I don't know why he was watching me. I have never seen him this far away from the cave before. Then the next thing I know, Jake is laying on the slab. There is no possible way he walked himself up there, Sheriff. It isn't possible. He was out like a light. The doctors said he had a high level of some type of venom in his bloodstream. You know exactly what that is from... Tori! She looks for young men to mate. I can't say a word of this to Lizzie. I know she had sexual relations with Jake. That is what she does to have another offspring. I am thinking that Benny for some strange reason must have seen this take place and saved Jake by removing him from wherever in the cave he was. You know as well as I, she would have killed Jake eventually." John tells him.

"I know, John. I just don't understand why she is back. I thought Kia said she was gone. When Jake wakes up, I have to ask him some questions. You might want to take Lizzie down to the cafeteria. I am going to have to ask him if Tori had tried to have any sexual relations with him. You don't want Kyle and Lizzie to hear that. Plus he probably isn't going to tell me much with them around." Sheriff Taylor says.

"I understand, Sheriff. I just hope when Jake wakes up he does talk to you. He hasn't talked much to anyone lately." John says.

John hears Kyle call him. He rushes back into the room. "Jake is waking up," Lizzie says.

John asks, "Should I get the doctor?"

"Sheriff Taylor said he'd get him."

"Hi, Jake? How are you doing, buddy? What happened to you, Jake?" John says.

Jake looks over at his dad and cries. Lizzie cries as well. The doctor comes in and asks them to step aside so he can check Jake quickly.   "How many fingers am I holding up?" The doctor asks.

Jake replies with a very hoarse voice. "Two!" The doctor checks his pupils, his heart rate, and listens to his lungs.

"Do you know where you are?"

Jake looks around the room and says, "A hospital?"

"Correct," the doctor says. "Do you know your name?"

Jake replies, "Ah...Jake Smith."

"Correct again," the doctor says and tells Lizzie and John they can talk to him now.

"Jake baby, what happened to you?" Lizzie asks as she hugs him.

"I don't know. I was in the bedroom and I fell asleep. I heard loud noises and buzzing sounds. I thought they were just bugs, or I was dreaming. Then I heard this whooshing sound like leaves blowing in the wind on the ground. You know, like in fall. Then the next thing I knew, I felt this sharp pain in my neck and I woke up. I looked up and saw this beautiful girl with long black hair and bright blue

148

eyes. She had this little dress on, purple with white flowers."

It's Tori. Jake's proving his feeling correct. Jake continues telling his story.

"It felt like my brain was being sucked out of my head. My body felt at first as if I was being pulled backwards through high speeds like riding a roller coaster backwards instead of forwards. That is when I felt like I couldn't move a muscle. I couldn't open my eyes. I couldn't move my arms or legs. It was as if I was paralyzed. I tried screaming for you and dad, but my mouth wouldn't open.

"Finally, when I did get my eyes open, it was pitch-black and I was laying somewhere cold and damp, on grass or something like that. I could hear these strange high-pitch screams and weird growling noises close to me. I was so scared. I knew it wasn't a person, but I could feel the heat of it pass by me. I could sense it on my skin. Then I felt a very strange breathing on my neck and something climbed on top of me. I could feel human hands like a girl's hands, but I couldn't move. I could feel my clothes being torn and ripped off me. I guess I passed out again. The next thing I knew, I woke up here." Jake tells them.

"Jake, the sheriff wants a word with you, son. Is that okay? He wants to know what happened to you. Make sure you tell him everything. Even if you didn't tell us everything, please tell the sheriff. He needs to know and he can't tell us anything you tell him. Don't worry about us finding out anything if you didn't want to say it in front of us, okay?" John tells Jake.

Jake agrees to talk to Sheriff Taylor. John grabs Lizzie by the arm and tells Kyle to follow them down to get a bite to eat in the cafeteria.

"Hi, Jake. I have heard a lot about you, young man. I am glad to see you're doing better. Looks like you put up a good fight. I would hate to see the one that attacked you. I bet he looks a lot worse than you do." Sheriff Taylor says jokingly, trying to ease the moment so Jake will speak to him.

"So Jake, can you tell me about what happened to you? Did you see what or who did this to you?" Sheriff Taylor asks.

"The only person I remember seeing was this beautiful girl with long black hair and blue eyes. She must have been the one that bit my neck. Whatever she did, she made me feel like my body was frozen stiff. I couldn't move a muscle and I couldn't yell for my mom and dad. I remember waking in the dark. I thought I was dreaming because I felt this girl on top of me."

"Was she having sex with you, Jake? I need to know, son. I won't tell your parents." Sheriff Taylor asks.

Jake hesitates on answering the question. "Yes."

"I could feel her already taking me inside of her when I woke up. I thought I was dreaming. That was the only time I could lift my arms up. She helped me by putting my hands on her breasts and squeezing my hands tight on them. She did all the work as far as moving up and down on me. She leaned down and kissed me. She bit my neck. The next thing I knew, I woke up here." Jake tells the sheriff.

"Very good, Jake. You're lucky to be alive, son. Do you remember how you got to the garage?" Sheriff Taylor asks.

"No, sir. I don't remember." Jake tells him.

"Thank you for talking to me, Jake. Don't worry. I won't tell your parents anything we talked about." Sheriff Taylor says and walks out of the room.

John and Lizzie walk up to the room as the sheriff closes the door. "Did you speak to Jake, Sheriff? John asks.

"He told me everything he could remember. Maybe in time he will remember more." Sheriff Taylor explains.

"Lizzie, go on ahead in to see Jake. I want to speak to Sheriff for a moment." John pats Lizzie on the back.

Kyle is in the cafeteria talking with a young girl that walks up. Kassidy Flynn, Abigail Flynn's sister. Abigail was murdered and Kyle's dad found her remains in the cave by the creek right after he bought the property. Kassidy didn't know that at the time she introduced herself to Kyle.

John walks with the sheriff down the corridor on the second floor of the hospital. John asks if Jake told him everything. The sheriff told John it is definitely Tori. John and the sheriff walk out of the elevator and Kyle and Kassidy are just stepping in as they are walking out. John tells Kyle his mom's upstairs with Jake and he was going outside with the sheriff.

"Do you know who that girl is, John?" The sheriff asks John.

"No, I have never seen her before. She walked up and introduced herself to Kyle while I was getting drinks. I didn't catch her name." John tells him.

"That is Kassidy Flynn, Abigail Flynn's little sister. I am surprised her parents are letting her volunteer as a candy striper here at the hospital after what happened to Abigail." Sheriff Taylor says.

"You mean that is the sister to the girl I found in the cave?" John asks.

"Yes it is." Sheriff Taylor says.

"Did you get a chance to call Victor yet, John?" Sheriff Taylor asks.

"No, not yet, but I can call him right now if you want to listen." John says to the sheriff as he pulls his cell phone out and dials Victor's number.

"Hi, Victor. This is John. Sheriff Taylor said you wanted to talk to me?" John says in the phone.

Victor explains to John what happened. "Will you help get Kia back?" Victor asks.

John says, "Of course, I will help."

"This is going to be very dangerous. They have Kia in a very secure location. I have no idea how to get into the place. It is about fifty miles away southwest of Beaver Creek." Victor explains.

"Well, just call me when you have a plan. I will meet you." John says.

"I am on my way to North Carolina to meet with the two doctors. My mother Mona is coming down to help from Salem, Massachusetts." John hangs up and tells the sheriff what Victor said.

John turns and walks back to the hospital entrance after Sheriff Taylor leaves. *How am I going to leave Lizzie and the boys at the property while I help Victor find Kia?*

Walking up to the room on the second floor of the hospital, John has an idea. Maybe the family can go on a little trip near the property. Tennessee or North Carolina for some family vacation.

Chapter 16

"Some people aren't what they seem"

"Hey, boys." Elsa says as she walks past Luther and Lucius sitting outside on the tailgate of Malik's Ford truck.

"You guys coming over for the party?" Dania stops in front of them and asks.

"Yes, ma'am. We were waiting for you two to get back and tell us when you want us over." Luther says.

"How about an hour? It will give us enough time to get everything ready. We have other friends coming over. They have rented three of the other rooms for the night. So it's going to be a big party." Elsa tells them.

"See you in about an hour, girls. Hey, do you want us to bring anything? Liquor, weed, rubbers?" Lucius says jokingly.

"Dude, that is so uncool! Grow up, idiot!" Luther says to Lucius punching him in the arm.

The girls laugh as they walk into their room.

"Yeah, bring all of that, boys. I am sure we will find use for it all." Dania says as she closes the door.

"What is wrong with you, dude? That was so not right!" Luther says.

They two brothers walk in and tell Damien the girls are going to be ready in about an hour if he is still willing to party. Lucius tells him that he needs to bring his own rubber in case he scores tonight.

Damien looks over from staring at the wall at Lucius. He glares at Lucius until he turns away and goes into the bathroom.

Luther asks Damien if he is all right. He notices Damien has been acting very strange the past couple of days. Something isn't right with him and Luther can smell a change in his odor. It is more masculine. Luther knows what that means and knows that they are to accept only one pack leader. Nevertheless, he knows his brother Damien is a loose cannon, just waiting for the day he and Malik fight for the position of pack leader.

Luther tries to spark a conversation with Damien. "So where is Malik, Damien?" Luther asks.

Damien just stares at the wall as if he never even heard Luther's question.

"Dude, I am talking to you." Luther says when Damien leaps out of his chair and throws Luther on the ground.

Luther yells for Malik. He notices that Damien's eyes are red as fiery coals. He has become violent as a hellhound — not a good sign. Once they get that far and develop that attitude, it is like a dog that kills animals. They never stop chasing the thrill of the hunt. Next thing you know, Luther sees Damien ripped from atop him. He sees Malik shifted in hellhound form. Malik stands holding Damien by the back of the neck and with one arm pulled high behind his back.

"What the fuck is your problem, Damien! This is your own flesh and blood. They aren't here to fight you. They are here to support the pack as a family." Malik says in a deep growling voice, one that would stop a person in his tracks if he heard him.

"Now when I let go of you, don't you even think about starting anything with me. I am sick and tired of your shit. This will be your last run with the pack. As soon as we get back, you're out. You can form your own pack or go on your own. Calm the fuck down, Damien." Malik says as he releases his grip on Damien very slowly.

Damien spins around and gets in Malik's face. Lucius comes out of the bathroom and sees what is happening. He doesn't move a muscle.

Malik waits for one move from Damien that is a threat. Malik rises up with a glare from hell, growls, and shows his teeth at Damien. He finally turns his head and walks around Malik and out the door.

Luther and Lucius just look at Malik. He stands in half-shifted form. Large human body covered in black fur, ears, eyes, and facial features of a hellhound. Glowing orange color on the fur around his neck, eyes glowing yellow, and long fingers with long sharp claws on his hands and his feet.

Luther and Lucius don't say a word or move. When they are in half-shifted form, they are easily agitated and fight.

Malik finally shifts back to himself. "Don't you two have a party to attend?" Malik says.

"Ya…Yeah, yeah, we were just leaving, Malik. We will be right next door in case you need us, okay." Luther says.

They both walk past Malik looking down to the ground. Damien is sitting outside on the bed of the truck.

"Where are you two idiots going?" Damien says under his breath watching them walk down to Dania and Elsa's room.

"We're going to a party, remember? Did you want to come, Damien?" Lucius asks with a quiver in his voice.

Damien looks up at them and gets a shit-eating grin on his face.

"Sure, that is just what I need about now. Someone to fuck." Damien says standing up from the tailgate of the truck. He walks towards Lucius and Luther. They turn and knock on the door of the girls' motel room.

You can hear music playing and people talking. Finally, Dania answers the door.

"Hello, boys. Nice that you all could make it." Dania says.

They all walk in and Dania asks what they want to drink. Lucius says a Bud Light, as does Luther, Damien asks for a shot of Jack or just the fucking bottle. Dania grabs the drinks and walks over to the guys. Handing the boys the beers and handing Damien a tiny bottle of Jack Daniels, the kind you find on the airlines. She hands it to him with a smirk on her face and one eyebrow raised as to say, 'Fuck you too, asshole.'

Damien looks at the bottle and smiles as he grabs it and says, "You're not going to open it for me? But you're the hostess, ma'am." Damien says with a smirk on his face and one eyebrow raised.

The boys all take a seat in the room. Damien, of course, turns and walks back outside and sits on the tailgate of the truck.

A young girl comes walking past him in a tight short mini skirt, tight shirt exposing most of her body except her breasts. Tall stiletto heels, black lace leggings with holes torn in them.

Damien smiles seductively as he watches her walk. She winks at him; he reaches out and slaps her on the ass.

She turns around and says, "Um, big boy. Are you all alone tonight?"

Damien stares purposely at her breasts and not her face. The girl walks a little closer to Damien until she is standing directly in front of him.

"See anything you would like to touch?" The girl asks.

"Yeah, I just did — your ass. I take a bit out those tits also." Damien replies as he reaches his arm out and pulls the girl in between his legs. Her breasts are perfectly in Damien's face. He reaches up with the other hand and lifts her shirt up exposing her full plumped breasts. They fall out from under the shirt and bounce enough to get his cock hard.

Damien grabs one of her breasts in his hand and squeezes it tight. She moans in pleasure of the touch. He puts his tongue on her nipple and teases it until it gets hard as a rock. Then he puts her breast in his mouth and he sucks on it, whirling his tongue around her nipple at the same time.

"Oh baby, that feels so good. Boy, you are one hot guy. I mean the heat is rolling off you like you're on fire inside." The girl says.

Damien pulls back from suckling her breast and says, "Wait until you feel me inside you. I will burn every desire you ever had and make you beg for more."

"Well then you sold me on that. What room is yours, sweetie? I am in need of a really hot, big horny man about now." The girl replies as she reaches down between his legs and grabs the hard bulge in his pants.

"Wow, you're a well-endowed big man. Let's find your room. I want to ride you like the wind and rain all over you." The girl tells Damien.

Damien stands up, swoops the girl up in his arms, and carries her into the room the twins have in the motel. They are not in there; they are in Elsa and Dania's room. Damien knows they are too nice of guys to force sex on any girl.

Damien carries the girl into the room and kicks the door closed behind him with his foot. He walks to one of the beds and drops the girl on it.

He pulls his shirt off, and unbuttons his jeans while she slides down her skirt, lace stockings, and G-string.

She positions herself on the bed with her legs spread open for Damien to feel her. Damien climbs up from the back of the bed and dives into the meat of her.

The girl takes a gasp of air; she wasn't expecting him to dive in so fast. She can feel him nibbling on her lips, and running his tongue all around her clit.

She moans in pleasure. When she feels him slip a finger inside of her, it sends her head back and she feels her orgasm release.

Damien can feel her wetness roll down and he licks it up with his tongue. Pushing his finger only deeper the second time, he pulls her wetness back out with it.

"OMG," she screams. "You're....OMG, and again..." she yells as she cums again.

"You are extremely good at this. Don't stop, ah, ah. I haven't ever felt anyone eat my pussy like you before. OMG, it feels so good." The girl says.

Damien slips two fingers inside her and she moans even louder. Just before she cums again, Damien pulls away.

"No, No! Don't stop! I am about to..." She says.

Damien pulls the girl up and turns her to the side of the bed. He puts his cock in her face.

"Your turn, bitch." He says to the girl.

She grabs his cock with one hand and looks up at Damien.

"Did you have an implant to make you this big? My God, I can't get that whole thing in my mouth." She says.

"Never know unless you try." Damien tells her.

She looks back at his cock and puts the head of it in her mouth. She rolls her tongue around the sensitive part of the head and sucks.

Damien eases his one hand behind her head placing it at the very back just above her neck and runs his fingers through her long brown hair. He pushes a little on her head and thrusts his hips at the same time, forcing his hard cock deeper in the girl's mouth.

She tries to take every inch, but realizes she can't and pushes him back a little bit. He releases his grip on her and she flows back and forth on his cock again. He thrusts his hips in rhythm to her sucking.

She tastes the sperm seeping out of Damien. It makes her hot and wet inside, thinking of how he is going to feel when he fucks her.

Damien moans and says to her, "Suck it harder. Don't you want it deep inside you? Umm, come on. Let me fuck your mouth with it and cum on your tits."

The girl pulls him out of her mouth and says, "Oh no, you're fucking me, and you're going to fuck me hard!" She tells him. "Where are the rubbers?" she asks.

Damien bends down and grabs his pants. Fumbling through his wallet, he pulls out a packet and opens it. He slides the rubber over the head of his cock and down the shaft.

"You ready to feel the ultimate fucking you ever felt?" Damien says to her.

"Bring it on, honey! I am waiting to feel that big cock inside me." She replies.

Damien grabs her, spins her over on the bed, pulls her hips up, and forces her chest down on the bed in a rough manner. He grabs ahold of her hips with one hand and rubs his hand on her vagina to stimulate her to get wet to make his entry slide in easier.

Sinking his finger deep inside her and pulling out her juices, he grabs his cock by the shaft and rubs the head of it up and down between her two holes, teasing her.

He slides just the head of his cock in her. She moans. He pulls her hair tighter and thrusts his hips until his cock rams inside of her hard. She screams in pain for a brief moment. It only excites Damien more. He pulls her hair tighter until he pulls her head as far back as he can. He kicks her legs further apart with each of his knees and thrusts harder and faster.

He can hear her moan and scream, the scream of pain from him ramming so deep inside her. His cock is too long, but he is forcing it all the way inside her. He hits her ass on the cheek so hard it leaves a whelp.

He feels her pull her head out of his grip, but he jerks it back to where he wants it and pulls his cock out of her for a moment.

He reaches down and pulls off the rubber, slinging it behind him on the floor. He moves his cock around her holes again and pushes it back inside her, thrusting harder and faster like no normal man would. She can feel him inside her every time he thrusts harder. The pain is taking the place of the pleasure. She can feel his body getting hotter. His cock is growing thicker. She can feel the skin on her vagina tearing, but Damien thrusts his cock deep inside her as if he is trying to break through the wall of her insides.

The girl turns her head to the side and looks back at Damien to see the look on his face. She can't believe what she sees!

"OMG, OMG, what are you?! Get the fuck off me, you fucking asshole." The girl screams.

Damien takes his one hand and pushes her back until she's pinned down to the bed with her ass still in the air.

Damien looks down and watches his cock grow thicker and the skin around her pussy torn and bleeding now. It excites him so much he cums.

His moan is like a growling howl. The girl still tries to watch out of the corner of her eye with her head pressed hard into the mattress of the bed.

She can feel him cum inside her. She then realizes he removed the rubber. *OMG! What the hell is he and what has he done?!* Her mind races with questions and fear of him.

Finally, she can feel Damien's cock shrink inside her and he pulls it out. He finally releases her hair. She spins around and crawls fast up to the top of the bed.

"What the hell are you? Why did you remove the rubber? Now I could be pregnant, you son of a bitch." The girl cries.

She looks down at the cover on the mattress where they were fucking and it has blood spots all over it from him forcing himself so deep and ripping her skin.

She panics and reaches for her clothes, but Damien grab her arm and pulls her up.

"Where do you think you're going, sweetie?" He says to her.

She looks him in the eyes and shakes with fear.

"What are you going to do with me?" She asks him.

"You're going for a ride, sweetie, to a big fancy house. Oh, you'll love it there. Plenty of time to fuck you whenever I want. Think of it this way: you won't have to worry about anything. You will be taken care of." He tells her as he throws her back on the bed.

He tells her to put her clothes on. He walks over and locks the door to the room. He turns back around and she is just staring at him.

"Put your fucking clothes on. NOW!" He yells.

The girl jumps in fear and puts her clothes on as fast as she can. She hears Damien yell something at her.

"What is your name?" He yells

"What?" The girl says softly.

"I asked you what your name is. What do people call you? Your friends, family?" Damien asks, much calmer now.

"Oh, Ellie. My name is Ellie Owens.

Damien hears the music blasting from next door. His two brothers are probably still over there just talking with those girls. Not even made the first move. They are such pussies.

Chapter 17

"The feelings"

Elsa is getting a little tipsy. She feels the alcohol kicking in. Her blood is flowing and so are her hormones. Making her want a man.

She walks through the door connecting the rooms to the next room and Dania is sitting on Lucius lap kissing him deeply. Elsa scans the room and her eyes lock with Luther's. He is sitting there alone and watching her.

She stares at his eyes there is something about his eyes that make her head feel like it's floating and a tingling in her stomach as if being pulled through the air. 'Why does he make me feel like that?' Elsa wonders.

Luther slowly drops his smile at Elsa and starts to use his talent to entice her feelings.
Tease her with his mind. One of the many powers they have that is fun to use.

Luther makes Elsa feel like someone is touching her body slowly from behind. Rubbing his hands up her sides slowly and breathing gently his warm breathe on her soft neck. He sees her eyes close and her head rolls to one side. 'It's working,' he tells himself as he snickers under his breath.

He concentrates harder making her feel him move his hands up and over her breasts, squeezing them tight as he kisses and sucks on her neck. She starts to moan and move her hands on her stomach as if she is holding his hand and rubbing herself as well.

She can feel him rub down her stomach and he starts biting her neck. He moves his hands to her pants line and stops for a moment. Her hand is on top of his. He waits to see what she'll do.

She takes his hand and pushes it just under her pant line. So he continues pushing his hand further down her stomach just before he gets to her sweet spot. He watches Elsa stand in the door way between the rooms just inside enjoying the feelings he is making her feel. She hasn't realize that he isn't physically touching her.

He starts to get aroused by the way she is moving herself around and moaning he gets up and positions himself behind her and takes the place of the feelings he is sending her through his thoughts.

He runs his tongue up the side of her neck to taste her scent then takes a deep breath to inhale the pheromones she is releasing. Testing them to see if she is ready to mate with him.

The animal instinct still has a lot of control of the younger boys. They still don't control their sexual feelings as well as older shifters can.

Luther tries to walk Elsa over towards the empty bed in the room. When he hears someone pounding on a door.

Lucius and Luther suddenly become on high alert. Lucius pushes Dania off his lap and rushes next to Luther.

Luther starts to feel himself shift and his eye are changing color. Lucius starts to force a deep growl from within his chest.

They are much more defensive because they feel the urge to mate and that even makes them more protective in the situation.

They hear a voice yell out.

"Damien, Damien open the fucking door!" Malik yells. Damien walks over and unlocks the door. Slightly opening it so Malik doesn't see Ellie on the bed.

"What the fuck man? Everybody could hear screaming in the room what are you doing?" Malik says as he pushes the door open and sees Ellie setting on the bed crying. Malik looks at Damien with a glare of disgust in his eyes.

"What? We are here to bring mother her requests for more patient's right? I was just satisfying this one's needs for a good fuck." Damien says to Malik.

"Load up your shit and her in the truck we got to go." Malik tells him.

"Why, what is going on?"

"Mother called it seems Phooka came earlier than expected. He has the prize already back at mothers. So get your shit and her in the truck we are pulling out of here in fifteen minutes." Malik tells him.

Luther and Lucius realize it is only Malik talking to Damien. Then they hear someone coming so they both step out of the room into the walkway. Malik is walking towards them with a disgusting look on his face.

"Come on boys, it is time to go. We have to load up and head back home. NOW!!" Malik says in an angered deep voice.

Malik turns and walks back towards the truck. He is pissed at Damien and his mother. She didn't even give him a warning she was sending out Phooka this early in the hunt. He should have known.

Malik usually just lets her decisions roll off his shoulders and move to the next, but this time he is pissed. They have some very good scents they picked up on and the feather he found is going to surprise the hell out of Dr. Brack and Monroe. They are going to want them back to capture the creatures they have discovered.

Luther and Lucius turn and walk back to Dania and Elsa. Grabbing them and kissing them passionate, leaving them with the feeling of ultimate desire.

Luther and Lucius walk quickly out of the motel room and into their room. Gathering all their belongings and throwing it in the truck they hear Damien say something to Malik and them.

"Wait a minute here! Why are they not loading those two girls in the truck? He says.

"What do you mean?" Luther asks.

"We are to take back new people for mother for her experiments. That means them two also and anyone else we can take with us. You know the drill Malik!" Damien says.

Malik looks at the Luther and Lucius and nodes his head and blinks his eyes in a yes manner. Luther and Lucius look at each other with sorrow.

174

They know what is going to happen to the two girls they like and they truly regret having to do it.

They walk back into the motel room where they left Elsa and Dania they see the girls curled up together on the bed. Luther picks up Elsa in his arms and Lucius picks up Dania. They take them and put them in the truck. The girls are so drunk they haven't a clue what is happening.

Damien walks back and takes his belt into the room he was in with Ellie. Strapping it around her hands so she can't do anything bad and he rips part of her skimpy shirt, enough to make a gag and forces it in her mouth and ties it.

"That should keep your mouth shut and you from starting any trouble." Damien says to Ellie and laughs as though it is a game and he has won.

Chapter 18

"Surprise"

It is midnight on the Plantation. Ada finishes her paperwork and schedules for the next event in a few days. She hears something walking heavily through the corridor outside the main entrance parlor of the house. She gets up and looks down the corridor from the side of the doorway in her office. She can smell something strange; her emotions rise within her. Her body becomes very alert and threatened by the smell in the corridor. It is an awful odor, like a goat and rotting flesh.

What can that smell be? Ada wonders. Looking intensively back and forth down the corridor, she can't see anything past the last light at either end. That is where the darkness starts. It seems to be coming from the direction of the stairway to the basement and lab area. Maybe it is something blowing up from the lab. They have all kinds of animals and strange things down there they work on. Probably exactly that.

Ada goes back to her desk when she notices the light flickering. She stops to watch it for just a split second when she feels a presence of something behind her. Ada jumps behind her desk and spins around to see what or who it is.

"OMG! What are you? What do you want?" Ada says in a frightened voice.

"I am Phooka. I am here to see Alexis." He says in a raspy high-toned voice that sounds like a goat trying to talk in human language.

"How did you get in here, Phooka?" Ada asks.

"Don't worry about that. I am here to speak with Alexis." Phooka says.

"I will have to go see if she is available to speak to you. It is a very late hour and she doesn't like to be disturbed." Ada replies.

"Then tell me where I can find her. I will go myself." Phooka tells her.

"Oh, that is not possible. Nobody is allowed up there." Ada tells him.

Ada reaches for the phone to call Alexis.

"What is it?" Alexis yells in the phone as she picks it up.

"Phooka is calling for you, My Lady." Ada says on the phone.

"Phooka, at this hour? What the hell?! He always comes at the oddest times. Tell him I will be right down." Alexis says in an angered tone. Alexis gets out of bed and grabs her satin night coat made from the finest materials money can buy. She pulls the doors of her bedroom open and comes face to face with Phooka.

"Phooka! How did you get up here?" Alexis says.

"We need to speak, Alexis. It has been a long time since I have last spoken to you." Phooka says.

"Well, I must say, Phooka, a job well done! I send my four sons out to do a job and every time they disappoint me." Alexis says.

"You have a problem, Alexis, with the one I brought to you." Phooka says.

"Why? What do you mean, Phooka?" Alexis asks.

"This human carrying child is followed by a strong force. A force I have not felt or been in contact for hundreds of years. This force is building and if it comes for this human woman you have, you will have trouble. Great trouble." Phooka tells her.

"I appreciate the gesture, Phooka, but do you really think with my age, my power, and my empire here that anyone can threaten to take me down? I am Alexis Ravenworth and I have powers beyond your imagination. I am building a force that nothing can stop." Alexis says in a loud voice.

"I am here only to warn you of what is to come. That is what I see, that is what I know. You don't have to listen to my warnings. By the way, the offspring that the human woman is carrying is the most powerful force. Don't underestimate your power for theirs." Phooka says and turns away.

Alexis stands there staring into the darkness of the corridor outside her massive bedroom doors, watching Phooka walk into the darkness and disappear into thin air.

"How dare he threaten me. That sorry excuse for a half-breed has stunk up the whole entire bedroom with his stench. Wait until I get a hold of Gabriel and Ada." Alexis says slamming her bedroom doors and stomping through the large room to her sitting area within the bedroom.

Gabriel walks into the kitchen. It is 5:30 a.m. and he is running late this morning to bring Alexis her tea. He usually has it there by 5:00 a.m.

"Where have you been, Gabriel?" Ada asks.

"I couldn't sleep, and when I finally did, I overslept." Gabriel tells her.

"Alexis is going to be furious with you being late, Gabriel. I would have taken it up myself, but she is already furious with me." Ada says.

Gabriel asks Ada why Alexis is so upset with her. Ada explains to him what happened earlier in the morning. Gabriel can't believe that Phooka would risk even coming into the house in fear of Dr. Brack.

Along with fresh fruit and flower arrangement cut this morning from the gardens, Gabriel grabs the sterling silver platter that has her best china teapot, sugar dispenser, creamer, and cup for her tea this morning.

"Hurry, Gabriel, before it gets even later." Ada tells him.

Gabriel rushes out the kitchen and up the stairs to Alexis' bedroom. Her bedroom is three quarters of the third floor. It is over nine thousand square foot of bedroom, bathroom, sitting room, and closets.

Knocking on the door, Gabriel trembles so badly that the tray shakes, making the china clang and bang. The doors open and Alexis stands there in front of Gabriel with her eyes in a glare. He knows she is upset he is late.

"Good morning, My Lady, look at the beautiful flowers from the garden this morning. How did you sleep, My Lady? Well, I hope you slept well." Gabriel says as he walks in fast and places the tray on the table in her sitting area overlooking the gardens below.

Through massive windows that allow the sun to come in as it rises over the mountains, the view is captivating. Gabriel stands for a moment in silence looking out the window although it is still dark outside with the orange, pinks, and yellows of the sun coming closer.

"Why are you so late, Gabriel?" Alexis asks standing beside him.

Gabriel snaps out of it, grabs the cup, and pours the tea, fixing it exactly how Alexis likes it while he avoids the question. She knows Gabriel has been having memories from the past and she knows he is trying to hide that from her. For good reason, she will have him removed or worse — fed to the animals. Gabriel is so nervous he is shaking.

"I am sorry, My Lady. I...I overslept. It will not happen ever again, My Lady." Gabriel says in a shaken voice.

"You're having bad dreams again? You know if you are having memories, you need to tell me. I can have Monroe and Dr. Brack give you something to take them away." Alexis tells him.

Gabriel turns and looks at Alexis, holding back the fear. He knows he has to act normal. If he doesn't, he will surely be removed. The thought of having Monroe and Dr. Brack analyze him intensifies his panic. He knows of the torturous acts they perform. And how heartless they are. *They have to be to do the sick things Alexis asks them to do.*

"I am fine, My Lady. Please do not worry yourself over me. I just drank a cup of tea too late and it kept me up longer than usual." Gabriel replies and hands Alexis her cup of tea.

"Is there anything else you will need, My Lady?" Gabriel says as he walks past her and over towards the doors. Turning and facing her, he bows down with his one arm out and a towel draped across just as a butler would.

"No, that is all. You may go." Alexis tells him and takes a sip of her tea.

"Oh, by the way, Gabriel, one more thing. My sons will be arriving today. Make sure their rooms are ready for them and notify me when they get here. We have another event to coming in about a month or so. This is the big one for the fall festivals. We will have more people coming in. I feel like celebrating for a change. Maybe a few days we will run it. Okay?" Alexis tells him.

"Yes, My Lady, that sounds wonderful. I will personally prepare your sons' rooms for their arrival." Gabriel says and walks out, closing the doors behind him.

Walking towards the staircase, Gabriel breaks. He panics. What am I to do? Alexis knows I am having memories of the past. She will have Dr. Brack and Monroe experiment on me again to erase them. I can't go through that pain and torture again. I am going to have to leave, sneak out. Maybe at the end of the fall festivals, she will be so busy with everything and her sons will be here, she will not even notice I have gone. I know she will send the boys to hunt me down, but if I can get a few days head start, I can run as fast as I can for a long ways. That is what I am. They gave me the DNA of....

Ada walks around the corner just as Gabriel comes down the stairs. She sees the look on his face. "Gabriel! What is it?" Ada asks.

"She knows, Ada. She knows I am having memories of the past. She wants me to go down and see Monroe and Dr. Brack. What am I going to do?" Gabriel tells her.

"Now just calm down. She probably is sincere about it, especially if she asked you to see them on your own. She likes you, Gabriel. You're her right hand man. You do everything for her and you make sure everything runs smoothly. She will not have anything happen to you." Ada tells him.

Gabriel doesn't respond; he just stands there looking at the floor while Ada talks in front of him. He knows that Ada is trying to make him feel better, but it is just talk. He has seen Alexis' eyes. He knows; he can sense what she isn't telling him directly. He knows she is not sincere in her words. She never is.

Ada grabs Gabriel, asking him if he hears her. Still staring at the floor as if he is lost in time, Gabriel simply nods his head. Ada hugs Gabriel and he just stands there, still lost in the moment.

"Good. Well, then. I need to get things ready for the day. I will check on you later." Ada walks towards her office down the other corridor.

Chapter 19

"North Carolina"

Victor and Kane pull up to the electronic gates at Dr. Redbone and Dr. Whiteriver's clinic. Victor presses the intercom button and waits for a response from someone. Kane turns to look at something he sees out of the corner of his eye. In the woods just off to the side of the entrance gate on the other side of the fence, he can see something moving slowly low to the ground. Kane growls deep within his chest. Victor spins his head over and looks at Kane.

"What...what is it? Someone follow us?" Victor asks.

Kane doesn't reply to his question. He just stares out the window of the truck, watching to see who or what it is moving towards them. With his wolf powers, he can smell and see things other humans can't. He is always on high alert; it's his natural instinct.

A voice finally comes across the intercom.

"Hello, may I help you?" The girl says.

"Yes, ma'am. It is Victor and Kane here to see Dr. Redbone." Victor replies.

They await a response or the gate to open as the movement Kane spotted a distance away now travels faster towards the vehicle. The gate beeps and opens slowly. Kane growls more furious than before. Victor tries to look at what Kane sees and watch the gate at the same time.

Kane opens the door and puts one leg out when Victor yells at him to get back in the truck. With no response, Kane climbs out and waits for whatever is coming at them. Hunched down and senses in overdrive, he is ready for the attack.

Victor slowly moves the truck forward, yelling at Kane to get back in the truck. When Kane slams the door and takes off into the woods, Victor looks out the windows, but doesn't see him or the movement coming towards them.

Victor pulls inside the gate and puts the truck in park. Getting out of the truck to see where Kane went, he can hear growling in the woods some distance away. He knows Kane has found something and he must be fighting with it. Victor gets back in the truck and heads up to the clinic to tell Dr. Redbone.

Dr. Redbone is standing just inside the doors waiting for Victor to pull up. He walks out as soon as Victor parks.

"Hi, Victor. Where is Kane?" Dr. Redbone asks.

"He was in the truck until we got to the gate. Then he saw something and took off after it. I waited for him, but it sounded like he was fighting whatever he saw. I could hear them in the distance." Victor replies.

"It is probably Warrick. He doesn't know your vehicle so he was stalking you when you pulled up at the gate. He must have sensed Kane and vice versa. Kane will figure out who it is. They will do the dominance fight; Warrick has been here protecting and leading the pack since Kane left. Kane must remember he is no longer alpha wolf here. He left and relinquished the rights to another wolf. Remember?" Dr. Redbone says.

Victor nods in understanding. "So you heard what has happened with Kia?" Victor asks as they walk into the clinic.

"Yes, I did hear from Dr. Whiteriver. How did this happen, Victor?" Dr. Redbone asks.

Victor explains to Dr. Redbone what happened based on what Kane told him. "We need to gather as many people in the clan as we can. The force that has taken Kia will more than likely experiment on her until the twins are born. After that, she is useless. The twins are much more valuable." Victor warns.

Dr. Whiteriver walks up as Victor and Dr. Redbone are talking in the lobby. He tells them he has everybody in the ceremony room just waiting for Victor.

Victor asks, "What they are doing?"

Dr. Whiteriver explains, "They are gathering everyone that is going to help search for Kia and strengthen their powers as a group."

"This is tradition, Victor. You don't remember this when you were a child. It was too many moons ago, my son. Come, let's get started." Dr. Whiteriver says.

The three of them walk towards the ceremony room when they hear something come in through the doors. They all turn around when they hear heavy breathing and a loud ruckus. They turn to find Kane and another person Victor doesn't recognize.

"I see you found him, Kane. I figured you two would have some issues to attend to before joining us." Dr. Redbone says.

Kane walks up behind him with a guy of the same size and build with bright blue eyes like Kane, except his hair is snow white and longer. They even walk alike, same stance and strut. Victor watches them get closer. Kane introduces the guy with him to Victor.

"Victor, I would like to meet my brother, Warrick. He is a wolf too. He was the one stalking us at the gate. He was actually doing his job. I didn't even recognize him when I saw him. He is getting much better at guarding than he used to be." Kane says.

Victor shakes Warrick's hand and they all walk towards the ceremony room. Walking into the big room, Kane notices they have altered it a great deal. They now have a different ceiling that they can actually open up by remote control to allow the spirit animals to come and go easier. It is all glass to see the night sky through it. They have placed more rocks, crystals, and different spiritual items like herbs, dolls, furs, and skins in the room. The skins are nestled on the floor, perfect for sitting. The fire pit is elevated so it will not burn the floor or any skins around. It also has a wire cover on it for extra protection. It has the feel of the traditional ceremonial areas previously set up outside.

Filled with people everywhere, Victor looks around and follows Dr. Redbone over to the medicine men. Walking around the people standing, Victor hears someone call his name. He looks to his left but doesn't see anyone. He keeps looking as he walks when he hears his name again.

"Mom!" Victor says.

Victor stops for a minute and Mona waves to him. She hasn't talked to Victor in a few months. He was going to call her to tell her what happened, but everything got way out of control and he just forgot. She left shortly after Victor brought her back. She wanted to go back to Salem to see her family and live up there. She felt like a burden with Kia and the twins on the way.

"Please, everyone. Gather around. We are about to start the ceremony now. We are going to need your strength, your power, and your love to find our Kia tonight." Dr. Redbone says as everybody gathers in their positions and sits down.

The drum starts low and slow, while Dr. Whiteriver tells everyone to join hands and strengthen the bond and power. Everyone joins hands and closes their eyes. The chanting begins faintly in the background.

Dr. Whiteriver talks and brings the spirit animals into the ceremony. "They will help guide us to Kia and they will protect her as much as they can." He says.

The chanting picks up louder; everyone joins in the chanting. A few minutes pass and one spirit animal comes in through the ceiling and flies around the room as fast as it can. It looks like a white streak it is moving so fast. Then suddenly it stops. Victor opens his eyes. In front of him is Kia's spirit animal. She looks upset. She lowers herself down until she is right in front of Victor. Everybody opens their eyes and watches the spirit animal.

It hovers just above the ground and reaches for Victor's hand. Victor lifts his hand up so the spirit animal can touch it. She grabs his hand and a flash of light like two electric wires touching breaks out from the touch. Victor jumps from the touch; it feels like an electric shock through his body. A flash of white light swirls around their hands. Everybody watches as Victor stares.

The spirit animal keeps her eyes focused directly into Victor's. The expression on Victor's face changes. He has fear in his eyes now. The others watch as two more white streaks come through the roof, circling the room and everybody, yet not as fast as the first spirit animal. They move in closer, settling slowly next to Kia's spirit animal. In a trance, he doesn't even see the other two spirit animals come in front of him.

The two spirit animals reach out at the same exact time and touch in the bond with Victor and

Kia's spirit animal. The light grows bigger and brighter with a yellowish gold color encircling the bond.

Dr. Redbone and Dr. Whiteriver sit next to Victor as they watch the event take place. Dr. Redbone looks over for a second at Victor's face and he sees tears running down. He knows as a medicine man exactly what is happening to him. The spirit animals are showing him what is happening to Kia and what the twins are feeling. It has to be done this way. It is harsh, he knows. He did take some of the responsibility to uphold the protection of Kia and especially his babies. Kane was there to help, but he wasn't at fault for the way the events unfolded. Victor should have never let Kane leave until he was able to follow behind them for guarded protection. Instead, Victor decided to catch up in North Carolina and allow Kane full responsibility to protect Kia and the twins.

Dr. Redbone puts his head down. He knows the hurt Victor is feeling. There's nothing more painful than to feel the agony of your children, especially when they are unprotected and scared. Kia can't help them and neither can he. This will give him more fight to get her back. This will give him the extra source for his powers to become stronger. He is going to need everything he can get.

The light fades slowly between the bond and Victor takes a gasp of air as if he hasn't breathed for a while. He comes out of the trance and one by one, the spirit animals drop off the connection except Kia's. She still holds Victor's hand. He looks at her and she turns her head ever so slightly and blinks her eyes. A soft grin comes over her face as she releases Victor's hand and the light disappears.

Victor blinks his eyes rapidly to clear the tears in them. He looks around the room quickly to see everybody watching him. Then he looks back at the spirit animals and realizes the other two are the ones from the twins. The buffalo spirit animal and the horse spirit animal. A single tear runs down Victor's face.

The buffalo and the horse spirit animal fly up, grab hands, and spin to face the others in the room. They put their other hands up and force a blue and green light out of each one. The light races around the room circling everyone and like a sparkler, flashes of light trickle down upon everyone in the circle.

After a few minutes, the flame grows higher and changes colors to a blue and green flame. Then Kia's spirit animal flies above them as if she is protecting them and with both hands, she sends out a bright white light. It is so bright they must all close their eyes.

The flash races around the circle at the speed of light. When it connects back to Kia's spirit animal, the flame in the center of the room touches with the light and pulls the blue and green flames up above the fire pit. With a movement of Kia's spirit animal's hand, the light moves across the room from the center all the way to the walls and disappears, passing through everyone in the room.

Then they take off through the roof and disappear like stars in the night sky. They open their eyes and Dr. Redbone stands to speak to everyone.

"What we have witnessed is truly amazing. The spirit animals have spoken to Victor. They have showed him the truth and have given him the strength to find Kia and the twins. They have also given us all the extra power and strength to help guide us in our journey to find them and bring them home safe. This is what the spirit animals have told us today. We must follow the words they have spoken. Victor will now guide us in this journey." Dr. Redbone tells everyone.

The drum beats again and the chanting starts out very slow and progresses louder. Victor looks around the room to see Mona sitting next to Kane and Warrick. She smiles at him; he just shakes his head. *Boy, she is changing fast with the new era she lives in. Hitting on two guys already.*

194

The chanting continues for another half an hour. Different people come up and dance to the ceremony, each giving a ritual for protection, safety, health, endurance and so on. These rituals all benefit everybody in the circle and this power will last until their task is done.

Once the ceremony is done, Mona finds her way out the door and waits for her son to come out. Finally, Victor walks out and she grabs his arm and pulls him aside.

"Why didn't you call me, Victor? You know I would have been down here as soon as you called. You should have never let it get this far. I could have stayed at the house with you, Kia, and Kane. One extra power might have stopped this from happening. You do remember I have more power than you do, and my powers are of ancient witchcraft. There isn't much that can escape them. What is your plan in finding Kia?" Mona asks.

Victor explains he followed this creature to an area a distance from where they live. "It's a big Plantation that is heavily gated and fenced. I noticed many statues of different creatures mounted all over the fence and the big house itself. I know what that means — it is protected heavily. They are creatures of the Raven Mocker." He tells Mona.

Mona's eyes enlarged. "Raven Mocker? I haven't seen one in ages. I thought they all had gone hundred or more years ago. Do you know the power a single living Raven Mocker can have on the people? She is the evil of all evil. She is fearless, careless, and she takes souls from humans. Sometimes, she will torment them by walking past their house at night, and in a few days, they die. She is usually waiting for them to pass; that is when she is seen collecting their souls to harvest for her longevity and powers. Only a medicine man can see her waiting to collect and the medicine man is the only one that can scare her off. However, it has to be a very powerful one. Dr. Redbone and Dr. Whiteriver are powerful, but this is a different power.

"This is one from a medicine man that doesn't practice just American Indian, but every tribe around the world. This is the only way to defeat her and make her run from us. I haven't seen a medicine man like this since I was a very young girl. I don't even know where to find one if there is any left. At that time, it was just the one. He was older than dirt itself, and he didn't look a day over thirty. I don't care how many shape shifters, witches, warlocks, or medicine men you have here, Victor. They are not going to scare this Raven Mocker off. If you find a way in, to get Kia away from her, you're doomed. She will have her hellhounds hunt you until they find you and tear you apart. We need to tell the two doctors about this, Victor. We are all going to need some more than what we have. You should have told them before the ceremony even started. It would have taken place so much differently." Mona tells him.

Victor puts his head down, disappointed in what Mona has told him and what the spirit animals showed him. He is so confused. All he wants to do is leave and get Kia back. Even if he gets her, he will gladly exchange himself for them.

Kane and Warrick pass by Victor and Kane pats Victor on the back as they keep walking. Mona watches them walk by and tells Victor that those wolves are some handsome species. She'd like to get her hands on both of them.

Victor spins his head over and looks at her with a disgusted look on his face. Mona looks slowly over at him; she is watching Kane and Warrick go down the hall.

"What…what are you looking at me like that for, Victor? I am female. Just because I am your mother doesn't mean I stopped having sex with men." Mona tells him and walks over to Dr. Redbone.

Still a little star struck, Victor tries to put all the information and thoughts in order so he can make sense of it all and figure out what to do. She needs to stay here until the twins are born. Hopefully, they haven't done anything by now to hurt them.

Another person from the ceremony walks up to Victor. Placing his hand on his shoulder, he tells him, "Don't worry, my son. The Great Spirit has sent us the spirit animals and they will help us find her. She will be safe and she will stay strong until we find her." Victor smiles and grabs ahold of his hand on his shoulder.

"Thank you, my friend." Victor says.

"I am your brother. Thank you, my brother." He replies.

"Thank you, my brother." Victor then replies.

Dr. Redbone turns around and looks at Victor with a blank face. Victor sees Mona standing next to him. She must have told him what we are facing. Where Kia is. Oh, no.

"Why didn't you tell us, Victor? This is a very different problem we have. You should have told me before we started. You should have told me before you got here, Victor. We might not be able to save Kia now. This force is one that has an empire behind it. We will be outnumbered, not just in people but also in power and strength. I will have to get ahold of every elder I know to see if we can find the true world medicine man and see if he can come here to help. For now, Victor, we don't do anything until I find him. Do you understand? If you do go after Kia now, it will surely be her death. The Raven Mocker will take her soul and leave her body to crumble to dust. She will more than likely take the twins as her own children and raise them." Dr. Redbone says.

Mona puts her arm around Victor, as he looks to the floor helpless, upset, and confused. He wants so badly to get Kia back and free her from harm's way, yet his hands are tied.

They walk down the hallway and Dr. Redbone tells them they have extra efficiencies. He is welcome to stay until they find the world medicine man.

Chapter 20

"Missing"

John comes back from town. Jake has been doing good lately. Pulling in the driveway and walking up to the garage, he looks over and sees Lizzie lying in the sun. It is September, but the temperatures are perfect eighty degrees in the daytime and fifties at night.

He stops a minute and takes in the view. She is a short woman all of five feet. With long strawberry blond hair, she doesn't have the model body as people live by. She has a small frame and is not fat or heavy; she is healthy looking, within her weight range for her height, maybe a pound or so over.

John turns and walks into the garage with the groceries to put away. Kyle is sitting on the couch in the garage where John has made a living area to stretch out instead of inside the camper. He is playing Xbox games; Jake is texting on his phone to his friends back home.

"Hey, guys. Dinner will be ready in about an hour and half." John tells them. Neither one of them act as if they hear him. He doesn't care. He has something else on his mind anyways. He has found a place he'd like to take the family for a day adventure.

While in town, he saw the fall festivals they are having all around and he brought back this brochure of a beautiful property with a tour of the gardens, and the grounds. For fifty-five dollars, one can visit the animals and learn the history of the area and the estate. They even serve a buffet lunch. It only happens one season a year. Shops are set up with vendors, and at night, they have a parade that is one exotic show.

We will have to go to this. It is in a week to kick off the fall festivals. Sounds exciting. I will get tickets and surprise the family.

John's cell phone rings. It is Ellie's mother.

"Hello, Mrs. Owens. How are you doing?"

"Not good, John. We can't seem to find Ellie." She says.

"What do you mean, Mrs. Owens?"

"She went off for the summer to meet with some friends. All three of them are missing. I was wondering if you have seen or heard from her I didn't want to bother you with this."

"No, ma'am. I'm sorry. I haven't talk to Ellie in a while since she was leaving. Have you contacted Sheriff Taylor yet?"

"I haven't yet, but the girls' parents have. Since they are not from this area, they called me and asked if I heard from them and I asked if they heard from Ellie. So none of us has heard anything for about three days now. It is unlike Ellie to not come call by now." Mrs. Owens says.

"I am sorry to hear about this. I would suggest you call Sheriff Taylor as soon as you hang up with me so he knows she is missing also, Mrs. Owens."

"Yes, I will. I just thought maybe she was staying in one of your cabins with a boy or something."

"No, ma'am. She hasn't come out for a while."

"Okay, then, thank you, John." She hangs up the phone.

John stands thinking for a moment. He is letting the news sink in and the feelings catch up to the thoughts. OMG, Ellie missing? He says to himself. I hope she is all right. She knows a lot of the history now and the creatures around. I wonder if she was doing some investigation work with her friends. I will wait to see if Sheriff Taylor calls me.

Lizzie comes in and asks John what is wrong. He has a worried look on his face. He tells her that Ellie's mother just called looking for. She hasn't called or been home in almost three months.

"Does she have friends she could be staying with?" Lizzie asks.

"I am sure she has friends. The strange thing is she was with some friends, her mother said, and they are missing also." John tells her.

"That is not good. I hope they find them safe and sound. Ellie is the one you hired for the research, correct?" Lizzie asks

"Yes, she is a nice young lady." John says.

"Dinner is ready, boys." Lizzie yells out.

They all gather around the table in the temporary kitchen in the garage. John would have moved into one of the cabins that he has done, but he thought if he did that, he would procrastinate on building the house. Therefore, he stays in the camper and garage.

A few minutes into the dinner, John's cell phone rings. "Hi, Sheriff, what can I do you for today?" John says.

"I am calling to see if you have seen Ellie Owens?" The sheriff asks.

"No, sir. I haven't. Mrs. Owens called a little while ago and asked me the same question." John replies.

"Yeah, she said her and the two other girls she was with are missing. Their parents called the other day, but we have to wait at least twenty-four hours. I wish Mrs. Owens had called as soon as she knew Ellie was missing. I would have looked into it sooner. Well, if you hear from her or anything, let me know first. Okay, John?"

"Of course, Sheriff. I will. I hope you find them. Safe and alive." John says.

Sheriff Taylor walks up to the front desk and tells Deputy Eldridge that he is going to the Beaver Creek Motel and talk with the clerk. "If anyone calls about Ellie, forward it to my cell phone." The sheriff orders.

Sheriff Taylor walks into the lobby of Beaver Creek Motel. The girl on duty is just closing out her cash register for the shift change at 8:00 p.m.

"Hello, can I help you?" A girl from the back walks out and asks the sheriff.

"I am looking to speak with the manager. Is he around?"

"No, sir. Sheriff Taylor, I am the only one here for the night. Can I help you?" The girl asks.

"A couple of girls were staying here a few months. Elsa and Dania. Do you recall them checking out or anything suspicious going on with them? Did you see anyone other than them?" Sheriff Taylor asks.

"I remember the girls. They left early. They had paid until Monday morning, but when the maid went there Sunday morning, they were not there. We figured they left and she made the room. Monday morning she came by to clean and their luggage, all their personal belongings were still here. The beds weren't missed up or anything. Therefore, we had to clean out the room. Their reservation was up. We put all the unclaimed stuff in lost and found until someone comes to collect it. And the car, was gone also.

"What about boys or possibly another girl with brownish black hair about five-foot six or seven, named Ellie?"

"I recall seeing a girl like that, but she was dressed pretty, if you don't mind me saying, slutty, Sheriff. Her description sounds correct. The two girls, they had been hanging out with the guys next door."

"Who were the guys next door? Do you recall their names?" Sheriff Taylor asks.

"I have it here in the computer. Let me pull it up. Yes, Malik Solomon with a total of two rooms and four guests. He paid for two weeks in advance. He also left earlier, except all their belongings are gone." She says.

"Do you mind showing me the rooms they all stayed in?"

"I would love to, Sheriff, but I have guests in them right now."

"I understand. When is the best time to come have someone let us in the rooms?"

"Tomorrow around 10:30-11:00 a.m., Sheriff."

"Okay, that is fine. Would you mind if I saw their things they left behind? In addition, for the car, don't move it or have it towed. It may be evidence in a missing person's case by tomorrow. I will have one of my deputies have it towed to impound." He tells her.

"No problem, Sheriff Taylor. Come around the desk and I will show you where we keep all the stuff left behind." She walks the sheriff into the back room and in a closet filled with miscellaneous stuff. She

206

pulls out all the stuff marked Room 10 for him to go through.

She leaves him alone to search the girls' belongings. Not to upset any incoming guests, the sheriff stays in the back room.

Sheriff Taylor opens the luggage from the girls' room. Sifting through, he notices nothing out of the ordinary: clothes, makeup, personal items girls would have with them.

"What do we have here?" Sheriff Taylor says under his breath." He finds the girls' purses and opens them to discover the wallets and their cell phones. He pulls out the cell phones from the purses and notices they are on stand by. The batteries are low, but they are on.

No signal, which would explain the low batteries. No phone calls because they couldn't get a signal where they have been stored.

He slides the home screen on the phone. Just like girls, they don't bother locking their phones either. Scrolling to the call history, he sees the same numbers phoned except one. He writes the numbers down and puts them in his pocket. He takes the girls' hairbrushes also and some items that he knows they had to touch and leave fingerprints. He places them in a bag and walks out of the back room.

"Done, Sheriff?" The girl asks.

"Yes, ma'am. I am done. I would like you to keep their belongings here until I come and get them or their parents. Please make a note of that on the luggage, if you would please." Sheriff Taylor says.

"Yes, sir. Sheriff. I will do that right now. You have a good night, sir." She replies.

"You too. Thank you." He walks out the lobby doors to his car.

The next morning, Sheriff Taylor and Deputy Eldridge pull up into the parking lot of Beaver Creek Motel at 10:30 a.m. They park in front of Room 10.

Sheriff Taylor sees the maid is cleaning the room. "Excuse me. May we come in and look around?" He asks.

"Yes, sir. Sheriff, take your time. I can move on to the next room." The maid says.

Sheriff Taylor and Deputy Eldridge walk slowly through the room, looking for anything unusual. The Deputy sprays door handles, tables, the bathroom, counters with Luminol spray, looking for bloodstains with a fluorescent light. He comes up with nothing. Sheriff Taylor collects some fingerprints around the room, picking up different ones to run.

"There is no evidence of any kind of struggle in here, Sheriff. They must have gone with the people easily." Deputy Eldridge says.

The sheriff doesn't feel right about the whole thing. It just doesn't make since. He asks the maid if she was on duty at the time the four men were staying in the motel.

"I do remember them. Let me take you to the rooms." She walks him down to Rooms 11 and 12. He asks if she has already cleaned them. She tells him she has and can unlock them for him if he would like.

"Please, if you would," The sheriff obliges.

Deputy Eldridge sprays Room 12 like the other one he did. Bathroom, door handles, counters; he even decides to spray the bedcover. Nothing shows so he moves over to room 11. Once again, after spraying everything, he finds nothing. He sprays the bedcover and he finds a stain of blood.

"Sheriff Taylor, you need to come here." Deputy Eldridge yells.

Sheriff Taylor walks out of the bathroom where he was taking fingerprints. Deputy Eldridge points at the bloodstain on the cover.

Sheriff Taylor tells Deputy Eldridge to take a sample and the cover also.

"Spray the bed after you pull the sheets off both. See what is on them also." Sheriff Taylor says.

They pull the sheets off the bed and faintly find traces of blood. Sheriff Taylor says they are old stains. Probably othing to be concerned about.

'Let's take this stuff to the lab and see what we come up with. There might be semen on the cover that we can identify."

Chapter 21

"The Argument"

Malik walks into his mother's office unannounced — something she doesn't like. She expects everyone to ask her permission first for just about everything on the Plantation. That is why most of the staff doesn't talk much amongst themselves. Alexis has cameras set up all around watching everybody. If they are caught talking secretly, she sends them down to see Dr. Brack and Monroe. Sometimes they come back; sometimes they are never seen again

"Hello, Mother!" Malik says as he pushes open her doors to her office. She sits behind her massive desk; so big, ten people could dine around it comfortably.

"Malik, how dare you barge into my office unannounced!" Alexis says viciously and stands up quickly, moving around her desk to meet him.

"What is so important that you couldn't have Ada call me before you came up?"

"Mother, chill out. Are you ever going to act like a mom? All our lives, you have handed us off to someone else to take care of us and worry about us.

You want responsibility, but yet you don't want us as your responsibility." Malik says.

"Malik, how dare you speak to me like that? I ought to have you sent down..." Malik interrupts her.

"Taken done to Dr. Brack and Monroe, your little lab rats, to do away with me? Go ahead, Mother. I am sick and tired of this bullshit game you play all the time. I am sick and tired of dealing with your idiot son Damien. He is the one that should be sent down to your little lab rats and have something done with him. He is totally losing it. I am done with him! He is not ever running with my pack again. He can stay here or you can send him out on his own. I will never let him come with me again. I will fight him to the death if he does." Malik snaps back at Alexis.

Alexis stands in one spot, eyes widened, teeth clenched, and defiant. Damien is her baby. If any of them were to be, it is Damien. He has always been the rebel and the hellion of the bunch, and she sees herself in him. They are a lot alike in that manner.

"What is wrong with you, Malik? You don't ever talk to me like that again, or I will have you sent away." Alexis yells.

Malik walks over and sits down on one of the couches in the office. He puts his arms across the back and crosses one leg on the other's knee, keeping a smirk on his face. He knows he has crawled under his mother's skin, something he's wanted to do for a very long time. He is normally a nice guy to her, never talking back, and listening to everything she asks and being at her beckon call whenever she wants him to be.

"Don't you dare walk away from me, Malik, and I didn't say you could sit down when I am talking to you."

"Well, I am tired of your fucking shit, Mother. You send me out on a job and before I even have a chance to capture the creatures, you have some excuse and send Phooka. Now I had creatures out there that you are looking for besides the silver-blood. We found some scents that tell us this is the fertile ground for these creatures. There's more creatures here than any other place we have searched. This is the gold mine, but you insisted on ruining it once again. I know you! You're going to blame me for your stupidity, Mother! Did you get the envelope with the feather I sent?" Malik asks.

Pissed off, Alexis turns, stomps over to her desk, and throws papers around her desk. She holds up a large envelope and says, "You mean this one, Malik? Yes, I got it!" she snaps back at him.

"Did you open it?" Malik inquires in a calm voice, knowing it would piss her off to no end.

Alexis grabs her letter opener and shoves it in the side of the envelope, tearing it as she struggles even harder.

A large brownish gold feather falls out on her desk. She looks down at it and puts the letter opener and envelope down. Slowly reaching down, she picks the feather up and brings it up near her face to get a better look at it.

It is the size of an eagle feather, but it isn't one. It is brown like glitter with hints of gold veins that run through the feather. There is only one type of feather made like this and the creature it belongs to hasn't been seen in hundreds of years.

"Where did you find this, Malik?" Alexis yells.

"Where do you think? The same place you had to pull us out of by sending Phooka in to take the prize." He says.

"You idiot! You didn't have to leave. You could have stayed, found this creature, and brought it back." Alexis tells him.

"I would have done that except your son Damien decided to… well, let's say he roughed up a girl. We brought her back with two others for your experiments. I had no choice; we couldn't let them go, especially after what Damien did to her. He mated with her." Malik says.

"He did what?!" Alexis stomps around the desk again and stands in front of Malik.

"How do you know this, Malik? You tell me right now."

"I can smell the difference between sex and impregnating a human with our kind. I am a hellhound, you know. I knew it when he opened the door. I asked him on the way back and he finally admitted to it. He wanted to have an offspring of his own and he knew if he brought this girl back pregnant, you would have Dr. Brack and Monroe keep her until the baby is born." Malik tells her.

"Great! That is just what I need — another headache like Damien running around. We should have something done with this girl so she doesn't have Damien's offspring. Dr. Brack and Monroe can take care of her."

"Really, Mother? You would do that when there are so few of our kind. That is typical for you. I should have known you would say something like this. Well, when I decide to have offspring of my own, I will never tell you about it. Now, what are we going to do about the feather?" Malik asks.

"You and your brothers are going back to find this creature and any others you come across, like you were supposed to in the first place." Alexis says loudly.

216

Malik smirks at her and laughs silently in front of her just to annoy his mother. Suddenly, they hear a knock on the door. Alexis throws up her hands, cursing all the way to the doors. She swings them open.

"Well, should we say happy to see you too?" Damien says.

"You're in trouble, mister. Get in here." Alexis says angrily.

Alexis hugs the two boys, Luther and Lucius. She knows they are innocent. They are good boys; they listen, stay out of trouble, and never cause any problems.

"So, Damien, what is this I hear from Malik? Is this true? Why the hell would you do such a thing? You know better. This is unacceptable, Damien. You are really pushing your luck, young man."

"I guess you did all the hard work again, did you, Malik? Thanks, man. I owe you again." Damien says as he sits down on the couch next his brother.

Malik just glares at Damien. He knows what Damien is trying to say. He set it up so Malik would tell Alexis about the girl so he didn't have to do it. *He thinks he is smart.*

"Since we are having a family meeting, let's get things straight. Damien, you are no longer working in this pack. Now listen to me before you even open your mouth, mister. I have heard enough from the past few years about you and the problems you are giving Malik and the boys. These are your brothers, your family, and your pack. A pack listens to the pack leader when they are on a hunt. That's it! Final! You, on the other hand, could never handle authority." Damien leans over to Malik and says just like her.

"I heard that, Damien. You have a choice. You can go hunt alone or you can stay here and work on the Plantation. Those are the two choices you get."

"Well…Mother, I guess I might relax a bit and hang here with my new girlfriend. At least my girlfriend until the baby is born. Then you can do what you want with her. I am slowly building my own pack. One by one." Damien says sarcastically.

"You want to be a smart ass about it all, do you? Well, you're not going to be relaxing, that's for sure. As far as your little girlfriend, she will be used as an experiment and that offspring is history. I will have Dr. Brack and Monroe dispose of that creature, maybe use it for testing." Alexis replies.

Damien's eyes turn orange then slowly fill with red. He knows what is going to happen. Alexis has pushed him too far this time. Damien can't keep his anger under control anymore and has gone where no hellhound should go. This is the final straw before they are put down. They will turn on everyone and everything. They get to this point and become nothing but an evil killing machine. Fighting every creature, demon, and human to death. Not much can kill hellhounds.

Malik jumps up and grabs Alexis by the arm before she can say anymore to Damien. He leads her quickly off and out of the office. The boys follow suit, not wanting to be anywhere near Damien when he changes.

"What are you doing, Malik? You know I can hurt you; you better let me go."

"Damn it, Mother. You have to push and push until no end. Don't you see Damien's eyes? Are you crazy? He is over the edge to the point of no return if you keep pushing him. Now go somewhere out of sight for a while and let him be. Just let him have this one girl, let him take care of his own offspring. Maybe this is what he needs to come back to being a hunter versus the killer he is becoming." Malik tells her.

Alexis stands looking into Malik's eyes in the long hallway. Down by the elevator they hear someone coming up the stairs from the other end. Alexis knows Malik is right about Damien.

"Ada, hi. Haven't seen you in so long." Luther and Lucius say.

"Hey, boys." Ada says and hugs them.

"My Lady, Dr. Brack and Monroe ask for your assistance in the lab as soon as possible." Ada says.

Alexis turns and looks at Malik. She knows exactly what they want. The new experiment subjects are here and they already know one is pregnant. She is sure of it.

Alexis reaches out and grabs Malik's hand for the first time; he can't even remember his mother's touch. It sends a cold chill right through him. One he doesn't like to feel at all.

"Ada, tell them I am on my way." Alexis says and walks towards her elevator. Malik, Luther, and Lucius look at each other and smirk. They know exactly what Malik is thinking.

Chapter 22

"The Lab"

The three of them walk down to the servants' stairwell. Waiting patiently for Ada to get out of sight, they sneak down the stairs like a bunch of children playing a game. Actually, they are playing a little game — to see what has really been going on downstairs.

Growing up as kids, all four boys were warned never to go downstairs. Alexis went as far as keeping one of the older hellhounds on guard at the time they all were just young pups. He would shift and scare each one. As they grew older, they became wiser and less scared of him. However, they would never let the younger ones know they weren't scared; this was a learning process for them growing up.

Finally, one day Alexis pulled the guard from the door and they never saw him again. The boys developed a relationship with him the older they got. The older guard was like a teacher to them. He knew what they were and he would give them different things to learn more about their abilities as a hellhound pup.

Alexis slides her card and puts in her code to enter the lab. The three watch from a distance down the corner of the corridor.

The door beeps. They hear Alexis open the solid white metal door. Malik nudges Luther, who takes off like a streak of light just in time to catch the door as it almost closes. He grabs the handle so it closes but not locks.

Malik and Lucius walk up and Malik takes the door handle from Luther. Opening it just a crack to see that Alexis is gone from sight, they slowly open it and walk in.

Sneaking around the room, they look at all the different tanks filled with bodies of different cross-DNA species. They are stunned what their mother has been doing down there.

Big glass jars litter one wall of the room filled with different sized half human half creatures. From babies to adult stages it is like all the bad experiments are kept as a visual reference for them. They see bodies laid out on stainless steel tables, twisted and distorted, some of them half shifted into creatures. It is as if their mistakes are on display so they remember not to do that experiment again.

The boys are horrified the more they look around. This is why Malik never liked Dr. Brack or Monroe when they would come up to see everyone or take a stroll through the gardens. He never put his finger on it. Well now, it hit him right in the face. They are as sick as his mother. No wonder she has kept these two around so long. They are playing Dr. Frankenstein with humans and different creatures.

They hear voices coming from a room on the other side of a big white wall with a plastic curtain hanging, like the ones in the meat department of a grocery store. Thick strips of plastic cut in ten-inch sections hang across an opening so you can pass through without a door.

They all sneak past the stainless steel tables that have human bodies also lying on them with tubes and IVs sticking in them. Each one looks in a different stage of transformation.

"This must be the newest experiment." Luther murmurs.

"Shhh… quiet!" Malik says sourly.

Luther and Lucius look at each other while Malik cocks his head to the side to get a better listen.

A scream echoes through the lab. The three jump, startled.

Luther says, "That sounds like Elsa?"

Lucius grabs his mouth and shakes his head at him. "No... not a word," and gives him a discouraging gaze.

"Where are we? What are you doing to us?" They hear one girl say.

"Well, well. What do we have here, Dr. Brack?"

"Alexis, we have a few questions for you. This one new patient here..." They walk around the two other stainless steel tables like in a morgue that has Elsa and Dania strapped down and gagged.

"This one here is pregnant, Alexis."

"That is what I just found out. You need to have something done with this one. Damien is the culprit of this. This is his doing and I will not allow him to have an offspring from a human that I have not chosen."

"What would you like us to do with her?" Monroe asks.

"You will have to remove the offspring and then you can experiment with a hybrid DNA strain."

"Why not try a hybrid hellhound strain? She has already accepted the sperm from Damien. We can use the unborn offspring, splice it with the silver-blood's offspring, and implant it back into this one until it is ready to be born. We can monitor and examine the type of creature it becomes. They grow so fast anyways. We will see progress faster this way." Dr. Brack states.

"Do what you think is best, Dr. Brack. I am behind your decisions. I still don't like the idea of having an offspring from my son Damien. The trouble he has caused his whole life, I can only imagine the creature this will become."

Alexis turns back and studies Anna and Dania, feeling the texture of their hair and skin, rubbing deeply to feel the muscle tone. Looking at their bodies lying naked on the cold steel table, she asks if these two have been mated yet.

"No, they are still virgins." Monroe said with a big smile.

"Oh really," Alexis says with a cock of her eyebrow. *Virgins… well that is even better. These two will make good surrogate mothers to the hybrid DNA tests.*

"I want you to take this feather," she hands the feather Malik sent her. "I want you to test it. I know what it is, but I want to make sure I am correct. This creature has not been seen in well over two-hundred years. Try to pull the DNA from the feather and see if you can splice it with the hybrid DNA. Let's see what we come up with."

Scanning the room, she sees Kia over by the animal cages. Walking over to see her prize possession, she notices Kia is awake and her eyes are moving around rapidly, just looking for a chance to escape. Alexis looks at her and sees she is in distress and pulling against the restraints trying to free herself. Alexis looks at Kia and smirks.

"Silver-blood, you might as well give up. You're not going to get out of here even if you do shift and free yourself from these straps. They will tranquilize you with more power drugs and you will sleep through the whole thing. Is that what you want? To sleep through the birth of your offspring?" Alexis says with a bitter voice.

Kia struggles harder just to spite her words. Alexis shakes her head and mumbles under her breath. "Stubborn silver-bloods. They are all the same."

Malik hears his mother's footsteps coming. He takes the two boys and they hide further down from the plastic curtain to the backside of the slab behind a corner.

The three of them watch as she walks out. Waiting until Dr. Brack and Monroe walk into the sealed part of the lab with Ellie, they see she is drugged up pretty bad.

They sneak over and, through the plastic curtain, they see a whole room filled with different humans strapped down on steel tables. They stand just inside the doorway looking from one side slowly across to the other side of the room.

"What the hell?" Luther whispers.

"This is crazy, dude." Lucius answers back in a soft voice.

"Mother is sicker than I thought she was. What is she doing with all these humans and creatures? I know there isn't that many in the gardens. She is trying to make a hybrid shifter for something. The question is why?" Malik mumbles to the boys.

Luther walks towards Elsa, and Lucius towards Dania. Malik grabs Luther's arm and then lets loose. He figures it might give the girls a little relief to see them. Maybe not though and takes off behind them.

"Whatever you two do, don't remove the gags." Malik whispers to them.

Elsa sees them coming before Dania does. She thrashes in the restraints, trying to get free. Luther grabs her and gently holds her down, trying to get her to relax. He looks into her eyes and she watches his eyes turn from a light brownish yellow to a calming green. He is hypnotizing her to calm her down.

About the same time, Lucius stands next to Dania. She looks at Lucius desperately with her big brown deer eyes. Lucius is a bit weak-hearted than his brothers.

Lucius reaches down and hugs Dania. Malik walks over and pushes Lucius out of the way. Looking into Dania's eyes, Malik calms her down with his. She stops resisting and is relaxed.

Malik moves out of the way and Lucius stands back to face Dania. She smiles up at him, happy to see him.

Malik walks over to see the silver-blood Kia. Her eyes catch a glimpse of something moving towards her. She looks down and sees someone getting closer. She notices it isn't anyone she has seen before. Then she smells a whiff of his scent. She notices he is a…

Malik walks slowly around Kia looking at her as if she was on display. *So this is what you look like. You're the one that escaped us that night. You are pretty. Smart too.* He can't keep from looking at Kia's skin. How it shimmers like tiny pieces of glass rubbed all over it. Then it stops and her beautiful reddish/tan color skin shows.

What is happening to you? Malik wonders. Kia's eyes shuffle back and forth with anger gleaming from them. If she could only get loose, she knows she would shift into a different creature. She can feel it stirring inside her.

Malik notices her eyes. Every few minutes, they change color from brown to blue to green, back to brown. He can't help but stare at her.

Watching her struggle, he tries hypnotizing her, but he soon learns it doesn't work on her. She can see past the gaze he offers and straight into his soulless body.

Malik stands up sharply, actually a little intimated by Kia's ability to see into him so deeply. Malik shakes his head for a brief second.

"Well, you really are something special, aren't you? Our powers don't work on you. That is interesting. But I do know you alone cannot harm us." Malik mutters and smirks.

Kia tries harder to push the drugs feeding her veins and keeping her from shifting into a creature and attack him. However, they overcome the feeling of being pure human and not of a shapeshifter. They are too strong for her and she has to stop fighting it. Her heart races so fast it feels like it is going to pound out of her chest.

She still hasn't felt the twins move in a few days now. She knows they're alive. They're just relaxed. She hopes it is from the drugs, and not her body trying to shift.

They all turn when they hear a commotion come from the other room.

"Hold her still, Monroe!"

"I am trying. She is stronger than I expected."

"Give her a tranquilizer, damn it!" Dr. Brack yells. Monroe grabs the bottle from his lab coat and a syringe. Quickly filling the tube with diazepam, he sticks the needle in Ellie's vein.

She stops struggling quickly and is fast asleep.

"Thank God. I think the offspring is giving this girl some sort of power and strength. We had better use some heavy-duty restraints on her. She actually has torn the thick leather straps and bent the metal!" Dr. Brack says to Monroe surprised.

"Maybe we should do this a different way, Dr. Brack. Maybe we should take the silver-blood's DNA strain we perfected in the lab this morning and just inject it into the offspring in this girl. Let it stay in and see what happens. I have never seen this happen to a human before."

"I think you're right, Monroe. I think we have something different here for sure. I will make a note of this." Dr. Brack turns and walks over to the small refrigerator. He pulls out a small vile for one dose. *Experimental SB DNA.*

Grabbing a long metal syringe equipped with a very long needle to go through her belly and into the unborn, Dr. Brack fills the syringe with the vile.

"Do you see that the unborn is growing fast within her? Her stomach has grown a lot since she's been here." Monroe says.

"Just wait until we inject this into it. It will grow three times faster."

Dr. Brack sticks the long needle slowly in through the lower abdomen. Her body twitches from a reflex of the needle penetrating through her stomach and into her uterus. She can feel Dr. Brack moving the needle side to side and up and down trying to find the area of the unborn. She tries with all her might to resist and get free from them and the restraints.

Monroe holds her hips steady while Dr. Brack guides the needle deeper and deeper into her abdomen. Finally stopping, Monroe looks up at Dr. Brack with a strange look on his face.

Dr. Brack draws back a tiny bit on the syringe to see if he gets blood or a clear fluid. A clear fluid seeps into the syringe. Dr. Brack gets an evil grin on his face and looks over at Monroe, giving him a wink of his eye.

He slowly injects the experimental SB DNA into the unborn creature Ellie is carrying inside her. Pulling the needle out, Dr. Brack and Monroe breathe a sigh of relief.

"Finally, after all these years we are testing the hybrid formula." Monroe says to Dr. Brack:

"Time to break out the expensive bottle of wine Alexis gave us years ago. Time to celebrate!"

They head out into the other lab.

"Oh, shit! They're coming!" Malik says to the boys.

Malik and the boys run to the corner they were hiding in before. Waiting until the two walk into their office, they watch from a distance as Dr. Brack and Monroe walk in and close the door.

Chapter 23

"What has Mother done"

The boys walk towards the door of the lab when they notice Malik has actually turned towards the area where Monroe and Dr. Brack were working on Ellie.

Curious, the boys follow suit, swiftly catching up to the back of Malik. They are all shocked at what they see.

"What are they doing to her?" Luther asks silently.

"I am not sure, Luther, but I think they are testing something on her."

"Yeah, I see that, Malik, but what? Look at the size of her belly. Ten times the size it was. That offspring is going to tear her apart. That is not right, dude. Not right at all. I don't care what Mother says. This is wrong." Luther replies. Shaking his head in disgust, his head fills with ideas of how he could destroy this place and free the poor creatures trapped in cages, strapped down, and drugged.

"Should we go over to her?" Lucius asks.

"I don't think that is a good idea. She might panic and hurt herself." Malik says.

They stand just inside the door, leery of walking any closer. They feel they might scare Ellie even more. Except, they are curious to see what she looks like up close. From where they are standing, they can only see her feet, legs, and a huge belly draped with a thin white sheet.

Malik points to the right and he walks to the left hoping that if they walk up on different sides at the same time, she will be distracted from one side to the other.

The closer Malik gets, the stranger the feeling he gets. He feels uneasy at first and suddenly sick to his stomach. By the time he almost reaches the table, Ellie is laying on. His head is pounding.

He reaches up and grabs it, bending over. Luther and Lucius see him on the other side and whisper to him. "Dude, you all right, man?"

Malik doesn't respond. Instead, he drops to his knees still holding his head.

The boys look at Ellie. She has a fixed gaze right on Malik. Her eyes have turned blood red around the pupils. Luther tells Lucius, "Don't get in the way of her stare, man. That is not good. Whatever she is doing is from what they have injected in her. She is something I have never seen before."

They yell at Malik as quietly as they can, "Dude, man, get up. We need to get out of here."

Both boys crouch down on their knees so Ellie can't see them. Finally, Malik stands up and faces Ellie.

"Damien, goddamn you!" Malik suddenly shouts. Luther and Lucius take off out of the lab and through the entry door like a streak of light. They know that tone and they are not sticking around to see the outcome.

Malik stands, eyes locked into Ellie's. He sees the creature she is becoming from the unborn in her. She quickly snaps one of the restraints and latches on to Malik's arm.

Malik jerks back to get free from her grasp. He watches as she changes. Her face bends and stretches, growing larger and longer. The skin on her face peels and drops off onto the table. Blood oozes from the flesh. She twists and moves almost as if she is trying to break out of her own skin. He can hear the crunching sounds from her body changing. He can see something dark, covered in a thick, wet gel-looking substance underneath.

He watches as her torso grows and changes shape. Her belly holding the offspring enlarges with the changing of her body. The sheet slides off and he can see it moving inside her belly. It presses as if it is trying to push through her skin.

Her human skin is half-attached and this creature underneath is trying to rip out from under it. Malik has never seen such a horrifying thing take place before him like this. He knows deep down this is not going to turn out to be good. He turns to rush out of the lab when he runs right directly into Monroe.

"What the hell are you doing here? How the fuck did you get in here?" Monroe says with his deep voice.

Malik takes a step back and tells Monroe he didn't do anything to her. He explains that he wandered in while searching for Alexis. Ada told him she was needed in the lab.

"I don't buy it, Malik. You know you're not supposed to be in here."

"Monroe, I know. I am leaving right now."

"No, you're not! I am calling Alexis and she can come get you."

"Really, Monroe? You don't intimidate me with your childish threats." Monroe looks over Malik's right side and sees Ellie. She has managed to get out of the other restraints. She turns and faces the back of Malik.

Monroe quickly pushes Malik to the side, grabs a syringe from his lab coat pocket, and injects it into Ellie's arm. Monroe looks at her. *I haven't seen anything like this before.* He watches as she stands up and takes a step towards Monroe. He backs up. Ellie collapses to the floor. Malik catches himself and spins around just in the nick of time to see Ellie fall.

"Well, don't just stand there, Malik. Help me get her up." Monroe demands.

Malik helps pick up Ellie's limp and slimy body. She is still bloody from whatever it is she changed into. He looks at her closely as they both put her back on a table.

"What the hell is she, Monroe?" Malik asks with a concerning voice.

"I really don't know, Malik. Examining her, I would have to say she looks part hellhound but she has a different fur and is huge for a female. It must be the hybrid DNA we injected. It sped up the growth of the offspring. It must have made a hybrid hellhound out of her. Alexis is going to be thrilled."

237

"What the hell is going on in here? What is he doing in here? Dr. Brack says standing in the doorway.

"I found him in here. Come see this, Dr. Brack. She got out of her restraints. She has partially shifted into something. It looks like a hybrid hellhound, doesn't it?" Monroe says looking at Dr. Brack as he examines Ellie.

"Yes, she does. How's the offspring? Did you check it yet? Look at the growth in the hour we were away. She is going to have this pup sooner than we expected. The hybrid DNA must amplify the growth process, doing something to the host that changes the DNA You know what that means, don't you, Monroe? When we use the humans for implants to harvest an offspring, the host will become something from the hybrid DNA mix. The only thing is what."

Monroe grabs Ellie's belly and gently rubs his hands around it, feeling the offspring inside. It relaxes. He can feel it isn't pushing outward so much. The drug must be taking effect on it also.

"Can I go now?" Malik says to the both of them.

"Yeah, yeah, go. You know where the door is." Monroe says and continues talking and examining Ellie.

Malik walks out and opens the lab door to exit the lab. Just as he closes it, he sees Damien turning the corner and heading towards him. His eyes are still an orange-ish yellow color. *At least they are not red anymore.*

"What are you doing in there? Damien yells in an angered voice.

"Just leaving. Why?"

"You are not allowed in there, Malik. What are they doing to my offspring?" Damien now stands face to face with Malik. His shoulders are up, hands tightened in a fist, face red with anger. He is holding back from shifting into a hellhound. Malik stands the same to Damien. He is the alpha; he can't back down or it will show Damien has become the alpha leader. Malik doesn't flinch.

"Why don't you go see for yourself, Damien?" Malik replies.

Damien, not getting anywhere with Malik, walks around him and slams his shoulder into his just as a sign to say, 'fuck you.' Malik turns at a half glance and huffs with a smirk on his face and shakes his head with disgust. Walking towards the stairwell as Damien beats on the door of the lab, he sees Luther and Lucius sitting in the stairwell, waiting for Malik to show up.

Malik looks up and says, "So there you two chicken shits are. What happened to you? I turned around and you guys were gone. I ran right into Monroe, thank you very much. You guys are some back up team. We need to work on that, especially now Damien is out."

Luther and Lucius smile at Malik and continue to play quarters.

Chapter 24

"The Secrets are never safe for ever"

"Ada, if anybody asks for me, I am busy until I notify you. I have something I need to take care of. Alone! Do you understand?"

"Yes, ma'am. My Lady, I will make sure nobody bothers you. I will take care of it like always, My Lady."

"Thank you, Ada. You are a good girl." Alexis says before hanging up the Bluetooth.

Alexis walks over to the other side of the library. On the shelf to the right is a book of Grim Fairytales. She reaches up and slides it out as far as it will go. It doesn't come out all the way.

A cracking sound of heavy stone moving slowly echoes within the library. The bookshelf opens ever so slightly on the left side. Alexis pulls it open far enough to walk into it.

Turning to the left, she pushes a metal lever and the door closes behind her. She walks down a long winding stairway carved from the wall of stone inside the secret passageway. The stairs have a beautiful stone railing that follows them four stories down.

The air is moist, cool, and dank. The lights dimly illuminate the steps down the stairway. This place has been a secret in the Ravenworth family for generations. This secret chamber is passed to one family member that possesses the right to know the secret of the chamber hidden deep under the Plantation. Nobody except the special persons knows about a secret place. It is passed to the first-born child and taught what is contained in each individual crystal and how to use them.

Alexis makes her way down the winding stairway, finally reaching the bottom. The stairwell comes out in the middle of a large long rounded corridor chiseled into the rock. It goes in two directions — one leads to the left and one leads to the right. There are no signs, just light fixtures that faintly illuminate the area.

Alexis turns left and walks down the corridor. The heels of her boots click and make a skidding sound as she walks. It echoes through the corridors. The closer she gets to the chambers the stones change and so does the floor.

The floor turns to black and silver marble that runs up the arched tunnel she walks into, bringing her to a massive stone doorway. White marble with

Latin symbols and writing lace the entire doorway. At the very top of the door is a larger piece of keystone. In the middle of it is a large red eye. Underneath, it reads, *'The Ocularis Infernum'* meaning 'the eye of hell.'

In the center of the stone door, it reads, *'Arcanum'* meaning secret, or mystery.

Under the Arcanum, it reads, *"A great secret of nature that the Alchemists sought to discover."*

Alexis takes one of her long chain necklaces from around her neck. On the one end, the charm that hangs is of a Raven with its wings out and feet as if it was landing. It is inlayed inside an amethyst crystal. She slips it over her head and puts it in the metal emblem in the stone. Her charm fits in and she pushes it inwards. A big shake comes over the door and it slowly opens. Moving down into the ground slowly, she waits, tapping her right foot in anticipation. She has no patience for things she can't control.

Once the door is down, she walks into a cream-colored room with thick bulletproof glass. Once again, Latin symbols and inscriptions lace the sides, top, and across the threshold of the door.

Inside, the cream color lines stone ceilings and walls. The floor is thick granite slate green with white veins in it. Walking through, she looks at these strange framed oval-shaped designs made out of twisted wood limbs. They are set up as if they have four legs, two off the backside that is lower than the two off the front sides. Each one is embedded with different crystals, with the same Latin writing on the sides circling the oval frame. The center, surrounded by the crystals and wood, has a glass-like mirror, but it is not glass at all. A clear thick quartz crystal, made into oval sheets of six-foot by four-foot wide, fit inside the frames. Hundreds of them branch off in different directions. Row after row, she walks swinging her chain with the Raven on it, looking at each one as she walks slowly past.

The chain stops swinging and sticks straight out of her hand as if someone pulled it with a string towards this one oval wooden frame. Alexis stops looking straight ahead still while the chain pulls to her right side as if it is pointing directly at this particular one.

Alexis slowly turns and faces the oval frame. She walks up to it, one small step at a time as if she is sneaking up on something. She lets the Raven charm go and it flies into the center of the clear quartz.

Alexis stands about a foot away when she reaches out and grabs the end of the chain to the charm necklace. Pulling, it gently releases. She stares into the quartz. Suddenly a strange hand touches the quartz moving slowly downwards and disappears. Alexis stands and watches intently as an image emerges from inside the quartz. She can faintly see a man's torso, skin beautiful brown covered in tattoos. Then a thick, muscled arm appears. It has a solid gold band around the bicep. Crystal light blue eyes move closer in focus. Alexis takes a sudden deep breath at the sight of this creature. She has forgotten how beautiful and hypnotizing his eyes are. Finally, he is in full view, floating in front of the crystal quartz. Alexis tells the creature inside she wants to ask him something. She waits for a response.

"Well, Alexis, what pleasure can I do for you? I haven't seen you in a while. What brings you all the way down here to see me?" He asks with a haunting monotone voice.

"I have a question only you can answer for me." She says softly in response. The beauty of this creature takes her aback. He has a black ponytail on top of his head; the rest is bald. He has a broad, square jaw, with lips and nose perfectly matched. Five o'clock shadow beard, and an Arabic tribal tattoo on each side of his neck.

He laughs at her response. Alexis, for the first time, feels intimidated by this creature and he senses her fear stirring within her. He has a very powerful magic even she can hardly avoid. His eyes gaze at her deeply. They change from whitish light blue to emerald green. A green smoke lingers within the chamber, changing colors with his eyes. She knows he is trying to lure her into his mind to control it, but with the necklace on, he can only get so far before the amethyst affects his powers on her.

"All I need is an answer and I will be on my way." Alexis says in a more demanding tone.

He laughs in his haunting voice to her. "You think you can manipulate me, Alexis? You know I am much more powerful than you are. Only a matter of time before this quartz won't hold me from coming for you. The answer to your question must first be asked."

"What is my doom? What is Phooka warning me about when he came to me?" Alexis asks.

"Ah, so you feel fear. I feel it racing through your veins. Finally, something has you on edge after all these years besides the fear I bring you. Yes, I see it and yes, Phooka is right. You have created your own doom. Only you with your greed, Alexis. Once they have summoned this great man, you will be..." Alexis interrupts him.

"Don't you tell me what fear I feel or what fear I have! You remember where you are! And you remember who holds the key to your freedom. If something happens to me, you're locked in that chamber of darkness for eternity. You remember that before you ever threaten me."

"I am sorry, Alexis. I did not realize I was being negative against you. Yes, Phooka is right. This person that will come has many men that help him. You will not defeat this man no matter how great of creatures you have. This one man knows all the secrets of the world; this man knows how to lock and unlock every power in the universe. He has done it before and he will do it again. This is what he lives for, to lock away evil like you. He is one who brings peace to the benevolent creatures and the other creatures in this world. You cannot defeat him."

"I am building a hybrid army. I will defeat anyone that crosses through them gates. I am building the perfect creature, one nobody has ever seen before."

"When he comes, Alexis, you need to release me from this darkness and I will make sure you will stay clear from harm. I can protect you and take you places they will never find you."

"I know this is a game you talk. You are not to be trusted. You don't speak from the truth; you speak from the desires you wish for, and you manipulate others into doing what you wish. That is why you are what you are. I don't think I would trust you to take me anywhere to protect me. You once tried to destroy me and that is why you are where you are now, Djinn. And that is where you will stay whether I live or die." Alexis tells him.

The quartz fills with white smoke and Djinn disappears in it. Alexis shakes her head in anger and walks back down towards the exit of the chambers room. Looking straight ahead as she exits, the giant granite door closes behind her.

Chapter 25

"The Fall Festival"

The fall festivals start this weekend all around Kentucky and Tennessee. John tells Lizzie, Jake, and Kyle over dinner on Wednesday night to see if they would be interested in going to spend the day at a local area attraction to kick off the season.

Lizzie is all excited about it, but Jake doesn't care at all. Kyle asks if he can invite his new friend Kassidy Flynn to go with them.

John and Lizzie tell Kyle as long as her parents don't mind he can bring her along. It is before school starts and the weekend before fall. Kyle can hang with her instead of walking with his parents or just walking through alone. Jake will walk off and leave him alone anyways while he tries to pick up girls.

Saturday morning, John is up early. He lets Hurley out and he watches to see where he goes. Hurley looks out across the field to the cabins. He stands for just a second then he takes off as if someone dropped the starting gate in a motocross race.

John laughs as he runs through the field jumping and playing all the way to the front door. The front motion light comes on when he gets within the area. Hurley scratches at the door and waits. Nobody opens it so he barks. Finally, the door cracks open and Hurley darts inside.

John knows someone is up to let him in. *Hopefully, they will stay up.*

Lizzie just gets out of the shower when John walks in.

"Do you think the boys are up, John?" Lizzie asks.

"Someone is. Hurley made sure of that." He replies.

"Well, you better get dressed and go make sure they are up getting ready. You know how they are. They will fall back in bed, sleeping with Hurley." Lizzie yells out of the bedroom to him.

John gets dressed taking his large cup of coffee with him. He jumps on the four-wheeler and slowly goes over to the cabin. He decides to take a long way around to see if any strange things lurk in the woods. Just the deer would be nice.

"Boys, are you up? John says as he walks in the cabin door. Hurley jumps off the couch and runs over to John. Kyle walks out of the bedroom scratching his head. He just got up. Jake doesn't answer from the loft. John yells up to him repeatedly. Finally, he tells Hurley to get him, but the dog turns away from the stairs and lies down in Kyle's bedroom. *What was that all about?* Suspicious, John decides to walk up and see what Jake is doing.

He gets to the top of the stairs and notices Jake isn't in bed. The light in the bathroom is on so he walks over to knock on the door.

"Jake, you okay?" John asks.

No reply. He knocks again and tries opening the door. Slowly pushing it open, he doesn't see anyone in there.

"Jake where are you?" John says looking for the light switch in the bedroom. He finds it and flips it on.

John jumps. A person sits in the chair next to the night table.

"Holy shit, Jake. Why didn't you answer me when I called for you? You scared the living day lights out of me, son." John says in a slightly upset and angered voice.

Jake just sits there with his arms locked around his knees tight, staring at the door that leads out to the balcony. John looks at Jake and notices something isn't right with him. He gently grabs Jake by the arm and shakes him.

"Jake, Jake, are you all right? What is wrong?"

Jake jumps suddenly and scares John again.

"What the hell is going on, Jake?" John says loudly.

Jake yells, "She is trying to get in!"

"Who is trying to get in?" John asks.

Jake stands confused, looking at his dad as if he is supposed to know about whom he is talking. John walks over to the door and tries to open it.

"It's locked, Jake." John opens the door and walks slowly outside. "Nobody out here, Jake." John yells back.

John looks all around. The sun is already coming up over the mountain. It is light enough to see anything there or in the woods around the cabin. He turns to walk back in the cabin and sees on the door grooves in the wood. Four long deep grooves like claw marks go all the way down almost to the bottom, as if someone or something was digging at the door, slowly trying to get in.

"OMG," John says under his breath. "What now?!"

Staring at the claw marks, he knows that Jake is terrified. Hopefully, he will get over this ordeal and with some luck, they might catch this thing. Tori, or whatever creature, is being violent towards other creatures and humans.

John places his fingers inside one of the grooves on the door to see how deep it is. Touching it, he can feel that it is from a very powerful creature. Not understanding why it didn't rip the door down, it must be playing with Jake, taunting him, trying to scare him. Maybe even get him to run outside and once there, it will attack him.

He rubs his hand down gently on the claw marks, imagining the fear his son must have been going through listening to the sound of something like this outside his bedroom door two stories up from the ground.

John puts his head down in sorrow, tears form in his eyes and quickly race down his cheeks.

I have to stop this! I can't let him be scared. I can't let him get hurt or worse… killed by something evil out here that doesn't belong.

Collecting his thoughts and clearing his throat, he walks back in to the cabin. Standing in the corner with his flannel pajama pants on and no tee shirt, Jake's long dark reddish hair sticking out all over. His eyes are swollen from crying most of the night and with hardly any sleep, scared from whatever is after him.

"Did you find anything? Did you see anything out there, Dad? You probably don't believe me anyways." Jake says and walks towards the bathroom to get ready.

John, still in shock, doesn't know how to answer Jake's questions. He is trying to figure out his own questions first.

"Jake… Jake, son, wait. Sorry, I was trying to figure this out." John says walking towards the bathroom, but Jake slams the door in his face. John stops just outside of it and puts his head down and his hand up on the door.

"Jake, look. I'm sorry. I believe you. I do. Trust me. There are many things going on out here. I was just trying to figure out how this thing got up to the second story porch from the ground. Jake… Jake?"

Jake doesn't respond so John goes downstairs. Kyle is sitting on the couch with Hurley.

"What's going on, Dad?" Kyle asks.

"Something was after your brother again. I mean something was trying to get in the upstairs door from the porch."

"Oh, can that happen? They would have to fly or they would have to come through the cabin to get up there. I don't remember seeing anybody or hearing anything last night."

"You mean you didn't hear anything going on last night upstairs?" John asks Kyle.

"No, I didn't hear anything. Why? Was I supposed to?"

"Well, yeah. It seemed to have been making a lot of noise. It would have to with the claw marks in the door."

"What claw marks? I want to see them." Kyle gets up and runs upstairs before John can say anything.

"No... Kyle!" John yells out, but Kyle doesn't stop. He is already upstairs and running towards the door. Standing there staring at the door, he grabs the handle and opens it. Kyle walks out on the balcony upstairs. The sun has risen over the mountain and it is bright out. He looks around quickly then spins around to look at the door.

"OMG!" Kyle yells. "What the…."

John finally runs out the door and closes it behind him. Standing in front of the door, he puts his finger in front of his lips.

"Ssshhh! Kyle, damn it. Jake doesn't know about this. I didn't want to upset him anymore. He is freaked out. He has been up all night scared from the banging and clawing at the door. He hasn't quite gotten over the other incident four weeks ago." John says to Kyle in a lowered tone.

John motions for Kyle to go back inside the cabin and they walk down the stairs. John follows Kyle. They sit on the couch and watch TV, waiting for Jake to come down.

John lets Jake drive the ATV back to the garage. Lizzie is ready, and has the truck stocked with drinks and snacks. They head out towards Kassidy's house to pick her up.

Driving down Highway 27, they find signs that list the fall festival. Driving down the countryside, they see a tall concrete fence that goes as far down as they can see on the left hand side of the road, running up and down the hills until it disappears into the tree line. They follow it for miles until they come up on a line of cars stopped on the side of the road.

"This must be the line to get in." John says.

"Yes, this is the Plantation Fall Festival. It brings one of the biggest crowds when she opens the gates." Kassidy tells them.

"Have you been here before, Kassidy?" Lizzie asks.

"Yes, twice. She doesn't open it that often to let people in. Every three or four years, she holds a big festival. Sometimes it might be in the fall, winter, spring, or summer. It depends on her mood, they say. She is a strange lady. She is an heiress to a fortune and this place. Nobody ever sees her unless they are one of the lucky ones that get in when she has her monthly drawing of twenty to thirty people."

"Monthly drawings? What do you mean? She has like a lottery or something?" Jake asks.

"Um, yeah, I guess you could say that. People are chosen that morning for one day to go into the Plantation and there are always some strange criteria. If someone complies with a request or wears a blue shirt, her guards will allow in the amount she asked for that one day." Kassidy explains.

They all fall silent thinking about what she just told them. The line moves quicker. A few people direct traffic to park inside the big brick and iron fence.

"Wow, look at the size of the gates. I thought that brick fence was tall. Wow!" Lizzie says.

Following the cars into the parking area, this strange-looking fellow motions them to continue down the line as if the cars were cattle. Settling in a parking spot Kyle can't get over the strange looking guy parking cars.

"Did you see that guy, Dad?" Kyle says.

"Now, Kyle, you know better than to talk about other people." Lizzie says.

"No, I am not saying anything mean. He just had long hair hanging off the bottoms of his arms and his legs. And did you see his face?"

"Okay, enough, Kyle. It is probably the costume they wear." John says.

They all walk up to the main gate to purchase tickets. It is nine thirty a.m. and they are one of the first few hundred to get in. Walking up to the ticket booth, John buys the tickets while the others stand out of line.

Jake nudges his mom and she turns. Her eyes grow wide as she sees these huge men, or buffalo men, in costumes. They stand over seven feet tall. Their heads look like a buffalo: the fur, the black horns on the sides of the head, their muscular arms are very large for a man, but the hands are two thick stumps. They have thick fur that runs down the back of them and runs just to the sides of the torso. The front of the torso is like that of a body builder — ripped stomach muscles, furry yet man-like chest. They have arms attached around their neck. A sleeveless, and thin metal plate runs down their abdomen and attaches to a thick leather and metal belt that wraps around the waist and flaps hand down just enough to spark a women's curiosity. Their legs are muscular like a man's with some fur on them yet medium-length and curly like a buffalo.

They stand motionless staring straight ahead. Lizzie, Kassidy, Jake, and Kyle watch to see if they are statues or real. They finally see them breathing, amazed at how magnificent they are made up and how huge the men are. Lizzie shakes her head and looks around to find John in line.

"Yes, I need two adults and three teenagers." He says with a slight laugh.

He pulls his wallet out and looks up at the young lady. His eyes do a double take. His expression changes suddenly. The young girl tells him the price of the tickets and John stares at her. He shakes his head, realizing he was staring at her. He looks up again as he thumbs through the money in his wallet.

"Wow, you have one heck of a makeup artist here." John says with a big smile, trying to break the tension between them. The young girl smiles and looks up at him. She flashes him her big green eyes at John. Her eyes are bigger than that of a normal human. She has brownish grey and silver fur all over her arms, neck, and most of her face. She has two white stripes of fur that run from the side of her cheeks all the way down under her shirt. Her ears are pointy and offset on the top of her head. You can't even see her human features or ears.

"You are amazing-looking, I do have to say. What are you supposed to be, dear?" John asks.

"Oh, I am a badger, sir. Here are your tickets, a brochure of the park and a schedule of events. Your ticket is good for the two-day event. You enjoy your day, sir." The young girl says.

Kyle turns and looks for his dad when he notices the girl behind the booth talking to him. John walks up to the others standing off to the side.

"What is going on? You guys look like you have seen a ghost or something." John says with a laugh and explains the events for the day when Lizzie stops him and asks if he has seen them.

John looks up at Lizzie, "Seen what, hon?" John asks.

"The huge creature men standing on the side of the Iron Gate?"

"No, I did not see them." John turns around and looks at the big guards. His mouth drops like all the others do when they notice them and see they are real. Everyone takes pictures of them. They look straight ahead like they see nobody. John notices something odd with them; they wear a black collar that looks like a controlling device.

"Wow! They are huge. I have never seen anything like that in my life that was real. They have some good makeup artists here. Did you see the girl in the ticket booth?" John asks.

"Yeah, Dad. I saw her as you walked over. That is a cool outfit she has on." Kyle says.

Lizzie looks over towards the booth. "What is she supposed to be?"

"She told me a badger." John says.

"Okay, kids. This is what is going on here today. Now if Kyle, Kassidy, and Jake want to go out on their own, that is fine. I will give you guys your own money and you can do what you'd like, as long as it is nothing bad or unsafe. You guys all have a cell phone so you can send us a message when you want to meet up. We will meet here in the middle at that big round bench area as the sidewalks split off.

Everybody got that? We meet back here in say two hours or less?" John tells them.

Everyone agrees and walks in to the main gates past the huge guards. John watches Jake to see how he reacts to them. He has hardly spoken to anyone today at all.

"What are they, Dad?" Jake asks softly, walking closer to his mom as they get further in the main area.

"I am not sure. They kind of look like a Minotaur creature from Greek mythology, but I don't know. I say that is some wild makeup though, isn't it? And they must have used wrestlers to dress up in the costumes. They are about the only huge humans I have seen." John replies.

Jake, Kyle, and Kassidy split off from John and Lizzie. They watch the kids walk past these tall thin people dressed in long black coats that hang down to the ground. An animal skull on their head with a black mesh fabric hangs over their face so you can't see them. They carry a long stick with a small animal skull on it and rattlesnake rattles dangles from the small skull. They are on stilts so they are like nine feet or taller. One sees Jake looking at him with fear in his eyes. He walks towards Jake one long step at a time. Jake's eyes grow wider with every step the strange tall creature takes.

Kyle and Kassidy smile and stop to watch what the tall man is doing since he is right in front of them. Jake slowly walks sideways until he is behind Kyle and Kassidy. The tall creature man stops and stands tall in front of the three of them. They all look up at him as he reaches into his long black coat and pulls out three beaded necklaces and hands one to each of them. Jake is hesitant to take his, but finally does. His favorite color — red. Then the tall creature man reaches into a small purse strapped to the side of him and puts his hand over the top of their heads. Motioning them with the other hand to look down, he sprinkles their heads with a white powder that glistens in the sunlight. The powder swirls and twists like a little tornado as it falls in a straight line on the tops of their heads and disappears. The tall man shakes his stick with the rattlesnake rattles on it at each one of them and says something in a foreign language.

"What are you?" Kyle slowly looks up and asks.

A strange voice, raspy and crackle says, "I am a witch doctor of voodoo. You have been enchanted with my powders. You will soon find yourself seeing the true animals we are." He walks away from them and they watch in amazement trying to figure out what just happened.

They all feel dizzy and their eyesight blurs. They reach up and rub their eyes, but it only makes it worse. Kyle turns around and looks at Jake, knowing he probably is freaking out. Jake's eyes are all glossy and have a pink color around them as if they are irritated. Kyle then turns to Kassidy. Her eyes are glossy, but they don't have the pink ring around them.

He asks Kassidy if his eyes look like Jake's. She looks at them both and says no.

They look around for a few minutes longer, and then their vision clears. They notice everything looks different as if they have special glasses on. Everything and everyone seems much closer than they really are.

"Wow, this is crazy." Kyle says to them. Kassidy and Kyle are laughing.

Jake still doesn't see any humor in it at all. He then turns and walks away, shaking his head angrily. Kyle yells at Jake, but he doesn't stop, ignoring Kyle and Kassidy's calls. They decide to let him go and head on their own way. Kassidy notices that certain people look very strange.

They walk down a path wide as a road and look at all the people and vendors selling different things. Some sell food, some clothing, most are all medieval things like they all come from another era.

Bang, bang, clang… they hear. It seems so loud. They look all around to see what it is. They stop and look at each other with surprise in their eyes.

"Do you see that, Kyle?" Kassidy asks.

"Yeah, do you?" he replies.

They watch as a half-horse and half-man sword fight in the middle of the walkway. People gather around and watch them fight, taking pictures and cheering them on. Each has a different color armor and long robe like a blanket that drapes the horse-like back. One has a white with red striped outfit and the other has a blue and yellow striped outfit. A mesh-like armor runs under the colors and along the torso and the arms of the strange creature.

They watch as they battle back and forth, one knocking the other down. People seem to cheer for the one winning in the blue and yellow. He is a golden yellow with blond hair and tail. They watch while he prances around wanting the crowd to cheer louder.

"This is a game, right?" Kyle asks Kassidy.

265

"I don't know. I haven't seen this before." She replies.

Kyle and Kassidy move around the fight and the crowd deciding to find something to drink from one of the vendors on the sidewalk.

"Over here," Kassidy says and pulls Kyle to a little old lady serving different drinks and snacks.

They look at the display and the woman asks them if they had seen the voodoo witch doctors when they came in. Kyle and Kassidy look at each other.

"Yes, we did. He gave us these necklaces." Kassidy shows with a big smile.

The old woman smiles, "I see. You know they only give them to special guests. These special guests are chosen by them personally to explore beyond what the other guests see."

"Really? Where can we go that they can't?" Kassidy asks.

"Oh, you can go through the house as a special guest. When you walk closer towards the house, someone will greet you and ask to show you a personal tour. Something only a few get to do." The woman says.

"Wow! That sounds fun. Doesn't it, Kyle?" Kassidy says nudging Kyle in the arm with her elbow.

The woman asks what she can get them. Kassidy tells her water. The woman walks behind the little old wooden wagon and bends down out of their sight. When she comes up, she has water in a fancy bottle shaped like a fairy that sparkles multiple colors as if a pearl luminesced from inside the water itself, with a cool blue umbrella and straw. Kassidy gets a big smile on her face when she sees the lady lift it over the counter to her.

"That is so pretty!" Kassidy says.

Kyle pays for the drink and Kassidy holds the bottle, fascinated by it and the glowing colors.

"It was especially made for you. Try it and see what you think," The woman says to her. Kassidy takes a sip and her eyes light up and glow like the bottle. Kyle's eyes widen and he smiles at her.

"How'd you do that? Is it something in the water?" Kyle asks the woman.

"Yes, each drink is made for each person. Something special is in each drink. This one is especially for her. She has an aura of the rainbow and when she touches, the bottle comes to life with the aura of each person."

"That is so cool, Kassidy. Your eyes change to the color of the liquid in the bottle." Kassidy holds the bottle up and watches the liquid inside spin slowly like a small tornado swirling. Her eyes glow with the smile on her face almost as if she is hypnotized by it.

The woman just smiles and tells them to make sure they visit the inside of the house.

"You will enjoy it." She encourages. Kyle and Kassidy move down the sidewalk looking at all the people.

Chapter 26

"What is happening to me"

Ellie opens her eyes, looking around the room. She remembers the events from earlier, thinking it was a dream. The harsh truth of reality sinks in quickly. Her eyes fill with tears and run down her cheeks as she tries to lift her hand. She realizes she is not dreaming. Trying to move her legs, she feels the straps on her ankles.

She is still groggy from the drugs in her veins. Suddenly, she feels a pain in her stomach. *What is that?* She thinks about the same time as another movement in her stomach. This time it is painful. She gasps for air, her eyes widen, and her voice is hoarse. She tries her hardest to scream, but only a squeak escapes her lips.

She lifts her head to look down at her stomach. She sees a large lump under the white sheet that covers her mid-section.

"OMG!" she tries to scream, again. Once again, hardly any noise comes out of her mouth.

"What has happened to me? I look pregnant. How can this be? How can I be this big! How long have I been here? How long have I been sleeping?

269

My parents! Oh my God! My parents!" Ellie tries to get the words out with hardly any success.

Heart racing so fast, she feels herself getting very warm. Her body tingles just under the skin. *What is going on with me?* Ellie's mind races with different thoughts, trying to figure out what is happening. She can't think straight with all the drugs. They are wearing off some but still she is fighting herself to think clearly.

"Oh, what have I gotten myself into? I am such a stupid idiot. Feelings, emotions, the need for a man's touch. Look where it has gotten me!" She cries harder when another movement within her stirs once again, reminding her that something is in there.

Ellie breathes heavily and she feels that tingling moving deeper inside her. Through the skin, into the muscle, it feels like a low current of electricity moving all through her body. She feels the hair on her arms stand up, almost as if it is moving or growing. Her skin feels like the sun shining on it and opening every pore on her body.

She leans up again, looks down at the white sheet, and notices her chest.

"What the hell is this? OMG!" She sees her chest covered in tiny hairs and rapidly growing.

She pulls herself out of the restraints again. Getting her strength back, she feels them loosening under her skin. She hears a rumbling deep in her chest as she moans. She doesn't understand where this sound is coming from. Shaking, she gets nervous and the movement inside her moves around as if it is coming through her skin. The pain is still there, but fear of the unknown takes over.

The harder she struggles, the tighter Ellie pushes down on her belly. A stabbing pain overcomes everything she feels.

"Oh, somebody please help!" Ellie cries out, her voice rattled and deepened by the change she is going through. It feels like the thing moving inside is ripping through her stomach.

Dr. Brack and Monroe hear a blood-curdling scream. They both jump and spin their heads towards the lab door.

"What the hell was that?" Monroe says.

They both run out of the office to the lab. Rushing towards Ellie, they hear her screaming and the sounds of metal banging.

They can't believe what they see when they reach her. Blood is everywhere! Panicked, Dr. Brack fumbles in his pockets for the syringe and a bottle of tranquilizer to sedate Ellie. Monroe grabs ahold of

Ellie's right arm to fasten the restraint back, but soon finds it has been ripped off.

They both can't believe that she is growing fur on her body and her face.

"Do you think she really is changing, Dr. Brack? She is almost completely covered in fur, her body is growing larger, and her eyes have changed. They are reddish amber color." Monroe says.

"Monroe, she is going to have this baby. We have to get her sedated and fast. It will rip her apart if we don't get her under so I can take the offspring out. Now, try to hold her arm down while I get the tranquilizer in her."

Monroe grabs Ellie's arm and, pressing it down on the cold steel table, Ellie feels the tightness of his grip. The beast that is trying to come out becomes fully aware that she is in danger and Ellie lifts up her arm from the table. Still hanging on to it, she slings Monroe across the lab into the wall. Dr. Brack stops and watches Monroe land on the floor.

"Oh hell, Monroe, Monroe, you all right? Can you hear me, Monroe? I need your help."

Dr. Brack still fumbles in his pockets for the vile of medication to sedate Ellie. He can't find it anywhere so he turns and grabs one from the counter behind him.

Trying to put the syringe into the vile, Dr. Brack realizes how badly he is shaking. He has seen many creatures come and go inside the lab, but Ellie is a different creature completely.

Finally, Dr. Brack has the syringe ready to inject into Ellie. He calls Monroe again. Monroe finally gets up, shaking his head. Dr. Brack notices blood running down Monroe's forehead.

"You okay, Monroe? Can you hear me all right?"

"Yes, Dr. Brack. I hear you. I have a hell of a headache, but I am okay. Let's get her sedated."

Dr. Brack notices Ellie's eyes are changing to blood red. He knows what this means. He has no more time to waste; he has to put her under immediately or she will tear the lab apart and them in it.

They both go to Ellie's side and hold down her right arm. Ellie is so strong; she fights them and knocks them both backwards. Screaming in pain, she pushes, trying to get the movement out of her insides.

Monroe sees the syringe on the floor. He reaches down swiftly, grabs it, runs behind Ellie, and sticks it into her upper left arm. He injects it quickly before she realizes it.

"Dr. Brack, are you all right?" Monroe rushes over and helps him get up. He slips and falls backwards when Ellie slings them off her arm. Monroe takes Dr. Brack over to the stool by the sink and helps him get cold water on a rag to place on the back of his head.

"I will be fine, Monroe. How is Ellie doing now? We need to get her in the operating room as soon as possible. We must perform a C-section and remove the offspring. Help me get up and we will wheel the table right in the operating room."

They slowly walk towards Ellie and see she is still thrashing around but it is slowing down. They grab the table and Dr. Brack looks into Ellie's now blood-red eyes. She gazes back at him. She can hear his heart racing with fear. She can smell the fear he has of her and it excites her.

"Monroe, now. We need to move now. You push the table in. I am going to grab a stronger sedative. I don't think that is going to hold her much longer. She has changed into a full hellhound. We must hurry, Monroe."

Just as Dr. Brack walks to the other side of the lab to get more sedative, he hears a crashing sound. Suddenly looking behind him, he sees the table is on the ground and Ellie is free from the restraints. Monroe tries picking the table up from

274

behind her when she quickly springs around facing him. She has gotten larger in size since shifting. She feels them as a threat to her and her baby so she has become very protective. The hellhound instinct has now taken over all human ones she had.

Pushing the table out of the way, she takes a large step forward towards Monroe. He moves backwards away from her slowly, not to rush. She will think it is a challenge and chase him. Ellie crouches down on the floor. He notices her eyes shift to a threatening gaze at him. He stops and stands tall, hoping the sedative will take effect sooner than later.

She moves towards him while he stands still. Monroe watches her stride become unstable with every step she takes. Soon she reaches him, now taller than he is. She moves in with a snarl. Monroe tries to act as if he is not scared of her. Fear will only provoke her more.

Suddenly, she wobbles and weaves. He watches her for the right moment. Knowing she is going to drop and he can't move a muscle, she could snap out of it so fast and rip his throat out.

Dr. Brack slowly moves up from behind her with another dose of the tranquilizer. She falls down to one knee. With labored breathing, she lets out a growling moan. About this time, Dr. Brack sticks her in the shoulder with a syringe. She tries to get up, but instead collapses on the floor.

"Help me get her back on the table, Monroe."

They put her on the table and run to the operating room. Transferring her to a new table, Dr. Brack straps her down and gets his scalpel when he sees something moving between her legs.

"Monroe, help me. The offspring is trying to come through. We have no time to waste. We have to cut her open now before her pelvis closes on it while it's in the birth canal."

Dr. Brack cuts her from hipbone to hipbone in one quick slash. Fluid and blood spews out all over the table. He reaches in and tells Monroe to hold the opening so he can see the head.

Pulling, he finally removes this blob of white, slimy flesh with dark coloring under it. They put it on the slab they brought Ellie in on, wiping it down to get the sack removed so it can breathe. Dr. Brack cuts it and more clear liquid spews from inside the sack.

A small human-like animal lies motionless on the table. Monroe looks at Dr. Brack with disappointment. Dr. Brack looks back down at this helpless being.

"I've had enough of this crap, Alexis!" He bends down, opens the mouth of the little offspring, and clears the throat. He places his lips and gently breathes into its mouth. Monroe grabs a couple of towels and blankets, placing them over the little creature on the table. Dr. Brack feels for a pulse. Monroe anxiously waits for a response, rubbing to stimulate the little fella.

Suddenly Monroe hears a faint coughing and then a cry. Dr. Brack looks up at Monroe and huge smiles come across their faces.

"You did it, Dr. Brack. You saved the little fella."

They rub it down and wrap blankets around it. Dr. Brack picks it up and bounces it as it makes a strange cry, almost like a human and puppy mixed.

"It needs to eat. We need to put it on his mother so he can feed."

"Do you think she has milk to feed the little fella?" Monroe asks.

"Well, let's check." Dr. Brack says as he walks over and grabs Ellie's breast. He pushes down then upwards and a white fluid squirts across the table.

"That answers your question, Monroe."

They prop the little one up and help him suckle on to Ellie's breast.

"That is the strangest looking thing I have ever seen. Cute as a button, but strange. Is this what the hybrid does, I wonder?" Monroe asks.

Dr. Brack shrugs his shoulders. "You do know Alexis is going to be pissed off that we saved this offspring. She wanted it gone." Dr. Brack tells Monroe.

Monroe hangs his head down looking at the little fella nursing on its mother. Shaking his head, he knows this is what they worked for. This is what they have been trying to accomplish and this one little fella is the outcome.

"The hell with Alexis and her bullshit, Dr. Brack. I am sick of doing the crap she wants us to do. She doesn't see the pain we put some of these people and creatures through. I am so sick and tired of torturing them to get her what she wants. This little fella right there is what we have been trying to do for years. He is the perfect little being. I am not going to let her destroy it and our work." Monroe says.

"I know, Monroe. Trust me, that is why I said 'hell with you, Alexis' and saved the poor thing. I want to see it grow up, and live a life. We have to make sure she doesn't touch it, or try to take it out of this lab. If she does, I am going to let the mother loose on her. She will protect the little fella; it is her nature."

"Is it a boy or a girl, Dr. Brack? I just assumed it was a fella."

"I never bothered to check. Let's see."

They gently unwrap the blanket of the little one. Dr. Brack reaches in and feels the belly, noticing that it now feels more skin than fur. Pulling the blanket open a little more so he can see the offspring, he observes that it is changing. Its hair is receding with more skin exposed, looking more human than creature.

"It's a little girl." Dr. Brack looks up and smiles at Monroe.

"It is a little girl and she is changing into a human baby now. Look, the hair is receding from the body. It must be the mother's milk." Dr. Brack says.

Ellie moans. Monroe quickly grabs the little girl and Dr. Brack talks to Ellie to see if she can hear him.

Ellie tries to lift her arms but the restraints are still on. Dr. Brack unbuckles one side, and then the other.

"Ellie, can you hear me? I need you to lay still, Ellie. Okay? I am going to look in your eyes now with a light. Okay, Ellie?"

Ellie nods her head. Dr. Brack looks into her eyes noticing the drugs are wearing off fast. A good thing since she needs to take care of her baby without being medicated.

"Ellie, we had to take the baby by C-section. Do you understand what I am telling you?" She nods her head yes again.

"Good. The baby is here. We need you to wake up and feed her, okay?" Ellie opens her eyes and looks around the room for her baby.

Monroe gets some pillows from the office and helps Ellie onto a hospital bed where she can be more comfortable with the baby. He helps her into a warm gown and puts blankets on her while Dr. Brack checks the baby's vitals one more time.

Ellie looks at the baby strangely. Dr. Brack holds the baby out for Ellie to take. She hesitates and looks up at Dr. Brack with eyes of fear. Monroe made a cloth diaper for her, wrapped her up in a blanket, and made a little hat for her head to help keep her warm.

"It is okay, Ellie. It is your baby girl. Take her; she needs you to survive. She had a very traumatic delivery into this world. It is going to be okay. The baby needs you. She needs her mother's love and care; something we cannot give her."

She looks down at the baby in the blanket and they see her eyes soften. Ellie reaches up and takes the baby in close to her chest.

"We will be right on the other side of this glass window in the office, okay? Monroe has gotten you everything you need. It is next to you on this table. Please, Ellie, rest and relax. We have a small incubator on the other side next to you to place the baby in if you get tired." Dr. Brack tells her and walks out of the room leaving only a soft light on for her.

Chapter 27

"Eyes Wide Open"

Kyle and Kassidy walk down towards the castle. Everything seems as if it's in slow motion except them. The people participating in the events all smile and take notice of them. Waving, coming up, and shaking their hands, some giving them small trinkets, and food.

Kyle and Kassidy talk about how the makeup is so real. They would swear the people are half-animal and half-human. The more they walk through the events the more real they seem to be. So many different ones, every different type you can imagine.

"Where is Jake? I wonder if he is experiencing this." Kyle says.

Just as Kyle says that, he feels his phone vibrate in his pocket. He pulls it out and it's his mom calling. Kyle looks at Kassidy with big eyes. "Should I answer it?"

Kassidy looks at the screen and swiftly glances to Kyle with a shocked look on her face. She shakes her head. *No, no, no, don't answer it.* They both seem to hear each other without saying a word.

"How'd you do that?"

"Do what, Kassidy?"

"Talk to me without moving your lips?"

"Well, how are you doing it, Kyle?"

"This is getting really weird, Kassidy."

"Hahaha, yeah it is, but this is awesome, Kyle.

"I wonder how many other people we can hear. I wonder if it is just us or can we hear other people?"

"I don't know. Let's go into a big crowd and see if we can listen to what people are thinking." Kyle replies.

They walk closer to the castle when they notice these strange little colored fairy-like things flying around. They are all of different colors — light blue, white, light yellow, light orange, light red, light green, light pink, and light purple. They have snake-like tongues, round mouths, long sharp fang teeth with three on each side, top, and bottom, human-like eyes with tiny black pupils, elf ears that are twisted at the top to a point. Their hair is human-like except for the color. They are just a shade darker than the color of their skin. They have ridges in their skin that run from their backs, and some up around their necks and down the front of their torso. They have no noses above their mouth; they are on their foreheads in an indentation. A wide V-shape with three small dots in a perfect arch with the fourth dot in the center a bit larger than the other three. Their wings are like a bat's flesh and bone-like with tiny little claw hooks on the ends like fingernails.

"Do you notice those little flying creatures, Kyle?"

"Yes, I do. I was going to ask you the same question. What are they? They are no bigger than my hand in length, maybe wider. Look at the teeth on them things."

"Why are they only after the teenagers and young adults? Did you notice that? We have been walking past them for like twenty minutes now and anyone over thirty they don't bother. Wonder what is up with that. I wonder if the people see them."

"I don't know, but they must feel them. They are swatting at their necks as though a mosquito is biting them."

They walk into a big area where people have gathered just outside this big wooden bridge walkway that lies across a water moat. Two big creatures stand guard on both sides of the wide wooden walkway.

"What?"
"Nothing"
"You didn't just try to talk to me in my head, Kassidy?"

"No. I didn't say anything. I am staring at the huge-ass guards, or whatever they are. Some kind of crazy half-human half-cattle looking things."

Kyle hears a strange sound, a voice, but it sounds like it's in a surround sound with a ghostly effect on it.

"Kyle..."
What the hell is that?! Kyle thinks, spinning side-to-side, trying to figure out what it is. He looks at Kassidy. She stares at the castle gate. Kyle looks

back at the crowd of people looking for anyone looking at him. Possibly playing a game with him.

"Damn it!! You don't hear that, Kassidy?"
"No. I don't hear anything."
"Please listen really hard. Tell me if you hear a ghostly voice."

Kassidy closes her eyes, puts her head down, and covers her ears. Listening hard, she blanks out her mind, tuning out everything to silence.

"Can you hear it?"
"Stop it, Kyle. I am trying to listen."

Kassidy's eyes open up, growing wider as she turns and looks up at Kyle. A surprised look on her face, "OMG! I hear it. I do. What is it or who is it?"
"I think it might be Jake. I am not sure, but how can I contact him?"
"Dah, dummy. The same way you're doing with me."
"You need to contact him, Kyle. Close your eyes as I did and tune everything out. Concentrate hard on sending your voice back to him in your

mind. See if it works. Somehow he has figured out how to contact you."

Kyle and Kassidy walk to the side of the crowd gathering outside the castle gate. There is a chain between the areas where the two guards stand. Most of the people are gathered to take pictures of the castle and the guards. The guards are as big if not larger than the ones at the front gates, with faces like a bull skull and a portion of the neck and back like one. The horns come out from the sides of the skull in the back, wrap around to the upper front, and extend at least eighteen to twenty-two inches past the head. They are huge and angled in an almost forty-five degree position. With small amber-colored eyes, fur covers their face and thickens on their back and shoulders. A silver ring hangs from their nose that looks pierced all the way through the flesh.

The muscles on their neck and back are like a giant human bodybuilder yet covered in thick long black fur with black horns with grey streaks in them. They have muscled arms and torsos, leather pants tucked into boots and laced like leather straps just below their thick knees. They stand with a long iron spear taller than they are. Grasping it with both

287

hands, they just stare out above the crowd —
fearless, emotionless. They wait.

Kyle and Kassidy feel a tapping on their
shoulder and they turn around. She is a small little
woman with the biggest smile on her face.

"Hi, my name is Shadow." Kyle and Kassidy
stare at her for a moment. She is different from the
other people they have seen. She looks like a
human panther.

"I am here to take you two inside the castle.
You have been chosen to be some of the lucky few
by our spooky witch doctors. At the entrance, they
pick the ones to come and visit behind the scenes.
You will visit the inside of the castle for drinks and
food, prizes and a free outfit. If you would just follow
me this way."

Shadow turns and walks towards the wooden
bridge towards the guards. Kyle and Kassidy look at
each other.

"Did you see her lips move?"
"No."
"Neither did I."

"Freaky?'
Yeah, I know, Kassidy. I know."

They both follow Shadow as she walks past the two large guards. They each look at them. At the exactly the same time Kyle and Kassidy step foot on the wooden bridge, the guards lift their spear and slam it back to the ground, as a sort of acceptance for them to pass.

Walking across the bridge and into the castle, Shadow leads them into a room where a bunch of young people just like them talk amongst themselves. Food and drinks are set up along the walls in magnificent displays: fruits, cold cuts, breads, vegetables. Everything looks so exotic and expensive.

"Help yourselves to whatever you would like. There is plenty of food, drinks, and dessert. If you don't see something, just ask and we will get it for you. The bathrooms are down the hall and to the right. I will be in here most of the time, along with some others like me. Just look for any of us with the purple and white shirts. We are staff inside the castle and any of us can help you." Shadow tells them.

"Thank you very much, Shadow." Kyle and Kassidy reply.

"What is she supposed to be? She is wild looking, isn't she? Wow! Purrrrowww!!" Kyle says.
Kassidy just looks at him quizzically.

"Come on, Kassidy. She is cool-looking."
"Yeah, she is."

"That makeup artist... I'm telling you... I need to have him or her do me up for Halloween this year. I wonder if they are hiring."

"Did you see the detail in her ears? You can't even tell she has human ears anywhere on her head. You can't even tell where the cat-like structure of the nose and mouth has been glued on. It is so good."

"Have you ever thought maybe it isn't fake, Kyle? With all the weird stuff I have heard about this place and what I have seen today? I watch the shows on cable and there is just no way this is makeup. The movement in the creatures outside. They would have to be remote or sensor controlled. I don't think so, Kyle. Look around again. Really look around at the staff, watch the way the lips move with the animal parts of their faces. They are as one, not as a fake piece."

Kyle looks around at the staff members. He sees Shadow standing over by the door. She is in a purple and white sleeve shirt, jeans and she has golden eyes, black fur covers her face, head, neck, and her arms. She has whiskers like a panther, her face comes out in a slope like a panther, continues down to the nose, and the lip is split. The bottom lip is black fur, but more human and so is the bottom jaw, but made to match the upper part of the skull. Her eyes are not shaped the same as humans; they are more tear-dropped and bigger. Yellowish green in color, her ears are where a panther's would be, just back and off the sides of the eyes. No traces of human ears at all, and smooth thin shiny black fur with small hands.

"I need to see if I can communicate with Jake." Kyle tells Kassidy.

"Let's go over here in this empty corner."

They walk to the far side of the room near a big column and a window. Kyle stands behind the column and puts his head down. Closing his eyes and calling Jake's name over and over, he faintly hears his name.

"Kyle... Kyle... is that you."

Kyle responds asking, "Jake?"

"Yes, it is me, stupid. Where are you?"

"I am freaking out, dude. There are people, animals, crazy shit happening, man. You haven't a clue what I am seeing. I need to get the hell out of here."

"Jake, calm down. Did you call Mom and Dad?"

"Hell no."

"Then call me on the phone, stupid, so I can find you."

Kyle feels his phone vibrate in his pocket he grabs it and answers it.

"Where are you, Jake?"

Kassidy listens while Kyle talks to Jake on the phone. She looks around the room as she watches Kyle pacing back and forth. She notices that he has caught the attention of a couple of staff guys. They are standing in the doorway. She can see that they are whispering back and forth, as they watch Kyle pace.

Kassidy watches them and then Kyle to make sure that is what they are doing. Looking behind him and her, she sees nobody else they could be watching. *What is going on here?* Nervous, she taps Kyle on the shoulder when he walks past her. He doesn't even realize she did. Kyle raises his voice a little louder and the guys stand a bit straighter. Kassidy is now nervous.

"Oh, shit. Kyle, shhhh! Quiet your voice."
He doesn't pay attention to her. They walk slowly towards them. Kassidy spins back around and grabs Kyle's arm. Spinning him around, he faces the two security people. Kyle finally sees what Kassidy has been trying to tell him. When he takes a good look at them, he stops talking to Jake on the phone for a second.

They both stare at the two guys while they walk right towards them. Long reddish brown hair past their shoulders by several inches, they have reddish-brown and black fur that comes across their forehead and down their broad nose. White fur runs down and around the rest of their face and neck. Their eyes stand erect, brownish in color, with a yellow center around the pupil, much like a coyote. Their faces are broader and extend from the center of the forehead through the cheekbones, just enough to look symmetrical with the human features on the lower half.

"Jake, dude. I have to go. I will be there in five minutes, okay? Bye. Ah, Kassidy, I think we need to get a drink or something, right?"

"Yeah, Kyle, like fast."
They both walk as fast as they can towards the other young people in the room and grab two bottles of water. Kyle tells her to act as if she is getting a plate of food while he figures out where the corridor bathroom is.

"Jake said he is hiding out inside a stall in the corridor bathroom we need to try to get to him if we can lose these two guys. When you walk in, go to the right and down a ways in line hopefully we can throw them off."

He sees the two guards standing over where Kassidy and he were. Grabbing Kassidy by the arm and leading her towards the doorway, they walk past the two guards and act as if they didn't even notice them.

"Keep walking and don't look at them. No matter what, Kassidy."

They walk swiftly down passing other people coming and going, looking for the sign for the restrooms.

"There it is, Kyle. The men's room is on the far end. He must be in there. Be careful. I will wait out here for you when I get out, okay?"

Kassidy darts in the women's restroom. Staff and guests move in and out of there. Other people talk about the makeup on certain people, but she notices they don't even say anything about all the staff.

OMG, it must be true. They can't see them! We must be the only ones that can. It has to be something with the witch doctor. Or that drink? I am looking right at that girl. She is a half-human, half-bird with feathers on her everywhere. She doesn't have clothes on, no human features, and no hair. She has a bottom jawbone, a beak, and her eyes are like a bird. She is looking right at me. She knows I can see her.

Kassidy watches the women in front of her look at the girl and don't seem to see anything different. Kassidy asks them when the girl walks past them.

"Excuse me, did you notice that girl that walked by?"

"Yes she had the most beautiful eyes, didn't she? Crystal blue. I have never seen such blue eyes like that before. They hypnotized you."

That is it. That is what they are doing. They can't see past their eyes.

She walks out of the bathroom and waits for Kyle to come out. Finally, she hears him talking and sees him and Jake come out.

"What took you guys so long? I figured it out, Kyle." She tells him.

"What did you figure out?"

"We are the only ones that see the people for what they are. They must see some of them like the big guards and the ones that want to be seen, but all these other ones. They don't see. I just saw a girl in the bathroom, a staff member. She was a freaking bird. I mean half-woman and half-bird. She had blue feathers with black around her face and a few white ones under her chin and neck with a beak and a human jaw, but on a human body with feathers. The key thing is she had crystal blue eyes, and when she walked past me, she stared right at me. I asked the two ladies in front of me if they saw her. You know what they told me?"

"A bird woman?" Kyle laughs.

"No! Damn it, Kyle. I am serious. They said she had the most beautiful blue eyes they had ever seen as if they hypnotized you. They look people in the eyes and they can't see past them. Unless they want to be seen."

"Hey, you are smart. You have a good point." Kyle says.

"How are you doing, Jake? Have you been experiencing the same things?" Kassidy asks him.

"If you mean seeing fucking weird people that are half-human and animal, I have. I have heard some really strange things the people working here talk about."

"What are they talking about?" Kassidy asks.
"We need to get back to Mom and Dad. It's been over two hours. I am surprised they haven't

been calling both of our phones. We can talk on the way; they will be watching us." Kyle announces.

"You wouldn't believe the things I have seen and heard today." Jake says.

Jake tells Kyle to call them so they can leave. On the way to meet their parents, Jake explains that he overheard two staff members talk about some young girl they had brought in to the lab from Beaver Creek and she had a hybrid baby. They also had another woman, some special one that had twins."

CHAPTER 28
"This Place is Strange"

"Lizzie, call the boys and see where they are. They might want to see the show. This looks like it is going to be exciting."

"Their phone goes to voicemail, John. I have tried twice now."

"They probably are out of range."

John looks around the crowd of people watching the jokers perform in the ring while they wait for the centaurs to come out and start the show. He notices a man just across the way watching the guards and not the arena.

What is he looking at the guards for? John wonders. *He must be security or something.* He keeps watching the guy as he glances John's way for a split second.

What the heck is that?
"Lizzie, I will be right back. Stay here." John says. He walks back around to the guy that he has

been watching. *He looks familiar for some strange reason.*

Why is he watching all the guards and exits? Is something going on? I know this man. I just can't figure out who it is with that cap and sunglasses on.

John slips beside the man and watches him for about ten minutes. Looking him up and down, he is sure he knows him. I would swear that is Victor, but he was supposed to call me first before he came from North Carolina.

John gets closer, stepping sideways until he is right behind him. John notices he is taller than Victor. John clears his throat loudly behind the man to make the man turn around.

"HHHUUUMMMMM."

"Victor?"

"JOHN?"

"What are you doing here? I thought you were going to call me to let me know when you were coming."

"Yes, I know, but I heard about the event and decided that it was time to scope the place out, and then call for the backup if I needed it." Victor says.

"What are you doing scoping the guards out so obviously? I can see you from way over there. You need to watch yourself."

"Ah, people would just think I am security."

"True, that is what I thought at first, but then I realized I knew you. The people here are going to figure out they don't have security in the crowds." John says.

"What are you doing here, John?"
"I am here with Lizzie and the boys. I thought it would be good to check out the place and for them to see some fall spirits while here."

"I need to find out where they are keeping Kia. They have her here somewhere and I need to get her out fast. By the looks of the guards, we are going to have a big fight on our hands." Victor says.

"Did you see the ones at the gate? They are huge. They are going to be hard to handle. I haven't been through the rest of the place to see anything else yet. We saw the strange characters fighting in the streets and thought we'd catch the show."

"So what are you planning, Victor? Do you want to get Kia out today? Or Tonight?" John asks.

"I need to get the layout of the place. Call North Carolina and tell them what I have found. Hopefully I will find Kia."

"I know this is a big place. I have only walked through part of the garden area and from a distance, seen that castle. It is massive. If I were you, I would look in there for her." John says.

"Yeah, I walked past it and tried to get in the castle, but they have a chain across and two creatures guarding. Can you believe they have Minotaurs guarding the castle? This place is like the Island of Dr. Moreau with all the strange creatures here. It's going to be interesting finding out what is inside there."

"Well, I can scout out areas again by the castle and get back to you later this evening, if you'd like, Victor. Comparing ideas might help." John replies.

John and Victor shake hands.

"I am going back to Lizzie before the show starts and I lose her in the crowd." Victor walks out of the crowd, looking for a way to find Kia. He knows she is inside the castle. With all the security and massive guards around the place, Victor's mind races with ideas, trying to put pieces together like a complicated puzzle.

Victor strolls down the walkway, passing the different vendors and their displays of medieval clothing, face paintings, trinkets, and music. Incense fills the air from the gypsy tent as Victor passes by. A palmist reads her customer's hand in one tent to the left, with a line of people waiting outside. Victor snickers and shakes his head. He knows who the true fortunetellers here are. She is not a true foreseer.

John makes his way back to Lizzie. Kyle, Jake, and Kassidy stand next to her. The show is just starting. The trumpets sound and the first two teams of centaurs make their way out into the arena. One goes left and one goes to the right, passing each other in the middle, and making a full circle back to the center as the other teams follow suit behind them. The crowd roars.

The different colors represent the various kingdoms invited to compete in the games. Purple, white, and gold are the Plantation's colors. The centaurs from the Plantation and of different families all stay on the Plantation, as do all the other creatures, shifters, and their family members.

"Oh, I see you found your way back to us. How do you guys like the place?" John asks them as he walks up, putting his arm around Lizzie and smiling. Jake, Kyle, and Kassidy look up at John and smile strangely, quickly turning back around to watch the show.

Victor's walk gets slower as he nears the big house. Something just doesn't feel right. He walks to the edge of the walkway and grabs the fence. He suddenly feels a sickening pain in his stomach. He leans forward.

OMG! What the hell is going on? Why am I so damn sick?

Holding his head down staring at the ground, Victor tries to clear his mind and make it go away. But it just keeps getting worse. He hears a soft voice, "Excuse me, sir? Are you okay? Do you need assistance?"

Victor turns his head and looks to see a beautiful young girl with jade green eyes, and a lighter green glowing ring in the center. She wears yellow, green, and aqua blue eye makeup with very small emerald stones tracing from her high rosy red checks, down the front of her little nose, above her eyebrows, and up to her forehead. Her eyes are lined with black makeup, just enough to feel the energy coming from her powder white skin and dark red hair, enhancing the green in her eyes and the little emerald stones. Her skin has a silky, shiny glow like a soft pastel rainbow and radiating from it, an energy that makes the hair on Victor's neck stand up. She has an energy that just shines from within her. Victor knows what she is. He hasn't seen one for many years.

"Yes, ma'am. Where are your bathrooms or wash rooms located?"

"The closest one is inside the main house, sir. I can take you in there and show you, if you need assistance."

"Yes, ma'am. I would really appreciate it. I think I ate something that isn't agreeing with me."

She lends her hand to help Victor to the main house. He takes hold of her hand and when he does, a sudden shock rushes through him. He squeezes her hand.

"Sir, are you okay? Sir, you're hurting my hand. Sir…Sir!!"

After a few minutes pass, Victor pulls his hand from hers. "Please young lady, don't do that again. I don't know what you are but you just sent me on a journey to somewhere in your mind. I have no clue where you took me."

The young girl's eyes widen. She knows that normal people don't have reactions like the one Victor is having. If she brings someone inside the main house that can read them by touch for what they really are then that is a threat to the clan, the Plantation, and the community within the Plantation itself.

"What if he is there to harm us?"

She panics and decides not to take Victor into the house.

"Maybe we should go to another bathroom not inside the main house," she tells Victor.

306

Victor knows why he is feeling this way. It is Kia. He is getting close to her. She is in pain and scared. If he can get inside the main house, he can find where she is being held. He has the power to get to her, but he would be going against his father and the others if he were to do so alone. This would cause great sorrow upon the people. He must wait and do as they have planned.

He agrees with the young girl and lets her take him to another bathroom. On the far side of the main house, as they walk past the entrance, Victor looks up at the guards standing at each end of the bridge.

Wow! Minotaur! How did she find them? They are extremely rare. She must have some kind of power to hold these types of creatures here.

"Here you go, sir. Do you need further assistance? I can call for a male assistant to come help you."

"No, thank you. You have really done plenty. Thank you so much for helping me." Victor says.

She smiles and bows ever so slightly to him. When she turns, he notices she has green see-through wings like a dragon fly except these are a thicker membrane like a clear green plastic but of flesh-like material. *She is a forest fae,* Victor mumbles to himself as he walks into the men's bathroom.

Kyle, Jake, and Kassidy try to focus their attention on the show, but they sense the most uncomfortable feeling. It slowly starts as the crowd gathers. Something just seems strange and the closer people get to them, the feelings become the same.

Kassidy finally nudges Kyle to get his attention. They stand to the side of his parents. She pulls him aside and asks him if he feels something strange like they are being watched.

Kyle says, "Yeah, I just thought it was that funny dust wearing off. It feels like something is touching me, a pinching almost."

"I don't think so, Kyle. Remember those creatures? We were glad they weren't flying around us. I think they are and we can't see them. I don't know why we can't see them right now."

"Yeah, I remember them. You're right, Kassidy. I bet that is exactly what it is. I don't know either. Maybe it is finally wearing off. But I do feel like something else is watching us. Not them little creatures — something else. I can feel the heat of them on my back like a hot coal."

"Exactly! What could it be? I can almost imagine it in my head. It is across the way, between the vendors' tents and that dark little area in the nestle of trees. If you stare right at that area, you will see the darkness changes from black to grey. Something is moving in there letting light in and

blocking as it moves. Watch it, and it is watching us."

Kyle turns and watches the area Kassidy points out. Jake looks over. He slings his hand back behind his parents, trying to get their attention when he realizes he feels something strange. He realizes they must be looking at whatever it is he is feeling.

CHAPTER 29

"She is Mine"

Damien is furious with his mother and Malik. Pacing through the corridors, he waits for darkness to come so he can go out without the bother of all the people in the fall festival. They will not let him keep his offspring, the girl, and they want him out of the clan. The tension builds more and more as he thinks about what his mother said.

"Fuck them all!!" Damien shouts through the corridor that connects to the lab. He storms back towards the lab with the intention of busting through. He knows what his mother will do if she hasn't already killed his offspring through Dr. Brack and Monroe.

His fists clench, he feels the hair growing thicker on his back and standing up under his shirt. He grabs his shirt in the middle of his chest and rips it off him. The hair rapidly grows like a rippled effect covering his muscled stomach. He turns his head to the side and then back again to allow the shift to readjust his facial features. He can feel his teeth and face growing into the muzzle of the hellhound. He feels his ears tingle as they lengthen. He shakes his head and punches his chest with both hands. A deep rumble starts in his chest as he breathes; the anger is getting the best of Damien. He can't control it anymore.

Turning the corner just up from the door of the lab, Damien in his hellhound form can smell things he normally wouldn't catch this far away. He stops and smells the air. His eyes turn yellow from glowing red. Something is changed; something feels different, smells different, and he stops to analyze what he smells. Taking big slow deep breaths of the air, he slowly approaches the door of the lab.

He suddenly feels strange; he has never felt this before. EVER! Standing confused at the door of the lab, Damien's anger has left, and something very different comes over him. A feeling of pleasure, a feeling of accomplishment, a feeling of being superior for once in his life. He feels like he has something… a purpose, a meaning to life, a feeling of love.

His heart pounds, sending blood flowing rapidly through his veins. Instead of anger, for once he feels the need to fight for something, rather than against everything and everyone.

He pounds on the door of the lab knowing that Monroe with probably answer and not let him in. Dr. Brack is too weak; he could never challenge Damien. Monroe is a larger man; he is younger and bigger.

Damien already gets his fur standing on his back just ready for the challenge coming when Monroe answers the door and tells him to leave. With his fists in a knot and his eyes gazing at the handle, Damien feels the anxiety boiling up from inside his stomach. Working its way up slowly through his body, he feels the heat from it raising his temperature, like a narcotic drug being absorbed through his body. The door handle turns in Damien's eyes; it looks like it is moving so slowly, as if everything has slowed almost to a crawl. It seems to take an eternity for the door to open. Anxious, he feels himself shifting, a rumbling sound echoes through the corridor.

The doorknob suddenly stops moving. Damien is furious; he can't hold himself back any longer. Something stirs within him that he can't control and he doesn't know why this is happening. These strange feelings he has never felt before.

Damien lunges into the door, knocking it open and hitting Monroe unexpectedly in the face. Monroe flies across the room landing on the floor. Damien rushes through, letting out a deep growl shaking everything in the lab.

"What the hell is all the noise about?" Dr. Brack walks out from the other side of the lab. He sees Damien standing at the door half-shifted. He knows why he is there, but he can't let him near Ellie

312

and that baby. She can't fight; she is still healing. It has been a week since she had the baby. He turns back around to get a syringe full of the narcotic Ketamine to knock Damien out, or at least drop him to his knees before he can do any harm in the lab.

"Monroe, hold him there. I am getting the Special K."

Monroe tries to figure out what happened. He stumbles to his feet when he hears Dr. Brack yelling. He turns and sees Damien.

"Damien!" What the hell are you doing, you son of a bitch!" Monroe yells out across the front of the lab area. Damien doesn't slow down. He heads straight back towards Ellie's bed.

Monroe stumbles forward and slowly picks up his step to catch up to Damien, hopefully slowing him down for Dr. Brack to inject him. Monroe grabs Damien's left arm. He stops only long enough to look, with his eyes bright yellow and red center. He has shifted in his hellhound form and he is not happy. He looks at Monroe and with a growl, he slings Monroe back across the room.

"Son of a bitch, Damien!" Monroe yells as he slides across two of the stainless steel tables in the lab.

Everybody and every animal in the lab fall silent when they hear Damien's first growl coming in the door. Now they are screaming in fear. Dr. Brack waits just on the edge of the corner for Damien to pass.

Dr. Brack watches him pass and doesn't hesitate. He slams the needle in Damien's arm so fast he doesn't even know he has been injected. He sees Dr. Brack move out of the corner of his eye. By that time, it is done. Damien swings his arm, hitting Dr. Brack in the chest and knocking him backwards on the floor. Monroe comes back around the tables and towards Damien. He notices Damien wobble. Monroe stops and watches to see if the drug will take effect on him.

"Dr. Brack, you all right?" Monroe calls out while watching Damien. Still in defense mode, Damien walks to the other side of the lab, towards Ellie.

"Shit! He is still moving, Brack! He is not going down!" Monroe yells.

"We will give him a few minutes. I gave him a big dose. He will fall flat on his face here in about two minutes or less." About the time Dr. Brack says that, Monroe watches Damien fall without flinching straight forward.

"Oh shit!" Monroe says as he leaps forward to keep Damien from hitting his face on the hard lab floor. Monroe barely grabs ahold of Damien's left arm to help break the fall. Turning him to the side, he slows some of the impact.

Dr. Brack walks over and looks down at Monroe lying on the floor next to Damien.

"Why in the hell did you let that stupid son of a bitch in here?"

"Are you kidding me? Do you see my face? I didn't even get the door opened and he busted through smacking me with it! I didn't let him in. I am not that much of an idiot, thank you. I am so glad you think so highly of me, Dr. Brack." Monroe mutters as he gets up without the help of Dr. Brack.

"Now what the hell are we going to do with him?" Monroe asks.

"You are going to drag his ass right back outside that door and leave him there. I will call Alexis and tell her to come collect her problem and keep him away from here." Dr. Brack instructs.

"You know he isn't going to keep away from here, Dr. Brack. By the way he is acting and where he is heading, he knows that is his child in there and he wants it. That is the instinct of the hellhound; it is in his blood. I am not sure what the mother will do if she sees him. They were not a loving couple, and this was not a planned pregnancy." Monroe says.

"I know. We are going to have to explain this whole thing to that bitch as it is. She wanted us to put that baby down. I just couldn't do it. All the work, all the suffering, all the torture, all the killings. Sure as hell, I am not going to destroy our one chance to see if this hybrid theory is even going to work." Dr. Brack says as he walks back to the table where he was doing tests before the interruption.

Monroe drags Damien outside the door. Everybody in the lab except Kia is finally calmed down and relaxed. Monroe goes in to see how Ellie and the baby are doing. When he passes by Kia, who is still drugged, he sees blood coming out from between her legs.

"Dr. Brack, we have another problem!"

He pulls the white blanket off Kia and sees she is in labor with her offspring. He rushes over and grabs some more towels. Dr. Brack gets the IVs out of the cabinet and ready for Kia.

"Let's take her to the room we used for the other one. At least she can have a comfortable table to lie on while having the baby." Dr. Brack tells Monroe

They wheel the table into the other room. Dr. Brack hooks up the IVs to bring Kia into a semiconscious state so she can help them deliver her offspring.

Monroe gets the room prepared for the things Dr. Brack will need.

Kia moves her head around. Dr. Brack watches her and checks all the restraints to make sure she can't get out of them.

"Monroe, you stand down at her head. Make sure you have all the surgical instruments laid out where you can reach them and she can't get to them. When I say put her down, I mean put her down. Do not hesitate because she will take us both if she comes out of the restraints."

"I am ready, Doc. Let's get this over with. I have a splitting headache from that son of a bitch Damien." Monroe snaps back.

Kia opens her eyes and looks around the room once again. The cold hard truth has sunken in to another person in the lab that it isn't a dream. She has no idea how long she has been there, how long she has been away from Victor, but she does know that she is in extreme pain and knows she is going to have the twins in that God forsaken place without her family, help, or spirit animals.

Kia screams in pain. Dr. Brack tries to adjust the table to prop Kia's legs up so he can see how far along she is. Very carefully, he pulls the pin in the table and quickly moves the left leg in position and locks it before she has a chance to respond. Dr. Brack sits back in his stool and looks at Monroe with a sigh of relief.

"Okay, let's try the next one, okay? I am only trying to help you here. We are not the bad guys. The lady upstairs, she's the bad guy. We just work here, lady. You are in need of our help right now. Understand? I am a doctor and I want to help you deliver these babies. With your help, we can all do this together and nobody will get hurt." Dr. Brack so charmingly tries to talk Kia into believing they are not going to harm her or the twins.

Kia tries to shift; her body changes only in certain areas of different creatures. With the drugs, the pain, the twins, she can't focus enough to fully shift. Monroe watches Kia instead of Dr. Brack. He can't believe what she is doing. He has never seen a shifter transform so fast between different creatures, let alone into several different ones.

Kia fights the restraints, the drugs.

"You must help us or you will end up harming you and your babies." Dr. Brack yells.

Kia still fights them and everything. Finally, Dr. Brack has had enough. He tells Monroe to put her down.

"I can't handle this bitch anymore." Kia snaps her head up and looks right at Dr. Brack. Dr. Brack looks at Kia and says, "I see that has your attention now, doesn't it?!"

"Yes, Doctor. I will do as you say. Please don't inject me with anything else. I promise I will not fight anymore. Just please help me." Kia says in a very soft broken voice.

Dr. Brack lifts the sheet up and looks at Kia's vaginal area. With a warm rag, he wipes off the blood and checks to see how close the head is in the canal.

He stands up between Kia's legs, places a hand at the top of her belly hump, and tells her to push.

"Push with all you got. You have to push them through the canal and out. I cannot do anything until they get their heads out. Do you understand?" Dr. Brack tells her.

Kia nods her head yes and Dr. Brack pulls slowly in a downward motion on her belly.

"Push, push, push hard, harder. It is crowning. Keep pushing. Almost got this one out. Keep pushing. Don't give up!"

Kia pushes and screams so loud Monroe covers his ears. Dr. Brack grabs the first baby and helps pull it out slowly as Kia pushes. Monroe watches with excitement as the first baby comes out and Dr. Brack cleans it up. He asks Monroe to wrap it up and hold it while he waits for the second one to come.

"Please let me hold my baby, please let me loose so I can hold it." Kia begs Monroe to let her touch her child, but he refuses.

"What is it? Can you at least tell me if it is a boy or a girl?" Kia asks crying.

"It is a girl." Monroe tells Kia.

Kia cries, wishing Victor were here, wishing she were with her Native family. She knows that she is to be killed after she has the last child. She knows that is the plan of the lady who runs this place. She only wants the hybrid children for the pure bloodline. How is she to escape with two babies and fight against these two and all the others that she encounters? Almost impossible for one person to think about in the drugged up state she is in.

Kia has reached a point she shouldn't be in. She has reached a point of giving up instead of fighting. She knows if she lets go, it will be easier for Victor and the others to rescue just the children. She doesn't even acknowledge the other child still in her. Kia's hopelessness is overwhelming and taking her over. She doesn't react to anything Dr. Brack says; she just stares straight up at the ceiling.

Dr. Brack panics.

"Monroe, I need your help. She is giving up on having these babies. Put that baby down and help me push her belly. We have to get this one out or else I am going to have to cut her open and take it out of her. We don't have much time, Monroe. Move it!" Dr. Brack yells.

Monroe grabs an infant cart to lay the newborn in while helping Dr. Brack push Kia's belly. They both push downwards on her. Dr. Brack yells out to Kia to push, but Kia doesn't respond. After about ten minutes of pushing and fighting to get the second baby down far enough, he stops Monroe.

"Let's cut her open. There is no other way to do this. She has given up all hope. She isn't going to push; she isn't going to do anything. She is like an animal with a broken spirit. She will not help get this baby out. She probably has sunken so deep in depression she doesn't even realize she is having a baby. Sad. I hate to say it. I don't like seeing them like this."

Monroe wheels over a stainless steel medical tray full of instruments. Dr. Brack cuts a line for the C-section to remove the child from Kia. One perfect swipe of the knife opens her belly and blood pours out. Monroe blotches and wipes up as much as he can while Dr. Brack takes one gentler swipe so he doesn't cut the baby.

Dr. Brack puts the knife down on the tray and quickly lifts up the skin and muscle to expose the uterus. He makes a gentle cut and opens it up. The baby slides right out with blood and thick fluid running all over the table and the floor. He quickly sets the knife down and cradles the baby with one hand before gently pulling it out.

"It is not breathing! Dr. Brack, it is not breathing. It is blue!! Oh no, you must help it!" Monroe quickly tells Dr. Brack.

Dr. Brack holds the baby up by his feet and spanks him on the butt once to see if he can get a response and open the airway. Still not responding, he flips it over, holds it in the other infant cradle, and starts CPR. Monroe walks around and cleans up Kia so Dr. Brack can staple her up.

Shaking his head, he can't believe how much stuff has happened in the past few hours. About that time, he hears a beep indicating the door has opened. *Damien busted back in, son of a bitch.* Monroe runs out of the room to see Alexis coming.

Oh shit! She picked the perfect time to walk down here. She hasn't been here in well over a month, since they first showed up here. She has no clue that Ellie has had her baby or Kia is having hers. She doesn't come down here very often, maybe a handful of times per year.

"What in the hell is going on in here, Dr. Brack?" Alexis yells out across the lab as she struts in the room. She stops and puts her hands on her hips with her brown leather pants, corset of leather, and vintage blouse. She looks like she stepped out of the 1800's steampunk era. You can hear her boots click closer to them as they work on cleaning up the area. Dr. Brack is trying to get the second child to breathe.

Finally reaching them, she looks in and her mouth drops and eyes fling open wide in shock.

"What the hell! Goddamn it, Brack. You should have called me and told me the silver-blood was in labor." Dr. Brack doesn't respond. He is still working on the baby. Monroe tells her that it happened so fast, they didn't have a chance.

"Bullshit, Monroe! Don't give me your horseshit and tell me what the hell happened to

Damien. He said you guys drugged him and threw him in the hallway." Alexis asks angrily, not caring at all about the situation at hand.

"He came down and busted in the door. Alexis, he threw me across the room. He was uncontrollable; we had no choice but to drug him." Monroe swiftly says back to her.

Alexis glares at Monroe until he looks away. She looks around and notices one baby in the cradle. Kia is cut open and Dr. Brack is working on the second one.

"What are you doing? What has happened here?" Alexis asks.

"We are trying to save this child; that is what is happening, Alexis." Dr. Brack comes back with a sarcastic answer.

"Move over and let me have this child." Alexis demands.

Alexis takes the child that is limp and not breathing from Dr. Brack. She holds it up to her face and puts her mouth right above its mouth. She opens up her mouth and a swirling black smoke comes out slowly. Dr. Brack and Monroe watch as Alexis' eyes turn bright red. Her mouth widens even further and the smoke crawls out as if it is alive. It is moving around as if it has tentacles. They reach out and grab the mouth of the baby that is not breathing, forcing it open. Then a long, black, slimy thing that looks like a finger, or a snake, moves out of Alexis' mouth and into that of the baby. All of a sudden, Alexis and the baby gravitate towards each other and the smoke-like fingers stretch and wrap around the head of the child. A glowing red light comes from the inside of their cheeks.

Dr. Brack and Monroe stand there in amazement. They have seen many strange things, but nothing tops this.

Suddenly the body of the baby convulses, and moves. Alexis tightens her grip, as it seems to be fighting her instead of coming to life. Alexis opens her eyes and suddenly pulls off the baby as if something has gone terribly wrong. She throws the baby back in the cradle and grabs her mouth as if she was in pain. Dr. Brack and Monroe look at each other.

"You little piece of shit!" Alexis yells as black smoke and spit drip from her mouth and down her face. "How dare this child challenge my powers? Who do you think you are dealing with, you stupid silver-blood!!!"

Alexis yells and turns around to see Kia lying on the bed not moving, just staring straight up at the ceiling. She then looks at Dr. Brack and Monroe.

"You know she is the sacred one. You had better make damn sure you bring her back. She has a place in the crystal dungeon. Her blood is so rare we will never get a chance again to have a silver-blood in our collection." About that time, she gets a call to come up to the festival. One of the staff has encountered a strange man that possibly is of a different origin.

"I will be back in a few hours. I better see the silver-blood in better condition than this." Alexis storms out of the lab.

Dr. Brack and Monroe rush over and look in the cradle to see the baby looking up at them. Monroe can't believe it. He looks at Dr. Brack stupefied. As he wipes the black goo from the baby's face, he wraps it in a blanket.

Dr. Brack has already stapled up Kia. He tells Monroe to undo the restraints on her and let her hold the babies.

"We have nothing to give them right now. She needs to feed them. I can't believe how quiet they are." He tells Monroe.

Chapter 30

"The Twins"

Victor is leaned over the toilet in the bathroom stall. Panicked from the feelings he is having his mind races with thoughts and questions to try and figure out why this is happening.

My heart… can it beat any faster? The strange feeling inside me — I can't figure out what it is, but it is making me ill. The ringing in my ears is almost deafening. It covers the sounds from the festival outside the bathroom. If I keep this up, I will so panic and draw attention to myself. I can't let this happen. If anybody finds out what I am, they surely know why I am here. Breathe, damn it, Victor. Breathe; take control. I really could use you, Kia. Honey, where are you? Even the spirit animals are having a problem finding you. There must be a powerful spell upon the place they have you in. That would be the only reason we cannot find you. Kia, if you can feel me, honey, or if you can hear me at all, I am here. Just show me, show me how to find you.

Victor opens the door and walks out of the bathroom. Putting on his sunglasses, he looks all around looking for anything, a sign, just one simple sign that would point to where she could be. Looking around the big house, he sees the crowd of people parting off to the sides and a lady walking towards him with four guards.

'Well, this must be the lady of honor herself — the one that has my Kia. She must be coming for me. Nice outfit. That is a dead giveaway, bitch. I know exactly what you are now. I can read you from the emblems you wear and the feathers on your corset. Oh and you bring none other than the four fawns with her. That is just great. I can smell them a mile away; their stench of a goat never can be masked with cologne.' John says to himself.

Victor turns to the left and walks quickly among the crowd of people trying to blend in. She is still furious over what happened in the lab today. Victor tucks his head and disappears within the people, moving quickly around towards the front gates. Alexis orders the guards with her to search the bathroom. One stands outside the door, one takes a position on the back of the building and two walk inside the bathrooms to search for him. The fawn guard stops the people walking in and tells them to wait or go to another bathroom. The people walking by notice that he is different and want to take pictures of him.

A crowd forms around the bathroom just outside the entrance. Everybody snaps photos with cameras and cell phones, videos of the fawn standing with his arms crossed and legs apart. He is not full human. The crowd awes over the costume and makeup. The fawn has curly brown, shoulder-length hair with a small beard that comes almost to a point at the chin. His ears stick out like goats, brown in color with black and white hair under them. Black rippled horns curve back around his head from just above his temple area. His eyes are bigger than a man's and very round, much like a goat's eyes — light brown with yellow rings around the black center. His upper body is like a man's except he seems to have more hair on his normal human arms, hands, and torso; the legs are different. Wearing leather pants that come just above the knee or hock, his legs bend as those of a goat, horse, and cow.

Alexis doesn't notice the crowd of people because she is standing about fifty-feet away talking on her headset to Ada, and pacing back and forth. The crowd grows bigger until soon she is approached and they crowd her space. She stops talking and looks around at the people. She can't see anything except the backs of people.

"What in the fuck is going on!!" Alexis *mumbles.*

She pushes her way through and sees everybody taking pictures of the fawn guard standing at the bathroom and the other two standing

329

behind him posing for pictures when they are supposed to be searching.

Victor walks around the big garden that circles the front part of the house. It sits in the middle and the walkway wraps around it and cuts through the middle. There is a big statue of a lady naked with a robe wrapped around her right arm. She is carrying a sword. In the left arm that she has above her head, she is holding a raven. It meets the wings that come out of her back. She has a snake wrapped up her left leg that is the main one forward in the statue. The robe drapes around and covers, making a three-quarter tear-dropped circle.

Victor looks up at the huge statue noticing it resembles the lady walking right towards him when he exited the bathroom. He slows to take a closer look at it. He sees a plaque in the front of it and decides to read it very quickly.

The Morrighan. Also known as the Morrigu, the shape shifting Celtic Goddess of War, Fate, and Death. She also presided over rivers, lakes, and fresh water, in addition to being the patroness of revenge, night, magic, prophecy, priestesses, and witches. Her name is interpreted in various forms... "Great Queen," "Phantom Queen," or "Queen of Demons." She was said to hover over battlefields in the form of a raven or hooded crow and frequently foretold or influenced the outcome of the fray.

Boy, that sounds like her. A witch, a priestess. That is why she is powerful and how she controls the big guards around the entrances.

As Victor walks away from the statue, he hears the sound of flutes playing and people clapping. He looks ahead of him and sees a group of dancing young fawns and Dryads. They are changelings, swirling, and dancing down through the crowd as part of the fall festival attraction.

The young fawns play their melodies on the small wooden flutes and the changelings sing and dance. The changelings are fascinating to see; they change with the each season. They are part of the forest creatures. They are in their autumn change so their hair is red-hued and skin is pale with a hint of green and glows iridescent like water on the grass in the rays of the sun. Leaves of yellow, red, brown, and green lace through their hair and down their arms to their hands. Sheer cloth in autumn colors is draped to accent them. Multi-colored sheer clothe with different trinkets wrap around their hips to hold the knee-length pants. Their legs are also different; they have a vine texture to them like a smooth bark. Tattoos are on the shoulders to the elbow of the five elements of the earth. Their eyes are the most unique thing about them; each one has a different shade of autumn red, yellow, brown, purple, green, and rust color.

Victor briefly stops and watches them dance around the statue and perform their song before moving on. He notices the crowd over by the bathroom as he looks over his shoulder to the right.

Looks as if I am in the clear; they have not noticed me. She is still over on the other side by the bathrooms. I had better get out of here while I have the chance. Now I know what she is and what we are dealing with to get in, I will make the call as soon as I get out of this place to the others.

Kia lays on the bed empty and lost; everything has gone dark. The sounds of reality have all blended into a noise. No certain recognizable tone, words, or sounds. Just... Static.

The light has gone. My mind is black. I have nothing left to give. I am better off in the spirit world. This is the only way I can be there to protect my family now here I can't do anything, but cause pain and suffering. I just need to let go and fade into this darkness. Victor will soon understand why I had to do what I...

A silent voice speaks. The feeling of loss and helplessness has taken its toll. The unforgettable pains of the leather restraints tighten around her until she can't move. She is left to lie in one position for almost two months. The pain is so great, not from the suffering, but from the loss of her love.

The twins are out of her and the darkness has grown to pitch black. There is not more feeling of life, no light to see, no feeling of survival in her blood anymore. Her heart and mind have given up on living. She must die.

She feels her heart slow; beat by beat, it slows a little more. Her breath becomes shallow, with only a few per minute. She feels the blood creeping slowly back up her body to her heart as if it is withdrawing back to its storage.

"Kia," a whisper comes through haunting, softly echoing through her mind so faintly. She is slipping so deep away she doesn't hear it.

"Kia, you need to focus." It says a little louder, swirling, haunting as if it was coming from an un-tuned radio fading in and out of reception. "Kia, hear me. You must come back. You need to focus on the twins. They need you now!"

Kia opens her eyes, darting them around the room. First reaction — *where am I?* Panic kicks in, her heart races. She tries to sit up and finds she is restrained. She pulls her arms and the agony of the shackled restraints and the harsh reality of why she was slipping into a dark and deadly sleep hits her. She tries to scream, but her voice is so raspy, she can hardly make a sound. Her wrists and feet are bound, her thighs, and waist are strapped down.

She lays back, breathing faster and faster, and then stops.

Breathe, Kia; just breathe, she tells herself. She breathes through her nose and out her mouth, trying to calm herself and stop the dizziness. She hears a voice, a different one she recognizes but doesn't know who it is.

A touch… somebody touches her arm. She can feel her body go into a defensive mode. She shifts; her skin feels like thousands of bugs crawling all over it, as the hair grows rapidly through the pores. Her skin tingles and burns as it changes underneath to compensate for the creature she is trying to shift into. The drugs are wearing off; she can feel that she is gaining her strength back. She pulls hard on the restraints and feels them giving.

"Easy, calm down. I'm not going to harm you. I just want to take these restraints off you so you can feed your babies. Do you understand?" Kia hears the male voice. It isn't Victor. She has heard it before. Not recognizing anything, she is scared not knowing what is happening.

Pain, I feel pain, terrible pain. Kia looks down at her stomach and sees a large cut with staples in it. Her eyes grow wide.

"Wwwhhaaatt… what has happened? Wwwwhhhaaatt is wrong with me?" Kia barely can speak; her voice is hoarse and raspy.

"You have two babies you need to feed. They are right over here. Can you see them?" Monroe points to the two cradles and Kia slowly turns her head. Everything comes back in a flash as if she is standing in the middle of a movie. The screen is wrapped around her, and it is playing all these events in different times. She tries to see each thing as her eyes scramble about to view the pictures, knowing it is a vision of what has happened. Finally, the one thing that makes her come back to reality. That smell! That smell of death, the smell of animals, the smell of different types of animals, and the smell of the hellhound!! That smell brings her back faster than all the others. She remembers the smell from the field when the wind blows in her dream, and she sees the hellhounds standing upon the cliff.

A beige and white image appears in front of Kia. Kia is in a field with the twins. She is chasing them around with Victor watching. The smell is so strong of hellhound. Rayne notices them also and asks her father what they are. Kia notices something different this time in the picture. Three hellhounds and a figure of a woman stand there with them.

"Can you tell me what they call you? Your name?" A man's voice again. She faintly hears it

335

while staring at this image playing out in front of her. Finally, she shakes her head for a second.

"Kia. My name is Kia."

"Kia, I am Monroe and this is your daughter. She is in need of feeding. She is about an hour old and has not eaten yet. Would you like a drink of water or a soda?" Monroe asks.

"Yes, sir. Please, I would like both if possible." Kia softly responds as she holds her daughter to nurse. "So you will be Rayne and your brother will be River. That is what the spirit animals told me in the ceremonial room." Kia whispers.

A tingling sensation emerges from her nipple, like a million tiny needles pricking at the same time racing up her breast. She looks down at her breast and sees a golden light moving up her skin as the feeling moves under it. Kia watches it spread over her chest moving up her neck.

Rayne places her tiny hand on Kia's cheek and Kia sees an image. She watches as a man standing at a fence leans over. A girl walks up and taps the man. When the man turns, she sees it is Victor. Kia takes a quick breath. The woman and Victor walk when she notices the woman grab Victor's arm and something happens. She sees another woman walking with four strange creatures towards Victor, but this lady looks familiar. *Oh, it is that lady. I know this lady,* Kia says. *She comes here.* Kia tries to look around at the surroundings as fast as she can in the image. *It has to be here. Victor has to be here looking for me.* Kia realizes that is exactly what Rayne is telling her. They are searching for them. Kia breaks the contact, kisses Rayne's little hand, and cries.

CHAPTER 31
"THE ACCIDENT"

Slamming the truck door, "Son of a bitch!" Frustrated, upset, and confused, Victor pulls out of the fall festival parking lot in a hurry. Heading towards Beaver Creek, all he can think about is the feeling he had when he got close to the house. Something is causing him to be sick. His mind fills with thoughts, trying to sort them out and the feelings that come with them before he has to call Dr. Redbone and explain what he has found.

What is happening? These feelings are crazy. I have strange pictures of objects, hallways, symbols, creatures, flashing random through my brain. What are they? I need to focus so I can figure this out. Ever since that girl grabbed my arm, something happened. She transferred something into me. What? I don't know. I have to figure this out. Think, Victor. Think!!! I need to tune in and stop worrying; worrying isn't going to bring Kia home.

The mental link that he has with Kia is blocked. He tries to find it; he pushes everything from his mind and struggles to find Kia as he drives. Getting close to her just for a few minutes to see her will give him more than enough will to find her.

Searching his mind for a clue, waiting for a response, he sends out without any response back.

Upon hearing a loud crash, Victor's truck spins out of control, veering off the road and down the embankment, over a small cliff, and down to the bottom upside-down.

A full moon illuminates the corner of the room as it inches its way through an opening in the curtains. Lighting up the get-well cards and flower arrangements in the corner of the room, the beeping sound from the rhythmic heart monitor is the only thing breaking the silence.

Outside, the night is much different from the quiet, dark hospital room. A super moon shines tonight, one of Celtic celebrations with the different night shifters that have moved into Beaver Creek. All the movement of the good creatures brings the hunters to follow. Many changes are happening with the following of November's harvest moon; it is preparing the beginning of birth and the spring for mating within the shifter community. Many events will be held and watched.

Inside, it is a different story. The moonlight has moved from the corner to light up the center of the room. In one cold dark corner of the room, two blue eyes glow, watching the moonlight move across the floor to the steel wheels and up the legs of the bed to the white sheets. Slowly, it creeps its way up one-half of the bed, revealing pale skin with dark whiskers on the chin and jaw that trace to the hairline. IV and wires are taped on the chest, arms and head, monitoring all vital signs of the person lying motionless in the bed.

The twitch of a finger that rests on the bed captures the eyes in the corner of the room. A jerk in the leg sets the alarm off on the bed. A ringing echoes in the room. The eyes step further into the darkness.

A woman comes in and checks the monitor and the patient in the bed.

"Mr. Donovan, are you awake? Victor, can you hear me? I am Nurse Marti. Mr. Donovan, sir, can you hear me? Hello?" She grabs Victor's leg and shakes it gently to see if there is a response. Victor doesn't respond. Nurse Marti checks all the wires, resets the monitor alarm, and leaves the room.

The moonlight has now moved higher in the night sky, illuminating most of the room. A tall dark grey silhouette stands in the corner, still and quiet, not even noticeable. With their eyes closed, he blends in with the shadows of the night. He opens his eyes and the moonlight reflects the spirit that dwells deep within. Shimmering like an ocean, the moonlight reflects like two bright stars. A shallow growl slightly breaks the silence within the room.

Victor's eyes snap open, with confusion and panic. Through the sound of dead silence and the beeping of a monitor, he tries to focus his eyes as he stares straight up at the ceiling. He slowly turns his head to look for the source of the light. He sees the moonlight shining through the curtains reflecting on the chair and table in the room. He doesn't recognize anything in the room. He moves his eyes slowly to the left; cards and flowers sit on a table. He stares at them for a minute. He looks about the room some more and sees the monitor, tracing the wires to him. It sinks in he is in the hospital.

A muttered curse escapes Victor's lips as he tries to sit up in the bed. Pulling the wires from his head, the beeps and alarms sound louder and louder. The mental fog is clearing from his mind and he takes a deep breath of air into his lungs. He then notices something in the air, a stench. He realizes he isn't alone in the room. Victor swings to the side of the bed rising to his feet. He sways and clutches the rails of the bed. It is as though he is struggling to get every ounce of strength he has just to stand up straight.

What the hell? His mind races. His heart beats so hard he can feel it move his chest. He takes a deep breath and pulls the IVs from within his arms. Blood sprays the white sheets. A deepened growl shakes the room once again. Victor stops and without hesitation, stands still as an arrow. He knows this sound. It is all racing back to him. He takes a one more deep breath. He feels the air move past him and about that time, he hears the door open and everything brightens. So bright he can't even see anything. He puts his arms up to break the light.

"Mr. Donovan, what are you doing, sir? You need to get back into bed. You're not well. You cannot be up walking around. Do you understand?" He hears a man's voice yelling, but he cannot see who it is. All he can see is white bright lights.

"What the fuck is going on?" Victor shouts as loud as his voice will let him.

Silence fills the room for a moment. The monitors and alarms stop, the crashing noises have stopped, and the sound of people muttering and yelling — all stopped. Dead silence.

"Someone answer me. What the hell is going on? Where am I and how long have I been here?" Victor says in an angered tone.

"Mr. Donovan, I think you need to get back in bed and relax."

Nurse Marti and a few of the other nurses help Victor get back in the bed and put all the IVs and monitors back on Victor.

"Mr. Donovan, you are in the Beaver Creek Hospital. You have been here for almost two months. Seven weeks, three days to be exact. You had a bad accident just across the state line several weeks ago. Your truck went off a cliff and landed upside down. Nobody noticed it for about twenty-four hours. You were in rough shape when you came in here, Mr. Donovan. Unconscious, lost a lot of blood, broken ribs, fractures to your skull, legs, arms, broken hand. You had to go right into surgery."

Victor can't believe what he is hearing. Then it all hits him. He was driving out of the fall festival. *OMG! Kia!*

"Has anybody come to visit or has anybody called for me?" Victor asks.

"Yes, lots of people come every day to see you and ask about you. Sheriff Taylor is here every day and so is John Smith. I will let them all know you have awakened."

Victor lays upright in the bed, letting the information he just heard sink in and trying to figure out what has been happened to his Kia. The twins have had to be born by now. He can't believe this has happened, that almost two months have passed. They must have never found out where she was or else she is…. *No, she can't be. I will not believe she and my babies are dead. Oh, what have I done? I have killed my only family, my true love. This cannot be right.* The life he was building with her and their unborn children, a life that made everything worth living. Victor puts his head back on the bed and the tears race down his cheeks.

The air moves in the room again, Victor feels the waves of air ripple past him like water in the ocean. He looks around in the dark room, but he doesn't see anything. A scent trails behind the air faintly filling his senses.

"Kane? Is that you? If you're there, Kane, I need to know it is you and not someone else." Victor says.

Nothing responds from the darkness, and then a growl faintly emerges and a dark shadow moves forward. Two bright blue eyes gaze through Victor as if he could kill him. The moonlight lights up the face of a tall dark-haired man with a muzzle, head, and ears of a wolf. It slowly moves closer to Victor.

Their gazes lock. Victor can feel the anger brewing within the beast to the point of rage and death. Victor finds himself helpless and hopeless, feeling that he has let his family die.

344

"If you want to kill me, Kane, go ahead. I would rather die than live without Kia and my kids. That is why you are here, isn't it? To punish me for messing up?"

Kane moves firmly to the bed and hunches over, placing his muzzle within an inch of Victor's face, clenching his fists, and growling with the deepest tone Victor has ever heard. One that makes the hair stand up on his skin in fear.

"I should rip your throat out, but I cannot do this. I am here to protect you from them, but you listen to me. I do not like what you have done. You have left her alone with them people. She is suffering. She should not suffer. She should not ever suffer or see pain. She is special; she is good and you do not understand how special she is to our people. She is the new hope we have waited for centuries and you mess it up."

Kane slowly moves his arm upwards towards Victor, still with a deep growl rumbling in his throat and snarling his lips at the side of Victor's face. He has a love for Kia, a love nobody knows about except for Kane. He has been doing very well containing himself from approaching Kia the whole time he has watched over her.

Chapter 32

"As a Young Girl"

Ellie stares out the window on the fourth floor of the Plantation. Damien caresses her neck gently with a kiss. Then moving slowly up her neck to her ear, he whispers, "I want another pup, my sexy fae. I want a male to join our daughter. To run with me in the pack. I need my bloodline to live on in a male. At least one, Ellie."

"I understand, Damien, but my blood is different than yours. I am still not sure what our daughter is going to actually be when she becomes a teenager. What if they take on my blood side more than your blood side?"

"I know how you feel, honey. The bloodline always follows the dominant males. If we have a male, it will be hellhound. Trust me on this; it always is. Females have a fifty percent chance. That is a known fact in the shifter community. They are the carriers of creation, carrying half of each their parents' bloodline inside them."

She turns and faces Damien, looking him in the eyes. She then puts her head down and walks to the bed to lie on her back and stare up at the ceiling. Damien follows her.

"I recall when I was a little girl, my father would go into the woods with me. We would sit along the creek shoreline or on logs in the woods and he would say, 'Now don't be afraid, Ellie. Okay? I want to show you what you are. One day you will use these powers as I am now. We are special people. We are different; we have the ability to go to other places, to be other people. Look, Ellie. Just watch the forest and you will soon see.'

"So there we sat on the log that had fallen almost all the way down to the ground. One end still stuck in the trunk that now has rotted away. Green moss grew on the sides and all over the trunk; mushrooms even grew in the valley of the trunk where it had decomposed the bark, and the heart of the old hickory. I watched the sunlight move slowly through the trees as it rose up into the morning sky. It had just rained the night before and the water still dripped slightly in the canopy of trees while we sat and watched as the sun caught the dewdrops on the plants and leaves that laid upon the ground. A rainbow of color reflecting in the clear liquid would dance in the flickering of the leaves as the wind blew. The light would break making it send the color of light shooting to the top of the canopy of trees. Like a bright pyramid, it shined so bright. A swirling mist slowly stirred inside the light and then he said, 'Look in the light closely, Ellie. What do you see?' My eyes widened and my mouth opened. I put my hand on his knee for safety as I inched closer to my father. There it was!"

"There was what? What did you see? Tell me?" Damien sits up and looks down at Ellie lying on the bed smiling.

"It was bright. It was green. I could see green grass like a field. It looked like a door opened in the middle of the forest and it was like a summer field. Yellow and orange hue beamed from it across the forest floor in front of us. The mist I could see slowly reaching for the other light like an arm pulling itself over into this light to grow bigger. It sparkled like chips of tiny broken glass when it reached this light. Then out of the corner of my eye, I saw something move very fast, but only within the light. Then again and another, and another and next thing I knew, a whole bunch of this tiny winged things flew around us. I remember thinking, 'Oh, Tinkerbell!' Actually they looked like her but different. My dad called them pixies and said they are friendly little spirit creatures.

"What was in the field? Did you every go into it?" Damien asks her.

"Yes, yes. A doorway opens when my kind comes around. I can access doorways to another dimension of time."

"Did you do it? Did your father take you in there? What happened?" Damien asks.

"Yes, we did go in there and it was like walking in the most beautiful field of flowers and grasses. It was perfect. There is no place here like it. The look, the feel, everything is different. I was very young and I had a lot to learn. I didn't understand what I was, what it was, or how I was to use my gift. My real father was killed when I was ten, before he could show me anything else. I never ever went back there because that was our special place to go."

Damien propped himself up next to Ellie. Looking at her, he moves down, kisses her neck, and sweeps his hand down her body from her breasts to her hips and back. Each time he comes up to her breasts, he kneads them a little harder and pulls on her nipples, making them erect and hard.

He moves his head down on her breast, sucks her nipples, and runs his tongue around the areola. He can feel Ellie move slightly under him and moan in response. Ellie moves under Damien, allowing him to get on top. He moves up her chest to her neck. Damien grabs Ellie by the chin and he pressed his lips so hard to hers it crushes her. She cannot feel it; all she can feel is the excitement Damien stirs within her. Ellie grinds her hips in rhythmic movements with Damien's. She can feel the excitement leak out of her.

Damien reaches his hand down between Ellie's legs and probes her body with his finger, sliding them in and out of her. She feels a tingling, numbing sensation instantly rocket through her body, making her hips grind harder and moan faster. Suddenly, Damien feels moisture oozing down inside Ellie like thick syrup.

He moves his hand out of her and positions his manhood at her entrance, rubbing it up and down, teasing her a little more. She moans and moves her hips harder against him in response. She bites his bottom lip and cries out, "I want you," and wraps her legs around Damien. He moves from her lips to her neck and kisses it at the same time he thrusts himself into her. Ellie lets out a cry of pleasure! Moving in and out, his shaft strokes her insides, stimulating every part of her female anatomy to its fullest. The more Ellie moans in pleasure, the harder Damien plunges into her. Faster, deeper, harder. He can feel each orgasm Ellie has, the wetter it becomes. Damien runs his hand tightly around her breast and down, tracing her curves to her butt, grabbing firmly as he moves with her with every roll of her hips.

He can feel the excitement closing in on him. Everything fades. The light in the room all fades to black as he closes in on the feeling of pleasure she has built up inside him. His seed is ready and waiting to find itself inside her, its place to reproduce to the strongest offspring. He can feel his energy drain suddenly into every ounce of his seed plunging within Ellie.

Ellie feels Damien's body tense above her. She knows he is spewing his seed inside of her and this sends her into an astounding orgasm of pure pleasure, knowing she is in acceptance to his seed. A wave of pleasure runs through her as she feels him release inside of her. She hears Damien moan in pleasure. The throbbing of his shaft makes her body feel like a million electric needles shock her all over.

He pulls out of Ellie and rolls over next to her. The room is silent and warm. The morning sun is shining through the windows and frost decorates the windowpanes letting them know the cool winter air is outside. The aroma of incense and coffee fill the air in their giant room on the third floor.

Alexis looks out her office window in the early morning. The sun has risen, shining the brightness of the sun over the courtyard and the gardens promising a warmer day with not a cloud in the sky. A front still laces the windows and snow has freshly fallen, leaving a blanket over the statues and benches in the garden and walkways. Neither a mark nor a footprint disturbs the white powdery blanket except for that tiny little trail over there. Alexis pulls her coffee mug from her lips and traces with her eyes the small trail of footsteps through the snow to the iron gate.

What the hell is she doing out there this early in the morning? That child is as stubborn as her father was when he was a child. Never listens. Alexis mutters to herself. *Come on, Raven. If you don't hurry up, Grandma is going to send someone to get you.*

The iron gate opens a little, then stops. Then it opens a little more, then a little more. Finally, a little girl squeezes through it. Long black hair, wearing a pink long jacket with white fur trim on the sleeves and face with boots to match given to her by Grandma Alexis.

Raven Elise Ravenworth, Grandma's first granddaughter was love at first sight. Alexis praises Dr. Brack and Monroe for not listening to her when she told them to do away with Ellie's child months ago. Raven is the joy of Alexis' life. She has never realized what it would be like without this little creature in her life. She is growing so fast even faster then a normal shape shifter because she has the hybrid DNA from the Silver blood mixed in her. They mature at a rapid rate to a eternal middle age.

Alexis smiles as she watches Raven walk alone through the snow-covered garden back to the house. *Brave as her grandma, she is.* Every morning it is theirs together. They have breakfast and spend special time together. Raven learns special things that a little creature like herself needs to learn from an experienced grandmother.

Watching intently over her little Raven, she notices as she stops and looks at something in the snow. Raven bends down and then stands up again, standing only for a moment before bending down on her knees and picking something up out of the snow. Alexis puts the coffee mug to her lips and takes a hard swallow. *What is this child doing?*

The snow begins to gently fall over the Plantation and the evergreen trees slowly move back and forth in the wind. Alexis still watches Raven hold something in her hands.

Come on, Raven, or Grandma is going to send someone out to get you.

She notices the snow is slowly spinning and moving around Raven, forming a tunnel effect within a few minutes. It is as high as Alexis can see in the sky. The snowflakes spin faster around Raven. A light glows in Raven's hands, growing brighter and brighter. The snow spins faster and faster. Alexis watches, trying to figure out what she is doing. She has never seen this happen. It is like witchcraft, but how would this child have this ability at her age? Alexis' mind races with ideas trying to figure out what she is seeing when a light bursts out from the center and all the snowflakes fall to the ground in the garden.

A bird flies out from Raven's hand into the air. Raven gets up and stares at the bird as it flies away. Alexis fumbles for her phone to call Gabriel to get Raven and bring her to her office immediately.

Gabriel rushes out the front door, slipping on one boot, then hopping and slipping on his other boot. Rushing down the steps, he laces his arms through his jacket and quickly zips it up, flipping the hood over his head and cinching it tightly around his face to keep the cool air from blowing in.

Standing on the walkway to the courtyard, Gabriel looks on both sides of the garden areas in search for Raven. He walks slowly forward in the sunlight so warm and bright, but a chill is still in the air; he can see his breath. He stops and looks closely at every statue, every bench. Turning completely around in a full circle, he hears behind him, "Boo! You're it, Gabriel."

Gabriel jumps, turning sharply around to see Raven dart down the sidewalk, up the stairs, and in the door of the house. Gabriel just stands there,

355

hands down by his side, and a puzzled look on his face. Now, he has to chase her through the big house. This little girl is very fast, faster than your average child.

He shakes his head in frustration and walks up the steps to the house. He can't help but laugh. She is such a spirited little creature, touching the hearts of everyone at the Plantation.

"Raven, I have a surprise for you." Gabriel says as he closes the front door behind him. Walking softly through the lobby, he listens for her laughter or little footsteps running through the corridors.

"Morning, Gab."

"Oh, good morning, Ada. How are you?"

"Fine. I see you're on Raven duty so early this morning in this cold weather?" Ada says.

"Yeah, she slipped by all of us and got outside again. Her grandmother wants a word with her ASAP." Gabriel tells her.

"Well, you didn't hear it from me, but... there is a little girl hiding out under the second level stairwell in the phone closet. However, please, you never heard this from my lips. They are sealed." Ada moves her hand across her lips as if she is zipping

356

them and takes her coffee into her office down the corridor.

Gabriel creeps quietly up to the phone closet under the second level stairway and slowly grabs the door handle. Ever so gently turning it, he pulls the door open quickly, jumps in, and says, "You're it, you little creep!" He hears Raven scream and laugh at the same time. "Okay, princess. Your grandmother awaits you." He bends down on one knee and Raven climbs onto his back. He whisks her all the way up to the doors to Alexis' office.

Gabriel gently puts Raven down in front of the doors before he knocks on them. He rubs his hand on her cheek and says, "You be a good girl, Raven. Okay?" He gives her a kiss on her forehead. Gabriel stands up and holds her hand as he knocks on the door.

The doorknob turns and Grandma greets Raven with open arms.

"Raven, my morning sweetness has arrived." Alexis grabs Raven, sweeps her up, and carries her in her office.

"Okay, Grandma. You're making my face wet." Raven said.

"But you're so sweet, I can't help myself." Alexis replies.

Raven laughs harder.

"I made your favorite breakfast. Eggs Benedict, with pineapple juice." Alexis tells her as she walks her to the table and puts her up in her chair. Raven responds with a huge smile.

Alexis slides the chair to the table closer for Raven to reach the plate.

"Raven, what were you doing outside this morning?" Alexis asks her.

"Oh, I was out checking on the creatures in the compound, Grandma. Don't tell my mom and dad, but I sneak out and help André take care of all of them sometimes. He likes it when I help." Raven tells her.

"That is very nice and very good of André to let you help him with all his work in the morning. I know he has many things to do and on cold mornings, it is even harder for everybody. Sometimes, the little animals around us die and we must bury them."

"Oh, but there was a little bird today and it didn't have to die anymore." Raven says and grabs a big drink of pineapple juice.

"What do you mean, sweetheart? If it has died, it is gone and the soul has left its body. The

358

spirit is free. The body is just a vessel and is no longer any use. It must be buried to return to the earth as it was once created."

"I can help them from being lost, Grandma. I know how. They don't have to be lost from their body. I helped a birdy today find his body and he was better. He was happy and just like a brand new bird all over again. He flew away singing and saying how happy he was to be back." Raven tells her as she eats her breakfast.

Alexis listens and sits back in her chair for a moment, thinking. This child, she knows her power. She knows what she can do and how to use it. Where did she find this and how did this get in her? She is half hellhound and the fae blood is not a healing creature. Oh... the SB hybrid that was injected, as the experiment; it accelerated the birth of Raven, and it must have become a dominating part of her. *I didn't think it would have created this!* A miracle healer by touch. Oh, this child is something very different. I need to have her blood drawn and run in the lab.

"So is that what you did today in the garden on your way back to the house? Pick up a dead bird and give him his life back?" Alexis asks.

"Oh yes, Grandma. Of course, I would. I love all living creatures. I hate to see any of them not happy. I can understand every one of them too, Grandma. When they talk, I can tell you what they are saying. André thinks I am making it all up, but I tell him every day that Gordy the bear shifter doesn't like carrots and André never listens to me."

"Raven, you must not tell anybody what you can do. I mean nobody can know that you heal animals and creatures, or that you can hear and talk to them. You cannot let anybody here know this. Do you understand me, young lady?"

Raven looks up at Alexis, her face blank, and her gaze locked into Alexis' eyes. Alexis stares back thinking if she wants to play mind games, she picked the wrong person for the challenge. Alexis stares back, glaring at her authoritatively.

After a few moments pass, Alexis hears a faint clanging noise. It gets louder and louder. She notices the silverware, the teacups, and glassware are shaking. At first, it is soft. The angrier she gets the louder and more violent it shakes. She looks back for a second at Raven and her eyes are glowing orange.

"RAVEN!!! You stop this right now, young lady. I am your grandmother. You don't act like this." Alexis stands up and uses a strict tone.

Raven's eyes deepen in color; Alexis knows that is the next step of shifting, but she is too young.

What is going on with this child? She must be controlled. Otherwise, she will be worse than her father.

Her eyes now red as burning embers, Alexis watches to see if she will change or if she can control the inner beast. Raven digs her fingers into the table. Alexis watches as her fingers take on a different form. Her face and skin on her body radiate and shine like a pearl in the bright sunlight. Something slowly emerges from the pores of her skin. Her face changes first. Her ears lengthen and become pointy, then her eyes slant and widen just a bit. Her face has soft feathers just around her eyes and faintly on her cheeks. Her hair around her face forms feathers and fur. She is growing taller and aging before her eyes. Raven closes her eyes, moves, and stretches her head and her back as if she is compensating for the growth in her body.

She opens her eyes and they are larger, rounder. She stands up and leans down on the table. Her shirt gets tighter and tighter. Alexis can hear Raven scream. Her voice changes and she can hear the sound of Raven's clothes ripping apart.

Suddenly, two large wings reach out from between Raven's shoulders. Black on the top half and blood red on the bottom.

Alexis takes in a deep breath, stunned by the sight of Raven. She can't believe that she is shifting into so many different things at the same time.

She can't understand what is happening to her. I have to call Dr. Brack up here right away. Alexis grabs her phone and calls Dr. Brack.

Chapter 33

"What Hit Me"

The air shifts like someone opened a window in the hospital room. It is so strong Victor can feel the breeze blow his hair. He realizes Kane exited the room. He sits up a bit and thinks about what Kane said.

He is right. I have to admit Kane is right. I let her down. She is alone, if she is even still alive in that place. It has been a few months since I was last there.

"Well, look who finally woke up after all this time. How are you feeling, Victor?" John asks.

"John, a sight for sore eyes. Man, what happened? The last thing I remember I was getting in my truck from the festival and heading back home." Victor tells him.

"I don't know, man, but I do know your truck looks like a freight train hit it. Whatever hit you could not have gone far. The sheriff and his deputies are still trying to find the vehicle that hit you." John tells him.

"John, I don't think it was a vehicle. I think it was something that followed me out of the festival."

"Why do you say this, Victor? I was wondering after talking to Sheriff Taylor and looking at your truck, I found no areas of paint from another vehicle, but I did find something. I kept it to show only you. I think you're the only one that can figure out what really hit your truck. Something didn't want you to come back looking for Kia at that place. I know after we left and got back to the house, Kyle and Kassidy felt drugged. They were sick for four days in bed after leaving there."

"What did you find? Can I see it? Did you bring it with you?" Victor asks.

"Yeah, let me get it. I have it in my truck." John walks out of the room and Sheriff Taylor walks in.

"Hey, John. Where are you going?" Sheriff Taylor asks.

"I am going out to my truck. I will be right back."

"Hey, Victor. How are you feeling?" Sheriff Taylor walks over and shakes Victor's hand.

"I am feeling better until I heard how long I have been in the hospital. I can't believe I have lost almost two months, Sheriff Taylor. I left that fall festival meaning to come back and get Kia out of that place. I will be honest with you, Sheriff. I didn't care what it took. I wanted her out of there. I know she was there. I could feel her. Thing is she has probably already had the twins and they might have already killed her by now."

"There is a very good chance of that, Victor. I will not kid you on that idea. However, I really need to ask you some questions about the accident now that you're awake. Are you feeling up to it?" Sheriff Taylor says.

"Yeah, go for it, Sheriff."

Sheriff Taylor questions Victor about the accident, who tells him the same thing he told John. He left the fall festival heading home and next thing he knew, he was in the hospital trying to wake up. Never knew it happened and never knew he lost two months of his life.

"Hey, John. Maybe you can help me to shake Victor's mind into remembering what happened the day of the accident."

"Well, let me show you this, Victor, and you tell me what you think. Maybe you will remember seeing something like this before it hit your truck. On the other hand, maybe you saw it at the festival that day. I know I saw some big guards that could do the damage your truck has." John pulls out a plastic bag containing brownish black hair with blood on it.

Victor takes the bag from John and holds it up to the light. Examining the contents on the inside, he suddenly gets a strange look on his face. He looks at John and sets the bag down in his lap.

"Do you know what this is?" Victor says in a curious tone.

"I think I do." John says,

"Well, I have no clue what that is. Let me see that bag." Sheriff Taylor says and Victor hands it to him. The sheriff examines it and says, "That looks like cow hair. No cows around here could do that to Victor's truck. It had to be another car that hit him."

Victor and John look at the sheriff. John says, "Well, I hate to tell you this, Sheriff, but the Plantation has animals that you have never seen before. They have animals that come straight out of Greek mythology. That place has animals big enough to do what happened to Victor. They have these things as guards inside and on the outside of the gates. They are massive, huge and that is not even explaining what they are. You would not believe the stuff there. Put it this way — the entrance of the place had two massive human/buffalo beings. They stood as tall as the iron gates and had to be almost twelve feet or more high. They're built like a giant man and buffalo. Then the two in the back by the gate to the house itself are even bigger and they are straight out of Greek mythology. Don't you say, John?

"I've seen them and the ones at the gate of the Plantation are massive creatures. They could do that."

Sheriff Taylor rubs his chin and thinks for a few minutes. "You know, ever since I have met you two, I have never in my life heard or seen such crazy and strange things. I have to say I believe you. As strange and crazy as it sounds, because I know I will end up seeing exactly what you are talking about like your crazy story of the black eternity and the spirit animals you told me before. Honestly, John, I thought you were nuts. Possibly living on that property was really working on a city boy's mind, but I was wrong."

Victor and John look at each other and laugh.

"So what is the plan? How are we going to get Kia out? Victor, do you have any ideas?" John asks.

"I had it all planned before all this came about. I need to get ahold of Dr. Redbone and the others. I know they have been waiting. By now, they should have found the world medicine man. All they need is a way to get into the Plantation and I think I might have the answer to that. She throws the lottery every month or twice a month for people. We need to all go and get in as a family. John, if you can find out when the next opening is at the Plantation, we can all get together and go. Sheriff, you coming this time for an adventure?"

"Why not? I find it interesting to follow you two around. The wife says it does me good when I go with you two. I am in a better mood for a few days." The sheriff laughs and shakes Victor's hand as he says goodbye.

"I will find out when the next opening is at the Plantation and let you know." John says as he leaves as well.

Victor lies back in the bed and relaxes thinking about what they talked about. He hears the door open. The nurse walks in the room to give him his meds and asks him what he would like to eat.

"When am I going to get out of here?"

"That is up to the doctor. I know he has a few tests for you to do yet. He wants to run some scans on you to make sure you have no damage or blood clots anywhere. Then you should go home, probably in another day or so."

Victor fills out the paper of the food request he would like for the day and takes the meds she brought. Laying his head back on the pillow, he can't help but think about Kia. *She had to have delivered the twins by now. I have let her down. I can't believe I let her down. With all the power I am supposed to have within me, why did I not even see the things right in front of me? I guess I was so focused on getting her out safely. I didn't even recognize what was going on around me. My head was in a fog. I wasn't thinking clearly and I should have been now. Kia and the twins are the ones that are suffering.*

Victor falls asleep from the medication he was given. The day now turns to night. The nurse comes to give him his diner.

"How was dinner tonight, Victor? I have your meds for the night."

"It was good, thank you. How long was I asleep?"

"Oh, I came on at three p.m., so three hours at least that I know of."

"Do you know if the doctor came to see me today?"

"I will look at your chart. Well, he did come by. He had them take you for tests."

"I don't even remember any of that."

"You were probably sleeping. That is fine. They like it when the patients are sleeping; it makes it go a little easier. He does have a note on here.

The tests look good; everything is healing well and you can check out in two days if you can walk on your own without help."

"Well, that is good to hear. Thank you."

I think over again my small adventures.
My fears, those small ones that seemed so big,
For all the vital things
I had to get and reach.
And yet there is only one great thing,
The only thing,
To live to see the great day that dawns
And the light that fills the world

Knud Rasmussen, poems of the Inuit Indians

Chapter 34

"Raven"

Alexis greets Dr. Brack promptly when he arrives at her office. Leading him to Raven, he can't believe the creature he sees. Alexis yells at him to do something to help her. Startled, Dr. Brack grabs his coat pockets looking for his tranquilizer and syringe. In the midst of fumbling to gather it and himself, he drops the bottle on the floor and it breaks.

"You idiot! Now what are you going to do to help this child? This is Raven. You have to stop this or it will kill her. She is in a fit of anger and she has shifted somehow." Alexis says.

"Calm down, Alexis. I have some in the syringe. Maybe it will be enough to subdue Raven. She is still a child. Let me see if I can get it in her without her thrashing about. She is changing into so many different creatures, but not a whole creature. She is like three or four different creatures in one. One fades and another one emerges. I have never seen this before, Alexis. This must be the combination of the hybrid DNA. It might be too strong."

Raven twists and moves about from the pain her body is going through. She spreads her wings and flaps them. They shrink, only to come back a few minutes later.

"Is she going to survive this, Dr. Brack?" Alexis says in a panic.

Suddenly the doors bust open in the office and Damien comes running in.

"What the hell did you do now, Mother?" He yells.

"Damien, help me hold her so I can get a tranquilizer in her." Dr. Brack says loudly.

Damien grabs the backside of little Raven that is now the size of a small adult woman. Her temperature is very high from the chemical changes rapidly transforming her body.

They finally get the tranquilizer in her. Alexis and Dr. Brack let go of her, but Damien still holds on hoping he can help calm her down.

Finally, Raven's thrashing slows down, as well as the changes. Her body shrinks, Damien notices as he holds her. Her fingers go back to normal. Her torso twists and shifts, then shrinks. Her ears slowly change, then her eyes, and her face.

The fur and feathers throughout her body recede along with the glowing light.

Damien feels Raven fall limp in his arms. Her picks her up and carries her to the couch.

"Get her a blanket, Mother, so I can wrap her up in it." Damien yells.

"She needs to come down and let me run tests on her in the lab to find out why this happened. Let me find something that will reverse this transformation." Dr. Brack tells Damien.

"I know. I don't want to have to say this, but you're right. Something is wrong here and she cannot go through this again. She is one hell of a strong girl, stronger than any hellhound I have ever seen in my lifetime. If so, she can survive it and she can learn and control them. However, I don't think I want to wait until the next episode to see if she can withstand it or die trying. As soon as I get her cooled down and new clothes on her, I will bring her down to you and Monroe." Damien tells him.

Alexis helps Damien wrap Raven in the blanket and wipe the sweat from her face. She puts a cool rag on her head to help lower her body temperature.

"Hey, what's up? What is going on with Raven, dude?" Lucius asks while he and Luther walk into the office. They walk over and stand behind the couch looking at her wrapped in the blanket.

"Whoa, what the heck happened to little Raven? She looks sick." Luther says.

"Yes, she is sick, boys. She is very sick." Alexis tells them and turns, putting her head in her hand and walking over to the chair.

"What is wrong with her, Damien?"

"We don't know exactly, Lucius. I heard from Ada that Raven was having some kind of fit so I raced up here. By that time, Mother had Dr. Brack ready to administer a tranquilizer to her. She shifted into so many things I couldn't even tell it was really Raven. She was taller, older. She had these wings, black, red, and silver-tipped. Her ears were like elves. Her eyes were as big as a deer. She had horns that would come and go. When they came back, they were a different type. Her skin changed from fur to feathers to — I can't even remember all of it. I just held on to her and kept saying, 'Raven honey, calm down. Daddy's here,' until she collapsed in my arms."

"So you found her like this? What could have started this? Something must have brought it on? Mother, you had her. What happened?" Luther asks.

374

"Yeah, exactly what did happen in here this morning to put her in such a fit?" Damien says.

"All right, I was watching her come across the courtyard. I noticed her tracks in the snow so I knew she snuck out and away from you and Ellie. I waited and waited until she came through the gate. She walked across, playing in the snow with her feet kicking. Then she stopped and stood there. I didn't know what she was doing. Next thing I knew, she was down on her knees. The snow just swirled slowly around her. I saw she had picked something up out of the snow and held it in her hands. Suddenly, a bright light shot out and the swirling snow fell. She stood up, lifted her arms up towards the sky, and let go of a little bird. When Gabriel brought her up, I sat down and asked her about it. She was fine until I told her never to tell anyone. Then she just snapped. Her eyes turned orange and everything in the office shook. It escalated to what you saw, Damien."

"What do you mean, she? I hate to say this, but you sound crazy, Mother, as if you're making up some crazy story. You must have yelled at her and upset her so bad that she went into a fit." Damien says angrily.

"Sounds about right to me. What about you, Luther?"

375

"All right, that is the truth, like it or not. I don't really care now. Let's get her dressed and down to Dr. Brack before she wakes up and has another fit." Alexis tells them.

"I'll take her down. You stay here, Mother. I will sit and wait with her until they are done." Damien says.

"We will go with you, Damien." Lucius says.

Damien, Lucius, and Luther take Raven down to the lab. Alexis cleans up her office when Ada calls her and tells her that the head guard Asterion needs her. Alexis quickly turns and tells the boys she will be down as soon as she can. She has to tie up a loose end.

Alexis goes out to the courtyard and walks through the side gate where Raven was that morning. Walking to the area where the guards reside in their homes, Alexis finds Asterion waiting for her. Standing with his arms folded at his chest, he is a massive creature. Even as a man, he stands over seven feet tall and is very muscular with a larger than normal rib and chest, smaller hips, medium-length brown wavy hair and dark brown eyes.

"I see you still have your shoulder in a brace, Asterion. I figured a big healthy man like yourself would be healed by now." Alexis says.

376

"Good afternoon to you too, My Lady. How have we been this morning?"

"Don't go there right now, Asterion. What is the problem? I need to be somewhere else in fifteen minutes, so make it fast."

"As you wish, My Lady. I have been doing as you instructed and I have an update for you. He is out of the hospital and home. He has a place, a cave. I followed him to where I can hear him chanting inside. He goes just about dusk and stays most of the night. There is a lot of energy and many different shifters in the area. I can smell their scent when they come close. The scents are stronger in the cave opening."

"So he is up to something after all. Hmm well, I felt he was of magic when he was at the fall festival. I just couldn't get close enough to pinpoint the right type, but now I believe I know exactly what he is. He is the other one on my list. Do not hesitate to do what has to be done. You know your orders. Carry on and if that shoulder doesn't heal up, go see Dr. Brack. Have him give you a shot of the new serum he has made with the special SB DNA we have. It will give you healing properties and strength beyond your imagination. Just keep it between the circle, or you know what happens."

Alexis walks back around and to the

courtyard. As she walks down the walkway, she sees Gabriel talking to Elsa and Dania.

"Gabriel, can I speak to you for a moment?"

Gabriel promptly answers Alexis as he rushes over to meet her, "Yes, My Lady. I am coming."

"Gabriel, I want you to take Raven and work with her. She likes you and she listens to you. She needs a friend, she needs someone she can trust other than her parents and I. She finds something special in you and you in her. I need you to work with her and get her to learn our ways. She is doing things that she shouldn't be. She has the skills to bring back the dead and I don't want her doing this!! She needs to learn my ways.

"I will have an order I want you to follow. You will check in with me on everything and every day. Report to me after you take her back. She has an anger that rages inside her that I want to control, anger like no other I have seen before. She is something special and I want to train her to be a Ravenworth, not some healer. As soon as I get her out of Dr. Brack's lab, you will take her from then on out and train her to what I instruct you to do. Understand me, or you know what will happen. Funny... I had to say that twice already today."

"Yes, My Lady. I will do as you instruct."

Alexis heads into the house while Gabriel goes back to Elsa and Dania to finish his rounds.

"Well, Mother, I see you managed to find time to come see your granddaughter when she is sick." Damien says sarcastically.

"Excuse me if I had business to handle! Dr. Brack, what have you found out so far? I would rather get the answers from you than smart ass over here."

"Yes, I understand. Well, she is perfectly fine, Alexis. There is nothing wrong with the child. The tests came back normal. She actually has several types of DNA in her body that function perfectly together, almost complementing each other in every way possible. As one would lack, the other will pick up and I have to say this... this hybrid is most outstanding. The best creature we have developed yet, My Lady."

"You just watch how you call a creature, you sick son of a bitch!" Damien bows up and steps for Dr. Brack before Alexis steps between, puts her hand into his chest deep, and cocks her head a little to the left. Her eyes swirl with black fluid filling up the whites of her eyes. Damien doesn't let it slow his anger down. He is tired of her bag of witchery tricks that she plays on the family. She isn't going to play it on his daughter's life any longer. He twists his head around and his body moves in reaction to the shifting. He suddenly changes; his face extends rapidly to a snarling vicious hellhound. His eyes turn red as fiery coals, with fur growing rapidly around his face, neck, chest, back, arms, and legs. He towers over everybody in the room by a foot and half. Raven runs and hides under one of the tables. Alexis doesn't back down from a fight. She sends a force from within through her hand into Damien, knocking him across the lab.

"I suggest you think twice who the hell you're messing with, little boy. I will send you to the crystal dungeon faster than your head can spin. You will never see Ellie or Raven again! You better lock your temper away right NOW!!" Alexis yells as she stomps towards Damien as he quickly stands and positions himself to attack.

"I am not going to let you treat Raven like a guinea pig any longer, Mother. She is a human being. She is my child. You have no right to experiment with her, and you have no right to touch her unless I allow you to do it." Damien tells her in an angered voice.

"You never had any respect for me all your life. You rebelled against me. I am your mother and I should have taught you years ago some respect. Instead, I turned my back and let you be a free soul like me, and you abused it. Well, this time you will learn to respect my authority on this matter, Damien. That is final. Do you understand me?" Alexis stands in front of Damien and with her hand and a force of white light, she lifts him off the ground, pinning him to the wall and ceiling. His chest is crushed in from the force and he gasps for air. He tries to move around still in his shifted form Alexis doesn't back down, making an example and hoping it will stick this time.

"STOP! You're hurting him!" A scream echoes loudly through the lab. Raven runs towards Alexis and Damien. Lucius and Luther turn around and grab her before she passes them.

"No, No! Let me go!!" Raven kicks and screams, trying to get free from them. They hold on to her tight.

"Don't let her go, Luther. If you do, she is going to get hurt. We will be at fault and I don't want to be the cause of that. I know, dude. I fucking know. Just help me hold onto her. She is like a snake here."

"What is that noise?"

"What noise?" Lucius asks.

"That banging noise. You don't hear it?"

"No, I am trying to hold on to her, damn it."

A loud banging echoes through the lab. Luther and Lucius look around and see the tables bouncing around on their legs. The noise gets louder, and louder. As everything lifts and slams down harder, Luther tries to cover his ears with one hand and hold Raven. Then he notices Raven's eyes are bright orange and she is staring straight at Alexis. Lucius squints with pain from the noise. Dr. Brack hides in the office with Monroe. Alexis and Damien are not even affected by the noise.

Then someone walks swiftly past them and Malik grabs Alexis from behind, twisting her in a neck hold, pinning her arms up so she cannot move. Two of the guards rush in; one grabs hold of Damien and another helps Malik with Alexis.

Dr. Brack watches and at the very moment they have them under control, he races out and injects each with a tranquilizer to calm them down and shift back to normal.

Luther and Lucius still holds Raven as she fights them to free herself, still creating the ear piercing noise within the lab. Malik lets the guard take Alexis as she falls limp, yet awake to a table. Malik turns to Raven and takes her from Lucius and Luther.

"Raven, calm down. It's okay. Your daddy is fine. He is not hurt. He is fine. He is relaxing now.

Look, I will take you to him. But you have to promise to stop this, okay? Raven, please stop banging."

The bang stops immediately when Malik picks her up and takes her to Damien. He has now changed back to himself, sitting on the floor against the wall. He is awake, but tranquilized.

"Daddy, Daddy, did she hurt you?" Raven says as she runs and hugs him.

Malik turns and looks at the guards, then around the room, and then at Dr. Brack and Monroe, shaking his head.

"What the hell?"

"Malik, I have..."

"No, don't even give me that, Monroe. What the hell happened? What the hell set her off? She has not shifted or acted like that in years!! Since I was about five years old. This had to be something bad, especially to be against her own son."

"Malik, it was all Damien, dude. Seriously, he provoked her. We watched. He just didn't back down when she said. He shifted and threatened to take her on because he was protecting Raven." Luther said.

"OMG, all over the grandchild. I should have known. This is her hybrid, her new toy, her experiment. Well, unfortunately, Damien was actually doing the right thing for once in his life. He stood up and protected his own blood. Except, he stood up to his own mother, one too powerful for all of us put together. Okay, let's get them upstairs and in their beds. Let them sleep this off." Malik says.

Malik reaches down and picks up Raven, who is still hugging her daddy.

"Come on, Raven. We are going to take Daddy upstairs to bed. You can stay with him there. Okay? Just let the big guys in so they can take him up to his room." Malik tells her as he bends down to the floor beside her and Damien.

Raven releases Damien and hugs Malik by the neck, crying. Malik hugs her tight as he stands up.

"It is going to be okay, Raven. Trust me, he is fine."

Chapter 35

"Protecting the Clan"

In the night, I call the moon

Hearken to our Joyous tune

North, East, South, and West

Gather my brothers and sisters

Join us tonight, come and join

The sons and daughters of

Mother earth and Father Sky

Embrace us all with your watchful eye

Give us the power we all Seek

To destroy this evil that lurks

Across the land this spell will go

Rid all the bad you try to send our way

Upon your own self will hold sway

All the acts of negativity

Will now return to thee

All of your actions, thoughts and words

Of hate will now become your…

Endless Fate…

Victor Donovan…

The smell of Juniper fills the air inside the cave, candles light the walls in the big room, and the flames flicker and dance their reflections off the water in the pond where Lily and her two children sit and watch the glowworms on the cave ceiling.

Listening to Victor read the spell throughout the cave, the echo carries far deeper and higher than within the walls of the cave. The spell flows with the wind, stirred as he conjures the spirit animals and the four elements when he first speaks the words in the ceremonial room. Victor's presence has been felt in here for the past few days as he has been trying to gain his powers back to get Kia and the twins out of the Plantation.

Tonight, he asks for the protection of the clan, for all to have protection and anything evil to be sent back. When they go to battle, they will have the power of their spirit animals to help them, to guide them, and the ones that are to join from other places will have protection from the ways of the warlock.

Victor almost completes his ceremony when Kane comes into the room. He stands in front of the steps leading up to the area Victor stands and watches for the first time the magic, the energy that builds and strengthens within Victor. He can feel the air electrifying with the energy of it. The hairs stand all over him like someone pulling a bunch of little strings tied to all the hairs and gently pulling all at once. The white and glowing amber lights swirl around above Victor in air. Lightning dances from the energy within, creating more power and strength illuminating the area in the room.

Kane stands with his arms folded, watching the show. He sees Lily and her kids out of the corner of his eye as they dive back into the water. He turns his head curiously.

'Hmm, now why did they do that?' Suddenly Kane smells something. The hairs on his back and neck stand straight up; he clinches his fists and lowers his head, tensing up in a defense mode as he rushes out of the cave toward the scent.

Outside, Kane gets a good smell of an odor coming from the south winds blowing towards them. A strong musky male odor, much like a bull except it has the tainted smell of human intertwined in it — a shifter.

He leaps up the rocks on the side of the cliff to reach the top of the ridge overlooking the creek and cave. Once on the top, he can smell the odor stronger and closer; whatever it is, it is coming their way.

Kane leaps back down and across to the other side of the creek. Going to the ridge on the other side, he can see them coming, but they can't get a good smell of him; he waits until he sees them coming into view.

A dark outline crests over the top of the south ridge; the moonlight shines through the trees, casting the perfect outline on the creature moving up on the rocks. Kane sees a pair of pointed horns cresting, followed by a massive outline of a head and a big body attached. He watches as the creature stands and looks down the creek. As he turns his head to the side, he can see a shiny ring reflect the light dangling from his nose. The steam rolls off from the heat of its body in the moonlight, reflecting behind him.

"*Goddamn, you're a big son of bitch!*" Kane mutters to himself.

The creature looks across towards Kane; he can see him raise his head and smell the air as if he has caught a brief smell of him. When he lowers his head, he sees two glowing orange eyes.

A snort echoes out through the woods. The big creature makes it known he has detected a scent of another shifter. Kane is sure it is him, but doesn't know what he will do yet. Kane waits to see if the creature will take try to fight or leave and return with his findings. Kane knows exactly where the creature has came from. He is the one that has been coming around for the past few months; the scent is very strong now he is present instead of days or weeks old.

Both of them instinctively know they are watching each other; they both feel the presence of each other. Either one will challenge, however it is not a fight the massive beast seeks, but a human; he knows the human he seeks has protection now.

Kane moves into the moonlight, becoming visible to his threat. He can see the creature's head and eyes lock upon him as he steps into the light of the moon. Kane stands tall and crosses his arms to indicate he is not intimidated at all by him or his size. The creature watches him for a moment, and then makes a growling moan and spins around, walking back down the ridge, returning to the south.

As he turns gracefully, Kane can see his upper body — the details of the muscle structure, the hair, some of the details of the face structure. The horns are the most prominent thing, thick, U-shaped, coming right out of the topsides of the skull, perfectly centered. The ears are small yet not human shaped, like a leaf oblong with more of a rounded point. The neck is thick, so thick there is no difference between that and the shoulders. The side of the face is somewhat extended and with an angled thicken jaw, broad nose by the length of the ring that hangs from it. He can see semi-long hair just shy of the shoulders fly up in the movement, as he thrusts his head around. Just as the light moves past the creature's arm, Kane catches a glimpse of a marking, but cannot make it out.

Kane waits until the scent of the creature completely fades away before taking a chance and heading down towards the cave, and Victor. Keeping the creature focused on him was the best defense Kane can use to protect Victor, especially while Victor focuses on gaining power for him and the whole clan.

Kane makes his way back down to the creek to wait for Victor. He shifts back to human form with just a twist of the head and move of the shoulders. He has been doing it so long and so much, it is like second natural.

Walking in through the cave, he can see the light of the candles still in the distance. Walking into the big room, Kane turns and looks to the left towards the pond. Victor is next to him inside a den made within the rock. As he turns and walks over to watch Victor, he sees something to the right. Defensive, he can't smell it, but he can see only slight movement; it blends in so well with the background. The one thing he can see is the piercing red eyes.

The creature clings to the wall, bobbing back and forth, watching Victor. Then he watches Kane glare at him. Kane walks towards the pond to get a closer look at the creature. He unhooks his small flashlight he has fastened to his belt and shines it up at the creature. The creature squeals and covers his eyes with one hand. Kane can't believe what he sees.

The creature hangs by one arm, kicking himself off the wall and onto a landing, darting down into a tunnel. Kane looks all around to see where it went when he feels someone tap him on the shoulder.

Kane jumps and spins around with an instant shift into his werewolf form, set to attack his opponent. A deep growl echoes through the cave from within his chest.

"Whoa! Hold on! What has got you on edge, my friend?" Victor asks.

Kane shakes his head and laughs.

"Goddamn, Victor, you just scared me. For once, I was totally taken off guard and that is very unlikely to do."

"What has you so on edge, Kane?"

"Are you done? I will tell you as we head back to the cabin."

"Yeah, I am done. Do you want to stay in the cabin? John made it with two bedrooms."

"I think I better. You have a tag, or shall I say a scout, sent out for you from that woman."

"Oh, she is still trailing me. After the hospital, I figured she would have thought I was dead."

"She might; I don't know. He has been sent to find out for sure and if he finds you, I am sure he aims to kill you or bring you back to her. So we need to get this show on the road soon, along with getting Kia out of that place, Victor. This is getting intense."

They walk up the ridge and back over to the other cabin that John had built for Kia as he promised her before she left for Virginia. It is a good thing too; Victor is using it. He is also keeping an eye on the property while John is back in Colorado for the holidays and work.

"Want a beer, water, soda, or tea?" Victor asks Kane.

"Water will be fine. Thanks."

"What is the creature she sent after me, Kane?"

"You have been around a while, right? You know the different creatures, history, etc."

393

"Yeah, actually I have and I do know all kinds of different creatures, shifters and yet, there are still new ones I don't know."

"The one that seeks you out is the leader, the one who leads the team of Minotaur's. He is the biggest, the bravest, the strongest, and he will fight for her every wish. They are dedicated creatures to the one who commands them." Kane tells him.

"My powers are strong now that I have sent a spell to protect us all against her and help battle her dark army. I can now call in the people to help us. Dr. Redbone has been talking with the world medicine man and he has an assistant that is of Dragon-born. Have you ever met one, Kane?"

"A Dragon-born? OMG! No, I have never met one. As a youngster, my pack would take Warrick and me along with some of the other family members for runs at night under the full moon. We would go to the edge of Lake Santeetlah in North Carolina where we lived, not too far from home, and take a break from the run. Warrick and I were just pups so when the adults would talk, we listened closely. They told us a story that I always remembered about a Dragon-born they had seen battling another shape shifter. They told us they have the body of a man or woman, but their soul is of the great dragon. They shift only when provoked to battle or war. They don't ever shift for pleasure or fun; that is forbidden within the Dragon-born. They aren't just your typical shape shifter — it is the assassins of shifters across the lands. They are rare and for a great reason. There cannot be two Dragon-born shifters in the same area; they will fight each other to death and nothing can stop them. No great power, no witch, wizard, shifter, or human.

"When they shift, they have the face structure of a human, but the skin on their bodies develops scales like a dragon. They can be hot or cold-blooded. They have DNA of many different reptiles and animals. They can even camouflage themselves like a chameleon. Their size is unbelievable. They reach heights of nearly ten feet and the wings are even bigger. The legs, feet, and hands change to those of a dragon, and they can breathe fire. They are the bounty hunters; they are the ultimate slaying machines of the shifters. The only thing that does kill a Dragon-born is a sword made out of the special metal one of the rarest metals on earth Iridium ore. That is if you are lucky enough to get close enough to do it and have the resources. Iridium ore is linked to the dinosaurs and the decomposition with the earth's crust."

"So in other words, it is nearly impossible to take the Dragon-born out when we get Kia? I just hope they are able to take the biggest of the creatures she has down before they come at any of us. We have a lot of power and many different shifters are coming to help, but after looking at the Minotaur's and the Tatonka's. I don't know. That is four massive creatures, and pissed off is a whole different ball game." Victor says.

"Yes, you are right, Victor, but I think we will manage to hold our share of the fight. By the way, when is this all going to happen anyways? Have you heard anything on a time or date?" Kane asks.

"We have decided that on the transition of the New Year would be less likely they would think of an attack. They would not expect us to be there during the celebration of the New Year. This way we all can gather inside the Plantation without any problems and it will be nighttime." Victor says.

"I thought they had a lottery to let people in for this event." Kane asks.

"No, not for the celebrations like the fall festival. She opens her gates and that is what we need to walk right in."

"Are you sure you will get past the guards, Victor? They already know you from the last time and now she has her man Minotaur hunting you. She will know and be on alert." Kane replies.

"Yes, you are right. That is exactly what we need to distract her from the rest of the clan coming in. She will have everybody in her security following me and she will try to get me, not paying any attention to the others."

"You know, you are absolutely correct. That is the perfect plan. She won't have a clue all of the rest are involved to free Kia and the twins."

Chapter 36

"Raven, Rayne and River"

"Good morning, Ada." Gabriel says with a big smile on his face as he rushes around the kitchen with the cooks, preparing breakfast for everyone in the house.

"Well, good morning, Gabriel. You are up early this morning, and cooking? Wow that is... hmmm... well, I say it is a great thing and a great way to start the day in such a happy go lucky attitude. We have a lot to discuss later, if you don't mind setting up an appointment in my office later today. To go over this New Year's Eve party she has coming up."

"No, not at all, Ada. I will be happy to go over it with you." Gabriel replies and hands her a cup of coffee.

"Oh, thank you. Wow, you are really chipper today, Gabriel." Ada says as she turns and walks out of the kitchen towards her office.

Gabriel takes Alexis' morning tray filled with coffee, tea, juice, Danish, eggs benedict for two, and fresh flowers from the garden. He gets to start his day working with Raven from this day forward. He will be the one responsible for how she acts and contains her anger around others. His job is to make her a kind and caring person. If he can't, Alexis will have to put a controlling device in her to control her anger.

"Good morning, My Lady. How is your day so far? Did you sleep well My Lady?" Gabriel asks as Alexis opens the door for him to come in the bedroom and place the tray on the table.

"I am fine, Gabriel," she replies.

"Good to hear, My Lady. Will Raven be joining you for breakfast this morning, My Lady?"

"Yes, she is and we need to talk about something while you are here."

"Why yes, My Lady."

"I am going to have two more children for you to work with soon. They will be Raven's brother and sister as far as she knows. Make sure you do not make her think any different, you understand?"

"Yes, My Lady. I understand."

"Raven doesn't know about them yet. I was going to tell her over breakfast this morning and have you go down with Damien and get them. Dr. Brack and Monroe. Damien should be here in a few minutes with Raven."

Before Alexis could ask Gabriel to sit down and wait, there's a knock at the door. Gabriel opens the door to see Damien and Raven standing there. Raven's eyes widen and a big smile comes across her face.

She grabs Gabriel by his leg and hugs him.

"Oh my, Raven, how are you feeling?" Gabriel asks as he rubs his hand on her head.

"I feel great, Gabriel. Are we going to play today? I miss playing with you."

"Yes, we get to spend most of the day together. Isn't that fantastic?"

Raven gets a bigger smile on her face and Damien grabs her by the hand and walks her into the room, lifting her up on the chair and setting up her breakfast.

"I can handle this, Damien. You go and take Gabriel down and get the things I need, okay?" Alexis says.

Damien nods his head and kisses Raven on the forehead.

Silences all the way down the corridor, the stairs, down the hallway to the lab. Just before turning the first corner, Gabriel asks Damien.

"What are we to do with these two new children, Damien?"

"What did Mother tell you, Gabriel?"

"Just that I will be watching them along with Raven from now on."

"Then that is exactly what you will do and you will not tell Raven anything about where these two children came from."

"I don't know where they came from. Alexis never told me anything."

"I am not sure I should tell you anything either if she hasn't said a word. I can tell you they will be staying with Ellie, Raven, and I. They will become our children and Raven's brother and sister. They are still young, and they are shifters, much like Raven. They are part of a different breed. Please be careful and they are not to be left alone or talked about to anybody. Do you understand?"

"Yes, sir. Damien sir. I understand."

Damien rings the buzzer on the lab door. Gabriel hates going to the lab; that fear will never leave him. The fear of torture, the fear of being killed by the hands of Monroe and Dr. Brack, but he cannot show fear. One thing Damien can sense being a hellhound is the smell of fear and if he smells it on Gabriel, he will know he is remembering past events. That is forbidden in the Plantation with the creatures. Especially the ones they turn from human to creature.

The door buzzes and Damien turns the handle, walking in with Gabriel right behind him like a shadow.

Slow down. Slow down. Act normal. Everything is fine. Gabriel says repeatedly in his head.

"Hi, Damien, Gabriel. How are you guys this morning?" Monroe asks.

"Good so far." Damien says with a short response.

"Here are your two new family members." Monroe walks out two tiny children with long black hair, one has green eyes, and one has a blue and a green eye.

"OMG! Twins? They look just alike, except for the eyes." Damien says.

"Yes, they are twins. Identical twins. A boy and a girl. They girl has the blue and green eyes. This will help you remember who is who. We called them number 1 and number 2. We didn't know what else to call them. We figured Alexis was going to do something other than what she has planned. They are a bit distant from humans because we really don't interact with them. As you know, it isn't our thing down here to get attached to any of these creatures that we create."

"Yeah, I understand what heartless bastards you two are. I will take the children, Monroe. Thanks so much for your time. I know how busy you are." Damien says with a sarcastic voice and takes the two children from him. After picking one up and handing him to Gabriel, Damien picks the other one up and turns towards the lab door. Dr. Brack walks out from the office.

"Oh, hello, Damien. I see you came to take our experiments away. Tell Alexis we found the exact type of creature that feather came from that she brought me."

Damien just keeps walking out the lab door and down the corridor.

"I swear one day I will tear them two apart. I hate them two sons of a bitch. They are the sickest individuals I have ever met."

"Yes, sir. I agree they are horrible and cruel." Gabriel replies in a soft broken voice.

"Raven honey, Grandma needs to tell you something, okay?"

"Okay, Grandma."

"You are going to have a brother and a sister. How do you feel about that?"

Raven puts her fork down and looks over at Alexis, surprised. Eyes widen, mouth open, then a huge smile comes across her face. "Really, Grandma?"

"Yes, your daddy and Gabriel are bringing them up right now."

"Oh, I can't wait."

Raven tries to climb out of the chair. "First, you must finish your breakfast, honey. Okay?"

"Okay, Grandma."

Alexis walks over and calls Ada on the phone.

"Hi, Ada. I need you to send up two more breakfasts and juices to my room immediately."

Damien and Gabriel finally get back to Alexis' bedroom with the twins. Raven climbs out of the chair as they set them down and stands next to Alexis.

"Grandma, are these my brother and sister?"

"Yes, Raven, this is your new brother and sister."

"But, Grandma, they look alike? And why does the one have two different colored eyes?"

"Raven, they are twins, identical twins. They are very special; they share the same thoughts, the same feelings, and a lot of other things."

"Do I share that with them, Grandma?"

"Well, you might. You will have to see as you grow and play with them. They haven't been around anybody like you or your dad before. You need to show them how to play and act, okay? You need to take care of them and teach them how to do things like talk, play, color, and play with toys."

"Can I show them the animals outside?"

"No, let's not do that yet, honey. They have to get used to it here first, okay?"

"Okay, Grandma."

Raven walks over and stands in front of the twins. Damien and Gabriel stand behind the twins and Alexis is behind Raven.

They stare back at Raven when suddenly she speaks and says, "This one is Rayne and he is River."

"What... what did you just say, Raven?" Damien asks.

"Her name is Rayne and his name is River."

"How do you know this, Raven? Are you making their names up? I think your mother and I need to choose the correct name for them, honey." Damien says.

"They just told me, Daddy."

"They did what? How did they tell you their names, Raven? Alexis asks.

"In my head."

Alexis looks up at Damien and Gabriel with her eyes wide. Damien stares back blankly at first, and then he turns to a smirk and giggle silently. Gabriel just stands there, shocked. He can't believe that he witnessed this between these kids.

"Can we have a minute please, Damien? Gabriel, Ada is sending food up for the twins. Can you put them at the table and get them ready to eat?"

"Yes, My Lady."

Gabriel takes the twins over to the table and puts them in the chair one by one, sliding them in. A knock at the door and Raven runs to answer it, struggling to pull the door open and two servants stand there with trays of food.

"Come in." Raven tells them.

They walk over and set the trays on the table while Gabriel takes the plates and puts them in front of each child. Setting the juice and silverware up for them to eat, he tells them to eat as much as they like.

Alexis takes Damien in her bedroom area within the massive bedroom and closes the door.

"Do you know what we have here? Did you see what just happened out there?"

"Yes, Mother. I saw the whole thing. I thought it was amusing honestly. All this time, you are dead set on making this hybrid shifter and here your own granddaughter is becoming everything you wanted to design. You are NOT going to use her for any experiments. You're not going to use her as a guinea pig… period!" Damien says with an angered voice.

"I wasn't planning on that, Damien. I wanted to talk to you about the twins. How do they already know their names? Where did they even get their names? And if they can mind read and communicate mentally, we have to find a way to suppress it. That means they can communicate with the mother and the father. He got away this time. Remember?"

"Oh yes, the father. He would be looking for him. I thought you had Asterion take care of the father?"

"I did, but unfortunately he lived. I sent him back about two weeks ago and he found something protecting him. Something I would never have guessed was in Kentucky."

"And what would that be?"

"A werewolf."

"A what? A werewolf? Are you kidding me? Where the hell did he come from?"

"I don't know, but he is in that Beaver Creek you guys got the silver-blood from."

"By the way, where is their mother?"

"Whose mother?"

"The twins. Where is their real mother? We brought her in. What did you have them do to her?"

"She is locked away deep in the Plantation, alive but hidden and locked away. They will never find her."

They walk out of the bedroom and see Gabriel has all three of the children at the table eating.

"Gabriel, can you send someone up with fresh clothes for these two?"

"Yes, My Lady. I will do that right now." Gabriel says and walks out the door.

Gabriel has to meet Ada anyways to discuss the new event coming up. He walks to her office and sees she is on the phone.

"Hi Gab, what are you up to?" Ada asks.

"Alexis wants you to send someone up with clothes for two children."

"Two children? Wait… where did she get two children? Or should I even ask this question?"

"Long story. I think she needs to explain this one to you, Ada."

"Okay, I understand. She must want this to be a secret?"

"No, they will not be a secret, but where or what they are will be a secret."

"I understand, Gabriel. Do you know how big the children are?"

"They are smaller than Raven by a few inches."

"Okay, I will call Zoey and have her take some up right away."

"So we need to discuss the new event. I need some details from you. I have a list here from Alexis of all the things she wants done in the grounds and what decorations to be put up. I will handle all vendors and that part of it. You handle the outdoor decorations, the gardens as usual, and the guards. I will have some of the others helping inside and out. Does that sound good to you so far?"

"Yes, that is fine. I know the decorations she wants to place at the gate and through the grounds. I will have no problems, Ada."

"Okay, that is all I needed from you, Gabriel."

Gabriel gets up and starts to walk out the door. "Thank you, Gabriel."

"You're welcome, Ada. Anytime."

Gabriel goes outside to conduct his business for the day so he can get back and take the children before Alexis has to do her rounds this afternoon.

In the main garden, he assigns Dania and Elsa to work with the plants within the house. He instructs them to cut the flowers in the morning and bring the arrangements they make and place them throughout the house. They also take care and replant the flowers along the borders of the house.

With no snow on the ground today, the sun is bright in the sky helping it keep him somewhat warm in the cold breeze.

"Hi Dania, Elsa, how are the gardens today?"

"Hi, Gabriel," they both say. "We are going to need some more fertilizer for the plants."

"Okay, I am making a list. I will have someone get some from town. Is there anything else you need?"

They both look down and hesitate for a moment.

"Are you girls all right?"

They look at each other and look back at Gabriel with a blank look on their faces. Finally, Dania says, "No not really Gabriel."

"What is wrong? You must tell me so I can have something done."

"No, Gabriel, there is nothing you can do for us."

"What do you mean, Dania?"

They both look at each other again before putting their heads down.

"We are both pregnant." Elsa tells him.

"You're what? I mean how… Oh I see."

Gabriel just realized that the girls have been impregnated with a shifter DNA that Dr. Brack and Monroe has conjured up in the lab. Dania and Elsa are the newest recruits. He knows all too well what happens to the young girls that suddenly become servants. They usually all have offspring a few times a year or until they die.

"Do you have any memories of any events other than here?"

"No, all we remember is being here. Why? Are we supposed to remember something or someplace else?" Elsa asks.

"No, just asking. Sometimes pregnancies make you think strange things. I was just checking. I will have Lucas help you with the heavy stuff. You two just focus on the cutting and arranging."

"Okay, thank you, Gabriel."

"Anytime. Just let me know if you have any other problems, girls. Good day."

Chapter 37

"DNA Testing"

Alexis swings through the door of Ada's office.

"Ada, oh, did I catch you off guard? Sorry dear, I will be down in the lab and I have some other things to attend to further. Please take all messages for me today. Also, can you keep an eye on Gabriel? He has his hands full. I have him watching three kids now. This will be his daily chore between eleven a.m. and five p.m."

"Oh, yes, My Lady, no problem. I will keep an eye on him."

"Thank you, Ada." Alexis walks out of the office.

"My Lady,"

"Yes," Alexis turns back around just outside the doorway of Ada's office.

"I need to ask you about the New Year's Eve event. Are you planning to have a dinner buffet, or are you going to have some other means of food?"

"We will have a buffet. We always have a buffet. That is why people come from miles around — to eat the finest buffet food. If they only knew what they were eating."

"Okay, that is fine. I need to know what exactly you want to serve as the main course for the buffet this time. And are you going to do a walk through the gardens beforehand earlier in the day?"

"Yes, I will do my ordinary walk-through with the guests. I know we will have a lot, but that is fine. And for the main course, we need a big creature, don't we? Hmmm, we will use one of the Minotaurs. I will arrange a fight or something as a demonstration early to get it ready for the kitchen by brunch. Sound good?"

"Oh, yes, My Lady. Sounds perfect. Thank you."

Ada watches Alexis leave, standing by her desk. *She is so heartless, simply cruel.*

"It's only a matter of time before they figure out you and Gabriel." A voice whispers in her ear. Ada jumps and turns around.

"What? What did you say? Who are you? Why do you keep haunting me with these things? How do you know these things about me?" Ada says as she closes the door of her office. Looking around the office, she sees nothing, but feels a presence near. She just can't tell who it is. The voice is female. Ada knows someone or something has been watching Gabriel and her.

Alexis heads down the corridor to the stairway down to the lab. Ringing the buzzer outside the door and waiting for someone to buzz her in. She rings the buzzer again. Tapping her foot in anticipation, she grabs her phone to call Dr. Brack to see what is going on. Just as she goes to hit the dial button, Monroe comes up behind her.

"Alexis, how long have you been waiting?"

"Holy shit, Monroe! What the hell are you doing?"

"I just went up to the kitchen to get some food. Dr. Brack is sleeping."

"Well, that is why nobody is answering the goddamn buzzer then. Okay. Unlock the door."

She steps aside to let Monroe unlock the door. She has a key but she figured someone was in the lab working. They walk in past the stainless steel tables lined up perfectly at the sink bays on the right and far left of the room. In the middle, they are scattered about in rows. Nothing on them, everything has been cleaned.

"Come in here, Alexis. What is it that you need? Can I help you or do you want me to wake Dr. Brack?"

"No. I just wanted to come down here and see about the feather. What exactly did you find?"

Monroe walks quietly in the office, sets down the food on the table, and walks back out, closing the door so they don't wake up Dr. Brack.

"Oh, that golden feather! Yes, that is amazing. Come over here and I will show you on the computer the analysis we found."

They walk over to the chemistry lab set up. The best money can buy. Computers for DNA testing, splicing, and combining the different shifters, humans, and creatures.

"I am glad you two are utilizing the equipment I spent a fortune on."

"Yes, this equipment is top notch, but we have a request to make, My Lady. We need a lab assistant, somebody who can help do the little stuff, like gather samples, draw blood, organize, wash the equipment, feed the shifters, creatures, and other things in here." Monroe asks.

"I think I can arrange that. I have a few people in mind. I will run it through Ada and see what she

417

has on the employee list that would fit exactly. Okay, now back to the feather."

"Yes, this is the DNA sample. Look in here, and then look here at the SB DNA combined with the DNA of the feather. Do you see how the DNA changes?"

"Wow, this is fascinating, Monroe! The DNA is totally reconstructed. It is bigger, and stronger. The colors within are almost glowing neon. Is this good, Monroe? I don't want a shifter that is going to look like it came from a chemical spill."

"Yes, My Lady. It will be perfectly fine. We already have two specimens with this DNA growing in them. We will have offspring soon."

"Who did you implant this DNA into, Monroe? And why are they not here in the lab?"

"We put the DNA in the two specimens that your sons brought back a few months ago. The ones with Ellie and the silver-blood that had the twins. We figured you wanted it to be tested right away. Now that we have the SB DNA, we can start building the army you wanted. Remember this has been your missing link; this is why you put a hold on making any other shifters, except for the ones we have within the Plantation that you use for the Lottery and staff."

"I understand this, Monroe, but what I remember of these two girls, they were not the type to be carrying such a priceless piece of DNA!! You could have found two better, stronger specimens than these two skinny young girls. What if they can't carry this type of creature? What if it is too powerful, too big?"

"It is okay, My Lady. We are monitoring them twice a day and they are doing just fine. They are accelerating just as they should. Would you like to see them and their progress since we started the implants?"

"Yes, actually I would; this shifter you have spliced together with them is one that has not been around for over a hundred or more years and this is very, very special. You have no clue what this will bring us when we need it to battle or to find anything outside the Plantation walls. This shifter will give us the bird's eye view of any threat that is outside of these gates."

"Yes, My Lady. I understand your concern. Let me show you the progress we have on the girls. Come look here at the files. This one is Dania; she has perfect blood analysis. The offspring is one month old and accelerating nicely. We are giving her extra injections of liquid vitamins and minerals to help with the pregnancy and the rapid growth of the offspring. This here is Elsa; she is pretty much the same but the offspring in her is a few centimeters smaller than the other one in Dania. Now, the only thing we can think is it is a different sex, possibly a female. We will know in about a week when we get the samples done that we just took this morning."

"Interesting. I do have to say, Monroe. Have you completed an ultrasound yet, to see the shapes or the structure inside?"

"Yes, actually we did this yesterday. Here, I have the papers in each file. See, this is what is strange. It is more creature than human. Usually it doesn't show this much of the creature in the development stage. We think it is the SB mixed in with it, causing the DNA structure to have changed. This is the result of the hybrid within them."

"Yes, I can see the skeleton. It is definitely a Harpy. The structure difference in the legs from the knee down is like a long foot with long toes, which will be claws. Big claws. Notice there are no full arms? Just small wings but you can see the bone structure in the folds. Let me look at the bigger one. Yes, this one is different. Wow! Look at this one closely, Monroe. Do you see the difference in them now? This one has a very different skeletal structure altogether. This isn't so much a male as it is a very different Harpy altogether. This one has arms and wings, and it looks like it has an extended tailbone. How far along are these two?"

"They are about a month into their pregnancy and they should only be about a month or month and half out." Dr. Brack says as he walks into the lab and over to the table where Alexis and Monroe are examining the ultrasound readings.

"Dr. Brack, how nice of you to join us, but I must say I have spent too much time here already. Thank you, Monroe, for the tour and the insight on the new shifters. Please keep me updated when they are to give birth. I want to be notified as soon as possible. Also, I will get you what you asked for earlier, Monroe. Give me a few days and I will have some assistants here. I must be going. Nice to see you, Dr. Brack."

"Nice to see you as always, My Lady." Monroe says as Alexis walks out of the lab.

"What the hell does she want to know all of this stuff for and why did you show here all this?" Dr. Brack asks.

"Because she came down here while I was out getting food from the kitchen. I came down the corridor and she was pounding on the door and buzzer, expecting me to open it. She wanted to ask you about the feather so I showed her what we found and the samples. I told her we have it in experiment right now and one thing led to another. She knows the creature this came from. She knows that each one is a different species. Something I didn't know. She also clarified why one is small than the other one."

"Yes, Monroe. Alexis has more knowledge about things than you will ever know. You haven't been around as long as I have and you haven't worked with her for as many years as I have either. Just remember what I am and how long I have lived, my good friend."

Dr. Brack pats Monroe on the shoulder, walks over to the microscope, and places a slide he had in his hand under the scope. Still studying the images from the ultrasound, Monroe is fascinated with the formation they have growing inside them. He can't wait to see what they will actually look like when they are out.

Chapter 38

"Back Home"

"Finally, we are back in Beaver Creek, guys. Wake up. We are stopping at Nell's Diner for breakfast before heading to the property."

Kyle and Jake are sleeping in the backseat of the truck and Lizzie is sleeping in the front. They are just returning from Colorado for the holidays. Victor had called John and explained that they will be going to the New Year's celebration on the Plantation. The world medicine man is coming to town on the twenty-seventh and they will be preparing everybody for the next three days.

John doesn't want to let Victor down. He wants to be there for him when this all goes down, knowing that it can be one heck of a battle to get Kia and the twins out of the Plantation, if she is still there alive.

"Okay, let's go, guys. Wake up. Let's get some grub in them bellies. We are going to have a lot of work to do and it is going to snow this afternoon."

The two boys climb out of the backseat and stagger up to the door behind John and Lizzie. Kyle rubs his eyes and looks across the diner at the people seated, having breakfast. As he looks through the people, his eyes stop on a young girl sitting alone with a cup of coffee and staring right at him. Suddenly Kyle realizes she is staring at him, shifting his eyes away and back to his parents.

Where do I know her from?

"Have a seat wherever you'd like." Nell yells out from behind the counter.

They all sit down at a table, with Kyle positioned where he can look at the girl.

Nell brings a pot of coffee over and fills John and Lizzie's cups. Jake holds his up for a cup also.

"Do you all know what you'd like to order?" Nell asks.

"I think we are ready." John says.

Lizzie orders, and then Jake, John, and Kyle just stare out across the diner.

"Kyle, what do you want to order?" Lizzie asks.

"Ah, yes the Lumberjack and sausage, instead of ham, with a large orange juice."

"Okay, it will be up in about fifteen minutes. I will be right back with your drinks." Nell walks back to the kitchen.

Kyle, still lost, stares at the girl across the diner. She looks up at him and smiles. Kyle suddenly feels flush and hot, embarrassed that he is busted for staring at her again, but he can't help it. Something about her eyes, he knows her from somewhere and it is driving him crazy. He fumbles for his phone after she notices him staring again.

He plugs in his ear buds and tunes on his music player, hoping he can forget about that girl. Jake surfs through his phone, texting friends as usual.

Kyle finishes eating some of his breakfast and plays with his phone. He texts Kassidy, telling her he is back.

"So how was your trip to the freezing cold snowy Colorado, bro?" Kassidy texts.

"It was exactly that, punk. Freaking freezing my ass off. LOL."

"So you are back in town? Your GPS on the messenger app is saying you're in Beaver Creek."

"Yep, just got into town about forty-five minutes ago. At Nell's Diner, getting some grub before heading home. So what are you doing later?"

"Nothing. Why? You have a plan? You want to hang out? I can get my mom to bring me over." Kassidy messages back.

"Yeah, that would be cool. We can find some cool things to do down at the cabin. Maybe hang out for dinner?"

"Cool, bro. See you then." Kassidy replies.

"Later, dude." Kyle texts.

Kyle sets his phone on the table and acts as if he is playing with the music. He turns it to the back camera, aiming at the girl he has been staring at. She looks out the window next to her, not facing him at the moment. He waits for her to turn back around and look at him. There is just something strange about her eyes they look so familiar and they draw you into them. Finally, she turns around. Kyle quickly snaps the camera several times to get as many pictures as he can in those few seconds.

Shit! She is looking right at the camera. Oh, she knows! Shit! Kyle moves the phone off the table so fast he knocks over a drink.

"KYLE!! What are you doing, son?!" John says as everybody jumps up, trying to get out of the way of the water that he just spilled all over the table.

"Well, I am glad we are done eating our breakfast before you decided to do that." Lizzie says.

"Sorry, Mom. I was about to drop my phone. I didn't mean to knock over the water." Kyle says.

He looks over at the girl and she is gone. He stops cleaning up the water and looks all around the diner, trying to find where she went. He doesn't see her anywhere.

Maybe she went to the bathroom.

"What is wrong with you, dude? Did you see someone that doesn't like you or something?" Jake says and laughs.

"Okay, boys, let's go outside to the truck. We have to go to the store yet. Here Lizzie, take the keys. I will be right out." John says as he gets up and walks to the cash register.

"Sorry about the mess. My son was playing with his phone when he knocked over the glass of water. We tried to clean it up the best we could." John tells Nell.

"Oh, no problem, John. We get accidents all the time. You have a good day and stay warm. Happy New Year." Nell says.

"Thanks, Nell. Happy New Year to you guys too."

Kyle walks out behind his mom while Jake still looks around for that girl in the parking lot. He doesn't see her anywhere. *Why can't I get her out of my head?*

He opens the door and gets in the backseat. Closing the door, he looks up and here she comes. She walks right past him in the truck. Looking at him the whole time.

Kyle has a blank look on his face as he watches her. Staring in her eyes, he suddenly sees them flash an amber glow at him.

"What the hell?" Kyle mumbles.

"What did you say, dude?" Jake asks.

"Are you all right, Kyle? You're acting awful strange ever since you woke up." Lizzie says and turns to the back to look at Kyle and Jake.

"Yeah, yes, I am fine, Mom." Kyle says as he watches out the window as the girl walks across the parking lot to a car and gets in it.

"Dude, man, what is up, bro? You know that chick or something? You have been staring at her since we got here and now she followed you out." Jake asks.

"I don't know. I think so but I can't remember where I know her from. It is driving me crazy." Kyle replies.

"Is that what you been doing, Kyle? Looking at that girl in the restaurant? For heaven's sake, knocking over drinks and everything. You need to grow up, son. Don't let your dad know. He will be upset with you if he knows that." Lizzie says, angry.

John opens the door just as Lizzie stops talking.

"Wow, what did I miss?" John says and looks around the truck at everybody.

"Nothing, Dad." Kyle replies.

"Hmmm, okay. Well, at least your mother isn't mad at me this time."

Kyle takes the mule to the end of the driveway, meeting Kassidy and her mom on the main road to bring her back to the cabin.

It is clear and sunny skies, but the temperature is only forty-two for the high and snow is on the way tonight. Kassidy's mom says she can

429

stay the night with them. Kyle wants to go exploring for spirit animals tonight in the woods so they told her mother they would watch a movie and have a cookout after Kassidy and Kyle catch some trout at the creek today.

"So you ready to go fishing? We can fish off the bridge, and then we can sneak out tonight to the cave. My dad said there are cave creatures in there and other things. It would be awesome to see some of them." Kyle says.

"Yes, I am excited. Where is Jake?"

"Jake is back at the cabin hanging. He didn't want to go fishing. He is playing on his tablet."

They stop on the bridge and sit in the sunshine for a few hours, catching fish. They get eleven Rainbow trout out of the creek and head back up to the cabin.

"Wow, you guys you caught a lot of fish! Go clean them and I will make up a batter for them for dinner." Lizzie tells them.

After dinner, Kyle and Kassidy hang out in the cabin with Jake. Victor and Kane have one cabin and John and Lizzie is staying in the other one for now until the house is completed.

"Kassidy, do you know this girl? I saw her at the diner this morning when we came into town. I know her from somewhere. I just can't figure out where." Kyle asks and shows her the pictures he took of her on his phone.

"Hmm, she looks familiar. Let me see them again." Kassidy says and takes the phone.

"When we were leaving, she walked past the truck on my side and no kidding, her eyes flashed and amber glowed at me. I swear I am not making this up." Kyle says.

"Oh, come on, Kyle. That is so childish. You are just fascinated with a pretty girl you saw at the diner this morning. That is all. You're just horny and every girl is hot right now." Jake says.

"Shut the hell up, Jake! Really, I know this girl. I talked to her somewhere but she looks different. I can't remember what she looked like when I talked to her, but I remember her."

"Yeah, so do I. I have talked to her too. Matter of fact, I think we both talked to her and I think it was at the fall festival." Kassidy says.

"Oh yes, yes, that is it. See, Jake? I told you I knew this chick. She is the girl that brought us into the house. Damn, I am trying to think of her name." Kyle says.

431

"Shadow, her name was Shadow." Kassidy tells him.

"Yes, Shadow. She was a panther, a black panther. Oh wow, maybe she really is one and she changes like the shapeshifters back and forth." Kyle tells them.

"Oh man, will you get a hold of yourself? I mean seriously, act your age. I am going to my room. I have heard enough of this crap." Jake gets up and walks towards the stairs to go to his room. He turns to them, "Trust me, if you want the real monsters, just go down to the cave and wait. She will come out." Jake says as he walks up the stairs and closes his door.

"Wow, sorry about that, Kassidy. He just hasn't been right for a while. First at home in Colorado, then all the stuff that happened here. He started changing, but now he seems like he is his old self again. He doesn't seem to remember anything we saw at the fall festival. Do you remember all the stuff we saw?" Kyle asks.

"Yes, I remember. I remember this girl well now and she is the one I swear followed us out, watching us when we felt something staring at us during the Centaur event. Remember?"

"Yeah, I remember that. What is she doing here in Beaver Creek? And why was she making sure I noticed her?"

"I don't know, Kyle, but maybe she has something to tell you or maybe just a coincidence. She might be here shopping or visiting someone."

Kyle agrees and they decide to sneak out and go down to the creek to see if they can see any of the spirit animals and maybe that creature.

They both walk out bundled up. It is lightly snowing and cold out. It is one a.m. and everybody but Jake is asleep. They sit down by the creek across from the cave, at the picnic table John has down there. Watching and waiting for any signs of the spirit animals to come.

Then they see something move across the creek in the trees by the shoreline. A faint black outline of something they can't make out. Then it looks over towards them as if it sees them sitting there.

Kassidy nudges Kyle as they watch the black figure slowly moving back and forth on the shoreline. Then it suddenly leaps and lands on a fallen tree that is halfway across the creek, walks down the tree, leaps again, and lands on the shore just down from where they are sitting.

433

They are both frozen with fear, not sure what it is and too scared to run. They can see it better now, as it is closer. It has yellow eyes and is down on all fours looking around at everything.

It stands up quickly! Kyle and Kassidy jump. It turns and looks towards them. Kassidy shakes with fear, squeezing Kyle's hand so tight. Since her sister was killed down in the cave, she is reliving some of the memories of the events her parents told her.

It starts to walk up the hill and doesn't seem to notice them setting at the table or it just is ignoring them for some reason.

"Holy shit, Kyle. We need to get back to the cabin. I don't like this at all, not at all. This is too scary. I thought I could handle this by now, but I don't think I am over what happened to Ashley. Sorry, but can we please go back?" Kassidy says in a shaken voice.

Kyle gets up and holds her hand close. They walk back towards the cabin and with every sound, they jump and cringe, scared. Almost up to the back of the cabin, they see something moving at the back of Victor's cabin.

Under the backyard light, Kyle and Kassidy can see it standing at the edge just outside the lit area. They decide to lay low and watch what it does. It looks like it changes as it walks into the lit area.

434

They can see it change into a human as it walks towards Victor's back door.

"Did you see that? It just shifted into a human, but from what?" Kyle asks.

"Yeah, I see it and I have no clue what it was. It was too dark by the time it got in the light. It was almost completely human and it looks like a tall lady with dark hair." They both say at the same time.

"OMG! It is that lady, Kassidy, from the diner. Shadow… that is her!! What is she doing here? What is she doing at Victor's cabin?"

"I told you, Kyle. She was here to visit somebody, whoever she is."

They watch as she walks up and knocks on the back door. A light comes on by the door and they hear talking. Then they see Victor walk out and talk to her on the porch.

"He knows this woman?" Kassidy asks.

"I don't know. I guess he does." Kyle says.

They watch to see what happens and to see if they can hear what they are talking about. Then they see Kane walk out and join the conversation.

"Hi, who is this?"

"I am Shadow I followed you here a while ago. I am from the Plantation. I am a servant there. I know you are looking for someone and I am able to help you find her. In exchange, I want you to kill Alexis Ravenworth."

"Whoa! That is a pretty big request." Kane says

"Yeah, it is, but it is worth it. Kane, she knows where Kia and the twins are. She can get us to them. If we can get in, she and her friend can get us there."

"Okay, then request accepted. How do you plan on getting us to Kia?"

"I know all the corridors, secret corridors, the dungeon, the lab, the secret rooms within the Plantation, stairways, everything. Even the room she keeps the DNA frozen from every creature and shifter she captures."

"Why would you want to kill your boss? She gives you a nice home and seems to take care of you?" Kane asks.

"Because she killed my mate and served him for lunch at one of the lotteries she held. See, we

436

are captured just as your Kia was. We are tied up and drugged for days, sometimes months. Hidden in a lab down below the Plantation. She has two men running this lab — Dr. Brack and then Monroe. They use us as lab rats, testing our genes, DNA, and then they splice it with a shifter. Some of us are impregnated with it and we end up changing as the babies are born. I was injected and so was my mate. We were brought in together as a couple. They decided to experiment on us as a couple. Then one day he started having issues, flashbacks of who he was before they spliced our DNA. That is not ever supposed to happen. When it does and she finds out, she waits for the perfect moment during a lottery or event and she uses the person as a showpiece in her walk-through. The people watch the whole thing and she and the employees tell the crowd it is all an act and it is part of the event. Then, the guests eat them during the buffet and they all wonder how she has the best tasting food for the main course. If the guests only knew what they were eating. This is why I come to you; this is why I want you to kill her. I know you have the power to do it. I watched you for months now, hidden out of sight. You had no clue I was there. This is one of my abilities as a panther, and with the other DNA I have been spliced with. I can disappear without a trace right before your eyes. I see you but you can't see me. I camouflage my surroundings to hide myself."

"If you can get us in, then we will bring someone that can take care of this lady." Kane tells her.

"I promise you… this is no trick. I am doing this for revenge for my mate. She is having a New Year's Eve event; this will be the best time for you to get in. You should find your way to the house. I will meet you; you will hear me before you see me. Now I must go." Shadow turns and disappears into the night.

"So what do you think, Kane? We have been followed without even realizing it. Now I wonder how many other ones have done this? I should have picked up on them but she is different. She seems sincere."

"I smelled her around here before. I just never thought she worked at the Plantation. I thought she was another shifter living in the area for safety. This is strange, but we are going in anyways. She doesn't need to know our plan and she definitely doesn't need to know about North Carolina."

Chapter 39

"Atreyu"

"Narden, hand me that leather bound alchemy book, the one from Romania. I just got a call from no other than Dr. Redbone. Now, we were just talking about him the other day."

"Yes, Sir Atreyu, we were. How are he and the clan doing over there?"

"He has a problem, a big problem, and needs our help. He said they think they possibly have a Raven Mocker that has been designing and making different breeds of shape shifters within her Plantation. She has also kidnapped a silver-blood about three months ago that was pregnant with twins; the twins are special to the clan."

"What do you have planned, Atreyu sir."

"We will have to go through and do our research, Narden dear. This one has the ability to reproduce other shifters. She has advanced knowledge of all shape shifters, so she will know how to kill each and every one that comes for her. Remember, a Raven Mocker can go on the ground or in the air; she is a deadly force and from what Dr. Redbone has told me during our talk, she has a big army at her Plantation and four sons that are hellhounds. That is her most fearsome protection there. A hellhound born from the evils of the shape shifters, the devil himself, that is about right for a Raven Mocker. She is a stealer of souls to add lives to her own; she is the blackest of the magic in the world. We are dealing with a very powerful woman and an army to back her up. We need to be prepared."

"Where is this lady located? Did Dr. Redbone tell you, sir?"

"I believe he said in Tennessee."

"Do we have anything on this Raven Mocker other than what you have mentioned? I need to get an idea of the books we need to research and the items I will need to bring with us. You know the history I know of the Raven Mockers; they are far and few left in the world. Much like myself, there are not many Dragon-born left, only a handful and we all know one another and where we live. Raven Mockers usually live in a wide area because they do not reproduce one of their own kind for many years. With the lives they save, they usually have plenty of lives to live. That should narrow us down to about one to maybe two people in the United States that is a Raven Mocker, unless they have reproduced and there are a few others. This should not be hard to find her and the information on her family. This way we know the history."

"Very true, Narden. Why don't you start looking her up and the history of this place while I see what I will need to make."

"Dr. Redbone, how is Atreyu doing? Did he say he would be willing to come here to help us find Kia and the twins?" Dr. Whiteriver asks.

"Yes, he was actually very interested in this. It has been quite some years since he has had to chase away a Raven Mocker; he is in need of a good workout. I don't think he realizes the task he is going to tackle with this Raven Mocker. By what Victor has told me earlier today on the phone, she is some piece of work. She has more than we can imagine behind those walls."

"She has built herself an army, I am sure of it. We are going to need everybody on hand for this event. All clans need to be contacted and all of the most powerful need to come help us."

"Yes, Whiteriver. She has Minotaur's as the main guards. That is what hit Victor's truck and caused him to crash. His friend John found a piece of flesh with fur on it, stuck in the metal of the truck when they found it. He saved it to show Victor."

"This would mean she knows about Victor, if that is the case. She must have them watching him. She will wait for the right moment and will send in her evilest to take him down. He had better prepare himself for everything until we can get there. Make sure he starts practicing and strengthening himself and his magic. He is going to need Redbone more than I do. You better call his mother to make her push him."

"Do you know everybody to contact to have them ready at the moment's notice, Dr. Whiteriver?" Atreyu says.

"I will get a list together. Let me go to my office, pull out my books, and gather up the most experienced and then some. Do you have an idea when this is going to take place? Has Dr. Redbone or anyone set a date yet? I know they are eager to get this done," Narden asks.

"They are waiting for us actually. I am going to tell them in a couple of weeks, about the twenty-sixth of December. This way we can get everybody ready. We need to have everybody on hand so we can set everything up and show them the weapons. Dr. Redbone said that other clan shifters will bring many of their own weapons I will have to enchant them before they go in." Atreyu says.

"Okay, so I will start on this in the morning. Tell everybody to be there on the twenty-sixth of December. I will call Dr. Redbone also." Narden tells him.

"I will see you in the morning, my dear. Pleasant dreams."

"Thank you, Atreyu sir. You too."

Chapter40

"Things are moving ahead"

Victor's cell phone rings at seven a.m. he is still sleeping from the late night. He couldn't fall sleep after Shadow came and told him and Kane the events at the Plantation. At least now, he knows he has a friend; hopefully she stays true to it to get them into the area Kia and the twins are in.

Reaching for his phone, he looks at the screen. Three missed calls from Dr. Redbone. Victor steps into the bathroom. Kane must not be up, as he doesn't smell the coffee brewing yet.

Slipping on his shorts and a shirt, he walks out to the kitchen. The morning sun shines in the kitchen windows where the dining room table sits. He starts making a pot of coffee and sits down at the table, waiting for it.

Looking out the window, he can see the pasture. The fog hangs just a few feet above the ground, thick like a cloud. The deer are feeding as snow blankets the ground this morning. Icicles hang off the edge of the porch roof.

Victor gets up, pours a cup of coffee, and heads back to the table, thinking about what Shadow was saying last night.

"Good morning." Kane says as he walks in the kitchen and pulls a cup off the hook from under the cabinet.

"Good morning, Kane."

"So what do you think about this Shadow and her story, Victor?"

"Not sure. I think she has sincerity. She seems to want revenge over her mate which I can understand."

"I was thinking of this all night. I hardly slept a wink. I think we will go forward and if she is in there when we get inside the house, great. If not, we didn't plan on anyone's help anyways. We must stay focused on the goal and not let anything interrupt this plan."

"Did Dr. Redbone call you this morning?" Victor asks.

"Actually, yes. When I was taking a shower, he did. I haven't called him back yet."

"I am going to call him here shortly. Hopefully they have good news."

445

"Hi, Dr. Redbone. How are you doing? I am fine, thanks. How is Mom doing? Is she a handful for you yet? (Victor laughs.) Atreyu, the world medicine man. Great… he has finally set a date for us to gather. Okay… sounds great. We will be there. See you soon." Victor hangs up the phone.

"Well, we need to gather our weapons. We need to leave here Thursday. Christmas Eve is the worst holiday to travel, but we need to get there and help them prep for the world medicine man. He is coming to train some of the clan members and to go through the plan with us all. Everybody from all over will be there. It is finally time, my friend." Victor tells him.

Wednesday morning Victor finds John and Kane in the garage loading the truck.

"What are you up to, guys?" Victor says as he walks into John's garage.

"Just gathering all the weapons and tools, and loading the truck for the trip." Kane says.

"So do you think this world medicine man can help me, Victor? I am no shifter or special Native American." John asks.

"Trust me. He will enchant you with some type of weapon or magical device. You will learn to use and it will protect you." Victor tells him.

Back on the Plantation:

Gabriel walks to Alexis' office to pick Raven up for the day. He knocks on the door and awaits an answer. The door opens and Ellie greets him.

"Gabriel, good morning. Come in. Raven is still getting ready for you. Would you like a drink or something while you wait?"

"No, ma'am. I am fine. Thank you."

"Gabriel, you have been doing wonders with my little Raven. I knew you could do it. I can always count on Gabriel. I am so glad I made you. You and Ada are the best servants I could have ever asked for." Alexis says.

"I am ready. I am ready, Mommy." Raven yells across the office.

"Wow, she has a voice on her. Okay, honey. Come on. Let's go. I will walk down with you and Gabriel to the second floor. Mommy has to clean your room and hers." Ellie says.

Raven runs over, hugs Alexis, and kisses her.

"Bye, Grandma. See you tomorrow." Raven says.

"Oh, bye, my sweet baby girl. Grandma will come tuck you in tonight. How does that sound?" Alexis tells her.

Raven beams a huge smile on her face while she holds her mommy's hand. Ellie just looks at Alexis, not smiling at all. Ellie is no fan of Alexis Ravenworth. She knows too much. She doesn't remember anything but the place she is at.

Ellie and Gabriel walk out and down the corridor to the stairwell. No words are spoken. Gabriel knows how Ellie feels about Alexis and he feels the same, but he cannot let anyone know. Gabriel acts like the perfect servant who doesn't know much.

They reach the second floor and Ellie kisses Raven goodbye.

"I will see you tonight. Have fun today and listen to what Gabriel tells you. Okay? Ellie tells her.

Raven smiles and shakes her head yes, and they continue down the next flight of stairs to the first floor.

"Today, we will help Zoey and Lucas. Okay, Raven?"

"Oh good! I want to play with the flowers. I want to grow my vegetable garden for my mommy

448

and surprise her. Do you think I can bring her some flowers today, Gabriel?"

"Of course! We will make a nice arrangement for her. How is that?"

Raven smiles from ear to ear with excitement. She has been very good with Gabriel. He talks to her and teaches her all about the animals, creatures, shifters, and plants. All the things Raven likes and he keeps her mind in a better place without having stress from Alexis.

Lucius and Luther are outside helping Dania and Elsa tend to the flowers. They will have their offspring very soon, by the looks of their bellies. Luther and Lucius don't like what Dr. Brack and Monroe did, but they are in love with the girls and stand beside them, trying to help them through this ordeal. Soon, they will have the offspring of them instead of a creation of their mother's chop shop doctors.

"How are we doing today, Dania and Elsa? You girls feeling okay today?" Gabriel asks.

"Yeah, we are okay today, but I don't know how much longer this will last, Gabriel. I think this thing wants out soon." Dania tells him.

"I understand if you girls would like to cut off early. That is fine and if you want to take time off, that is fine as well. Zoey and Lucas can handle the work. Plus, Raven and I can help."

"Thanks, man. Really appreciate all the good you are doing for the girls, and for little Raven." Luther says.

"I second that." Lucius says.

Gabriel and Raven continue the way in the cool morning to take care of the other deeds for the day. Gabriel has included Raven. It seems to help keep her mind occupied on good things. She loves to see all the animals and they seem to love her and the rest of the staff that live in the village behind the big house.

Alexis walks out of her personal elevator and storms down the corridor towards Ada's office.

"Ada, have you found us our sacrifice yet for the New Year's Eve party?" Alexis says as she walks into her office.

"Ah, yes, My Lady. I have been looking for the particular one you asked about — a Minotaur or Tatanka, but I haven't found a specific one. I have been monitoring each one and the reports from the leaders of each group. I have four of them. I need to eliminate three. I just want to make sure we do the right thing."

"Your job isn't to do the right thing; it is to do what I ask you to do. So lose the sympathy for these damn creatures and find one before we have nothing to serve. And if we have nothing to serve, I will make you the main course." Alexis says as she slams her hand down on the desk and leaves.

Shaken from what Alexis just said, Ada gets up, runs out of the office, and outside. Down the steps and around the corner, she runs into Luther and Lucius with Dania and Elsa.

"Oh, sorry. I didn't mean to frighten you." Ada says, crying, and runs past them.

"Looks like Mother strikes again." Luther says.

"She must be in a lovely mood today." Lucius replies.

Ada runs back to the village where the others live.

"Gabriel, wait up. I need to talk to you." Ada yells out across the walkway.

Gabriel turns around and sees Ada crying.

"Raven, go see how Asterion is doing and get his log book for the daily necessities. Okay?"

Gabriel turns and walks towards Ada.

451

"What is wrong? Why are you so upset?"

"Alexis; she is ruthless, just evil. I can't stand this anymore, Gabriel. I have to do something. I can't do this." Ada falls to her knees, crying hard. Gabriel grabs her, picks her up, and takes her over to sit on a bench outside one of the huts in the village for one of the Plantation staff.

Gabriel looks around and knocks on the door, waiting for someone to answer, but nobody does. That is what he was hoping. What they have to talk about, nobody needs to hear, or they risk execution themselves.

"Calm down and tell me what happened. Maybe I can help you."

"She came into my office and startled me as I was working. She asked me if I had a creature for the main buffet meal for the New Year's Eve event. I told her no, but I have some prospects. I just have to make sure I pick the correct one. I didn't want to pick wrong and kill an innocent. All are innocent, but by her rules, they are betraying her so they need to die."

"Yeah, I understand. You do this for every event. So what is the problem?"

"She told me if I don't find someone soon, I would be the one she uses. It is not my job to judge but to do as she says — period."

"This is also true, Ada. You know the rules and I understand how you must feel. I couldn't choose who lives and who dies either, especially knowing how they become what they are. I know it is sad; it is hard, but if you want to save your own life, you must do what she asks of you. Do you understand? If you don't, she will kill you. She has no feelings, no regret, and no remorse. She is pure evil; that is what she is."

"I know, Gabriel, but this time it is harder. I have five choices from the logbooks that are possible. They remember where they came from and who they were, but when I send back for concrete proof, they say they can't give it yet. Apparently, it was told from another, that heard them talking. I can't choose one on this type of evidence. I need a direct account."

"Listen, Ada, I will ask around directly with some of the leaders here. I will find the truth and give you the evidence you need. Then I will order the event to happen during the New Year's Eve ball. Okay? You don't have to do anything. Just act like you are doing it if she asks. She will never know."

"Okay, Gab. Thank you. I knew I could trust in you."

Ada hugs Gabriel and Raven comes skipping down the walkway.

"I got it, Gabriel. Asterion gave me a lollipop too." Raven says with a big smile on her face.

Gabriel continues on his way, with Raven hopping and skipping with her lollipop. *She is one glowing spirit when she is away from Alexis.*

Alexis gets a text message from Lucius. "Get the lab ready for delivery now. We are heading down."

"What the hell is going on now?" Alexis pages Dr. Brack on her headset as she makes her way down to the lab from the great dining area on the first floor.

"Dr. Brack, Lucius is coming down. He said to get ready for a delivery. I am assuming he means an offspring. I am on my way down now."

She rushes to the elevator and goes down to the third level, underground the lab and testing facility. Stepping out and walking down the corridor, she hears screams coming from the other corridor leading up to the main level. She doesn't allow anyone to use her elevator. They have to use the manual service one, the stairs, or the ramp.

"What is happening? How long has this been going on?" Alexis asks Luther as he carries Elsa and Lucius carries Dania.

"They are having their babies, Mother. The ones you created as usual. I just hope they pull through all right. They have been having a bad time." Luther tells her.

"Oh, they will be just fine. I am sure Dr. Brack and Monroe will take care of them. I will see to it. I know you two care a lot for these two. I will not let anything happen." Alexis replies.

The lab door is open when they get there and they all rush in.

"Back here. Bring them back here; we have the beds ready for them and the equipment." Monroe says as he waves them back to another room inside the lab.

Dania lets out an echoing scream of pain. They are both pale and sweating profusely. Elsa has already broken her water and she is incoherent.

"Did you give them anything? She looks like she has taken something." Dr. Brack says.

"No, we never gave them anything. They texted us and said they were having pain and didn't feel good. When we arrived at their room, they were like this." Lucius says.

"I would bet they have done something to cause this." Dr. Brack says and grabs a needle, sticking it in the vein of Elsa's arm and drawing blood to test it. Then doing the same to Dania.

Monroe preps them both for a cesarean birth. Alexis asks Dania, "Did you take anything before you came here?"

Breathing heavy, huffing, and puffing from the pain, Dania finally finds the words to answer her, "Yes. Pain relievers." Dania says.

Blood comes rushing out of Dania. Monroe yells for Dr. Brack as he rushes around to the back of the table. Lucius and Luther jump back.

"OMG! Someone help her! Monroe, do something."

"I am trying to, Lucius. Grab me some more towels off the counter over there. And I will need to strap her down; this is going to get rough for her. You hold the towels here. I am going to start the IV to calm her down for Dr. Brack."

Just as Monroe gets one IV started, Elsa screams in pain. Monroe asks Alexis to strap her down while he starts the IV. Alexis walks past her and notices her belly. She can see what looks like an impression of a small wing and a claw-like hand. Her eyes widen with surprise.

"Did you see that?" Alexis says.

"See what, Mother? I am trying to clean this up." Lucius says.

Dr. Brack comes rushing in. "Okay, let's get them under now. They have been taking a strong pain reliever and it seems to have set the labor of the offspring. I think they took more than they should have."

Dr. Brack slides the towels out of the way, hands Monroe a syringe, and tells him to inject this into their IVs. He takes his scalpel and slices under the bulge of the belly. In the crease, he holds the bulge of her belly up with his hand and does another cut, this time gentle and precise.

Blood and fluid rush out of the cut and onto the floor. Luther and Lucius squint and turn away. They can't watch what is happening. Alexis watches and waits to see what they are going to pull out of them.

Dr. Brack reaches in as he holds up the skin, pulling a foot of something out. He looks at it and slowly pulls it until another one pops out.

"Monroe, here. Hold this up so I can use both hands."

Monroe holds open the incision while Dr. Brack grabs both feet and slowly moves it back and forth, revealing the offspring.

Alexis watches as this strange creature comes out of Elsa. It has clawed hands and feet half-human, with long boney digits and sharp little claws. The body looks human except for the small skin-like membrane attached just behind the arm on the shoulder blade. It is a small wing with three small claws, one on the top where it bends and the side, and one at the bottom. It also has a strip of feathers golden in color running down the back.

He clears the mouth, wipes of the face of it, and hands it to Alexis. The offspring screams a strange cry. Lucius and Luther turn around quickly and can't believe what they see.

Dr. Brack tells Monroe to hold the bulge up on Dania. He cuts her open, spewing fluid and blood all over. Luther and Lucius turn back around, holding their mouths.

Dr. Brack pulls out the next offspring. It has the same claw feet as the other. Slowly, he pulls, revealing more of it. A strip of brown, orange, and yellow feathers covers most of the back area with feathered wings not like the other one. The head has the same colors of feathers, but the orange is human hair. The feathers run down along the face and has a V shaped in the center of the forehead. The hands are the same as the other one.

As he dries it off and clears its mouth, it opens its eyes. Dr. Brack says, "Whoa, look at the eyes on this one. They look like an owl's eyes."

Everybody rushes over to look at the offspring. It has all human facial features except the eyes.

"Wow, they are green and yellow. So bright." Luther says. "What does the other one have? The same?"

Alexis looks down. Its eyes are closed, so she shakes it a little. When it opens its eyes, she is shocked to see them.

"Mother? What do they look like?" Lucius asks.

"They are black as coal. The whole eye. I don't know if it is blind or not." Alexis replies.

She holds it up for them to see. They can't believe how hideous it looks. The face is like flesh over bone, the black eyes are sunken in, and it is pale color with a tint of grey to it, with feathers down its back and strange hands and feet with a set of bat-like wings.

"Oh my God. What is it supposed to be, Mother?" Lucius asks her.

"It is a Harpy. That is what she wanted. That is what I spliced with the DNA. There are two types of Harpies and it seems they each had one of them, which is a good thing. They carry different powers. One is a humanoid-type creature with the face of death, greyish-colored skin, and wings like a bat this type is the one that malevolent one. The other one is a benevolent, a kinder creature, not ruthless. They both are females Harpies always are females and they like to steal things, and steal food from others. The Benevolent one you see is more elegant, stunning colors and beautiful." Dr. Brack explains.

Alexis hands the offspring over to Dr. Brack. He takes her and puts her in the incubator. Monroe has the other one in the incubator next to Dania.

"So boys, what are you going to name your two children?" Alexis asks them.

They look at her with disgust and look back at the girls.

"Oh, they will not stay like that long. They are in the shifted form because the Harpy is defensive. It is normal for them to act like this. With the shock of the birth, it will go away as soon as they start to feed on the mother's milk." Dr. Brack explains.

"Okay, boys, let's go. We have other things to tend to. You can come back later after they wake up."

Dr. Brack sutures Dania, while Monroe cleans Elsa to be sutured next.

Chapter 41

"Before we go"

"Before we leave, Victor and Kane, I want to go see Lilly. I want her to know I will be gone for a week and that we are going to get Kia and the twins."

"Okay, I will finish loading with Victor while you go."

John jumps on the mule as Hurley climbs aboard and they head down in the fresh snow that fell early this morning. The creek is down a lot, so it is easy to walk across. Of course, Hurley doesn't mind getting wet anytime of the year. He is a Burmese mountain dog and Border collie mix; he loves to swim.

John turns his flashlight on as he walks into the cave. The temperature inside the heart of the cave stays about sixty-seven to seventy-one degrees.

Approaching the big room, he hears noises. He stops and listens before walking around the corner and entering.

He can hear two young kids laughing and splashing about in the water. Then he hears a strange noise. One seems to talk, but it is jumbled, more of a moaning in different tones. John listens, trying to figure out who it could be. Then he hears a familiar voice.

"Children, be nice to him. He doesn't know how to play with you. I will be right back. You stay here with him."

Lily swims to the shore and walks up on the sand in the big room.

"John, is that you I feel?" Lily asks.

John is surprised by Lily noticing him. He steps out and around the corner. Entering the great room, he sees Lily standing in human form, waiting for him.

"Hi, Lily. How are you?" He hugs her.

"Oh, I am fine, but I sense you are very worried. John, what is wrong?"

"I come to tell you I would be leaving for a few days. Victor, Kane, and I are going to get Kia and the twins back."

Lily's eyes lighten and a smile comes over her face.

"Oh, finally, she will be set free. I bet Victor is happy and anxious to see his offspring."

"He is and we all are actually. We have a full army of Native American shifters from all around. A world medicine man is coming to help us get her out."

"I know you all will be successful at this task. But I need to tell you one thing. Don't trust the one you used to trust when she was here. She is not what you remember her as and she will not remember any of you. She will instead try to kill all of you." Lily replies.

"Yes, Lily, I understand. Thank you for the warning. Lily, can I ask you a question?"

"Of course you may, John."

"Who were your children talking to? I heard a strange mumbling sound respond to them as they talked."

"Oh, that is the cave dweller. He has been visiting us about every day and the kids and he play. He is very playful. I think the kids are too rough with him; he is intimidated by them, but he tries. He looks at me and smiles; he is the strangest looking thing."

"Benny? He is actually communicating with you? I can't believe it. That is great. I always knew he wanted to when I saw him a few times. He always seemed to want to say something but was too afraid. He also brought Jake back that morning to us. I knew he had goodness somewhere in there. Lily, I will see you when I get back. I am sure Kia will be here with the twins to see you." John says and hugs her.

"Okay, John. I will be waiting." And she turns around and walks back to the water.

John gets Hurley and they head back to the garage, thinking about what Lily said not to trust the one I used to. He is trying to figure out to whom it is she was referring. It can't be Kia, so who else could it be? Puzzled, he gets out and puts the mule back in the garage.

"I'll be right back. I am going upstairs to put Hurley in the apartment with Jake and Kyle. They wanted to play air hockey last night, so they ended up falling asleep watching movies." John says as he leads Hurley out the back of the garage and up the stairs to the apartment.

Redbone/Whiteriver Clinic North Carolina

December 24

John, Victor, and Kane almost make it before sundown. They pull up to the gate of the second clinic in Maggie Valley, North Carolina. Up in the mountain, this exclusive clinic sits on two hundred

465

and fifty acres, limiting anybody from hearing the big ceremonies they have up there.

"Welcome. I am glad you guys made it. Everybody is here. We were waiting on you three before we ate dinner." Mona tells them and hugs Victor, John, and Kane.

They follow her in, and some of them help take their luggage and put it in their rooms for them. They continue into the great dining area. It is filled with people. They can't believe how many clan members came.

"Wow, how many people did he ask to help, Mother?" Victor asks.

"Oh my, Victor, there is two hundred people here. They are all shifters from all over. Atreyu and Narden, the world medicine man and his companion, are over there talking with your father and Dr. Whiteriver."

"I had no idea this many would come to help us get Kia and the twins. I am totally beside myself right now." Victor says.

Kane walks over and greets Warrick with a chest butt and a high five.

"Come with me, you two. I want you to meet the world medicine man. He has been waiting for you, Victor. I have not talked to him. You are my son. I didn't want any of this to interfere with your quest for Kia and the twins. I will leave that up to you, son."

Mona takes them over to Atreyu, Dr. Redbone, and Dr. Whiteriver. They decide to go in and talk privately about the plan to get Kia out.

"Atreyu, this is Victor. He is a warlock and his friend, John. John is the one that owns the property where they found a lot of the shifters, spirit animals, and other things that brought all this on."

Atreyu shakes their hands and introduces Narden. He explains she will be coming with them on the trip to the Plantation. She is the one who will take the Raven Mocker out. As a Dragon-born, the Raven Mocker cannot defeat her. Only two can take down a Dragon-born. Himself and another Dragon-born.

"I will need you two to help me enchant weapons. The other clan members need to know the plan. I have made various mojo powders for different situations. They will need to learn how to use them and how to defend themselves, as well as the different shifters and creatures they will come in contact with."

"No problem. Just show me what you want us to give them. I know most of the mojo powders from being a warlock." Victor tells him.

"Good. I have them here if you would walk over to the table and look at the items we have put together. I have Goofer's Dust, which is an old voodoo witchcraft. It will harm or kill the victim that ingests or inhales it. You will have to keep this in the pouches without demonstrating it. Second, we have the herb Devil's Shoestring. This will confuse whoever inhales it. They will forget what they were doing and you will knock them out, capture, or what you will. Another one here is Devil's Dung; it is used to protect you from evil. It will help your powers work better, and physical strength will be enhanced. All this and a few weapons, unless you brought your own. I will enchant them for you to help you in the battle." Atreyu tells them.

"Everybody will get one of these red bags that tie on your belt. It will have all the different herbal combinations for each protection. Please use them wisely and cautiously." Dr. Redbone says.

Dr. Redbone lays all the pouches out as the clan members come to take one. The weapons that have been enchanted by Atreyu are sorted and checked by Mona and Victor, and then handed to Narden and Warrick to give to the clan members.

"Everything must be collected and everybody must understand what they have in their possession. Each one of you now has the red bag and your weapons. Now it is time to celebrate and have our ceremonial fest before leaving tomorrow for the Plantation." Atreyu announces.

"Wow, there is a lot of people that came to help. I can't believe so many clans came together to help Kia and the twins." Victor tells Atreyu, Mona, Dr. Redbone, and Dr. Whiteriver.

They all watch as everybody moves into the ceremonial area outside; it is already set up for the feast. Almost five hundred different clan members from over seventy-five different shifter clans have joined forces to fight for the twins' safety.

Morning of departure

Atreyu stands outside, waiting for all members to gather before they head towards Tennessee to the Plantation.

"Tonight, we will fight for something we all have waited for a very long time. I will send as much protection out as I can once we get inside the Plantation. You must focus on surviving. We will go in pairs, or groups of four members, except for the Fire Dancers. They will go in five, as that is all they have in their clan. Remember to use everything in your power to take down the enemy. If you don't,

469

they will take you down. I can only protect so many once I am inside the Plantation. We all will be on our own until the end. Good luck to all and may the spirit animals protect and fight with us all."

They all gather their gear, load into the vehicles, and head towards the Plantation.

Chapter 42

"New Year's Festival"

"Welcome, welcome, my friends and thank you for coming to the New Year's Eve event here at the magical Plantation. The event today will have one winner. Choose your favorite and cheer him on to achieve his win." Alexis says.

The crowd cheers as the first Minotaur comes out to the center of the arena. He is massive, big, muscular, giant half-human, half-bull with an armor shoulder and chest plate, armor briefs, and an armor piercing Pollaxe. Alexis announces his name after he walks into the arena and looks at everybody with his Pollaxe slung upon his shoulder. He walks towards Alexis above in her podium, looking high above the event complex.

"This is the great Minotaur warrior Asterion!" Alexis says loudly through her headset, echoing through the grounds. Everybody cheers for Asterion as he bows on one knee to Alexis. She tosses him a purple and gold sash.

"And his opponent today is Magar." Alexis announces. He walks forward towards Alexis. He is not as big and massive as Asterion, but he is still very muscular and stout with almost complete black hair and dark skin. He wears only a chest and brief armor, and carries a battle-axe upon his shoulder. He bends down on one knee under Alexis and she drops the sash down for him. His colors are red and gold, the colors of the Kingdom of Ansteorra from the West. The crowd cheers as Magar gets up and walks past them to the opposite side of the arena to ready himself for the fight.

The crowd stands and cheers them on as they stand across from one another in the arena. Alexis waves her arms and cheers with them, getting the fighters hyped up for the battle.

Asterion makes the move towards Magar. He walks straight and solid with his steps showing no fear. Magar's walk is more swiftly, as to hurry and get the job done. He shows anger in his face, something Asterion picks up right away and knows he can use this to his advantage.

Magar swings his battle-axe at Asterion, and misses as Asterion steps off to the side. Asterion takes the chance as Magar is slightly off balance and thrusts his Pollaxe into the torso of Magar, stabbing him with the head spike and then swinging the butt spike of it around and knocking Magar off his feet.

Magar swiftly rolls out of the way, as Asterion thrusts another blow towards Magar. Angered, Asterion rips his Pollaxe out of the clay ground and his eyes narrow at Magar as he tries to get away to see his wound before turning and fighting Asterion.

Asterion's steps are felt through the ground into the stands. They cheer him on.

"Kill him, Kill him," They shout out through the arena. Asterion doesn't even hear them. He has one thing on his mind and that is to take Magar down as instructed by his master.

Magar turns and swings his battle-axe just in time to block Asterion's Pollaxe. The clash echoes throughout the arena like a fresh strike of lightning hit. Almost a deafening noise, the crowd awes in response.

Alexis watches as they battle, hitting once and blocking the other's blow. Finally, they get close enough. Asterion pushes with both hands against the Pollaxe, sending Magar stumbling backwards. As he tries to catch himself, Asterion rushes in and as he does, he quickly glances at Alexis. She gives him the nod of her head to finish it.

He raises the Pollaxe up, stepping firmly forward, and swings high, catching Magar in his right arm and grazing off, hitting his throat and slicing it. The crowd roars with cheer for Asterion.

Blood sprays all over Asterion, but he still goes in, pushing Magar to the ground and pinning him down with one foot until he stops moving.

Small elf-like people come rushing out and drag Magar out of the arena. The crowd falls silent and just stares, wondering what actually just happened.

Alexis quickly steps up, commending Asterion on a great performance. The crowd slowly claps confusingly.

"Please, people, it is a show. This is all an act; nothing happened to Magar. As soon as he is cleaned up from the fight, he will be right out. Give Asterion a big cheer for his performance today, winning for the Kingdom of the East!"

Finally out comes a Minotaur and Alexis announces for them to give Magar a big cheer for his part in the show. Everybody cheers loud as Asterion and Magar stand facing Alexis as she points for them to leave the arena.

"What took your people so long to come on and remove him from the arena?" Alexis says in her headset as she storms off the podium and out of the sight of the crowd.

"Take him down to Narsis. Remember, time is of the utmost importance. We need to get the brunch started. They are waiting for this to finish the main course meal."

The servants take Magar body down below in the tunnel system.

"Gabriel, thank you for doing this for me. I know it was a lot of pressure trying to find and choose which one will be used for the sacrifice. I say to make it seem a little better than just killing." Ada tells him as they stand and greet people coming into the dinner buffet for the evening before the show starts.

"Your welcome, Ada, I had Asterion help me. He knew right away which one to choose for his opponent." Gabriel says.

The people flood into the royal dining area. They have big pavilions set up outside for the guests to dine also. She hasn't wasted a dime on luxury for the event.

Sitting above the ground about three feet to give the appearance they are floating, the pavilions are magnificent. They seat one hundred guests. The buffet area sits on the far wall, overlooking a lake and the other pavilions built around the lake. Fully self-contained with bathrooms with attendants to service guests, music specifically for the guests to relax and enjoy. A porch and walkway wraps completely around each of the pavilions and a covered walkway connects to each one.

    After the dinner, the people compliment the staff on an extraordinary meal, one they have never tasted so unique with the seasonings.

Chapter 43

"The Battle"

The festival grounds are packed with spectators, waiting for the fireworks and the countdown to the New Year to come.

It is eleven p.m. and the place is filled with the sounds of music, people yelling and carrying on. The little stores are filled with people buying up everything on the shelves — snacks, tee shirts, souvenirs from the event there, and the vendors outside with the food and the lady that sells the water for each person's specific aura.

The shifters are all working this year with the amount of people. It has tripled since last year's attendance, bringing a big profit for the Plantation.

The wind slowly starts to move across the ground. No snow in the forecast and no storms coming. The breeze picks up and blows the cool air through the pathway to the event stands. The trees slowly rock back and forth; bare are most except the evergreens.

People walking through the pathway past the vendors and stores start to feel the breeze blowing harder, making them put on their hats, jackets, and scarfs. There is a strange chill in the air, heaviness almost like it isn't air, but someone blowing the wind down the pathway. Some start looking around, but they still head down towards the event stand to get a good seat for the show.

The clan pulls in and even though they are late to arrive, the gates are still open for anybody to come in and see the show. At their surprise, they pull up without anybody noticing the amount of people. Most are already in the event, but Victor, John, Kane, Warrick, Atreyu, Narden, and a few large groups of clan members pull up in several large vans.

They move swiftly through the grounds of the Plantation. One by one, they follow the plan that Atreyu set to follow. They need to get Victor into the Plantation castle with the help of Gabriel and Shadow. They will take him to Kia.

Everybody breaks up into teams of two as they cross the grounds in the night celebration. Victor and John stay together as they come up on a Satyr guarding the pathway that leads around the first big circle heading up to the Plantation.

The Satyr tells them to go back. They're not allowed to go any further than they have been. Victor insists he move out of the way, but the Satyr doesn't. He stands his ground.

John steps aside while Victor and the Satyr argue. Suddenly, he sees the Satyr swing at Victor. Victor quickly moves to the side, but catches a blow to the shoulder. Spinning around and stepping back, Victor places his hands a few inches apart and a red ball of energy forms. The Satyr stands, waiting for Victor to make his next move, not realizing what he is about to do.

John watches from the side, keeping a lookout for any other guards coming. Watching the red ball grow, thousands of pink lightning bolts dance viciously through the ball.

Victor throws the ball at the Satyr, hitting him in the chest. The Satyr drops to his knees as the red ball of energy engulfs his whole body. The Satyr falls to the ground on his side in convulsions.

"Goddamn, Victor, you didn't kill him, did you?" John asks as he looks at the Satyr's body convulsing on the ground.

"No, he will be fine in about an hour. It is like a bad Taser hit. It just knocked him out for a while. Come on, before anymore come. They usually come in a pack. I can't believe this one is alone out here."

Victor and John move towards the house when they see two of the Minotaur's moving towards them down the walkway.

"That doesn't look good, does it?" John and Victor hear a voice come from beside them. It is Kane and Warrick with four other Native American shifters. The other shifters are big enough to take on the Minotaur's; this will let the other four get by and head to the house.

"What are we going to do with these guys, Victor? I am no help here, man." John says as he watches them come closer. The ground shakes with each step these massive creatures take.

Kane and Warrick look over at the other four shifters.

"Well, this is your chance, my friends? This is what we have been waiting for the past couple of months. Give them everything you have." Kane tells them.

"Yes, my brother. We will fight like warriors. There are four of us and two of them. We should handle this one. You guys take care and good luck. We will do our best to come behind you and take down anything coming after you." Logan says to them and they walk towards the two Minotaur's.

"They aren't going to challenge them like that, are they?" John asks.

"No, they will shift and when they do, we need to be on the other side of this walkway heading towards the house. It will not be pretty." Kane says.

They head the opposite way down the walkway around the first main circle. John still watches the four Native Americans, curious to see what they shift into. Just before they get past the podium in the middle of the circle, the four shift into these huge creatures.

"Come on, John. I know you want to watch, but we need to move. Look at this; shifters are coming from all around now. They must have spotted us and figured out what is going on." Victor says.

The four Native Americans shift into two grizzly bears and two Tatanka warriors they are like Minotaurs, but look like a half man half buffalo.

Victor, John, Kane, and Warrick hurry down the walkway when they see people running from the sides in the garden areas and past them as they fight with other shifters.

These shifters are making a path for the world medicine man and his assistant. She needs to get to Alexis and take her down. Once they do, the other creatures should stop fighting.

Victor watches side to side as people shift from human to animals, and battle each other. Some taking blows so hard they fly up through the air and hit the walls, fence, trees, and ground.

"OMG!! Did you see that? That bear shifter just pulled up that post and hit the other one with it, sending him airborne." John says.

"Heads up, guys. We have two fauns coming at us." Kane says.

"Yeah, I see them. On your left, we have three more coming. They are not fauns; they are bigger. Shit, more Satyrs. Okay, guys, this is it. We are all going to have to fight here. John, sorry, man, but I will try to help you if I can take this one out fast." Victor tells them.

They form a small circle, looking in all directions as the two fauns and three Satyrs rush in and challenge a fight.

Kane makes the first move with Warrick right beside him, taking on two of the bigger Satyrs, leaving Victor the other one and John to deal with the smaller fauns.

Kane leaps in the air to tackle the Satyr. At that time, he shifts into his werewolf and Warrick does the same.

The Satyr sees Kane and reaches up to grab him as Kane comes down on him. Kane bites down on his neck with force, shaking and ripping flesh from the Satyr. The Satyr punches Kane's back as hard as he can to get him to free his grip, but Kane grabs the Satyr's arms and holds him back. Then Kane moves in for the kill, biting the Satyr right in the throat, piercing the jugular vein. Blood squirts all over, covering Kane's face and his chest. The Satyr drops almost instantly.

At the same time, Warrick is not having as good of luck. The Satyr has Warrick by the head, squeezing him until he is almost unconscious. Kane jumps on the back of the Satyr and bites down on the back of his neck near his head. The sound of bones crunching echo. The Satyr's grip on Warrick releases and Warrick falls on his knees, gasping for air. He can hear the sounds of bones snapping. He gets up and sees Kane on top of the Satyr as he lies on the ground. Covered in blood, he knows Kane is fine and turns to focus on the other faun that is after John.

Victor is playing with the faun that is after him. He can't figure out how Victor can move so fast. The faun spears at Victor, but Victor moves so quick, the faun doesn't even see him move until he misses him.

Angrier and angrier the faun gets, snorting and stomping the ground while Victor laughs at him.

Warrick takes on the one faun that is on the left side of John. John is doing a good job holding them back with a magical staff the medicine man gave him. With the crystals on it, it helps John fight off the faun using the earth plane and John's aura to power the staff, creating energy that he can shoot out at the faun and stun him enough to knock him back for a few seconds. He shakes it off, giving John enough time to get the upper hand on him.

John takes the end of the staff and swings it up, knocking the faun under the chin and he stumbles backwards. John hits him again with the staff, and then shots another beam of energy, finally knocking him completely down to the ground. John walks over and hits the faun in the head, knocking him completely out.

Warrick grabs the other faun by the horns and throws him on the ground headfirst.

"Head butt me, you son of a bitch." A deep voice comes from Warrick.

The faun gets back up and Warrick grabs him by the side and slams him down on the ground once again. The faun gets back up and as soon as he does, Warrick punches him in the face, sending him flying backwards into the concrete statue in one of the gardens, immobilizing him.

Victor finally gets tired of playing with the faun and using his power, lifts the faun off the ground, and slams him into a metal post, piercing the faun through the leg. He can't go anywhere; he is stuck on the metal rod unless he breaks it off and pulls it out of his leg.

"Everybody all right? John, you okay?" Victor asks.

"Yeah. I am good. That was exhilarating! Woo! I am ready now; just need something to break the tension. OMG! Kane, what happened to you? Man, are you all right?" John asks.

"Yeah, I am fine. Why?"

"You are covered in blood, my friend." John replies quickly.

"Not mine. Don't worry. It will take more than a faun to bring me down." Kane says.

"Follow me. I will get us into the house." A voice comes from the back of them. They all turn around to see Atreyu and Narden.

"I will help you get in the house safely. I need to get in there to face the Raven Mocker." Atreyu says.

They all follow him and Narden without question. Battles continue between shifters throughout the grounds. They can hear the screams of people in the distance, running for safety out of the Plantation.

The centaurs come through the one main walkway with their bows and arrows with which they wounded several of the clan members. Atreyu with his power as a medicine man points his staff at the centaurs and the wounded shifters speaking an enchantment:

Taking them back, before they came

To battle here once again.

Return the weapons that wounded

Them lame.

Sending them back to do the same.

A green light travels down the staff and out the end towards the battle of the clan's shifters and centaurs. The light bounces from one to the next and so on until everyone in the battle is pierced with the green light.

Their bodies stop and freeze in time as if they are statues. The clan shifters suddenly disappear and reappear at the edge of the garden. Standing there, still frozen in time, still all connected within the green light.

The centaur's light disappears and arrows rain down upon them from the sky, piercing and wounding them. The clan shifters' light slowly fades. They move about, looking around and then back to each other, realizing they are not wounded anymore. They yell and take off in groups to attack the other guards that are coming out of the darkness.

Kane and Warrick stop. Looking into the darkness, their hair goes up on their backs.

"There is something out there. I smell them. We will return to you shortly." Kane says as he and Warrick take off into the darkness while the others keep moving towards the house.

Kane stops suddenly in the darkness and Warrick stops behind him, walking slowly up to him, standing just off his right shoulder. Glowing red eyes appear just ahead of them. Warrick steps out from the side of Kane to stand directly beside him. One of the eyes moves off to the right and Warrick follows them. Kane stares at the other, waiting for the shifter to appear closer.

Damien's eyes narrow as he looks at Warrick. Warrick returns with a snarling growl. Damien slowly moves towards Warrick, and Warrick bows down on his legs enough to spring up in action at the right moment.

He moves closer Warrick then lunges out towards him at the same time Warrick springs up and they both clash in the air. They bite and tear each other's flesh viciously clawing. Warrick rips his claws down Damien's arm, slicing it deep. Blood squirts out like an exploded blood bag.

Kane moves in closer to view his opponent. Two alphas take a different approach to fighting than the others do. This is a fight for dominance, a fight to win and be king over both sides.

Now Kane faces Malik just a few feet apart. They stare with angered eyes. Malik's eyes are as red as burning embers.

Kane shifts his body to the side, bowing up his arms and pushing out his chest. He slowly walks to the left. Malik follows, moving at the same pace as Kane. Circling each other slowly, checking out each other, Kane sees Malik is bigger than he is. He is taller by almost a foot and the weight about twice that. Malik's arms are much longer and thick with muscle. Kane knows if he grabs him, he will feel the blow of his strength. Kane thinks things through as he moves, looking up at Malik's red glowing eyes, waiting for the right moment to fight.

Kane takes the first move, deciding to swing a fist first to see how tough Malik is. Malik puts up his arm right away, blocking the blow to his face. Malik is pissed now; he returns a growl.

"You have no strength against me." Malik says.

Still circling, Kane turns and swings, once again hitting Malik in the face, and knocking him back a few steps. Kane takes the opportunity to follow through and throwing a few more blows to Malik's face. Malik tries to swing but Kane ducks and steps back. They both stand there for a moment. Kane snaps a limb from a tree he is standing near and breaks it in two, making a club out of one end.

Still viciously fighting, Warrick and Damien finally break apart for a brief moment. Damien once again takes the first move towards Warrick, but Warrick dodges Damien, letting Warrick move quickly around the back of Damien, and jumping up on his back, biting his neck and shoulder deep.

Damien bends down trying to shake Warrick off him, but doesn't succeed so he reaches back and grabs Warrick by the back of the head and slams him on the ground. Warrick lands on his back knocking the breath out of him.

Warrick tries to get up quickly, but Damien slams him in the face, knocking him back down on his side.

Kane, now with a wooden club, swings it at Malik, who jumps back, but Kane swings again, and again, finally landing it into Malik's rib cage. Kane knows he now has advantage over him so he swings the club as if he is clawing the skin off Malik.

Malik falls down. Kane stops, looking down at him, waiting for Malik to get up and fight again. Malik sits for a second, trying to get up. He knows his ribs are cracked and it will take a little bit of time to heal them in shifted form. Longer than Kane has the patience for. Malik knows he must get up and move. If he doesn't, Kane will win the fight. If Malik leaves injured, he will forfeit the fight and leave it as though it is not finished.

Malik gets up, faces Kane, and steps backwards, holding his left side. Malik turns and walks away from Kane. Kane stands and watches him leave, slowly limping away. He knows he forfeited so he can come back and challenge him again.

Damien, still on top of Warrick, swings and claws, biting and tearing at him. Kane walks towards them, fighting to help Warrick when Damien hears Malik calling him. Frustrated, Damien doesn't want to leave. He looks over and sees Kane walking towards them with a wooden club in his hand.

Damien realizes he isn't a match for two werewolves and one with a weapon. Damien leaps off Warrick and disappears into the darkness.

"That was a lot easier than I expected it to be with a hellhound." Warrick said

"Really? Have you looked at yourself? Your fur is covered in blood. You're not even white anymore."

"It's not all my blood, just some of it." Warrick says.

They both take off to catch the others that are almost to the house.

"The Minotaurs are not at the gate. That means they have put something else in place to guard the house. Keep your eyes and ears open." Victor tells them.

"The Minotaurs are in the field battling the clan shifters. It is okay. Narden will be here to keep a look out for anything as she waits for the Raven Mocker to come out." Atreyu says.

As they walk across the wooden bridge closer to the house, Narden shifts into a Dragon-born. She is almost ten feet tall, scaly skin like a reptilian.

491

They all watch as she changes into a Dragon-born, fascinated by her appearance.

"I will be right up there on the third level, watching and waiting for the Raven Mocker to come out. When she does, she will try to fly away, but she will not get far." Narden says.

They head to the front door of the house. So far, nobody is around. Everybody is out fighting.

Once they reach the massive wooden front doors, Atreyu takes his medicine staff and with a slight shake of his hand, the top half of it glows like iron in a fire. A flame bursts out at the very end of it. The staff is made of special metal Ruthenium; hot, cold, and acids don't affect it. It is one of the strongest metals.

He shakes the staff and the door bursts into flames. Little embers of the door fall towards the ground and turn to ash.

Chapter 44

"Battle Scars"

Alexis is in her office, watching out the window as the event happens. She gets a call on the headset that there are two men sneaking through the barricades and heading into the garden. Alexis knows it is Victor and she knows this is it. The time has come and the battle is in place. She must send everybody to the grounds now.

She calls Gabriel and tells him to get her sons on alert. It is happening now. They are here in the Plantation and the battle is starting. She hurries to get her keys and she slips down the back entry to the crystal dungeon. Trying to reach Malik on the headset, he is not answering. Then she tries Damien, who finally picks up.

"Damien, where the hell is Malik? I need you and him in the garden now. They are coming to get the silver-blood. I am going down to get Djinn and Tauran. You give Raven to Gabriel and have him take her. He knows where to hide her so they don't hurt her and Ellie." Alexis tells him and hangs up, rushing down the stairwell to get to the crystal dungeon as fast as she can.

Running down the hallway and to the door of the crystal dungeon, she takes a deep breath. Unlocking the door, she walks quickly past each corridor until she gets to the one where her key rises and pulls to the left. She walks down, passing the massive crystal quartz one by one until the key yanks so hard, it pulls out of her hand and into the one crystal quartz with the green smoke bubbling up in front of it.

Djinn knows already what is happening. She knows this could be bad for her because he is one of the most evil creatures on the earth. But she has no choice; she needs his help against the world medicine man. Djinn has a partner, the Tauran, a huge bull that strictly battles in wars back in the Arab countries they both come from. When Alexis was over in the Arab countries, she tricked them both and captured them for her collection. She had them brought back and placed them in the crystals that suspend them in infinity of time. Time doesn't exist anymore; it is like the fourth dimension.

Alexis' hand shakes as she reaches for the key that is stuck in the glass. She releases it quickly and shakes her hand. Reaching for the key once again, the green smoke bubbles thicker and she can faintly hear a laugh from within the crystal.

"Hahahaha, so it is time, is it? Time to release me to protect my capture. Oh, this is ironic, now isn't it, Alexis? Hundreds of years ago, you tricked Tauran and me, stuck us in this infinity hell, until you have nothing else to save you. So you come to us. Hahahahaha! I told you, didn't I, Alexis? You will never trick me again!" Djinn tells her from behind the crystal as he emerges to face her.

The key slowly absorbs into the crystal and Alexis stands back as the solid crystal liquefies within the frame. Rippling ever so slightly, a puff of green smoke comes out the center of the liquefied crystal and then another follows until a small stream of green smoke slowly bubbles out.

The liquid crystal ripples faster and more green smoke comes out, thicker and faster. A shape forms within the green smoke. It swirls around and around, growing higher. Alexis steps back further as it grows taller.

The smoke stops to dead silence in the dungeon. Bright lights that run down the corridors above the crystal frames dim. Alexis feels her skin crawl. She hasn't felt this in years. A laugh emerges from inside the green smoke. All of a sudden, the smoke is sucked up to the top.

Alexis feels her skin change and she shifts. Two wings grows out of her back, her body grows taller and slender, and feathers line the back of her arms, leaving the front human skin. Her head grows feathers and they mix within her long black hair. Around her eyes, small bluish black feathers grow in the shape of a bird flying with its wings opened up, covering both eyes to the hairline.

She looks up at the green smoke with her orange glowing eyes. Fear has left every part of her. She walks towards the green smoke. Just as she gets to it, a huge mass of muscles of a man steps out of the green smoke.

"Well, it is nice to see you still have it in you, Alexis. I am so glad I can bring the best out in you. You wear it very well. Now, let's go get Abigar out. I will need his help." And he turns and walks down the corridor towards the back to find Abigar's crystal cell.

Alexis follows behind, lifting another key from her necklace and pulling it off with a quick snap. Whispering to it as she lets go of the key, they follow it to a crystal on a huge thick stand.

The crystal is black with no movement inside. The key hits the crystal and sticks to the outside of it. They wait and watch for some sign of movement and the glass to give.

The key starts to slowly crumble to metal dust and falls towards the floor. The crystal is still black, and then suddenly a hand slowly emerges from within the crystal.

As it comes out of the crystal, they hear crackling like someone grinding or stepping on broken glass. Further, the hand emerges, reaching and grabbing with its fingers. The sound of cracking glass echoes loudly as the hooved foot comes through, followed by a thick muscular human leg. Slowly trailing up to a muscular torso, the head and shoulders appear out of the crystal and it falls completely with bigger chunks crashing to the floor.

Here stands a giant half-man, half-horse creature with tribal tattoos all across his chest and back, right arm and neck. His head resembles a horse, attached to a thick long human neck. He has a leather breechcloth that covers him in front with a belt that wraps around the top of it and wide leather hangs like a scarf down to his knees with two braided ropes attached to the side of the belt. He has in his hand a Pollaxe, a fourteenth century long axe on the back and another on the end of the shaft for thrusting. It has a blade axe on the one side, round and sharp for piercing armor.

Abigar shakes himself off; crystal glass and dust blow out around him into the air. He looks at Djinn and nods his head. He turns and sees Alexis standing there in her shifted form. He stops for a moment, looking at her, and then he realizes she is the bitch that tricked him. He raises his Pollaxe and takes a step towards her.

Djinn yells out, "No, Abigar! No, she is here to let us out. She needs our help. There is a war going on outside." Djinn tells him.

Abigar puts his ears up and listens. With a loud snort, he blows out his nostrils, "I am ready, My Lord." Tauran says to Djinn.

Alexis turns swiftly and walks towards the exit of the crystal dungeon. Djinn and Abigar follow behind her, side by side. As they get closer to the door, she casts a spell,

"I command the ancient ones to stop and come forth, for this is the call for need

Bring us the strength to abolish these creatures sucking the life out of our veins

And let the illness spread on those who came and drank the magic waters

Rise and fight with me, build the dark army from the deepest depths of hell and fire

Come rise the ones that have our mark."

499

Chapter 45

"Release Djinn"

They walk slowly through the door with Atreyu leading the way. He stops in the middle of the medallion on the floor of the entry. It is a huge tile medallion inlaid in the floor of a large female creature with feathers down her arms and through her hair. She holds a sword with ravens sitting on her and flying around her.

Atreyu looks at the image well. With a disturbed look on his face, he looks at Victor and then continues to glance around the house for other clues.

"We are not dealing with a Raven Mocker here. We are dealing with two very powerful creatures that somehow became one, one very powerful creature. This image here we are standing on is the Morrighan and the Raven Mocker. We are dealing with a creature that shifts into several creatures, and this female monster is what we call the "Goddess of War." Those words alone should answer any of your questions. She is a fighting war machine. We need to bring in some more powerful help. A witch, necromancer, witch doctors, someone that can help Narden and me take this creature.

Victor, is there anybody you know that has power like you, preferably stronger?" Atreyu asks.

"Yes, I do. My mother, Mona. She is a witch from the old Romania. You met her in North Carolina when we were preparing for this."

"Yes. I remember her. We need her here and now. Can you find a way to get her here?"

"Yes. I will get her. Hold on a minute, I will contact her. She is outside in the parking lot."

Victor contacts Mona, telling her to get into the Plantation and meet them inside the big house.

Then they hear a voice from down the corridor. It is dark with a very dim light shining from a doorway at the very end. They see a shadow moving in the light, but can't see what it is.

"Follow me." A voice from nowhere softly echoes in the entry.

"Who said that?" Atreyu says.

"Follow me this way." Everybody looks around, trying to find out where the voice is coming from. It sounds like it is right behind them.

They look to the end of the corridor and a black silhouette stands down at the end. They all stand there looking at it, not saying a word.

501

"That must have been the shadow moving in the light, or was it a person walking back and forth the whole time?" John whispers.

"Who are you and what do you want?" Atreyu calls out.

Another figure walks out and stands next to the black silhouette. You can see this is a creature and half man. They motion for them to come. Everybody looks at each other in question.

"Well, let's go. We came this far. I am not giving up." Victor says.

"Wait!" Kane yells out. "I know her. This is Shadow. You don't recognize her far away, Victor, but I can see her clearly. She said she would lead us to the area Kia was held captive. She also said she would have another person helping." Kane walks towards Shadow and the other person. The others follow a few steps back hesitantly.

"Hi, Kane, Victor. This is Gabriel. He is Alexis' right hand here. The other one is Ada. These two people are the only two people Alexis puts her faith in to run the place. He also is the one watching your twins." Shadow tells them.

"Oh my God! You have my babies? Where is Kia?" Victor says frantic, stepping up closer to Gabriel.

Gabriel steps back, intimated by Victor's demeanor.

"I… Yes, I do take care of Rayne and River. I also take care of Raven, their stepsister." Gabriel says.

Kane grabs Victor by the arm. Victor tries to pull away, but Kane pulls him back forcefully and Victor finally realizes he needs to focus and lose the feeling of despair.

"Sorry, I let my feelings take over me for a moment. Who is Raven, may I ask?"

"Raven is Damien and Ellie's daughter. She is very special. She is a healer and they are trying to kill that in her, making her see more of the bad than good. I have been teaching her to let it out." Gabriel says.

"Oh my God, Ellie? Ellie is here? We have been searching for Ellie for months with no luck. It all makes sense." John says.

"We have no more time. We must go before she comes back. She is down in the crystal dungeon. She is bringing something back to fight. This will not be a good thing. Kia is being held down there. We must be very careful. I will go ahead and make sure everything is clear to go." Shadow says and walks towards the corridor. They watch her as she disappears into thin air.

"Follow me and be very quiet." Gabriel says.

Victor, John, Kane, and Warrick walk behind each other as they follow Gabriel. Victor looks back and notices Atreyu isn't following them. He still is standing back at the corridors. Victor stops and turns around, motioning for Atreyu to come. Atreyu nods his head at Victor, who shakes his head in agreement, and turns back around to follow the others.

Atreyu walks back to the entry of the house and outside, waiting off to the side for Alexis to come out. The coldness in the night air on the Plantation doesn't bother Atreyu; he watches the battle grow as he awaits her exit from the house. Spirit animals come from all around to help battle the shifters. The sounds of fighting echo in the cold dark night. He listens closely as he hears someone approaching from a distance. The intruder pauses in her steps as she comes closer to the door of the house. Atreyu waits for her to come closer into view before he says anything. He knows she is no threat.

"Hello, Atreyu," the woman's voice gets closer as she walks up the steps and greets him with a hug.

"Mona, how are you? And thanks for coming to help." Atreyu says.

"My son called for me to come in. I was going to come, but they insisted I should stay outside in the van until I was called for so here I am."

"You're Victor's mother? Well, I should have realized that when he said his mother was a witch from Romania. I didn't even realize you two where related even at Dr. Redbone's clinic. I guess I was too busy with the preparations and never got a chance to talk to you. They were in such a hurry and we had little time and a lot of work to do."

"I know. I have been following this place since Victor told us about it. Little does he know what mothers do behind his back."

"I am glad you're here. I will need you to stay here for now. They have gone inside and two shifters are helping them to get Kia. Narden, if you remember her, she is up above us on the third level waiting and watching. I do have to tell you this is not just a Raven Mocker, but also a Morrighan. You know what they are capable of and what they are able to shift into."

"A war goddess and a Raven Mocker? What a hell of a combination. She is going to be very hard to bring down."

"Yes, Mona, I know. I didn't say much to the others; they will figure it out when they get back. We need them to stay focused on Kia and the twins. We will stay focused on her." Atreyu says.

"There is energy, a strong one. I can feel it getting closer. Do you feel it, Atreyu? This is an evil energy that I have felt only once before in my lifetime." Mona says.

"She must be coming. I feel three presences coming also. Narden, get ready, my dear." Atreyu yells out.

Mona and Atreyu stand to the side of the door against the concrete rail that circles the huge lanai.

They hear the sound of hooved feet with heavy steps coming from a distance. They can hear and smell the stench of death oozing through the center of the door. They both know she is coming. Atreyu gets ready with his staff. This time it has a bluish white light running up to the end of it, as if his body is charging it.

Alexis comes through the door. Her size is larger than they imagined her to be. Djinn and Tauran follow side by side behind her. Djinn notices Atreyu and Mona, but Alexis doesn't. She leaps up and flies off. Narden sees her and takes off to follow her.

Djinn smiles down on Atreyu and Mona. Abigar moves towards them when Djinn tells him to go battle in the fields. Abigar agrees with a loud moan and turns away, running out towards the great battle.

"So what do we have here?" Djinn says.

Atreyu holds his staff up towards Djinn, but he jerks it out of his hands so fast Atreyu can't grasp it hard enough.

Atreyu looks down at his arms and hands. Latin writing appears rapidly down his arms and bluish white lights pulsate down his veins as if it was blood. It travels all the way up his body, his face glows the same, and Egyptian writing mixed with Egyptian symbols form on his face. The powers of the world are drawn in through Atreyu. The power builds inside him with energy and the forces of the elements. His eyes glow indigo.

Atreyu's face pulsates with little lightning bolts moving around under the skin like veins. Then he looks up at Djinn. He throws his hands towards Djinn and a bright light shoots out of his hands. Atreyu's whole body pulsates with these bluish white bolts of energy racing from the ground, up his legs, through his body, and out his hands, feeding the source of power that engulfs Djinn, knocking him off his feet and suspending him in the air like a Taser hitting him.

Djinn is immobilized. He is trapped within the force of energy. Mona holds Atreyu by the shoulder, reading the writing that appears on his skin.

"Listen to me, Djinn. I have captured you. By the laws, you must obey what I ask of you. I want you to go forth and walk away from this place. I set you free from your master's grasps and any others that stow upon you now. You are to leave without harming anyone in my clan, but you have the right to harm anyone that is doing harm to my clan or to you. Now, I will release you and you will not harm us or I will lock you away as your master herself has." Atreyu tells him while he is in suspension of the magic he holds on Djinn.

Atreyu's face slowly changes. The tiny bolts of white and blue run down his neck and arms, through his torso and legs, returning to the ground swirling, and the light disappears. Djinn lands down on his feet, angered, but he is bound by what Atreyu has said to him.

"My Lord, I will do as you ask and thank you for kindly sparing my life. For this, I owe you a life in return." Djinn says.

"It is agreed, my dear friend. We meet again and we shall meet in another time. You are free, free to go away from here. May your journey be pleasant, my good friend." Atreyu says.

Djinn bows to Atreyu, and when he stands, he shakes Atreyu's hand, nodding his head. He then turns and jolts upwards like a rocket into the night sky.

Narden, tired of Alexis' maneuvers to lose her, decides to attack. Narden flies above Alexis, hovering and gliding in the wind as though it is so easy, while Alexis struggles. She hasn't used her wings in so long her body needs to strengthen as she flies. Her wings will adjust and hold her more accurate and stable. Narden arches her big wings upward and she drops like a brick on top of Alexis. Alexis struggles to get her off, flying into tops of trees, swirling and turning, but with no luck. Narden sinks her sharp teeth into Alexis' shoulder, locking her long claws into her legs. Alexis pulls her wings close and spins fast as they barrel towards the ground.

Smashing into the ground and sliding over dead trees and rocks, Narden leaps from Alexis, letting her slide across the ground and into a big rock.

Narden slowly walks towards her. Alexis, stunned, tries to get to her feet. Narden laughs at her and says, "Finally, after all these years, I have found you once more. This time you will not escape my wrath, you filthy Raven Mocker half-breed.

Alexis throws something towards Narden. It hits her and bursts into fire and smoke. It knocks Narden back a few steps, but doesn't stop her.

Alexis does it again and again. With each hit, Narden is knocked back further and further. Finally, Alexis gets to her feet and walks towards Narden. Narden walks quickly towards Alexis, with squinted eyes and a smirk on her face.

"You think you have power against me. Your little smoke booms don't faze me." Narden tells her.

"Well, I think you believe I can't harm you. Little do you know, I have killed one of your kind, and I can kill you just as well." Alexis tells her.

Narden stops and stands. She takes a deep breath of the cool crisp air filling her lungs and she breathes out a fiery flame towards Alexis. Alexis spins and wraps her wings around her to protect herself from the blast of fire. With one leap, Alexis jumps up towards the night sky and flies away from Narden. Trails of fire and smoke linger in the air.

Narden takes off like a rocket. Barreling through the treetops, she sees Alexis. She flies faster until she is right behind her. She reaches out to grab her and throw her back down when Alexis darts directly down and into the trees. Narden passes her and spins around, pissed off. She scans the woods below, looking for Alexis. Narden tries to find an area she can get fly through, but when she finally does, she can't fit through the trees to chase her.

Even more pissed off, Narden lets out an ear-piercing screech, echoing through the forest. "I will get you, bitch!"

Alexis takes refuge in a nearby cave to mend her wings from the fire. Narden also bit through the bone on her shoulder and it is affecting that wing when she flies. She must take time to heal it.

"Damn, why didn't I try the SB DNA on myself. I would be healed right now and stronger than anyone." Alexis says as she slams her fist into the cave wall. A loud cracking noise echoes through the cave system. Alexis lets out a loud scream that sounds like a flock of ravens in distress. The anger boils her blood as her mind races with flashes of the events at the Plantation. She paces back and forth with blood running from the gashes and bites. The smell of burned flesh lingers up around her as a reminder that she is defeated.

The longer she paces the angrier she becomes. She wanders further and further into the cave. Suddenly, she stops. She smells the air; it is no longer thick and moist, but that isn't it. The scent that comes through like burning incense has her attention.

"That smell. I know that smell." Alexis says as she follows it through the tunnel. The smell gets stronger and stronger as she comes up on a den.

"Someone lives here. I know this smell. I know the one who lives here. I haven't smelled their scent in over a hundred years." Alexis says softly as she slowly walks into the area.

Chapter 46

"Kia and the Twins"

Gabriel takes Victor and the group down to the crystal dungeon, walking up to the massive and solid granite doors.

"How are we going to get through these doors?" Victor asks.

"I have a special key." Gabriel says as he lifts the specially cut crystal key from under his shirt and around his neck.

He holds it in his hand and it hangs from the lock. Then it jerks around and sticks straight out. Gabriel holds the end of the leather strap so it doesn't take off, and places it into the hole especially for the crystal key. The hole is covered with a brass-laced lining that circles the hole.

They watch as Gabriel slowly moves towards the massive doors. The key slips into the hole. The key turns on its own and a rumbling sound echoes through the corridors as the door opens slowly.

They walk into this huge marble room with ancient writing all over the arched doorways and on columns through the area. Long hallways of hundreds upon hundreds of mirror-like structures are set everywhere, perfectly spaced apart. They also have ancient writing and symbols on the wooden frames, the floor, and columns as they walk.

Victor deciphers the symbols and words as they move further into it. "The writing on the frames and the doorways are spells and enchantments to keep each creature and each shifter inside their realm. Within each realm, they are suspended in time. They do not age nor eat, but live a life in like an awakened coma state.

"They can see the light from the outside, but they are stuck between dimensions, more or less a living hell. They know there is life outside the lighted area, but cannot ever escape their realm. That is, unless their specifically designed key breaks the spells that holds them inside." Victor explains as they turn down the far row of mirror structures.

"You mean this is where Kia is? Locked in like a third dimension?" John asks.

"Yes, and every one of these are holding something or someone inside. She has thousands of creatures and shifters down here. I would probably say, even other things you couldn't imagine." Victor replies.

Gabriel comes to a light wooden frame crystal mirror. They all stop and watch Gabriel, still holding the crystal key as it shakes violently in front of the mirrored crystal. Gabriel can't hold on to the strap any longer. The key moves so harshly, it pulls out of his hand and into the center of the crystal mirror. It slowly absorbs into it and fog rolls out from the bottom of the frame and onto the floor, moving across it. The air is very cold inside a tunnel with wind blowing through it.

"Kia..." Victor yells into the darkness of the frame. "Kia, are you there?" He yells again.

No answer. Victor moves towards the frame as if he is going to climb into it when a hand slowly merges from inside, covered in a slimy oily clear substance. Victor grabs hold of the hand and Gabriel stops him.

"Don't pull. She must come out herself or you will lose her inside forever." Gabriel tells him and releases Victor's arm.

Another hand comes out and grabs Victor's arm. John can't believe what he sees. His heart is beating with anticipation for Kia to come out safe. Kane steps forward, nudging Gabriel out of the way and grabs the other hand that has emerged from the darkness. They both have tears running down their faces as they just hold tightly to the hands.

"Gentle, Kane, gentle. We can't lose her again." Victor whispers as they both let her hands use theirs as an anchor to pull herself from within the dark realm she is in.

Finally, they feel the resistant force release. They slowly walk backwards, watching as the arms, then a leg steps out, and then a face emerges.

Victor softly speaks her name.

"Kia, oh my God." Victor breaks down at the sight of Kia. She is very skinny and pale. Kane and Victor help her out and she collapses. Kane grabs hold of her and with one swift swing, he picks her up in his arms. Victor falls to his knees crying. John puts his hand on Victor's shoulder, trying to comfort him as much as he can. John is also crying at the sight of Kia. They can't believe how bad she looks, almost near death.

"We need to go before she comes back and finds us here." Gabriel says and turns to head back out. Kane carries Kia and Victor and John follow up behind them.

"Victor, we have Kia. She will be all right now. Okay? But I need you to focus, Victor. We need to find the twins. Don't forget, we must find the twins." John tells him as he holds onto Victor's arm.

"I can't hear them. I can't hear anything down here with all these spells. It blocks everything. She must have spells all over this place. That is why I could never hear Kia or the twins when I came here." Victor says.

As they make their way up the corridor to the stairs, Gabriel tells them they need to go to the second level. That is where Ellie has the twins.

"Kane, take Kia, and keep going. Don't turn back and don't wait on us. Just keep going. My mother and Atreyu will be outside the main doors. They will help you get to the truck and take her back home." Victor tells him.

"Will do, Victor. She will be protected. Warrick and I will make sure she is not harmed." Kane replies.

Gabriel turns and heads down the eastern corridor to the second level. Walking fast towards a door at the very far end, they suddenly see Shadow appear walking towards them.

"Hey, did you guys find her?" Shadow asks.

"Yes, we found her and she is on her way home. Thank you, Shadow, for your help." Victor replies.

"No problem. Glad I could. Okay, the twins are still in the room with Ellie and Raven. They haven't come out. I have been down here watching in the shadows of the darkness. The only persons that have been here are Malik, Damien, Luther, and Lucius. They are all in there with them. I don't know how you plan on getting them out with all of them." Shadow says.

"The only thing we can do is fight, John. Do you still have your pouch of herbs and powders?" Victor asks.

"Yes, I do."

"Okay, pull out your Goofer's Dust. It is the only way we can win. As soon as they come towards you, throw a handful into their face. It will put them out long enough for us to get the twins and out of there." Victor tells him.

They reach the door and hear Damien and Malik arguing inside. The sound of the kids crying makes Victor angry. He tries to communicate with the twins. Since he is so close, he might get them.

He closes his eyes and concentrates. Searching for any voice to respond.

"Daddy?" He hears a voice and he loses concentration. He is overwhelmed. He finally got them. He focuses and concentrates again.

"Hi, baby. Which one am I talking to Rayne or River?"

"Rayne."

"Where are you inside the room?" Victor asks.

"We are on the sofa. They are yelling."

"I am right outside. Don't let anybody know we are here. I want you both to lay face down on the sofa and do not look up until I grab and pick you up, okay?"

"Okay, Daddy."

Gabriel knocks on the door; John and Victor hide off to the sides of the door so they can't be seen.

The door opens and it is Malik. Victor spins and steps in front of Gabriel, pushing him out of the way. With a handful of Goofer's Dust, he throws it in Malik's face, burning his eyes and inhaling it. Malik falls to the ground within seconds and is unconscious.

Damien comes running over to see what is going on. He sees Malik on the floor and Gabriel standing there.

"What the hell did you do?" Damien yells and starts for Gabriel. Damien's eyes turn red almost instantly in anger. Gabriel can see his body start to shift to a hellhound. Gabriel's eyes widen with fear. He takes one step back when Victor pushes him out of the way again and throws a handful of Goofer's

Dust in Damien's face. Damien coughs and then collapses on the floor.

They rush in. Ellie screams, and Luther and Lucius jump up, facing John and Victor. Then, suddenly Ellie notices John, but he doesn't really recognize her. She has changed.

"John, is that you?" Ellie says.

"Yes, Ellie? Oh my God, Ellie. We have been looking everywhere for you." John replies.

"What the hell are you doing here, John? This is no place for you. You must leave before they kill you." Ellie says.

"I am here to get my twins from you." Victor says to her.

"I can't let you do that. They are mine now. I have to protect them." Ellie says.

"No! They are mine and you are not touching them." Victor says angrily. As he says it, his voice changes and he lifts his hand up towards Ellie. A light hits her in the chest, lifting her off the ground, paralyzing her. He tosses her off to the side unconscious.

John stares at Luther and Lucius, waiting for them to make a move. He will hit them with a handful of Goofer's Dust. Luther and Lucius bow their bodies in response to being threatened. They start to shift, but not fully.

"Step aside, you two, or I will get you also." Victor says as he has Ellie pinned to the ground.

"I am not going to let you take them!" Ellie says as she struggles, trying to break free from the force Victor has on her. The more she fights the stronger he pushes the strength of his power.

"Come here, Rayne and River. Hurry, we don't have much time." Victor says.

Rayne and River come running over to Victor. He still has Ellie pinned down. Finally, he lets her go after he has drained her of power, making her useless. He tosses her off to the side, slamming her into the wall. She falls to the floor limp and unconscious.

"Where is Raven?" Gabriel asks.

Luther points to the chair on the other side of the room. He looks and sees Raven standing there with that look on her face. Gabriel knows exactly what that look is. The look he has taught her never to have again.

Everything in the room lifts off the counters and tables, shaking with a tremendous force. Raven stands, her orange eyes looking straight ahead.

Gabriel knows they will soon turn red and she will have everything flying at them in the room, trying to protect her mom and dad.

"Raven, Raven? It's Gabriel. Please listen to me. It's all right. Remember what we did? We learned not to have these bad episodes. Raven, please concentrate on my voice." Gabriel says and he reaches out to grab her hand.

After a few seconds, everything in the room settles back down on the tables and counters, as if they never were disturbed. Gabriel holds her hand tightly until the color of her eyes changes to normal. Raven looks up at Gabriel, grabs him, and hugs him.

"Gabriel, where have you been? I missed you." She tells him, as if nothing has happened.

He grabs her, puts her on his hip, and turns to carry her out with John and Victor in front of him, each carrying one of the twins. Luther and Lucius don't make a move; they just watch. They are not leaders; they are still young and they will not do anything unless Malik tells them.

They rush down the corridor to the first floor and head straight for the main entrance.

"Keep moving. Don't stop and don't look back. Atreyu should be right outside the doors, waiting for us." Victor yells out.

They all pick up the pace. The dust has worn off Malik and Damien. They shake off the effects. It doesn't last but twenty minutes with a hellhound. It will affect each shifter differently, depending on their breed and health. Luther and Lucius help their two brothers stand. Groggy and confused, Malik and Damien look around. Malik sees Ellie lying on the floor unconscious. He races over to her.

"What happened to her?" He spins around and looks at Luther and Lucius.

"That guy that came for his twins had a powerful magic. He threw Ellie up at the wall, and then she struggled to breathe. She passed out and he threw her to the floor." Luther says.

"Yeah, and then they grabbed the kids and ran. They just left. If we hurry, we can catch them before they get out." Lucius says as he walks swiftly out the door and down the hallway.

The front door seems like it is so far away. They turn the corner out of the main corridor that leads to the dungeon. Victor turns his head as he walks fast. He hears movement in the distance behind them.

"I think we need to start running. The hellhounds are coming and if we don't make it to the door, we are not going to get out of here with the kids." Victor says.

Gabriel starts to run with Raven, with Shadow leading the pack.

"I will get you guys to the main corridor to the entrance. After that, you guys go ahead. I will try to slow them down." Shadow yells back.

"Don't be crazy, Shadow. You can't hold them off. What is wrong with you? Just keep going; we will get out before they get to us." Gabriel says.

They reach the big corridor to the main entrance doors. The hallway is long and wide. The main corridor is two stories tall with big windows from floor to ceiling all the way down it. Once they get halfway down the corridor, they hear Shadow scream! Gabriel stops and turns around. Victor grabs his arm and tells him, "Come on. We can't help her. We must get the kids out of this place now!!" He turns around and runs.

Busting through the front doors, Gabriel doesn't stop. He keeps moving. Atreyu watches as he goes past. Victor and John stop.

"Where is he going?" Atreyu asks.

"He is scared and panicked. Come on. We have four hellhounds coming behind us. We need to move fast." Victor says.

Atreyu tells them to go on ahead, and turns to the doors, pointing his hand. He casts a spell on the door to lock it tight.

Take my power

Full and fight

Seal this door, with all your might.

Strength of the wind

Powerful as a storm

Make this lock bind and conform

No escape for those within.

The door slams closed and the center split lights up with a bright whitish blue light moving together from top to bottom, and stops in the middle.

Atreyu puts his hand down and the light fades. The door becomes solid wood with no handle to open. He turns to walk down the stairs and he hears a thunderous noise coming from the door. The hellhounds beat furiously on the door, slamming into it. But the door stays strong as commanded. It doesn't move; it doesn't open. He can hear them howling from inside as he walks onto the Plantation grounds. Then it stops.

Victor and the others keep moving as fast as they can to get to the parking lot. He looks across the grounds in the darkness. All that he can see are bodies, smoke, and small burning fires. He can see several injured shifters slowly moving about. However, he doesn't have time to look for the good versus the bad ones. He hurries to the others.

Then a strange breeze blows above him in a circular motion.

"Narden, is that you?" Atreyu stops and looks up to the starry sky.

The breeze changes and suddenly is behind him. He turns around and sees Narden.

"Are you okay, Narden?" Atreyu asks.

"Yes, sir. I am fine." She replies as she shifts back to her human form.

"Did you get Alexis?" Atreyu asks.

"I lost her in a deep cave a ways up to the North. I tried to get in the passages, but they were too small for my passing in my shifted form." She replies. "I injured her bad enough. She will not be coming back for a while. She will need to heal before she can fly again."

"Good. We need to go. It's only a matter of time before those hellhounds use another door to get out," he says.

Chapter 47

"Home"

Victor races out of the truck and towards the house as John pulls into Victor and Kia's driveway.

Busting through the door to see Kia, John brings the twins and Raven, who are still belted in the backseat yet. Gabriel helps John unbuckle and carry the kids inside.

Kane has Kia in her bed. Mona, Dr. Redbone, and Dr. Whiteriver are there also with medicinal herbs burning. Kia is sitting up, drinking an herbal tea mixture Dr. Redbone has made her, to gain her strength back fast.

Everybody turns as Victor rushes into the bedroom. "Kia, you're home! You're finally home." Victor kneels down next to the bed and wraps his arms around her.

"Yes, honey. I am home. I am feeling much better, thanks to Dr. Redbone, Dr. Whiteriver, and Mona for the herbs they have been giving me." Kia says as she rubs Victor's head as he sobs in her lap.

"Where are the twins, Victor?" Mona asks.

"John and Gabriel are bringing them in," he replies.

John walks into the bedroom with Rayne and River on each hand. Kia hasn't seen them since they were born. The others turn and greet them with open arms.

"Oh my God, my babies! I have been waiting to see you two. I am Grandma Mona, your daddy's mommy." Mona tells them as she hugs them.

"And this is your Grandpa Redbone and Dr. Whiteriver. We have been waiting for you two for a very long time. But I know someone who really needs your help right now. Do you know who that is?" Mona asks.

"Yes, Grandma. It's Mommy. She has been sick for a while." River says.

Mona takes them over to the bed. Victor hugs each one and puts them up next to Kia.

"Hi, babies." Kia says and kisses each one with a long kiss on the forehead.

Mona turns around and Gabriel steps out from behind John with Raven. "Well, who is this beautiful little girl?" Mona asks.

"This is Raven. She is the twins' stepsister." Gabriel says.

"Oh well, Raven, it is very nice to meet you. I am Grandma Mona.

"Mother, she is part Fae and hellhound. She is the first child with Kia and the twins' DNA. I was told that she can heal birds when they stop breathing." Victor says as he stands up and winks at Mona to let her know to watch what she says.

Victor still has a bad feeling about Raven, something he can't put his finger on yet. But he will not show any bad emotions towards her. He knows she is smart and she can feel the emotions of everybody. She carries a strange presence with her that most can't feel, but Victor can.

A strange sound comes from the other side of the house. They all turn to see three white streaks shoot in above everyone in the room and circle above Kia and the twins.

Gabriel darts off to the side of the room; he doesn't know exactly what they are.

"Gabriel, it's okay. They are Kia and the twins' spirit animals. They will not hurt you as long as you are calm, and with us." John says.

Kia looks up at the spirit animals and smiles. Her spirit animal moves down and hovers just in front of her. The other two, for the twins, move behind, side by side. The twins' spirit animals touch Kia on the forehead.

Little white lights slowly circle the connection between the spirit animal and Kia. It grows larger until it is all around Kia's head.

The twins hug Kia tighter and the light moves down until all three of them are in the light. Everybody watches as Victor gets up and steps away as the light moves further down around the twins. John looks at Gabriel as his eyes widen in amazement of what is happening. He has never seen this. John is a little unsure of Gabriel's reaction, so he keeps focused on him, just in case he tries to do something or run.

Everybody looks around quickly as a phone rings, trying not to disturb Kia and the spirit animals. Gabriel fumbles with his pockets. John watches him, thinking the worst. Alexis is calling him or one of the sons.

Gabriel turns and walks swiftly out of the room as he answers the phone. John turns and stands in the doorway, watching him.

"Ada! Where are you? I looked all over for you. Are you all right? No, I am not anywhere around the Plantation right now, and neither should you. Okay, I will be back as soon as I can. Just stay where you are. They will not find you there. Bye."

Gabriel disconnects the call and turns around. He sees John watching him. He gets a strange look on his face and looks down at the floor.

"It was Ada, a friend of mine in the Plantation. We are very close and I couldn't find her when all this happened. I need to get back to her before Alexis and her sons find her. They will punish us all. I need to get her to a safe place." Gabriel tells John.

"It will be okay. I will take you back as soon as I know everything in there is all right. Okay, Gabriel? Just give me a few more minutes here and we will go." John replies.

Victor and Kane walk out just as John replies back to Gabriel.

"What's going on, John?" Victor asks.

"Gabriel needs to go back to the Plantation. He has a friend that is stuck there. She needs his help." John says.

Kane stands over by Gabriel, making him even more nervous.

"Is this true, Gabriel?" Victor asks.

"Yes, it is." Gabriel replies.

"Well, we have a problem, Gabriel. We risk a big chance going back there. Those sons of hers will be out looking for us. We will have to find you another way to get back without endangering anyone." Victor says.

"I will take him. I am not scared. Warrick and I will handle it." Kane says.

Gabriel looks over at Kane, then John, and Victor, waiting for a response.

"Okay, Kane. If you think you two are willing to take the ride, you have my blessing. Take him back; just watch yourselves coming back that no one follows you. We need more time for Kia to heal and get strong before letting anything like another fight start right here."

The morning sun has just risen from the tops of the trees. The sunlight is bright, heading into the east at this time in the morning.

Kane is driving while Warrick is in the back, keeping an eye on everything. Gabriel is in the front seat next to Kane, staring down at the phone.

"What are you so gloomed about, Gabriel?" Kane asks.

"I was just thinking." Gabriel replies.

"About what, if you don't mind me asking?"

"About what we are going to do. What are all the ones that survive going to do? Alexis is going to come back and she will punish us all. This isn't the first time something like this has happened. The last time it did, she killed every creature and shifter except Dr. Brack, Monroe, the sons, and me. She says they failed her so she has no more use for creatures that cannot protect their own homes and master. And she started the hunt for a silver-blood and building a super creature that was to be her slave, like the rest of us." Gabriel says.

"Wow, I didn't know this. Gabriel, Alexis isn't coming back. She has been injured, and chased away from the Plantation. You will have to run it now, Gabriel. Maybe you and your friend?" Kane says.

"I still have Malik, Damien, Lucius, and Luther to confront when I get there. If anybody will run it, it would be Malik. He is the first born." Gabriel says.

"Dude, you passed the turn. It was right there!" Warrick says.

Kane spins his head around quickly to look.

"Goddamn it! This sun is extremely bright this morning. It's blinding me." Kane yells.

"Gabriel, where is Dr. Brack and this Monroe guy? We never came across them in the Plantation. They have to be hiding somewhere?" Warrick asked.

"It's a long story. They have been with Alexis for a very long time. They are very bad people. They had orders to take all the DNA samples from the vault and flee with them. This is Alexis' safety protocol if or when something very bad happens." Gabriel tells them.

"This is interesting. So you're telling us these guys escaped through all the fighting and just walked out with a vault full of special shifter DNA?" Kane says.

"Yes, that is what I am saying. Their blood is from the Dhampir, giving them the ability to shift invisibly when they want. Something like Shadow could; she had a mix of their DNA in her."

"That is a very old breed. I do know a little about them, more or less. They are a hybrid vampire? This would sure explain a lot." Kane replies.

Gabriel holds his phone up. Kane turns and looks at him.

"Are you waiting for it to ring? If you need to make a call, man, just ask. You can use my phone. I have a signal." Kane says.

Gabriel looks over at Kane and back at his phone. He starts to dial a number.

"Ada? It's me, Gabriel. I'm not too far away. Are you all right? With the sun up, have you looked outside yet? Do you know if the boys are still there or did they go?" Gabriel says into the phone.

"Good, I will be there shortly. Just stay there. If everybody is gone from the house, then you should be able to walk around. Okay, I will see you soon. Bye." And he hangs up.

Kane and Warrick watch him, waiting for him to tell them anything, but Gabriel puts his phone down in his lap and stares out the window.

"Well, are you going to fill us in? What is going on there, before we risk our lives to take you there?" Kane says.

"Ada and two girls she found with two offspring. Another one of Alexis' lab experiment." Gabriel says and puts his head down in disgust.

"Two other girls? Who else would be their not fighting?" Warrick asks.

"Two girls that came to us. Malik and Damien brought them back a few months ago. They have been in the lab and experimented on with their offspring." Gabriel replies.

"That leads me to ask... is there anybody else still in the lab?" Kane says.

"I guess I will see when I get there." Gabriel response.

Kane slowly pulls up to the gate to the parking lot. Smoke fills the grounds like thick fog. Visibility isn't good with the sun rising and reflecting on the smoke, making it even harder to see. Slowly, they drive through the parking lot, following it back to the main entrance.

"If you turn here, it will take you around the main entrance and into the back of the Plantation. It's the truck delivery route. You can pull all the way through without being seen." Gabriel says.

Kane and Warrick look at each other and shake their heads in regret.

"Why didn't Victor know about this? We would have been in before they even had known." Kane asks.

"I don't know. Just follow it back and you can drop me off in the back of the house and leave." Gabriel says.

They head down this long road with brick walls on both sides of the roadway. They come to the end of the brick fence and it opens up to the backyard of the Plantation and a huge circular driveway for trucks to turn around and back into the bays to unload supplies.

Kane looks around as well as Warrick. They see nothing moving through the smoke and fog, but they do notice the lights on and the one bay door is open.

"This is good. You can drop me off here." Gabriel says.

Kane stops the vehicle and Gabriel gets out without saying a word. Warrick gets out and walks in front of the car, passing Gabriel, who doesn't even make eye contact. Warrick watches him as he passes, feeling uneasy. Warrick turns and looks at Kane with a worried look on his face. Out of the smoke and fog comes a big black figure running towards Warrick and the vehicle. Kane yells to Warrick, "Look out!"

Before he could turn around, Warrick feels something hit him like a brick, knocking him into the hood. Kane puts the vehicle in park, but before he can get out, Warrick's blood is splattered on the windshield. Kane panics, which quickly turns to anger.

Gabriel turns around when he hears Kane yell and sees what attacked Warrick. He runs as fast as he can to the bay door to close it before it notices him.

Kane shifts into his werewolf and attacks the creature that has Warrick. Shaking Warrick around like a rag doll, Kane attacks the larger creature. Kane jumps on the back of it and sinks his teeth into the base of its neck, pulling as hard as he can until he rips flesh and bone.

The creature staggers and falls like a brick to the ground. Kane jumps off and rushes to Warrick. He picks his brother up and puts him on his lap as he shifts back to human again. Warrick coughs up blood.

"Come on, man. Don't you leave me alone. I need you, Warrick. Please don't let go. Fight. I know you have it in you. If you could shift, you might heal." Kane tells him.

He watches Warrick's body start to shift but doesn't complete the shift. Kane, trying to think of what he can do to help save his brother's life, turns and yells with a deep growl for Gabriel.

Gabriel hears Kane and rushes back out to see what he wants.

"Gabriel, please help me get him inside, so we can try to save him. Please. I beg you." Kane asks.

"Come on. Let's get him into the lab. I know enough that I can inject him with something that will change him and save his life." Gabriel grabs Warrick by the arm and with Kane on the other, they rush him inside and head to the lab.

Chapter 48

"As you lay dying"

"He has lost a lot of blood. If he could shift, he would live." Kane says, sobbing.

They lay him on one of the steel tables in the lab. Kane rips his clothes off him to dress the wounds. Gabriel disappears into the other side of the lab area. Kane looks around for clean towels to wipe the blood. He notices something and he feels a change in the air. He looks down and stares at Warrick, quickly placing his hand over his chest to see if he can feel a heartbeat.

"Oh my God, he is gone!" Kane yells out.

Gabriel rushes back with a syringe in his hand and a vial.

"Hold on, Warrick. Hold on!" Gabriel says as he flips the bottle up, sticks the needle in it, and fills the syringe with a clear substance with a, rainbow liquid swirling inside.

He slowly injects the liquid into Warrick's arm. Kane watches as his arm changes as the liquid runs up the veins. A light breaks through the skin and shines the color of the liquid as it travels further up and rapidly through his body.

Suddenly, Warrick's body twitches, which then turns to convulsions. Kane stands firmly, holding Warrick down on the table until Gabriel is finished with the injection. Gabriel finally pulls the needle out and he lays silent on the table. Kane slowly releases his grip.

He feels a change in the air. Warmth and a brief wind blow past him. He looks down and Warrick's eyes open. Kane's skin crawls. His body senses something in the lab. He lifts his head and turns it slightly to the side. He growls and shifts into a werewolf.

Angered, he scrunches up his back and shoulders in defense, lowering his head. He snarls and growls, as he smells another presence in the room. Gabriel watches and then realizes as a voice comes from a small closet far back in the lab. "Ada, is that you?" Gabriel says.

"Gabriel? Are you there?" The voice replies.

Kane walks towards the voice, ready to attack, when Gabriel yells, "No!! No, Kane. It is Ada, my friend. Stop, please. She is waiting for me to come." Gabriel says.

Kane stops and looks at Gabriel, still angered. "There is something here, something strange. It is not your friend." Kane tells him.

"No, Kane. Go take care of Warrick. I will go to her. Please, just let me get her to a safer place." Gabriel begs him.

Kane suddenly shifts back to human. Looking back over his shoulder, he sees Warrick. The light is still glowing, covering his whole body. Kane turns back and stands next to him, watching as the wounds heal with a bright white light that circles the edge of each one, welding them back together as the light moves onto the others.

Warrick stares straight up, not even looking at Kane. The light travels down from Warrick's head, his neck, and his arms as if he is being reborn. The light slowly fades to the heels of his feet and flickers before fading completely away.

Kane is shocked at what he sees. All of the wounds are completely healed with no scars, no blood, and no trace of anything. His skin looks renewed.

"Are you going to stand there or you going to help me off this freezing cold slab?" Warrick says.

"Warrick, my God. You are alive."

"Yes. What did you expect me to be... dead?"

"Actually, brother, you did die. Thanks to Gabriel, he saved you."

Warrick sits up with the help of Kane and spins to the side of the table.

"What? Seriously? By the look on your face, you aren't joking."

"No, Warrick. Something attacked you when you got out of the car. It tore you up bad. Don't you remember?"

"I remember something, but I thought it was a dream."

Suddenly, Warrick leaps from the side of the table and looks towards a noise coming from the back of the lab. He can hear people talking. Kane tells him Gabriel has found that girl he came to find.

They both watch Gabriel walk out with a thin, pale lady with brownish hair. Behind them are two more people they can't see.

Gabriel walks up and introduces Ada to Kane and Warrick. The other two step out from behind, holding two offspring. When Kane and Warrick see them, they get defensive and Gabriel knows why. They have two offspring Harpies.

"Now, guys, please let's all get along. Nobody here is going to start anything with you. The threats to any of us have left, I believe." Gabriel says.

Kane listens and backs down, but Warrick is still growling deeply. Kane puts his hand on his shoulder and tells him, "Brother, it is fine. They are no threat. They have a different smell; they are strange shifters to us. Let them pass without any harm." Kane says as he pats his brother on the back.

Chapter 49

"Family"

Victor walks Dr. Redbone and Dr. Whiteriver to their vehicle.

"Remember, Victor, to keep giving Kia the teas. They will help her recover faster. I have a feeling something sinister is stirring in the air. That child you brought with you has bad energy surrounding her."

"I know. I can feel and I can see it. I just haven't put my finger on it yet. It is a very dark place in Raven's eyes. They are almost black. Something controls her. I just haven't figured out what it is." Victor replies.

"If she starts to act strange, you will have to keep Raven from Kia and the twins. She is drawing strength from them and they don't know it yet." Dr. Whiteriver says as he gets into the car.

"Call when you arrive back to the clinic. I will make sure Kia and the twins stay in our bedroom. I will stay with Raven in the living room until we figure out what to do." Victor says.

The doctor's pull out and head back to North Carolina. As Victor walks back towards the house, the wind from the cold front picks up and the scent in the air stops Victor in his tracks.

This isn't good. I know this smell.

He continues to walk towards the house, looking around the house as he goes. Suddenly, he notices someone in the window looking out at him. Startled for a moment, he realizes it is Raven. Her eyes have a red glow to them. He knows she is evil. To control it is not going to be easy.

"Raven, are you hungry? Why don't we make something for everybody to eat? Just you and I?" Victor says as he walks in the door.

Raven continues to look out the window so Victor walks behind her, feeling the energy surrounding her is furious with anger.

"Come, Raven. I would really like you to help me cook, sweetheart."

Raven finally turns around and her eyes are back to the dark color. She reaches for Victor's hand and they walk together to the kitchen.

"How about we make your favorite food for everybody? Sound good?"

She nods her head shyly and tells him that she loves spaghetti with meatballs. Victor agrees that is his all-time favorite and gets the stuff ready for them to make.

"Am I going to see my mommy?" Raven asks.

"Well, sweetie, if we can find her. Yes, you will. Do you know where she could be?"

"Is Gabriel coming to pick me up?"

"Possibly. He might be coming back soon, but for now, you get to stay here and play with your stepbrother and stepsister. Tomorrow, we will go to town, and you and I will shop for some clothes for you. How does that sound?"

Raven looks at Victor once again. Her eyes have changed. This time they are green. He thinks this is how mood swings are detected with this girl. Now he knows what to look for. It's always in the eyes. They never lie.

Victor walks with Raven into the bedroom where the twins and Kia are fast asleep. Victor tells her that they will eat and make plates for each one and wrap them up. He takes Raven, gets her some clothes for bedtime, and makes up the couches for them to sleep in the living room.

The phone rings. Victor gets up to answer it. Raven is captivated by the movie she is watching and doesn't pay any attention to Victor.

"Hello, Kane? What is wrong? Slow down. I can't understand you. You're talking too fast. What? Is he all right? Okay, I will see you guys when you get here." Victor hangs up the phone, goes back, and sits down.

He hears something coming up behind them on the couch. He jumps up and there stands Rayne and River, rubbing their tired eyes.

"Daddy, we are hungry." Rayne says.

"Great! Raven and I made you both and Mommy dinner while you were sleeping. Come to the table. I will get it ready for you."

"Kia honey? Hi, would you like some spaghetti? Raven and I made it earlier for everyone."

Victor kisses Kia on the cheek as he sets the dinner plate in front of her. Whispering in her ear that he needs to talk to her in private later. Kia looks up at him and nods her head in agreement.

Rayne and River sit next to Raven on the couch and watch the animated movie, giving time for Victor and Kia to sneak off to the bedroom and close the door.

"Honey, what is it? What is going on now?" Kia quickly asks.

"When I was outside, when the doctors left, the wind from the north had a scent in the air. A scent I will never forget. The day you were taken I smelled this same scent and it's here again. Now, it isn't close, but it is here in Beaver Creek somewhere. I have locked all the windows and doors, closed all the blinds, and set the alarm. I am going to sleep out in the living room with Raven. I don't trust her to be in the room with you and the twins."

"Victor, that isn't nice. She is just a little girl who doesn't know any adult here."

"I know, honey, but I am telling you. Something is wrong with her. I just haven't figured it out. She misses her mom and dad. I don't want her to go searching for them or worse, call them here."

"I understand. I will keep an eye on her. I didn't know you felt like this."

"You need to eat and drink your tea. Dr. Redbone said you must stay on the herbs and teas until you are strong and your powers come to full strength."

Kia agrees and they walk back out quietly to the kitchen to clean up.

Victor wakes with a knocking at the door. He jumps up from the couch.

"What the hell? Who is it?" He says with a mumble, trying to wake up. Walking towards the door, he realizes it is only three thirty a.m. in the morning. Who would be knocking on the door at this hour?

He approaches the door, cautiously unsure, but expecting anything could happen. Looking through the peephole in the door before he turns any lights on, he doesn't see anything. He waits to see if they knock again.

After another series of knocks on the door, a small draft of cold air squeezes under the door, just enough for him to smell the scent lingering outside.

Victor rushes to the bedroom to check on Kia and the twins. Opening the door softly trying not to make any noise, he sees the three of them sleeping safe on the bed. He turns around and feels a presence in the house. Walking slowly out to the front door, he notices Raven isn't on the couch. The TV is still on and the light from it barely lights the room, but just enough to see something behind the curtain in the living room window.

He whispers softly for Raven.

"Raven, is that you standing by the window?"

551

No reply. He slowly walks over and pulls it back gently to find Raven staring at something through the blind.

"Raven, what are you doing up?" He says, trying to sound like he is concerned.

She doesn't answer. Just stares out the window as if she is in a trance.

"Raven, you need to come back to bed."

He grabs her hand gently and she turns her head in surprise, looking at Victor with glowing orange eyes. Victor holds his thoughts and softly asks her again to come back to bed.

Raven squints her eyes in anger at Victor. Victor prepares himself for a fight, building his energy within to knock her back if she attacks.

Suddenly, her eyes change in front of him and she turns to walk back to the couch.

"Raven, did you see anything outside?"

"Yes."

"Can you tell me what you saw, Raven?"

"I saw Grandma's friend. I haven't seen him for a long time. He is very strange, but I know what he smells like. He can talk to me without being in front of me."

"What do you mean by that, Raven?"

"He knows what I say in my head and he listens. And he answers me if he wants."

"What is his name? Do you know it?"

"Phooka."

Victor knows the answer before she utters it, but he just needs the confirmation.

"What is he doing here? Did he tell you?"

"He asked me to be quiet. He was only passing on his way to meet Grandma."

Victor sits with her until she falls back to sleep. Then he sneaks into the office and closes the door to call Kane and warn him not to come to the house. Phooka is out here somewhere, looking for Alexis. Kane tells him they just got into Beaver Creek. They will go to John's and wait for him in a few hours.

"What is that stench, Kane?" Warrick says as they get out of the vehicle at the cabin on John's property.

Kane smells the cold air as he spins around and faces the creek. "I know this smell. The creature John warned me about, that was near his house, is coming."

"What the hell does he want?" Warrick replies.

"He is after Kia and the kids. I bet he is taunting everyone, trying to scare us all again."

They walk towards the cabin. Kane is exhausted and Warrick is full of energy.

"Wait... There is something else." Warrick stops and turns back around, looking into the woods behind them.

"Can you smell that, Kane? Do you know what that smell is?"

Kane turns around and sniffs the air.

"I don't smell it, Warrick. How the hell can you smell it?" Kane says, looking at him, puzzled.

"Seriously, Kane, you can't detect the smell of our enemies? Brother, what is wrong with you? It is plain as day, man."

Chapter 50

"She isn't dead"

The evening Kentucky sky is almost at sunset. Light blue, yellow, orange, pink, and burgundy dance with each other before the sun drops from the sky and the colors turn black, bringing out the moon and stars.

Victor, Kia, and the twins walk through the field on the property. Rayne and River walk ahead of them with Raven. They laugh and hold hands.

The grass is tall in the field, with black-eyed Susan field daisies. Chicory and other meadow flowers soak up the last of the spring sunlight before it goes down behind the mountain. The smell of the air is cool and crisp, blowing down from the north. The change of the season is coming and the flowers already know it.

The spirit animals zip across the field, chasing and playing with each other, darting through Rayne, River, and Raven. The deer watch quietly as they walk by, knowing they are no threat.

Kia and Victor find a spot on the rolling hills of the pasture on the property. They sit down and watch the sunset going down slowly. They hear the three kids laughing and playing, chasing each other around and playing with the spirit animals.

"Thank God they are out running the last of their energy out. They will be exhausted tonight." Kia says.

"Yes, maybe we can finally get some time alone, so I can make love to you like I never have before." Victor replies.

"Uumm that will be nice." Kia says and leans over to kiss Victor. Slowly releasing, she opens her eyes and they stare at each other. Gently he puts his hand on her face and he leans in to kiss her passionately while the kids are still playing in the field.

Then, everything becomes silent. Kia notices no noise while she kisses Victor. She stops and slowly pulls her head away, still staring into his eyes. Suddenly, she smells a haunting scent, one she never wanted to smell again. She shifts as she stands up quickly. Victor is still sitting on the ground.

"Kia, what is wrong?"

"Where are the kids? I don't hear or see them."

"What is wrong? They probably are sitting down in the field."

"No, Victor, you don't smell that stench in the air?"

"Stench? No, I don't smell anything strange." Victor says as he gets up.

"They are here. They are back. Goddamn it, Victor! I thought they were done with."

"What are you talking about, Kia?"

Kia calls for the kids as she rushes down the hill in the field to find them. She sees them standing in a line and the spirit animals all hovering above them, staring in the same direction. Victor comes running up behind her.

"What is the problem?"

"You can't smell anything in the air, Victor? You can't smell the scent of death? We need to get the kids and go now."

They get to the kids and Kia bends down to Rayne.

"Look, Mommy. They are back." Rayne points to the ridge behind Kia as she kneels down in front of them.

Kia turns slowly, noticing Victor stop behind them, looking in the same direction with a blank look on his face.

She slowly turns and starts to stand up when she sees three hellhounds standing upon the edge of the ridge, looking across the field.

Kia and Victor stare at them for a moment when another figure comes up out of the tree line. From the shadows stands a woman looking down at them also.

"Do you see this, Kia?"

"Yes, this is what I was telling you. The stench in the air. They are back. I thought they were run off somewhere, Victor."

"So did I, Kia. Come on. We have to get out of here."

"Mommy, what is that?" River asks.

"It is my dad and Grandma." Raven says.

The animal spirits stop and stand in front of the children as a shield of protection, blocking the view from the ones on the cliff.

They grab the kids and move quickly through the field towards the cabin. As they get inside the cabin, Kia closes the door and looks at Victor.

"I had this vision when I was pregnant with the twins. Now this vision has come true, another vision is happening." Kia puts her hands on her head and shakes it with regret.

Victor takes the kids and puts them on the couch. "Wait here while we pack some things."

"Kia, it is going to be all right. This is what you do you have visions and you should know by now. The visions are not a dream that never happens, but a glimpse of what is to come in the future. You must learn from them. None of them will tell you exactly when it will happen. You will need to study them and learn from the signs. Now, come on. We have to get the kids' clothes and things to leave for North Carolina. It is the safest place for the kids to be."

There is a knock at the door. Kia jumps and runs towards Victor and the kids on the couch.

"Victor, Kia... It's John. Open up. I need your help. Kyle and Jake are very ill." John yells from outside the door.

Kia sighs with relief and rushes to the door to unlock it.

"What is wrong, John?"

"Kia, thank God you guys are here. I need you to look at Kyle and Jake. They are very ill. They look very bad and they are burning up with fevers."

"Did you call the doctor?"

"No, he said there was nothing he could do for them. If we brought them into the hospital, they would turn them away; they have too many in there now, with no room for anymore."

Kia tells Victor to stay here and lock the door. John and Kia run to the cabin.

Kia walks in and sees the boys lying on the couches covered up with blankets. Both are very sick and sweating. Kyle is pale and looks like he is shifting into something Kia notices. She doesn't say a word to Lizzie or John about what she sees.

Kia reaches down and places her hand on Kyle's forehead to check his temperature. When she touches Kyle, she gets a shock. A vision races through her mind. Flashes of events unfolding somewhere in time, somewhere in the future.

It is raining and dark, very dreary outside. She is walking in the mud. Water is standing in small puddles that form from horses hoof prints. She can smell that stench in the air. The hellhounds are there somewhere. She looks around as she walks through the rain. She can smell stables, the smell of horses. The smell of death also fills the air. The wind blows to the side of her face. Within it are screams, screams of pain and suffering. They are in the wind as though racing through this 1800s-like abandoned village.

She keeps walking down the small road when she sees lights coming from this big abandoned hospital or clinic. She walks towards it slowly. She sees white strikes racing out of the windows and down through the road, as fast as the wind. When it passes by her, she can hear screams, terrible painful cries.

She suddenly is inside the abandon place, standing in the hallway looking at row after row of cots filled with young people. Shifters rush around, tending to the people on these cots. The screams and cries come from all around. Then she sees two familiar faces walking towards her, looking at each one on the cot as they slowly walk past them.

OMG! That is Dr. Brack and Monroe!

Kia tries to hide, but there is nowhere to go. She just stands there, waiting for them to notice her. They get closer and closer. Kia's heart starts races with fear, but she stands still, and they walk right past her as if she isn't there at all.

Kia walks down the corridor past the beds, looking at the patients. Some have patches of hair missing on their head, as if it is falling out. Others are completely bald, and the further she goes down, she sees the last several cots. She stops and stares at them.

The faces of the people are pale. Their eyes are sunken into the sockets. The skin on their faces looks like it is gone and the skull is exposed. The eyes are glowing blue lights. The bone structure is thick as if they are some sort of fierce fighter. She watches as they lead two of them out in front of her, a faun shifter on each side, holding the arms of these creatures.

Kia follows them out and she walks into another room. Same thing. Hundreds of cots filled with people young people. These are different. They have hair, lots of hair. Some are in the first stages, and then the next stage. As she walks down, she notices their feet are not human, but hooved. She walks further down and watches as a faun shifter leads a black horse through the corridor and out.

Suddenly, Kia's vision is gone and her hand comes off Kyle's head. She looks closely at Jake. She notices his eyes are sinking into his head and the skin is very thin. She walks over and rubs his head, pulling it up slowly. She has hair all over her hand — Jake's hair. She looks down and sees a bald patch and loose hair dangling off the rest. She holds her hand in front of her and stares at it with a blank look.

"I noticed his hair is falling out also. It just started this morning." John tells her.

Kia looks up at John and asks, "Has anybody seen Kassidy?"

I do not sleep, but I do eat

I am the many winds that blow,

I am the reflection in the snow

I am the sunlight dancing on the frozen ground,

I am the dew on the ground.

I am the gentle breeze that blows in your face.

I am the flock of birds that fly high in the air

Swiftly diving and circling, watching all that is

Below,

I am the star that shines at night,

Don't think that I have gone away; I am here

just waiting in each new dawn that rises.

I wait for my chance to get revenge upon you all.

Alexis Ravenworth

I hope you enjoyed the second book in the Sulfur Mountain series. Please go on Amazon.com and leave a rating I am a self-published author and the ratings help me get my book noticed. Thank you for your support.

Cover Design:

Vicki Adrian

Image: iStockphotos.com

Inside Images by Vicki Adrian

Coming Soon....

The Dark Army

Book 3

A brief passage from chapter One of **The Dark Army.**

"Jake's arm is turning Black" Lizzie yells to John as he walks in the door.

Black lines run through his skin like veins of black blood his fingers start to slowly turn black. Lizzie turns and looks at Kyle on the other couch she notices he is changing also. He is turning a pale white color and his veins seem to becoming closer to the skin and the blood is not normal red color it is a dark red it is also changing.

The eyes in both Jake and Kyle seem to be sinking deeper in to the sockets. Dark black circles start to form around the eyes.

The doctors have no clue what it is he said many young teens and young adults are falling ill just like this something is going around and they don't know what it is or how to treat it.

"Kia honey what do you think it is?" Victor asks.

"This is a curse they have been plagued with a very strong curse and nobody has heard from their friend Kassiday?" Kia replies.

Kia holds her hand up to show the others. Her hand is covered in Jake's hair it is falling out.

"OMG!" Lizzie screams. John grabs her and holds her tight.

"What the hell is this John what is happening to our boys?" Lizzie says crying.

A knock on the door finally Sheriff Taylor brings a friend who is a doctor she is Internal medicine and has experience with the backwoods traditions in Folk Remedies and she knows about different witchcraft in Native American tribes, Gypsies, and other origins of crafts.

ABOUT THE AUTHOR

AUTHOR NAME is

Find out more at http://www.amazon.com/Vicki-Adrian/e/B00L8BAXB6

Or visit

We are on Facebook:
https://www.facebook.com/Authorvickiadrian/

OTHER BOOKS BY (AUTHOR)

Devils Attic a Sulfur Mountain series,

Devils Attic is the first book in this series.

Is available on Amazon paper copy and Kindle edition. The links to the first book are here:

http://www.amazon.com/Devils-Attic-Sulfur-Mountain-1/dp/0692236007/ref=sr_1_1?s=books&ie=UTF8&qid=1451772868&sr=1-1&keywords=devils+attic+sulfur+mountain+series

www.ingramcontent.com/pod-product-compliance
Lightning Source LLC
Chambersburg PA
CBHW051929020726
47501CB00001B/45